On the Plus Side

ALSO BY JENNY L. HOWE

The Make-Up Test

On the Plus Side

A NOVEL

JENNY L. HOWE

ST. MARTIN'S GRIFFIN
NEW YORK

First published in the United States by St. Martin's Griffin, an imprint of St. Martin's Publishing Group

ON THE PLUS SIDE. Copyright © 2023 by Jenny L. Howe. All rights reserved. Printed in the United States of America. For information, address St. Martin's Publishing Group, 120 Broadway, New York, NY 10271.

www.stmartins.com

Designed by Omar Chapa

Library of Congress Cataloging-in-Publication Data

Names: Howe, Jenny L., author.
Title: On the plus side: a novel / Jenny L. Howe.
Description: First edition. | New York: St. Martin's Griffin, 2023.
Identifiers: LCCN 2023031029 | ISBN 9781250837882
    (trade paperback) | ISBN 9781250837899 (ebook)
Subjects: LCGFT: Romance fiction. | Novels.
Classification: LCC PS3608.O946 O5 2023 | DDC 813/.6—dc23/
    eng/20230707
LC record available at https://lccn.loc.gov/2023031029

Our books may be purchased in bulk for promotional, educational, or business use. Please contact your local bookseller or the Macmillan Corporate and Premium Sales Department at 1-800-221-7945, extension 5442, or by email at MacmillanSpecialMarkets@macmillan.com.

First Edition: 2023

10 9 8 7 6 5 4 3 2 1

This one's for you, Katie DeLuca.
Because you always get it.

AUTHOR'S NOTE

Dear Reader,

My characters and I use the word "fat" throughout this book, but it is meant as a neutral descriptor, nothing more: no different from thick, wide, round, soft, plus size, etc. Like many in the fat community, I want to reclaim this word, disempower it by using it neutrally, and hopefully help to evacuate the harmful connotations so often associated with it. So when Everly and other characters in *On the Plus Side* refer to themselves as fat, please know that it comes from a place of self-love, a place of understanding that this word does not need to be a weapon.

Being fat is a varied and complex identity, the same as any other, and we need stories that represent the host of different experiences and feelings that come with living in a fat body. For me, challenging fatphobia through my stories means creating main characters who love themselves and feel comfortable in their bodies, no matter their size. When we meet Everly, she is struggling with *who* she is, not what she looks like, though sometimes the two can feel intimately entwined—she tends to hide herself in shapeless or colorless clothes because she wants to disappear, while being on a makeover show gives her a chance to celebrate who she is by what she puts on her body.

But I believe that to challenge fatphobia, we also have to look it in the eye. We can't pretend it away. So I tend to situate my characters in a world that reflects our own. And unfortunately, one of the first places fat people often encounter fatphobia is in our own homes. Everly and her mother have a tenuous bond, the cracks in the foundation largely the result of her mother's internalized fatphobia and her misguided attempts to protect her child. I have worked hard to approach Everly's relationship with her mother with care and sensitivity. I hope I have done it justice. And if this topic is difficult for you, please take care while reading.

Other content warnings for *On the Plus Side* include mentions of cancer and the death of a loved one (in the past), mentions of emotionally abusive parents (in the past), and a brief mention of the death of a family pet (in the past).

As much as this book deals with some fatphobia, it also celebrates the joys of finding community. I hope I have adequately illustrated the absolute glory of having someone (or better yet, multiple someones!) who relates to your lived experience—being able to commiserate with someone, to share your wins with them, to know you can turn to them and find true understanding, is a precious gift. And if you haven't found that yet, I hope that maybe this book can be a starting point. Because no matter who we are and what we look like, we all deserve a mirror. We all deserve to be understood. We all deserve to be seen.

xoxo,

Jenny L. Howe

On the Plus Side

CHAPTER 1

No one should be expected to exhibit self-control before ten in the morning.

Especially when their coworker, a practical photocopy of Chris Hemsworth, was leaning over their shoulder to dig through the dregs of the company candy jar.

The fact that Everly Winters hadn't audibly inhaled his bonfire-built-of-air-fresheners scent or brushed her knuckles across his stubble should win her some kind of gold medal. She hadn't even had a sip of her latte yet, for god's sake.

This was torture.

She contracted her muscles until they were stone and held her breath. Not since her last attempt at yoga had she achieved such levels of still-ness. Inside, though, her heart was dancing an uncoordinated rumba.

Get it together, she told herself. *This is your workplace, not a meat market.* She homed in on her monitor and changed an item in the open spreadsheet, only for it to crash for the third time this morning. "Bas-tard," she grumbled.

"Everything okay, V?" James's words blew warm across her arm, summoning goose bumps to the surface of her skin. He was the first person at Matten-Waverly to give her a nickname, and she loved it, despite the fact that V wasn't the most logical abbreviation of Everly.

"Will you bail me out of jail if I murder this computer?"

James flicked aside a perfectly good Twix to grab a Snickers like the true monster he was. "Depends on how much." The right corner of his mouth kicked up in a grin.

"Wow. A fickle friend you are." Everly swiveled in her chair so he wouldn't see her gaze raptly at his fingers as they peeled away the candy wrapper.

He circled her desk to put himself right back in her line of sight. "Some crimes need to be punished."

"This document has crashed multiple times. We're looking at a clear case of self-defense." Under her sweater, Everly's skin had grown warm. Her little exchanges with James rarely went on for this long, and the prolonged attention was inducing hot flashes. Sometimes she wondered how people that attractive managed to exist without combusting.

"You know, the computers in Design are better quality," James said around a bite of nougat and peanuts. Once he swallowed, he bent over the chest-height counter to plunge into the candy again. He was so close now that the strands of golden hair that had fallen out of his bun brushed against her cheek.

For the second time in ten minutes, Everly performed a reverse Pygmalion: woman transforming into statue.

"I like it over here in Reception. It's cozy." And stable. Everly knew exactly what was required of her and could fulfill those tasks with ease. It wasn't like a creative job, where there were so many opportunities to get it wrong.

Clicking open a browser, she navigated to her email with the precision and focus of a neurosurgeon, trying with all her might to ignore the way James's biceps strained the sleeves of his button-down shirt.

Too many of her best daydreams starred those muscles, and Everly, clutching them as he saved her from an icy sidewalk, or, in her more daring fantasies, from falling down the second-floor stairwell where they were making out on their lunch break. (Once, there'd been this whole intergalactic motif right after she'd watched *Gravity,* but it was really hard to make space suits sexy, even in her imagination. Too many clips and gadgets and whatnot.)

In her head, Everly could hear Becca clucking her tongue. As her best friend *and* sister-in-law, Becca had decided long ago that it was her duty to have an opinion on every part of Everly's life. And she had a whole host of them about James and his yet-to-be-expressed feelings for Everly.

And maybe Becca was right. Maybe the eye contact they shared every time he crossed from one end of the office suite to the other *was* meaningful. Maybe the finger guns he seemed to only shoot at her, the nickname only she got, all suggested that he might be interested in being more than work pals.

But if Everly didn't ask him out, if she didn't push at this, then there was never the chance that those maybes were nos. The possibility of him . . . of *them* . . . persisted into infinity.

He was Schrödinger's date.

She tilted away from James's wayward strands of hair and cut her eyes to the computer. She'd barely caught a glimpse of a notification from the forums of her favorite makeover show, *On the Plus Side,* in her inbox before he rounded her desk.

"If Bob knew how good you were, he'd have transferred you over to us by now."

Everly shook her head. Her boss had never asked for her portfolio. She was pretty sure he was waiting for her to approach him, but she appreciated that he didn't push her. This reception job allowed her paid benefits and a livable paycheck, and being at a marketing firm meant that, if she ever wanted to, she could use her visual arts degree, so college didn't feel like a waste of time and money. As far as she was concerned, she was exactly where she needed to be.

"I get to dabble a little in everything here. I've learned a ton." As she spoke, Everly tugged on the middle of her buttoned black cardigan to add a tad more room to the waist. Stupidly, she'd put it through the dryer last weekend, and now it hugged her curves more than she'd hoped. But as she fussed with the buttons (her kingdom for some that didn't gape at her breasts), Jazzy Germaine's favorite line from *On the Plus Side* echoed in Everly's head.

People see you the way you see yourself.

She forced her hands still. If she thought her sweater fit fine, everyone else would, too. Including James, who, after grabbing another piece of candy (a Mounds, *gag*), kneeled beside her chair.

"Fiiine. I'll stop trying to recruit you for Design. But can I show you this one thing?"

Everly shrugged because what were words? His proximity erased everything from her brain like her mother claimed magnets used to do to credit cards.

He clicked around on her screen. "Your advice last week about the lines being too uniform in that logo for Ivy was so on point."

His file opened on her oversized monitor, revealing a social media banner for Bartleby & Sacks, the men's style consulting something or other their firm had recently nabbed. The layout was all blacks and grays and straight lines, summoning a yawn from the creative side of Everly's brain.

The smoky scent of James's cologne overwhelmed her senses, and her heart had no idea what a rhythm was, but she tried to focus on the layout, tried to let herself fall into the logo's shapes and lines as she studied the screen.

For Everly, art was something she felt as much as saw. And immediately, that itch of wrongness burrowed under her skin.

"Something's . . . off," James mumbled. As he waited for her feedback, he picked up a vinyl figurine of Kermit the Frog off her desk and passed it back and forth between his hands. There were a good two dozen of them, mostly from *The Muppet Show* and Disney films, characters Everly had loved since she was a kid, plus the custom ones of her favorite book boyfriends from romance novels that Becca had been gifting her for her birthday for years. Meticulously organized by categories that made sense only to her, they were arrayed along the front of her desk like a museum display.

Everly pursed her lips. "It's the lettering. It's too whimsical," she concluded.

Setting Kermit down (beside Ursula and Ariel, of all places), James pointed at the monitor. "I thought the ampersand really fit their brand."

"It's got too many curves and loops." Everly reached out and shifted Kermit to his correct spot between Fozzie and Miss Piggy. "I'd use it for a children's clothing company or maybe the cover of a fantasy novel." The font was called Woodland; the whimsy was right in the name. "The brand manager said they were looking for something sleek and contemporary. Totally minimalistic." Because god forbid anything masculine be playful.

She highlighted James's lettering and replaced Woodland with Cooper Hewitt. The difference was immediate. What had once been a chaos of curves and lines was now starkly linear. Harmonious, even.

For some light contrast, she tinted the letters a stone blue, then sat back, satisfied.

James let out a low whistle. "Damn, you're good." He tapped his knuckle to her desk an inch from her hand, setting her whole body aflame. Imagine if he'd actually touched her? She'd have burst into ash like a molting phoenix.

The sharp ring of the phone made them both jump. Though a call was usually James's cue to cut their visit short, he took to sorting the chocolate bars by color as Everly pressed her earpiece. "Thank you for calling Matten-Waverly. This is Everly. How can I direct you?"

Dead air hummed against her eardrum, followed by the telltale click of a hang-up. In the age of email and texts, Everly wasn't sure why the company still had a landline. Ninety percent of the calls were wrong numbers or bots.

James watched her disconnect the call, then cleared his throat. "So . . . V . . ."

Her heart stuttered at the hesitation in his voice. "Hmm . . . ?" Even that one syllable failed at sounding cool and collected.

His fingers fiddled with the lid of the candy jar, and from the way he was swaying slightly back and forth, he seemed to be passing his weight between his feet.

He looked nervous. Everly tried to catalog all the possible reasons why, but her brain kept coming back to one.

He was going to ask her out.

No. No. No. Her monitor blurred against her stare.

He couldn't do that. She wasn't ready for her daydreams to become reality. She'd only be disappointed. Or worse, get her heart stomped on.

Her fingers frantic, she clicked open the *OTPS* email, desperate for her favorite show and its fans to save her from this impending disaster. If James saw her absorbed in something, maybe he'd reconsider whatever he was about to say.

Everly studied the list of thread updates and replies. As the only lifestyle makeover show catering exclusively to fat people, *On the Plus Side* had cultivated quite the online community, and she spent most of her free time on its forums. It was one of the few places lately where she felt seen. As much as Becca was always sympathetic, she'd been thin her whole life. She didn't know what it meant to have the world literally be designed to forget you or to make you feel wrong.

But for an hour on Thursday and Sunday nights, the hosts of *OTPS*—Jazzy and Stanton—and their guests reminded Everly that she wasn't alone. And for the rest of the week, the forums were the closest she could get to injecting that feeling into her veins and carrying it with her everywhere.

She scanned the email, searching for her favorite users. After two years of lurking on the forums, they were as familiar to her as her closest friends. Annette's speculations about the upcoming season had gotten hundreds of likes, and everyone was participating in Bridget's poll on their favorite episodes to rewatch.

Everly was dying to respond to the poll (the ultimate rewatch episode was obviously the season one finale with the hot plus-size male model), but James was still hovering in her peripheral vision, encouraging her pulse to spike. At this point, he'd moved on from color coding to dividing the candy by ingredient. For some reason, the peanut butter and caramel bars were shoved to the side like he was trying to hide them.

It was criminal. No one put peanut butter or caramel in the corner.

Everly fought the urge to ask how his candy feng shui was going, or why, exactly, he hated delicious things. She tried to avoid being even remotely flirty around him. It was safer that way. No chance of accidentally opening that box.

She was just shifting her attention back to her email when a clamor of boisterous voices broke out in the hallway. Matten-Waverly was one of the few office spaces currently in use on the second floor, and the emptiness of the surrounding suites amplified the acoustics until it sounded like an entire parade was marching toward them, megaphones and all.

"What the hell?" Everly jumped from her chair and, rounding the reception area, yanked open the door.

The way everyone on the other side yelled her name, it was like she'd stepped into a surprise party.

Her stomach leapt into her throat as two people split from the group to rush at her, arms wide, ready to scoop her into a hug.

"Everly Winters!"

"Look at you, you *queen*."

Their embrace was inviting and warm, two sets of arms squeezing her tight. One of them smelled like strawberries and cream, the other like a summer day at the beach, and someone's shirt pressed to her cheek, blanket soft.

When they finally stepped back to appraise her, her knees and hands were trembling.

Everly wanted to lie down on the floor. "What . . . how . . . ? *What?*" She didn't realize she was crying until she rubbed at her eyes with her palms, and they came back wet.

Was this a dream? That was the only way to explain how the hosts of *On the Plus Side* were standing in front of her right now. Somehow, they'd stepped out of her TV into her real life, and they knew her name. The realization made her head fuzzy, and her chest felt too full.

As Everly glanced around in disbelief, the details of her surroundings sharpened, as if it were the other way around, and *she'd* stepped through a hi-def screen like a modern-day Alice in Wonderland.

Her mouth had lost the power to form words.

This couldn't be real.

She repeated that over and over in her head as her hero, Jazzy Germaine, took Everly's hands and said the catchphrase Everly had never expected to hear in real life: "Everly Winters, will you let self-love in?"

READ-IT FORUM: ON THE PLUS SIDE

OTPSfan23456 *over two years ago*

I don't know if there's anyone else in here but I needed somewhere to go after watching the first episode of OTPS. I'm a bit of a reality TV junkie—there's not much else to do in my tiny town—but this show is like nothing I've ever seen. It seems more "real," if that makes sense? Probably not. Lol

I guess this is what people mean by seeing yourself in a piece of art or a book or whatever. All the things Jazzy and Stanton were saying about being fat in the world, I felt them all. It's the first time in a long time I've felt normal, not like this person who lives slightly outside everyone else's plane of existence. It makes me wish I knew more fat people.

I'll stop babbling into the void now.

TL;DR: I loved the first episode and I wish there were a hundred more shows like it.

24 ♥ 4 👍 16 ✦ 0 👎

Annette98 *over one year ago*
Hi friend! Everything you wrote here speaks right to my SOUL!!!!! The premiere was EXCELLENT. OMG. I will fight anyone (WITH SWORDS) who tries to take this beauty off the air.

5 ♥ 10 👍 31 ✦ 0 👎

KelseyR0305 *over one year ago*
omg I thought I was the only one who felt this way

9 ♥ 12 👍 28 ✦ 0 👎

RosyTea *over one year ago*
i officially declare you all my people

11 ♥ 22 👍 18 ✦ 0 👎

CHAPTER 2

"Holy fuck."

Those were the first words that popped out of Everly's mouth when she finally peeled her hands from her face.

On the Plus Side had two hosts: Stanton Bakshi, who focused on the guest's career and lifestyle, and Jazzy, who consulted on appearance. Together they tried to give the show's participants a true makeover, transforming every part of their life.

Everly loved them both, but Jazzy had always been her favorite. She was funny and smart and stylish, and her ability to look at a guest and instantly understand how to bring out all their best qualities was truly an art.

Now she was standing in front of Everly, probably doing that exact same thing to her.

How was this happening? And to *Everly* of all people.

"Holy *fuck*," she muttered again.

Somewhere nearby, a frustrated groan broke through the shock that had left her ears ringing. "There goes that take."

Everly cut her gaze toward the gruff voice. It came from a guy standing slightly apart from the rest of the group, an expensive-looking camera balanced on his shoulder. He'd angled it to the side so he could judge her with his whole face. Whatever he saw caused his frown to deepen beneath his dark, close-trimmed beard.

Jazzy sighed. "Logan, they can bleep it out."

"Get this man a trash can and glue some green fur on him," Stanton declared.

A laugh burst from Everly's mouth. With her two idols standing in front of her, she was too excited to hold it back, and the sound bounced loudly off the walls around them, drawing people's eyes.

If her mother were here, she'd be cringing and apologizing. Everly's cheeks flushed. "Logan the Grouch?" she asked more quietly.

Stanton shook his head. "Oh, honey, you have no idea."

The description was fitting. She'd been in the camera guy's presence for half a second, and already, she could picture him as the grumpy green puppet.

Except with a killer jawline and piercing blue eyes.

Logan set the camera on the ground and crouched to fiddle with some of its buttons. Though he was barely two or three inches taller than her, his presence filled the small hallway. Maybe it was the breadth of his shoulders and arms: he was the kind of broad Grandma Helen would have said was meant for carrying oxen, his muscles challenging the give of his navy-and-white-checkered flannel with every movement.

Hefting the equipment back on his shoulder, he approached the group, close enough that Everly caught the pine-y, wintry scent wafting off him, like he'd just stepped out of a forest. This guy was basically an urban lumberjack. Or a woodsy metrosexual. Whatever the term was for an attractive, bearded, plaid-donning dude who was not presently chopping up trees.

"You know our format means fewer opportunities for edits," he said to Jazzy.

On the Plus Side aimed for a more "documentary" style of reality TV. It only had four guests per season and showcased each for eight episodes, airing as they filmed to keep things as raw and realistic as possible.

Jazzy's burnished brown eyes only glinted with more amusement at his scolding tone. "I've also seen plenty of censoring done when needed."

Everly snapped her gaze back and forth between them. She'd been so awestruck by the sudden appearance of *On the Plus Side*'s hosts that she hadn't even considered what their presence (accompanied by this plaid-covered man and his camera) meant. "Wait, you're already filming?"

This was the biggest thing that had ever happened to her. She'd be watching her episodes on repeat for the rest of her life. They had to give her a minute to get ready, right? At least to run a brush through her hair (had she done that this morning before stumbling out the door in a caffeine-deficient haze?) and catch her breath?

She smoothed down the front of her dress as if her hands had suddenly developed the power to eliminate wrinkles.

Look out, Marvel. Here comes your next superhero: Iron(ing) Girl.

"We'll only use it if you sign the contract. Otherwise, it gets trashed." A statuesque woman stepped up beside Stanton. Her hair was a sleek sheet of gold that fell to her shoulders, and her pale face was covered in a spread of freckles half hidden under thick black glasses. Unlike Everly, who carried her weight in her hips and thighs, this woman's was mostly in her midsection.

Everly recognized her immediately from media coverage of *On the Plus Side*. Sady Sanders, the showrunner.

"Right now, all you have to worry about is saying yes," Sady explained.

Everly bit her bottom lip. No wonder the guests always looked like deer in headlights in the first episode. This was a literal ambush.

The showrunner's hazel eyes scanned her. "We want to tell your story. There are so many people out there who will connect to it."

What story? Everly's list of fun facts included that she detested guacamole enough for it to be a defining character trait, she and her mother saw eye-to-eye on exactly nothing, and she knew zero fat people outside of the show's forums. Not exactly the stuff of legendary TV.

For a second, she imagined herself sitting with Stanton at a fancy Mexican restaurant in Boston, cameras zoomed in to a close shot of their booth by the window. Sun glinted off the pane and caused the traffic lumbering by to glitter like diamonds. Stanton leaned in, his silky black curls falling across the rims of his round glasses. He knocked the strands out of his eyes. "Tell me about your hatred of guacamole, Everly," he said seriously. Then he dug a tortilla chip deep into a mound of that green abomination and held it out to her. "We'll face it together."

Oh yeah, the Emmys would stream in.

Still, if they wanted her, the last thing Everly would do was talk them out of it. She was going to be on her favorite TV show. How many people got to say that?

"Let's do it!" she declared, glancing up to catch the gaze of Sady or one of the hosts. Instead, her eyes locked on Logan, and as much as Everly tried, she couldn't look away.

The first episode for a new *On the Plus Side* guest was always pure chaos. Jazzy and Stanton would burst into their home or workplace, exuberant and loud, chatting with everyone around them and rifling through their belongings to get a sense of who their newest participant was.

When they watched at home, Becca and Everly would speculate about how they'd react if they were the guest. Becca would cry. No question.

Everly, they'd both agreed, would follow in the hosts' wake, picking up every mess they made.

Except Everly was learning that the reality was even more out of control. There was no time to clean up when Jazzy was making James and the rest of the design team laugh as she tried on an old, pilly sweater Everly had left at the office, and Stanton was settling in at her desk, pawing through her Tasks folder and rearranging her figurines by size and color.

It was like being at a circus when all the acts were performing at once. Everly didn't know where to look. What to do first.

Stanton leaned back, his tall body filling the chair, his camel-colored loafers propped up on the edge of the desk. The phone's headset squashed his curls. "Is this what you looked like when I called a few minutes ago?"

Everly choked at the idea of Bob Matten, CEO and quintessential granddad, seeing her lounging at Reception like it was a resort pool. "That was you?"

Stanton had deep sable-colored eyes that practically twinkled when he grinned. "We had to confirm you were here before we came up."

"Has that ever happened? That the guest wasn't where they were supposed to be?"

"Episode one. Ashley had called in sick at the ice-cream parlor and no one told us. We burst in on this poor overworked teenage boy and about ten customers. Half the people dropped their cones on the floor in shock. Kids were crying. It was mayhem."

Everly laughed, mentally filing away that tidbit to share with Becca. They were both obsessed with behind-the-scenes *OTPS* gossip.

"We learned our lesson after that. Always check first. The ice cream, though, was excellent."

Stanton had set his feet back on the floor and was now unearthing Everly's pens and markers from their (very strictly organized) mugs. If it had been anyone but Stanton Bakshi cultivating anarchy on her desk, she might have lost it. But as far as Everly was concerned, he and Jazzy could do no wrong.

She barely had a chance to inventory the pens he was tossing haphazardly into her drawers before Jazzy appeared at her side and slung an arm around Everly's shoulder. "Soooooo . . . I've been looking at your social media." She held her phone up between them.

Everly swallowed, knowing exactly what was coming. Jazzy hated when guests only wore dark colors. And since the end of her junior year in college, navy was probably the lightest one in Everly's wardrobe.

But she wasn't trying to hide her body like most of the show's guests. It was more that she was trying to blend in.

Disappear.

With a perfectly manicured scarlet nail, Jazzy tapped open a photo slideshow. "What do you see?"

Everly cleared her throat. "An extensive palette of gray and obsidian hues," she said with a hopeful grin.

Jazzy barked out a laugh. The sound, so familiar from years of watching and rewatching *OTPS,* eased the growing knots in Everly's shoulders. Jazzy and Stanton had always felt like home to her. They were their whole selves. They let their voices be heard. They didn't let anything steal their joy.

The same way Grandma Helen had taught Everly to be, before she died. Before Everly was the only one left in her family who was, as her mom loved to say, "a bit too much."

She wanted so badly to hug Jazzy. To thank her for all the times that her very existence had helped Everly feel less alone. Hopefully, sometime over the next few months, she'd find the courage to do it.

"Spoken like a true artist," Jazzy said, still flipping through the photos.

"Wait." Everly gestured to a picture of herself in a black-and-white-striped jumpsuit, which was now buried somewhere in the back of her closet. She'd forgotten how cute she looked in it. "Look. There's some white."

"With black," Jazzy said.

"But it's a color."

"Technically, it's the absence of color," Stanton pointed out.

From the opposite corner of Reception, Logan coughed. Everly had forgotten about him and the fact that she was being filmed until he forced himself back into her consciousness. "White is the presence of all colors." She was about to thank him for proving her right when he added, in the flattest of tones, "So you're both wrong."

This man was clearly the life of the party. Everly couldn't wait to spend weeks of her life with him following her around. Long hours of being frowned at and corrected in monotones. What a hoot that was going to be.

Jazzy snorted. "Okay, nerd."

Logan rolled his eyes, but there was no venom in it, as if he were used to their teasing.

The last set of pictures on Jazzy's photo reel were from Matten-Waverly. A few of Everly behind her desk. Two of her watching her co-workers do a ropes course at a company retreat. Another where she was handing out refreshments at the charity soccer game.

"Why weren't you playing?" Jazzy asked.

"I suck at soccer."

"We all suck at soccer," Stanton echoed. "That's what makes it fun."

Everly tugged at the cuff of her sweater sleeve, stretching out the cotton material. This was part of the experience, she knew that. *OTPS* focused on all aspects of the guest's life. It wasn't just about getting new clothes or a fresh haircut. It was about questioning her choices. Digging into who she was.

On the Plus Side changed people's lives. They'd helped Philip go from social media influencer with a small following to the runway, helped Brenna launch a daycare center in her neighborhood, helped Hannah come out to her family, helped other guests open businesses, find birth parents, attend auditions, confront trauma.

But Everly didn't have big dreams. She was settled and comfortable. Her job was fine. Her apartment above her brother's garage was cozy and perfect for one person. She lived across the driveway from her best friend. She had a hot friend at work, but none of the pressure of dating him. She didn't need anything changed. So why had they picked her? What did they expect her to do?

A tingle at the back of her neck drew her eyes from the floor. She flinched when she discovered Logan and his camera a few feet away, the lens trained on her face.

"You're going to be perpetually on camera for a good two months. Try to get used to it," he said gruffly. "Just pretend we're not here."

"Says the person who has probably never been in front of a camera before." The last time Everly had been filmed, it was for the series of drawing videos she did freshman year of college, and she'd been the one controlling the lens.

"Pretend I'm someone you'd actually want to have following you around, then."

"My best friend would be insulted if I imagined her in all that plaid." Everly waved her hand at his shirt.

She'd hoped for a laugh. Or at least the ghost of a smile. She liked to think that maybe those blue eyes crinkled at the corners when he grinned.

But all she got was a frosty stare and a camera homed so steadily on her that she wondered if it could read her thoughts.

And what that might mean for the next few months of her life.

CHAPTER 3

The moment the clock hit five, Everly raced to her car.

Though her fingers had been itching to text Becca all day, finding out you were going to be on your favorite TV show was not the kind of information shared via some grammatically incorrect typing. This needed to be done in person, so they could properly yell.

Which meant Everly needed to get home *now*. Posthaste. Before she exploded from holding the news in for so long.

But as she navigated the darkening streets of Monmouth Cove, it seemed like everyone was intent upon slowing her down. By the time she was within two blocks of her brother Ellis's house, Everly was leaning on the horn, swearing under her breath, and nursing a healthy bout of road rage.

Not that any of that stopped her mind from whirling. She had a contract to review and contact information for the hosts and Sady saved in her phone, and yet she still couldn't believe she was going to be featured in *On the Plus Side*.

Why had they chosen her? Most of the previous guests had some huge event that their episodes built toward. Everly had none of that. Really, she had nothing going on at all. How could Sady possibly think she would be good TV?

And who had nominated her in the first place?

And could she even do this? Be on TV? In front of thousands of people?

As each thought invaded, she whacked it away like one of those plastic moles in a carnival game. This was not the time to be scared. She should be celebrating!

When she got home, Everly found Becca in her usual afternoon spot: curled up on the couch in front of the big bay windows in the living room, making the most of the last rays of natural light. She had her sketchbook propped up against the mountain of a dog lying beside her. Bagel was a mix of yellow Lab and pit bull and had somehow managed to inherit the largest genes from each breed.

Holding up her free hand, Becca signaled that she needed another second of silence to finish her pencil strokes. She'd been an artist basically from birth, and her first love was making character sketches for fans and creators, but her steady income came from illustrating picture books. One of her college professors had helped her to get a foot in the door, and by the time she'd graduated, she already had enough books on her résumé that Ellis had filled the upstairs hallway with poster-sized reproductions of their covers.

It was one of the many things that Everly loved about her best friend. Becca hadn't hesitated to chase her dreams, while Everly didn't let herself have any.

Another box she was too afraid to open.

Maybe *that* was what *OTPS* could help her change.

"Okay. Done." Becca gently eased her sketchbook closed and set it on the coffee table.

A whoosh of air escaped Everly's lips. "Thank god, because holy crap do I have news." She didn't even make it across the room to the couch before blurting out, "I'm going to be on *On the Plus Side.*"

Becca's eyes widened, the palm of her hand that had been smoothing Bagel's short tan fur coming to a stop. "Wait. What?"

"Jazzy and Stanton showed up at my office this morning. Out of nowhere."

Becca shook her head. "Shut. Up. *What?*"

"Stanton took my desk hostage. He was answering the phones and going through my drawers. He dismantled my tea station."

Everly had spent her first three months at Matten-Waverly painstakingly building that setup. She'd found this perfect little apothecary cabinet that housed each of the teas and an adorable mug tree and matching tray to display cups and fixings. It was organizational nirvana. And Stanton was Godzilla.

Becca clutched her chest. "Not the tea station."

Everly tossed a pillow at her head. "Jazzy was charming everyone, as usual. At one point, she was holding court with the entire design department, giving them all fashion advice." Everly grabbed Becca's hand, as if her best friend wasn't already captivated. "She talked to *James.* Forever." And despite his scorching levels of hotness, Jazzy had shown no anxious tics. No weird hesitations. No silences that stretched out into the great beyond. And they were laughing so much. Not once did Jazzy cut herself off or force a tight-lipped smile to strangle the too-loud sound at the back of her throat. Jazzy Germaine never thought she was too much.

"*No.*" Becca rose up on her knees to lean her small frame across Bagel. She grabbed Everly's hands and waved them wildly in her own. "NO!"

"YES," Everly yelled back.

Here, with her best friend, in her brother's house, she could do that. It wasn't like at work or out in public, where Everly worried what people would think of her and her naturally loud voice. Or her tendency to get overly excited. Or her unfiltered sense of humor. All the things that made her mother tense up when Everly didn't rein them in.

The relief of it, of letting her voice, her whole self, just *be,* was like releasing a breath she'd trapped in her lungs for too long.

"They were just *there*. In the flesh. Like they'd stepped right out of the TV. And so was the showrunner, Sady Sanders. And some cameraman." Everly wasn't sure why she'd added that last part. Obviously, there was a crew: it was a TV show. But Logan, with his rough voice and plaid shirt and uncannily blue eyes, was still stuck in her head. A splinter she couldn't dislodge. "They hung around the rest of the day taking . . . what did he call it . . . B-roll? For some special they're going to air the week before season three starts."

"I can't believe you met them." Becca was practically bouncing with excitement. "And they're going to totally bibbity-bobbity-boo you." She flicked a hand in the air like she had a magic wand. "This is amazing."

"It *is* amazing." Everly's voice caught a little on the last syllable.

Becca dropped back on her heels, her features scrunching together. "But?"

Everly heaved out a breath. There were so many contradicting thoughts in her head it was hard to shape them into something logical. "Obviously, I want to do this. But I don't know if I should. If I *can*."

"What do you mean? Of course you should. You're an *OTPS* superfan."

"But all those people . . ."

Bagel had set his head in Everly's lap, and she ran his short, folded ears gently through her fingers. Something about the presence of an animal—their warmth, the way they were so uncomplicated, loved so easily—had always helped to ease her nerves, and already she could feel her heartbeat slowing.

"I don't want to humiliate myself in front of a TV audience."

Everly's mother, half of social media, random passersby on the street, everyone had their own ideas about how someone who looked and acted like Everly should exist in the world. And navigating it all—insisting that she had the right to live exactly as she was—was exhausting. It was easier to blend in. Be quiet.

"Impossible."

"Hi, have you met me? I'm the girl who sat across from you at Jay's Pizza in the middle of the dinner rush, narrating my first biblical encounter with Sean in enough detail that the family sitting near us got up and left. The one who professes her love to everything with a pulse the minute I have a sip of alcohol. You think I'm going to survive weeks of filming without embarrassing myself? Or you all, for that matter?" Everly stretched out her arms to indicate Becca and Ellis, and by extension, their mother.

"None of that's embarrassing. It's you. And it's going to make the audience, and Jazzy and Stanton, love you. It's why we love you."

"Not my mom."

Becca waved her off. "She doesn't count."

Everly snorted. If only that were true.

"Oh my god." Becca slapped her arm, then pointed at the wall above the TV. It was full of art that Everly had made over the years. Most of the frames held little caricatures that the two of them used to send each other when Becca had moved hours away to New Hampshire to live with her grandmother while her mom was deployed. They'd sketched out little comics every week to keep each other updated on their lives. Sometimes, when she and Becca wanted to make fun of Ellis without him knowing,

ON THE PLUS SIDE
25

they'd draw scenes on scraps of paper and pass them to each other across the couch while watching TV. "You could do the Collective." Becca pulled up the calendar app on her phone and then counted on her fingers. "The timing should work out if filming starts soon."

The Cape Cod Collective was the premier art event in southeastern Massachusetts. There was a huge craft show and contests and a gala, and creators from all over had booths to showcase and sell their work. After years of dreaming about participating, Grandma Helen had helped Everly secure a booth four years ago. But then she was diagnosed with cancer, and she died a month before it opened. Everly couldn't imagine doing the Collective without her, so she'd given up her booth. And never tried again.

"I know you've always regretted not doing it junior year. This could be your chance. You know Helen would want you to."

Everly narrowed her eyes. "That sounds suspiciously like the rationale of someone who nominated me for this." It made total sense. No one was more aware of Everly's love for the show than Becca.

Splotches of red seeped over Becca's pale cheeks. A clear sign of guilt. "Oh my god, I wish."

"Uh-huh. Thank you for the early Christmas and birthday present."

Everly's heart was racing. Could she really apply for a booth at the Collective again? It seemed like exactly the kind of event *OTPS* could use for her episode arc. And it would force her to stop hiding her art. Give her a reason to draw again for the first time in years.

Becca shook her head. "No, Ev. Seriously, it wasn't me."

"Of course it wasn't." Everly flashed her a teasing grin. The nominator's reveal was one of the biggest surprises on the show, so Becca probably had to sign a bunch of NDAs and couldn't admit anything until after all the episodes had aired.

Her friend sighed in surrender.

Bagel had rolled over on his back, letting both of them scratch his belly. Joy settled into Everly's limbs. Being on the show would be scary. She'd be putting herself out there, giving strangers a chance to peek into her life, judge her choices, judge *her*.

But Jazzy and Stanton focused on the best parts of each guest, inside and out. They redefined beautiful so everyone could fit within it. Everly wanted to be a part of that. She wanted the chance to spend time with people who intimately understood what it meant to live in a body like hers. She wanted to let herself be an artist again.

She'd seen firsthand (well, via the TV screen) how *On the Plus Side* could transform a person's life.

She just had to let it.

ENTERTAINMENT NOW,
BUZZ-WORTHY TV EDITION
"MEET THE STARS OF *ON THE PLUS SIDE,* THE MAKEOVER SHOW
THAT'S POSITIVELY PLUS-SIZE!"
Samantha Quain, Media Desk

Not since *Queer Eye* has a makeover show created such a stir in
the world of reality TV as *On the Plus Side,* following its premiere on VuNu three weeks ago. In a world where fat is viewed
as ugly and unhealthy, the show and its two stars are working
hard to unpack and reimagine the way plus-size people are seen
by encouraging self-love and acceptance, and leaving conven-
tional ideas of beauty and success behind. A novel concept in
an industry so focused on cookie-cutter perfection.

So who are these champions of body positivity?

Jasmine "Jazzy" Germaine has worked as a beauty

consultant in the fashion and entertainment industry for a decade. Five years ago, she started her #fatisfab movement across social media, styling herself and other plus-size women in hand-sewn replicas of couture to remind the world that beauty comes in all sizes. The hashtag blew up, eventually becoming one of the main spaces where influencers from across numerous industries discuss their experiences with fatphobia and how they overcame them, as well as celebrating body positivity and fat liberation. These days, when not filming episodes of *OTPS,* Jazzy travels the country as a speaker and media consultant for fat representation. Her *On the Plus Side* role is to help the guest with makeup, hair, and fashion. As she says herself, "I want our guests to figure out what *they* love, what makes *them* feel good, not what the world tells them they should like or how they should dress. You can't love yourself until you can actually *be* yourself."

Stanton Bakshi spent his childhood dreaming of entering the comic book industry. After attending art school he landed a job at one of the most prolific comic book publishers in the US, only to be quickly disillusioned by the lack of body diversity in superhero stories. His online campaign to make superheroes fat—because, as he says, superhuman strength does not require muscles—went viral, gaining him thousands of fans, but blacklisting him in the comics industry. Stanton says his shift to the fashion world was inevitable: "With a mother so obsessed with *Sex and the City* that she named me after a character, I was bound to follow in Carrie Bradshaw's footsteps—or more aptly, Manolos." He's thrilled to be part of *On the Plus Side,* working with guests on their career aspirations. "As a fat man, an Indian man, and a gay man, I have unique insight into the ways that our various intersections affect us in the workplace, and I hope to help our guests figure out how to achieve their goals and break through the many walls that get put before us."

CHAPTER 4

The Boston office of New Mood Media was a funhouse hall of mirrors.

Everywhere Everly looked, her face stared back at her. From the façade of the skyscraper, in the marble tiles of the lobby, on the reflective glass of the entryway; you name it, and the evil queen from Snow White could use it to ask who was fairest of them all.

It had been almost a month since Everly agreed to be part of *On the Plus Side*'s third season, and even though her signed contracts were tucked in her purse, her heart was still tap-dancing against her ribs.

There had been too much time over the past few weeks for her to think. Too much time to worry about how she would come across on camera, if she'd embarrass herself, if the audience would care about her quiet little life. Her mom certainly hadn't helped matters by responding to Everly's announcement about the show with a very pointed "Why would you do that to yourself?"

But every time Everly thought about using *OTPS* as a way to participate in the Collective, whenever she thought about how amazing it had been to meet Jazzy and Stanton, and how comfortable she'd felt with them, her choice to be on the show felt more solid. It felt true to her. To the real Everly. The one she spent far too much time squashing down these days.

As she waited for the elevator to make its snail-slow descent from the top floor, she scrolled through the *OTPS* forums on Read-It and tapped open one of the more popular posts.

- -

KateD *5 minutes ago*
If you had a chance to be on OTPS, would you? Hypothetically speaking, obv.

100 ♥ 42 👍 22 ✦ 0 👎

- -

RosyTea *5 minutes ago*
HELL YES

i'd love to be pampered

get new clothes

cut the lines at disney like daisy did last season

40 ♥ 33 👍 11 ✦ 0 👎

- -

CourtK *4 minutes ago*
I bet the grueling production schedule makes it feel a lot less like pampering

29 ♥ 7 👍 8 ✦ 0 👎

Bridget80 *3 minutes ago*

Right???? Someone I know from college went on one of those bachelor-ish shows and she said you get almost no time to yourself, and you're never alone, and the whole thing was so stressful

19 ♥ 3 👍 15 ✦ 0 👎

Annette98 *2 minutes ago*

But for those shows you live on location and are filming the whole season. With OTPS, they come to you and they're only there for a few weeks.

Who wouldn't want to spend a few weeks with Jazzy and Stanton??!?!?! I bet they're a complete DELIGHT!!

10 ♥ 4 👍 11 ✦ 0 👎

KelseyisHere *now*

I would totally do it. I love the idea of viewing myself through someone elses eyes. When Jazzys picking out their clothes and doing their hair and makeup, its like she sees this person, this light, that no one else does, and she brings it out in the guest. Makes it shine. I'd love to know what my light looks like. If that makes sense?

5 ♥ 4 👍 3 ✦ 0 👎

Everly thought about replying—she currently had some very not-so-hypothetical experience with this topic—but it had been so long since she'd last posted anything on the forums that she couldn't bring herself to do it. As much as she loved reading everyone's messages, she wasn't really a part of the community. Just a shadow looming on the periphery.

Instead, she let herself get sucked into a comprehensive ranking of every one of Jazzy's outfits from season two until the elevator doors dinged open in front of her.

Putting her phone back in her bag, Everly used the ride up to the fifteenth floor to smooth the front of her black A-line dress. The fabric was jersey and practically Velcro. She hadn't been near Becca's cat, Cream Cheese, this morning, and yet she kept finding clusters of white fur everywhere.

She was picking at a third patch of it when the elevator stopped and she found herself face-to-face with Logan.

He was also taking advantage of the endless array of reflective surfaces in the building, scrubbing at the skin around his close-cut beard and wide brow like he was washing his face, though there was no water anywhere. "That's what I get for coming in on my day off," he muttered to no one. "Turned into a fucking art project."

Everly snorted. She couldn't help it. There was something almost boyish about how put out he looked that clashed with his beard and muscular arms.

Glancing up, he startled at the sight of her. "Oh. Everly." The heel of his left palm still rubbed idly at his cheek. "What are you doing?"

"Riding the elevator? What are *you* doing?" It seemed like the more reasonable question.

His eyes narrowed, and his (not-at-all-unpleasant) facial features scrunched in confusion. They were both quiet for so long that the elevator doors closed again.

Everly's laugh bounced off the walls. What was happening right now? Was this some kind of setup for the show? Was she being filmed? She peered into each corner of the ceiling to check for cameras, but there didn't seem to be any. Logan hadn't even been holding his.

She pressed the button to reopen the doors, and there he was again. Hoping to avoid another round of elevator peekaboo, Everly hurried forward into the office suite.

Now that she was closer, she could see why he'd been fussing with his face. Across his forehead, down the straight slope of his nose, and streaking his cheekbones were heavy layers of gold, glittery powder.

"Oh," she said. "You've been Jazzy'ed." Jazzy's intense love affair with powdered highlighters was well known among the fandom.

His frown deepened into something more like a scowl. "I look like Rocky from *The Rocky Horror Picture Show*."

"Wait. Does that mean she got you . . . other places as well?" Everly arched an eyebrow. Though she tried not to imagine him in a gold loincloth, she failed in spectacular fashion. He probably had fantastic thighs—thick like his arms. Muscular. Delicious.

Not a hint of humor marred his stony expression. "I ran before she could start painting my beard." He caught her amused gaze and added a surly ". . . or anything else." As he talked, he resumed wiping at the glitter, this time with his knuckles. All he managed to do was smear it into his hairline.

For someone who'd never really been interested in having kids, Everly had a deep maternal streak, and it set in before she could consider what she was doing.

Popping open her large leather tote, she started rummaging. It was stocked with all the essentials: makeup, granola bars, pens and paper, candy for emergency stress eating, toothbrushes and toothpaste, extra underwear, a flashlight, menstrual products, condoms, and a pharmacy of over-the-counter drugs. There was no crisis that couldn't be handled by something in her bag. She'd be a dream to be stranded with on a desert island. It would be more like a vacation.

She unearthed a travel pack of face wipes and offered them to Logan. "Makeup remover."

He took one gingerly, like the cloth was soaked in venom, and dragged the whole thing across his face with the palm of his hand, like a little kid trying to wash up by himself for the first time. It was adorable.

And entirely ineffective.

After a few more rotations, he pulled it back and glanced expectantly at Everly. Most of the powder from his nose and cheeks was gone, but thick clumps clung to his sideburns and the edges of his beard.

She considered pointing them out, then thought better of it. Quite frankly, this man needed a little levity in his life. Maybe resembling an Oscar award for a while would do him some good. "Can you point me to Sady's office?" she asked. "We're supposed to have a meeting."

Logan dragged his glittery palm down the hem of his maroon-and-gray plaid shirt. Apparently, flannel was his look. "Head straight back. It's the biggest one. Tell her I'll be there in a second."

With a grunt Everly chose to interpret as a goodbye, he disappeared in the opposite direction.

Everly removed a few more cat hairs from her dress to distract herself as she wandered toward the back of the suite. The production company's office seemed to take up the whole floor, and the entire exterior wall was windows, tinted a hazy blue to keep the sun's brightness at bay. The rays moved like ocean waves across the tightly piled carpeting. A number of the cubicles Everly passed were empty but she could hear soft voices and the sounds of typing drifting toward her from farther down the hall.

She stopped at an open door with a silver plaque bearing Sady's name. The showrunner saw her immediately and waved her in.

"An early bird," she said. "I love it."

Everly shrugged. "You can never trust Boston traffic." Plus, she had been up since six, her nerves buzzing too much for sleep.

"Grab a seat." Sady gestured to one of two chairs opposite her desk. "My assistant's out today, but I can order you some coffee if you'd like."

"I'm okay." Everly brushed away some lint on her knee in an effort to avoid fussing with her outfit. "The large cold brew I had on the drive up was probably enough caffeine for the rest of the year, but thank you."

"That stuff's a gift. It's gotten me through more than one night shoot."

Everly wanted to ask if any of those were in her future, but a loud knock interrupted them, and she turned to see Logan shadowed in the doorframe.

The front of his shirt was drenched in water, more of it glistening in his dark hair. All of the highlighting powder was gone, except for a stain of gold in the shell of his left ear.

"Did you swim here?" Sady asked.

He grunted as he shoved a tablet under his arm and closed the door behind him. "One of your *stars* ambushed me with her face paint."

Sady arched an eyebrow. "I heard you volunteered."

"Are you kidding? She was brandishing that stuff like a weapon." Shaking his head, Logan dropped into the seat next to Everly. "Can we make this quick? Alan and Ravioli need their walks."

Everly's eyes widened. Ravioli? What an amazing name for a pet. Assuming, of course, that was what he meant, and not that he preferred to take his pasta for a jaunt around the block before eating it. "Um . . . who?"

Sady cracked a grin. "Logan adopts dogs—"

"It's not important," he broke in.

Everly cut her eyes to him, only to find him already staring at her. They were close enough for her to see that his blue eyes had streaks of gray, like lightning. "Dogs are always important," she said.

He grunted (again). "I have two."

That cleared things right up. But Everly didn't press him. It might have been kindergarten logic, but if he didn't want to tell her about his dogs, then she didn't want to hear about them. Even if, in her head, she was already trying to guess what breed Ravioli was. She mentally cataloged the various kinds of dogs she'd met at her grandmother's animal sanctuary when she was younger. Which seemed most likely to be a Ravioli? A puggle? A sheepadoodle? An English mastiff?

"So are you . . . the director?" Everly asked instead. He'd been present when Jazzy and Stanton had surprised her at Matten-Waverly, and here he was again. But this time they weren't filming.

"No. I'm barely the cameraman."

Sady snorted. "He says, like he's not the unofficial DP."

DP, Everly knew, was short for director of photography. They were in charge of the camera work and lighting, or so she had learned on one of her many Google spirals into TV production over the past few weeks. "Unofficial?"

"Dan McKay is our actual DP," Sady says, "but he's—"

"A hack."

"No—"

"Unreliable."

"Logan."

"A complete donkey."

Everly's laugh was loud enough that she slapped a hand over her mouth. Her shoulders tensed, and her cheeks burned, and she glanced at Sady and Logan, expecting them to be staring at her in shock or at least looking mildly uncomfortable, but beyond Logan's arched brow, neither of them reacted. "Sorry. I've just never heard anyone say the word 'donkey' with such gravity."

"Is ass better? I was trying to be professional." His beard moved a little, like he might be fighting off a smile.

Everly let herself relax into her chair. She met his maybe-grin with a definite one of her own. "It's always best to say what we mean."

"He's an ass, then."

She snorted.

Sady rolled her eyes. "Dan is Dan. We're lucky to have Logan here to back him up. And none of this is Everly's concern, anyway." She leaned forward and folded her hands over her closed laptop. "We're here to talk about the production schedule, but I always like to give our new guests a little insight into the show. *OTPS* is my baby. I conceptualized it, I'm the showrunner, and New Mood gives me complete creative control. My goal is to celebrate bodies and people who are too often ignored by the media. And to do it without adding to the stereotypes and microaggressions that are such an ingrained part of our culture when it comes to fat people."

"Like when someone tells you that you have such a pretty face," Everly muttered. It was one of her mother's most favorite phrases.

"Exactly. Or when straight-size people complain to us about being fat."

"Or the way most stores are only 'size inclusive'"—Everly tossed air quotes around the words—"online. Because, god forbid we're allowed to try anything on. So now we have to pay extra shipping to return things, as if we aren't already paying more for our clothes anyway." She didn't realize until she stopped to take a breath how fast and forcefully she was speaking. She cleared her throat. "Sorry, I get real riled up about the fat tax."

Sady held up her hand. "We don't apologize for speaking our truth here." She shook her head. "The 'fat tax.' I love it. Share that one with Jazzy and Stanton for sure." Flashing Everly a welcoming smile, she went on. "All right. You obviously get where I'm coming from, so that's the end of my spiel. Let's get down to brass tacks. I'm assuming you've taken a look at the contracts?"

"I did." Digging into her purse, Everly produced a manila envelope with the signed copies inside. She'd studied the contract for hours, looking up every legal phrase she didn't know and pestering her cousin in law school when that didn't help. There didn't seem to be anything out of the ordinary in it, but she still felt a bit like Faust, signing her soul away.

Sady accepted the envelope, and pulling out the stack of papers, flipped to a particular page. "I like to point out to our guests that, unlike most reality shows, we do not include a right to defame in the contract." She angled the document toward Everly. "This protects you from being misrepresented by the network or the show, and, I hope, will set up a good-faith relationship between us."

Everly nodded. "Got it." It was easy to trust Sady on this. From what she'd seen on the reunion specials and read online, there was very little negativity from guests about how they were portrayed on the show. Only Veronica, who complained that they'd overplayed how much she disliked her makeover. But Veronica had been a drama queen throughout her episodes, so Everly wasn't sure how much she believed her.

"Great." Sady gestured for Logan's tablet, then scrolled through it for a second before finally tapping on an icon. "So, the schedule . . ." She set the device between them, a multilayered spreadsheet open on the page.

Everly's heart sang. It was beautifully color coded.

"We will be starting next week, and filming usually takes about a month and a half, maybe two. We've booked some rooms over at the Seahorse Inn in Monmouth Cove, but we'll be back and forth between there and our Boston offices. Except for travel days, we'll do most filming Friday through Monday—"

"Wait. We won't be filming every single day?" What a relief. Everly had assumed she'd have a camera on her nonstop, and the thought had

had her on edge. No one could be expected to be perfect at all times when they were being watched twenty-four seven.

"We will for the first week or so," Logan chimed in. "I'll basically be following you everywhere as we gather shots for the early episodes."

Everly's eyes snapped toward him. "Everywhere?"

"Everywhere."

This sounded like a complete nightmare. "What if I have a date?"

"I'm coming."

"Dinner with my mom."

"And me."

"Shopping? The gym? A mani-pedi?"

"I'll be there."

"What if I want to hang out with my vibrator?" Something about this man summoned the side of Everly that she tended to curb in public. But she just wanted to see him laugh. Smile. Do anything but glower.

Logan's eyes popped wide, and under his beard, his tan skin flushed. *Bingo.* This time, Everly didn't try to hide her laugh.

Across from them, Sady chuckled. "Whoa, whoa, whoa. Poor Logan is easily scandalized." She shot him a playful wink, earning the first real smile Everly had witnessed from him. It was tiny, the smallest lift of his lips, but his blue eyes brightened like a light someone had just switched on. "He'll be shadowing you within reasonable limits, obviously. Mostly at work or when you go out. The point is to get as much pre-makeover footage as possible so audiences can really see how you're changing over the course of the episodes."

She pointed back at the tablet and its various columns and rows. "After that, the show will be airing as we film, so Logan and I will spend the mid-week up here reviewing footage and seeing what the editors are putting together. We'll follow the usual format. Two weeks of you bonding with the hosts: interviews, wardrobe day, a few outings, that kind of thing." Her purple-painted nail traced over the schedule. "Then the next three weeks, we ease into the transformation stuff: shopping, a few trips, time with your family, career planning, the actual makeover, etc. And the last week or so is dedicated to the finale."

At the end of the document, Sady paused. "As you probably know from watching, every guest has an arc that builds toward an important goal or event. Something that really commemorates the big shift happening in their lives."

Those finales had always been Everly's favorite part of the series. Getting to watch people make their dreams come true or reach what they thought were impossible goals or see themselves in ways they never thought they could was pure magic. Sometimes the best episodes were the ones with the most modest endings. Like Nelly, the freshman in college who just wanted to find a style she loved and felt good in and ended up looking like she belonged in an early Taylor Swift video, all fall vibes and country comfortable. The way she (and Becca and Everly) had sobbed when she went to her first sorority pledge event and everyone lost their minds over her new look was etched right into Everly's heart.

She cleared her throat. "I've actually been thinking a lot about this. I don't have big dreams or anything like some of the other guests, but there's this art festival, the Cape Cod Collective, and I was supposed to do it a few years ago, but . . . it didn't end up happening." She wasn't ready to admit to this person she admired that she'd quit. Or the many reasons why. "Maybe this would be a good opportunity to try again?" Though she tried to keep her voice steady, she could feel herself stumble over the words. Why was this so hard? She wasn't asking for that much. The exposure for the Collective alone would be enough for them to give the show a booth. It wouldn't be a hard sell, even with the event just over three months away in December.

Logan seemed to note her hesitation. His gaze flicked from the tablet to her face, those halting blue eyes prying at her. She tried to stare back, but ended up making intense eye contact with his left earlobe.

Sady's smart pen flew across the bottom of the screen. "I love that idea. I'll have our PR person get in touch with the festival immediately."

Everly leaned over the desk. "What else do you have on that list?"

Sady flapped one hand at her and angled the tablet away with the other. "You'll find out soon enough. We need some surprises. They make good TV." She arched an eyebrow over the top of her glasses. "But what else do you *want* to be on the list?"

"Getting a tattoo. One I design myself." The words flew out of Everly's mouth. It was the first time she'd spoken them, and her heart fluttered at their strange shape on her tongue.

She was fascinated by tattoos. She loved scrolling through ink hashtags on social media, seeing the unique ways people expressed themselves, reading about the meaning behind them. She often lay in bed at night imagining the kinds of sketches she might design for herself, for Becca, for people at work.

But it had always seemed too silly to admit to anyone (even Becca) when Everly didn't have any tattoos of her own and had never actively shown an interest in them. At least not out loud.

Logan's brow furrowed. "You're into tattoos?"

"I don't have any yet, but they're one of my favorite art forms." Everly wrung her hands together in her lap. Her heart was beating wildly in her chest. Could this be part of her *OTPS* journey? A tattoo? Maybe even designing some samples for the Collective that people could buy?

Sady shoved her glasses farther up the bridge of her nose. They changed the shape of her face, highlighting the incline of her cheekbones and accentuating her hazel eyes. It made Everly regret preferring her contacts to her own cat-eye glasses, which she'd once thought were so cool and retro and now worried were too much.

Too loud.

"Tell me more," Sady said.

Everly pursed her lips, shuffling through words in her head to find the right ones. "I love how bold they are. The way you can't help but notice them. They're unabashed and loud and the people who get them are usually proud of that." She ran her finger along the side of her left forearm, where she always imagined her first tattoo would go. "And I love how they all mean something. The most mundane heart or butterfly or whatever has a story when it's on someone's skin, even if that story was, 'I got a little too drunk' or 'I lost a bet.'" Tattoos were a kind of memorial: they remained when everything else—the moment, the feelings, the people—were gone.

Sady shifted to face Logan full on, wiggling her fingers. Her mouth moved like she was trying to remember something. "You have that friend . . . that artist guy . . ."

"Goro?"

"You know Goro Adachi?!" Everly gaped at Logan. "His stuff is *stunning*."

Sady nodded, like this was scripted and they were reading their lines perfectly. "Maybe he can do Everly's tattoo? Help her design it? That could make for some great footage."

Logan shrugged. "I can ask."

Everly's gaze bounced between them. Were they delusional? She couldn't collaborate with one of the world's premier tattoo artists. "Um. Maybe we could wade into the kiddie pool first? I've never designed a tattoo. I don't even have one. Working with Adachi would be like asking a kindergartener with some new finger paints to join Jackson Pollock in a session, don't you think?"

Sady's eyes narrowed, but Logan cracked an actual, legitimate smile. And it was a good one. "Pollock's stuff looks like finger paints anyway."

"My apologies. I didn't realize you were an art expert." She sounded more flirty than sarcastic, so Everly rolled her eyes for extra effect. He, of course, didn't even blink in response.

Sady kept writing and talking as if they hadn't said anything. "Jazzy wants to take you to Kisses and Hugs, too. She thinks they're a perfect label for you, and they recently opened a new boutique on Newbury Street."

Everly's fingers squeezed the hem of her dress. She shopped thrift stores, sales, and clearance exclusively, and, even then, often with coupons. She'd never stepped foot into a high-end fashion boutique before. "Wow, their stuff's . . ." She didn't know how to finish her sentence without sounding like she was worried about money.

"The show covers everything, so price isn't an issue." Sady glanced at Everly over the rim of her glasses. "I like that this makes you a little uncomfortable, though."

"Oh?" Everly's stomach cramped at her tone.

"The best TV happens outside your comfort zone."

"And the biggest disasters," Everly muttered.

Sady gave her a wink from behind her glasses. "Well," she grinned, "that's also good TV."

CHAPTER 5

In a moment as rare as a Loch Ness monster sighting, Everly's brother and mother were both standing in her apartment at the same time.

In her bathroom, to be exact. Well, technically, Ellis was loitering awkwardly outside of it, but their mom's tiny body filled the space until Everly's lungs tightened like there was no air left.

"Explain this to me again."

Everly sighed. "You know what's going on, Mom." Though she'd told her family about being on the show weeks ago, her mother had not taken it well, nor had she stopped reminding Everly at every opportunity that she disapproved of this decision. So Everly shouldn't have been surprised to find her on her doorstep this morning before her alarm went off. It was the first morning of filming, and Penny Winters was not exactly known for letting a topic go before she had beaten it fully to death.

Everly tried to focus on her reflection in the mirror. Logan would be here any minute to get her geared up, and she was trying hard not to succumb to her nerves, which felt as raw and electric as a live wire.

Her mother's presence was not helping matters.

She frowned at Everly. "I just don't understand why you would want to be on a show that encourages people to be fat."

A frustrated groan rammed its way up Everly's throat, but she swallowed it down. "That is not what it does. It shows people how to feel good about themselves exactly as they are."

There was so much more she wanted to say. Like how after watching the episode where Hannah tried on a crop top for the first time, Everly had cut the bottom off an old T-shirt to see how she'd feel in one. And she'd cried because she'd looked just as good as any thin person. She hadn't had the courage to leave the house in it yet, but she wore it around her apartment, and it was the most skin she'd shown outside the shower in years. She wanted to tell her mom about the forum post she'd read where the poster was determined to stop calling themselves fat when they were having a bad self-esteem day, because they realized the damage it caused after watching Nelly's episode. This show made a difference every day.

"Which makes them not bother to lose the weight," her mom declared.

Strangling the handle of her brush, Everly pulled it through her straight, reddish-brown hair. This was why it was easier to shut down and stay quiet. The road of least resistance and all that. She would never change her mother's mind. For Penny Winters, weight loss was the magical cure for everything. A bad day at work? Lose five pounds. Money trouble? Just diet a little. Global climate crisis? Drop a size. But losing weight was not easy, or even safe, for everyone, and, as earth-shattering as this fact might be to her mother, being as small as possible was not what everyone wanted. It wasn't what *Everly* wanted.

"*Ma.*" Her big brother to the rescue. Ellis and their mother exchanged a glance that stopped whatever words might have been poised to leave her mouth, as if the two of them were twins who shared a secret language.

They might as well have been. Though almost a foot apart in height, Everly's brother and mother had the same slim shoulders, straight back, and blond-copper hair. Their chocolate-brown eyes, bow-shaped mouths, and high-arching cheekbones all a match. It was like someone had photocopied her mother and then stretched her out and squared her off to make Ellis.

Meanwhile, the only thing Everly inherited from her mother was her congenitally missing teeth, which had led to a fun half decade of braces.

The rest of her echoed her father—average height, round cheeks, greenish-blue eyes, hair somewhere between auburn and brown. Every time Everly glanced in the mirror, she saw his face and wondered how he could leave her behind when everything about her claimed him. Ellis insisted they didn't need him, but their father was an internal scab she didn't know how to stop picking at, even fifteen years later.

Her mouth a taut line, Everly's mother swept her daughter's hair off her shoulder. "You should add a little more makeup." She frowned at the mirror. "And maybe have gotten a haircut and a new outfit."

Everly ground her teeth. "Mom, the whole point of this is to be myself. I don't need a makeover *for* the makeover show."

"But you're going to be on TV. You want to look your best. That's the point, right?" Her mother had somehow armed herself with a powder brush and was aiming for Everly's cheeks.

Shaking her head, Everly ducked toward the door. The point was to learn to be comfortable as herself. And to reclaim some of the person she'd lost over the past few years.

Imagine *that* Everly. She'd have a booth every year at the Collective. And her own chair at a tattoo studio. She'd be wearing the bold, bright, *loud* patterns she loved. And she'd probably have asked James out by now. Maybe they'd be dating—living out some of the stairwell fantasies

she'd only allowed herself to think about in the privacy of her own bedroom, covered in darkness.

The thought alone brought enough color to her cheeks that her
mother set down the brush. Instead, she turned to exalting the miracle
(according to her) that was shapewear as she followed Everly into the
living room/kitchen combo that made up most of her apartment above
the garage.

Everly almost jumped when her mother grabbed her hand and
squeezed. "I just want you to be happy," she said. "That's why your brother
and I are here. We wanted to make sure you were okay for your first day."

It was clear she meant it, even if she didn't understand what happiness looked like for her daughter. This had always been the way with
her mother: the best of intentions, the worst executions. Everly squeezed
her mom's hand back. "Doing this will make me happy." Her gaze cut
between her mother and her brother. "And having you both be a part
of it."

Out the window, she saw a shiny black SUV pull up to the driveway. Logan slid out of the passenger seat a moment later. He was wearing yellow-and-green plaid, his sleeves rolled up again. The muscles in
his thick forearms flexed under the weight of the boxes he hefted out
of the back.

"They're here," she announced. The words kicked her heart into high
gear. The moment she stepped outside, this would be it. No turning back.

Her limbs were stiff enough to creak as she trailed her family down
the stairs that stretched the side of the garage, watching Ellis disappear
back into his house, and her mom climb into the red Toyota she'd had
since Everly was in junior high. She rubbed at her arms to try to quell
the nervous thrum that buzzed beneath her skin.

How was she supposed to do this? What if she was so awkward or
loud or weird that the viewers hated her? What if she didn't like any of

the clothes Jazzy picked out? What if Jazzy and Stanton didn't think her art was any good? What if James came to talk to her while Logan was filming?

That final thought had Everly wishing she could lie down on the stairs. The very idea of her and James on film, for anyone to watch, to speculate about, to laugh at, blew her knees right out.

She had to grip the railing to pick her way down to the driveway.

Logan tipped a chin in greeting.

"Thanks for agreeing to go in so early," he said. "It will give me a chance to set up all the equipment."

"No problem."

It wasn't like she'd slept last night anyway. All she could think about was what would happen today. What footage would they get? What kind of story would Sady tell about her?

Logan crouched on the ground to dig through a big black bag. Uncoiling a wire, microphone, and battery pack from the side pocket, he gestured for Everly to come closer. "Put this lav mic on." His eyes swept over her, presumably looking for somewhere to anchor the device, but her heart galloped anyway. Damn him and his hypnotic blue eyes.

His jaw tightened. "You had to wear a dress."

"Was I not supposed to?" Everly's shoulders went rigid. There'd been nothing about wardrobe in the contract or the call sheets Sady had sent her.

"It's a pain in the ass. Now we're going to need to . . ." His voice was rough with frustration, and a furrow appeared in his brow. ". . . get this under . . ." He held up the mic, then shook a hand at her dress. ". . . that."

He reminded her of a thirteen-year-old trying to say the word "vagina." It hinted again at the possibility of something softer, more bashful, under his gruff exterior, and the urge to break through it hit Everly like a truck. She gave in to it, slowly dragging up her hem above her knee.

He yelped. "What are you doing?"

"You said you needed to get under my dress." She could barely stifle her laughter. He was so easy to fluster.

Plus, teasing him was really helping to ease her own nerves.

"I meant—" He stopped short, and his mouth pressed into a tight line. "Put that down," he said, gesturing to the skirt she was still holding. His voice hitched a little at the end, and his face was flushed.

Everly took the mic pack from his hands with a smile.

As soon as the garage door shut behind her, she got to work on the microphone. Its battery pack had a waist strap, which she tried first, but it was a good four inches too short for her midsection. The clip fared no better: the battery was too heavy for her satin underwear, causing the fabric to roll down her ass if she moved so much as an inch.

She was searching her half-full laundry baskets and the shelves of detergent for some way to fasten it securely when Logan knocked on the door.

"Everything okay?"

She stared dejectedly at the black Velcro in her hand. Nothing like having to tell a guy you barely knew that you were too big for his standard-sized equipment. She swallowed. She'd hoped that they would be prepared for this inevitability when working on a show specifically for plus-size people. *On the Plus Side* should be one place where Everly didn't have to feel this way. She let that righteous indignation seep into her voice as she said, "Having a bit of a wardrobe malfunction."

He was quiet for long enough that she could hear the dance of the wind through the trees outside the window. "Your wardrobe or mine?" His voice was closer, like he'd pressed to the door.

"I can't see you so I have no idea how your clothes are doing."

He groaned. "Is it the mic?"

She fisted her fingers around the device. "Yeah. It—"

"Greg packed the wrong strap, didn't he?"

Everly didn't know who Greg was, but she liked the idea that the problem was him, not her body. "Maybe?"

"I told him to throw out everything but the extra-large. The other sizes barely fit kids, for Christ's sake."

Some of the tension released from her shoulders. "What do I do?"

"Let me get a second one."

"Are we going to pull a MacGyver?"

"Fewer explosions, but sure."

Everly had only seen one real smile on Logan's face, but she thought she could hear another in his voice now. She hoped his eyes were crinkling at the corners. And that maybe a dimple had appeared beneath his beard.

Then a thought hit her. "You're not filming, right?" This didn't exactly set the tone she wanted for her episodes.

"Of course not. You don't have a mic on."

"So wait, otherwise, you *would* be filming?"

He groaned. "Just take this."

He jiggled the door handle until she flipped the lock and opened it a crack. His hand and part of that muscular forearm slid into her vision, another strap hanging from his fingers. When she peeked at him on the other side of the door, his eyes were closed. As if she might be indecent.

"What are you doing?"

"Giving you privacy."

"You think I'd open the door naked?"

"Who knows? You were yanking up your dress in the middle of the driveway a minute ago."

"Oh my god, you're dramatic. I lifted it like two inches."

His eyes flicked open, and Everly's heart leapt a little when they caught on hers. Lethal. Those things were lethal.

She grabbed the strap and shut the door again.

It took a little ingenuity, but she managed to secure the two belts together and get the battery pack strung around her waist beneath her loose navy-and-white-striped dress. She snaked the wire up through the V-neck collar and hooked the mic near her shoulder, which was closest to her mouth, and, she assumed, the best place to pick up sound.

The wire tickled her skin as she moved, and it was going to be an uphill battle not to fuss with the battery pack every time she sat down. Between this and a camera in her face, she wasn't sure how she was supposed to act like today was a regular day.

Logan was leaning against the garage when she opened the door, his fingers jabbing at his phone. "All good?" he asked.

Everly flashed him a thumbs-up.

As it turned out, her car needed a host of equipment, too. Logan fixed two GoPros around the driver's seat—one under the rearview mirror, the other mounted beside her window—and put a third in the same place on the passenger side.

"Do you have people in the back a lot?" He tilted the small camera this way and that, checking it on his phone to see how the angle looked.

Everly skimmed her hand along the steering wheel. "You overestimate the amount of people I know."

He let out a noise somewhere between a grunt and a laugh. "You probably won't be driving that much anyway. Jazzy and Stanton have a tricked-out SUV for your retreats. This is mostly to catch the quiet thoughts you might have when you're alone."

Her head whipped in his direction. "I hope you're suggesting that your camera can read my mind."

Logan stared at her long and hard, as if determining how much she was joking. "You're going to have to talk out loud. Narrate things. Tell us how you're feeling."

Everly groaned. "Isn't there usually a producer there to prompt me?"

"Yeah, but Sady—"

"Wants the realism."

"Yup."

Great. Half the thoughts that popped into Everly's head weren't appropriate for public consumption.

Logan settled into the passenger side and snapped his seat belt on. His gaze shifted to her, but she continued to look out the windshield at the dew gathering on the garage door.

"You're going to be fine. Just be yourself."

"Except I don't normally talk out loud in the car. Or walk around with a gaggle of cameras in my wake."

"A gaggle?"

"A parliament? A murder? What's your preferred term?"

"There's no gaggle. Just me, remember? One camera." Though still low and rough, something softer had snuck into his voice. "They want something they can use for the premiere special and to fill in the occasional gap among the other footage, that's all. Mostly, you'll have Jazzy and Stanton there."

"Easy to say from the passenger seat." And behind the camera.

Everly turned the key in the ignition. Being on camera was scary. There were so many ways she could embarrass herself. So many opportunities to say the wrong thing, to laugh too loud, to be too much. But if she wanted a chance to be in the Collective and do right by Grandma Helen, if she wanted the push she needed to get the tattoo she'd dreamed about, if she wanted to figure out what her career could be, who *she* could be, then she had to get used to being filmed. And maybe try to find a way to enjoy it.

Maybe she could torment Logan endlessly until the final shoot. So far that had been plenty enjoyable. She fought off a smile at the thought.

"You ready?" He adjusted the camera in his lap so it was aimed at her profile.

She nodded.

His eyes lingered on her face for a moment, then he flicked a switch on the side of the camera, and a red light popped on.

Filming had begun.

SIX YEARS EARLIER

@EverlyWinters on YouTube

Video #67

Video opens to a younger Everly sitting at a desk in her small dorm room. Her hair is piled messily on top of her head, and she's wearing a tie-dyed sweatshirt with the collar cut out so it hangs off her right shoulder. "Claymore University" is written across the rainbow colors in white.

She arches her eyebrows at the camera.

EVERLY: Hey all. I wasn't planning on posting anything this week, but people were shook by my reimagined cover for *Romeo and Juliet* with a fat Juliet—which, to be clear, was probably closer to accurate Renaissance beauty standards. Go look at some Renaissance art if you don't believe me. Plump ladies used to be scorching hot. Fuck it. We still are. Have you seen our boobs? Our hips? They call them love handles for a reason. It's something to hold on to.

A blush sweeps across her cheeks, but she grins slyly at the camera and winks.

   EVERLY: Anyway. A lot of you asked about how I draw fat bodies, so I thought I'd do a quick how-to with a guy's body this time.

The camera shakes as she spins in her chair to face her desk and attempts to fasten her phone to a mount. It clatters loudly to the desk.

   EVERLY: Shit.

There is a loud snort, then a louder laugh.

   EVERLY: Well, I guess that's staying in there since I suck at editing videos, and I don't have time before chem to start over.

There's more shaky footage of her desk as she mounts her phone more securely. When the image steadies, it is focused on a sketch pad resting diagonally across the desk. Her right hand is holding a charcoal pencil.

   EVERLY: I always start my figure drawing with circles. Usually three. One for the head, one for the upper body, and one for the lower body. How you space them out, and the varying size of the circles will determine the figure's height and shape. So if you want to draw someone who is middle-heavy, you'd want the last two circles to be similar in shape and to intersect. Like this . . .

CHAPTER 6

"What seems more retro to you? A disco aesthetic or a cottagecore vibe?"

The phone hadn't rung for the last hour, and half of upper management was at a conference, so Everly had taken to mocking up a few designs for clients to pass the time. Over the next few weeks, Stanton would push her to think about her career goals, so this could be a good way to decide if brand building and marketing was something she actually enjoyed.

Currently, she was assembling a style sheet for a bakery that had requested something feminine and retro.

"You're not supposed to talk to me," Logan muttered from behind his camera. He'd been standing in the corner of Reception since the office opened, like a garden ornament without a garden.

"It's hard when you're right there." And he'd been right there since they'd left her house—beside her in the car, filming as she fed the parking meter (dropping her quarter and having to chase it down the sidewalk must have made for *enthralling* footage), taking the elevator up to the office, making a lackluster cup of coffee in the break room because she'd been so nervous she drove right by her usual coffee spot and was too embarrassed to turn around.

Though she was doing her best to forget about his camera and relax, she couldn't seem to stop sneaking glances at him.

She'd thought she was being stealthy about it, pretending to flip through papers or fiddle with the phone whenever she faced his direction, but then he'd groan and drop his head back against the wall. "We're not in an episode of *The Office*. Stop looking at me."

If only he knew how impossible that was. His face was somehow both rugged and elegant at the same time, like a duke in a romance novel who had been lost out in the wilderness for too long, and his whole look was rendered all the more appealing by the way his jaw and brow were always frowning and furrowing. Then there were those damn eyes that stripped Everly down to nothing.

"Everly."

Her name sounded different in his low, graveled voice: the syllables more complex, more interesting. It caused her heart to flip in her chest, and she shifted her gaze back to her monitor.

Two seconds passed in silence.

"Cottagecore is less retro and more 'milking goats on the prairie.'" Each word was clipped, like she'd forced them from his mouth.

"Ah yes, those classic children's books."

"You know what I mean."

She flashed him an amused grin. "I love that you know what cottagecore is."

"You can't work on a show like this and not pick up some things." His plaid shirt rustled as he adjusted his stance. "Now stop looking at me."

She swiveled her chair so she was aimed directly at her computer. "Disco makes more sense anyway. The bakery is called 'Hot Stuff.'"

He strangled a quiet laugh, clearly opposed to sounding even the tiniest bit jovial.

Everly squinted at the chevron stripes on her screen. They looked more contemporary than retro. Attempting something a little more obvious, she set the lettering over an actual disco ball, only to delete it a second later. Obvious had never been her style.

She was cycling through rows of clip art when James strode around the corner. Immediately, her back pulled straight like someone had tugged a cord, and her fingers fussed with the hem of her skirt, pressing it to her knees. She'd been too distracted by Logan to pay attention to the time. Two hours before lunch was James's trail mix break. He even ate the raisins.

Horrifying.

Everly's pulse jolted into a panicked rhythm as James draped himself across the reception counter. Logan was still here. Still filming.

James's melon-sized biceps flexed with the weight of his chin resting on his hand. "Hey, V," he said. "What's up?"

Everly stared at his mouth, as if it had formed sounds that weren't quite words. She always joked that when she was nervous, she looked like she'd just smelled something vile. God, was that her expression right now? Did she appear to be sniffing a particularly ripe chunk of cheese? What would viewers think if this footage made it to air?

What's up? That was all he'd asked. The same thing he greeted her with almost every day. Yet each response that popped into her head was more ridiculous than the last. Her brain seemed incapable of interpreting the phrase anything but literally.

The ceiling? The light fixture? His fly? Ugh. No. That last one was a fast pass to HR.

"Uh . . . the elevator?" she finally offered. Her tone sounded as pathetic as she felt.

James frowned. "What?"

"Nothing. Nothing's up. Totally boring over here." It was not a good save, but she leaned in anyway.

Logan snorted from his spot in the corner. She leveled him a glare, sharing a long, decisive moment of eye contact with the camera that she hoped ruined the shot.

Then, because she didn't want to give him the satisfaction of getting under her skin, she swung her chair back around to face James.

In her head, she was grace and nonchalance.

In reality, her elbow swept wide across her desk as she spun (a bit too fast), creating a tchotchke avalanche. Her metal water bottle rolled loudly over the faux wood before crashing to the floor. Pens clattered. Her vinyl figurines tumbled like dominos. Mr. Darcy slammed into Gonzo who face-checked Statler who smashed into Flynn Rider who toppled onto Ursula the sea witch. In the quiet of the office, it sounded like a set of pots and pans being banged together, a toddler's symphony.

"Oh crap." As if she was the one who'd fallen, James rushed around the desk. He must have been a runner along with all his CrossFit because he was in front of her in the blink of an eye.

At the same time, they both bent over and reached for Gonzo.

Their temples cracked together. Loud enough that Everly was sure the camera caught it. Or at least her sharp yelp as pain shot through her skull and white stars burst behind her eyes.

When her vision cleared, she saw James cradling his forehead with his hand. He looked as dazed as she felt.

"Are you okay?" they asked at the same time.

He was smiling sheepishly, and heat flushed her cheeks. If they didn't already know each other, this would have qualified as a meet cute. Or a meet awkward at least. For a second, Everly could almost imagine telling her friends about it someday, she and James sitting across from them in a restaurant booth, holding hands like they were molded only to fit each other.

But that pleasant image shattered as reality set in, and she remembered Logan was still there. Watching. Filming.

Slinking off her chair, she landed on her knees and cowered under her desk. She pretended to be cleaning her mess, but really she was trying to grab a moment of privacy to reset.

Until James crouched next to her.

"Sorry I'm a disaster," she mumbled.

James shook his head, the corners of his eyes squinting against his smile. "You're doing great. I don't know how anyone can act normally with a camera around." He nudged her so gently in the arm that she wasn't sure how she was still in solid form. Something about a strong guy touching someone like they had to be careful not to break them always squeezed her in all the right places.

He set his pile on the desk. "I know you have a system for these, so I'm not going to try to put them back."

"Smart." She hoped she sounded teasing, even as her cheeks reinvented the color red. She never knew James noticed her desk organization. Or anything about her besides her design skills.

"I think that's everything." He rose to his feet and wiped his palms on his pants leg.

"Me too." Everly slid back into her chair.

He grinned again. This guy probably smiled in his sleep. "Time to go ice my head." He tapped his temple, then grimaced like there was a bruise.

"I will pray for no subdermal hematomas." Good god, she was doing it again. Forgetting to think before she spoke. She watched too many damn medical dramas with Becca.

The expression on James's face as he walked away made her want a panic room in which she could hide from herself.

Everly wasn't one of those people who could let embarrassment roll off their backs. She was an obsesser. A re-liver. She would replay this moment over and over in her head like a new song she'd just heard until nothing else existed.

She was so lost in humiliation hell that she didn't realize Logan had come closer until he cleared his throat.

Within range, of course, to have captured that entire encounter with James.

Everly silently begged someone to throw her a bone and cut a hole in the time-space continuum that she could fall into.

"You were doing good until that whole hematoma thing. What was that?" There wasn't so much as a smile in his voice to suggest he might be joking.

"Thank you for the unsolicited opinion." She slotted her felt-tip pens in their black floral mug with a little more force than was strictly necessary. Suddenly, now that it didn't seem to matter, she was doing a great job not looking at the camera. "Please don't use any of that."

"I'm just the guy with the camera. I don't make those calls."

She sighed. "Then you couldn't have helped me out?"

"You seemed to have it handled."

"No, I mean, leave me some dignity. You don't need to record *every* one of my awkward moments. Some could conveniently disappear from the footage."

Talking to the monitor instead of Logan felt like addressing a ghost. Or an imaginary friend. Someone nonexistent. It wasn't like they could use this part anyway, since he was in it.

She faced him head-on.

The camera obscured his expression. She could only see his left eye and a corner of his bearded cheek. He looked colder this way; everything that had felt softer, easier to poke at before James had appeared was now hidden behind plastic and glass. She was surprised by how alone it made her feel.

"It is the sacred duty of the cameraman to record all but not get involved," he said.

"Do you have to swear that on a fish-eye lens before every gig?"

"Yup. Then we slice our palms and smear blood across the memory cards. It's a whole ritual."

Despite her embarrassment, a smile fought at her lips. "So, if I were to choke on a piece of carrot while sitting here, you'd keep recording and let me die?"

"If there was someone else nearby to help . . ."

Her eyes widened. "Oh my god. What if we're alone?"

"Why are we alone at your office?"

Quite a few options ran through her head, but Everly managed to get her tongue under control for once. "To allow my hypothetical scenario to play out." Crossing her arms over her chest, she leaned back in her chair, taking him in slowly. Like a challenge. Daring him to say yes.

But since she was the antithesis of intimidating, she probably looked like she was checking him out.

And then she was. Because those forearms. The way the right one flexed as he balanced the camera on his shoulder, his muscle so taut it looked sculpted from stone. A tattoo peeked out from the end of the rolled cuff. All she could see was the bottom half of a black circle.

She shook her head and resumed eye contact with the camera.

"Of course I wouldn't let you die."

She nodded sharply in approval.

Then there was a rare tug of his lips toward a smile, a hint of playfulness under the roughness of his voice as he added, "But I'd get it on camera if I could."

CHAPTER 7

The warehouse sign was large and brightly lit, with a slightly off reproduction of Wreck-It Ralph shouldering a pile of bricks and broken wood and metal at its center. Below the image, angry block letters spelled out THE WRECK-IT ROOM, then in smaller font, *Where you can rage against more than machines.*

Everly cocked an eyebrow. "This place likes to live on the edge when it comes to copyright infringement."

"Okay, but we're here for pleasure, not work," Becca said with a laugh. She flattened her palms against Everly's back and urged her forward.

Everly, Becca, and Ellis had been instructed to meet Stanton here at nine thirty in the morning. They'd been told nothing except to dress comfortably, and already, Everly was regretting not taking that more seriously.

As if reading her thoughts, her brother pointed at the mascot's red overalls. "You should have worn that."

A rage room definitely wasn't the best place for Everly's jeans and heeled black booties, but she wasn't about to take fashion advice from Ellis, of all people. "Says the guy who only knows how to dress like an accountant." Even his loungewear included pressed khakis and a collared shirt.

"They say to dress for the job you have," he replied.

"It's dress for the job you *want,* dork," Everly shot back with a smirk.

Ellis shrugged. "They're the same for me."

Everly's stomach twisted. What was that like? She didn't hate working reception at Matten-Waverly, but it wasn't exactly her dream job either. She hadn't dressed up as a secretary for career day at school. No, she'd been a painter, a veterinarian, and one year, when she was feeling particularly ambitious, both at the same time (she'd worn paint-splattered coveralls under a pristine lab coat and carried around one of her stuffed dogs). These days, though, safe and comfortable won out over everything else.

But safe and comfortable could never be something Everly *loved.* Passion and excitement came with an inherent risk. You might lose, fail, be let down. Wasn't that why she'd backed out of the Collective the first time? Because without Grandma Helen there, her mother's doubts had sunk too far into her skin for Everly to pluck them out.

On the Plus Side was going to help her overcome that fear. She'd have a booth at the Collective. And she'd find a career she loved. Maybe it would be doing tattoos. Or marketing. Maybe she'd go back to sketching book covers like she used to do in her old YouTube videos. Maybe she'd be like fourth-grade Everly, and do them all at once. That was the beauty of this show. She didn't have to make any decisions right now. *OTPS* was the start of a journey, not the end.

The entrance to the Wreck-It Room was spacious, sparsely filled, and a headache-inducing shade of pure white. Clearly demarcated into two sections, one was dedicated to T-shirts, sweatshirts, hats, and other merchandise with the company logo. On the other side, a metal counter stretched from window to wall, the large TV behind it shuffling through footage of guests participating in various stages of destruction. But the focal point of the space was a set of large barn doors that led into what Everly assumed was the warehouse proper, *Let the Rage Begin* scrawled across them in black spray paint. Rock music pulsed loudly enough from behind the distressed wood to cause the floors of the entranceway to tremble beneath her feet.

Stanton and Sady waved from where they were leaning on the counter, talking to an employee. Logan, who'd been wandering around getting B-roll, swung the camera toward Everly.

Her stomach flipped. It hadn't even been a day since she'd last seen him, following the now (in her mind) infamous vinyl figure fiasco with James, yet her body reacted like this was the first time she'd ever laid eyes on Logan.

Her gaze caught his briefly, then she glanced away before she had to suffer another lecture on the ills of breaking the fourth wall.

Stanton rushed to meet them, a wide smile spreading across his light brown cheeks. His dark curls spilled out of the hood of what looked like a white hazmat suit. He had another one draped over his arm, presumably for Everly. Once again, she regretted her choice of footwear.

"Are you ready to smash your negative feelings?" he asked.

On the TV over his shoulder, a man slammed a golf club into a wine bottle, the pieces of glass exploding across his feet like shrapnel. Everly cringed. There was nothing safe or fine about swinging heavy objects at breakable items. But that was the exact mindset she was supposed to be challenging. "Uh. Sure." She did her best to muster some enthusiasm.

"Us too, right?" Ellis's brown eyes grew into rounder and rounder Os as he took everything in. Their whole lives, Everly's brother had loved taking things apart—the toaster, their mom's hairdryer, Everly's dolls—to see how they worked. And more often than not, he did this by smashing them open. Everly's Barbie graveyard had been a macabre sight; thank god they'd gotten most of them for cheap at thrift stores.

"How else are you supposed to help Everly break through her barriers?" Stanton wagged an eyebrow.

Doing a little fist pump, Ellis dragged Becca off to get changed into their protective gear.

Stanton directed Everly to another dressing room behind the counter so she could do the same. When she emerged, Sady and Logan were positioning her brother for an interview.

Which meant that, for a brief second, Everly wasn't the center of attention. She took it in with a sigh of relief and leaned against the wall to enjoy a little peek at the inner workings of her favorite show.

Sady gestured for Ellis to stand in front of the barn door, so the invitation to come break things perfectly framed his head.

She peered into the camera's viewfinder, then cut her gaze to Logan. "Do you think it's too . . . ?" She waved her hand to indicate something. Everly had no idea what she meant, but Logan clearly got it. Nodding, he stepped forward and guided Ellis to a blank wall.

"What about this?" He and Sady glanced at the camera's screen again.

They both cringed and said "No, too bright" at the same time, like some sort of hive mind.

Everly's cheeks warmed. She'd never been as in sync with anyone— even Becca—as these two seemed to be. How many projects had Sady and Logan worked on together?

After rotating Ellis through a few other spots, they finally agreed on the right lighting and background and began his interview.

It was too awkward to have someone talking about her like she wasn't standing two feet away, so Everly wandered toward the merchandise. But when she heard Sady ask Ellis what he wanted for his sister, Everly froze, listening without meaning to.

"I want her to find herself again."

"What do you mean?" Sady prompted.

"She used to be one of the most confident people I knew. But over the last couple of years, she's started to doubt everything. It's like she's afraid to be herself or something." Her brother's face was more serious than Everly had seen it in a long time. "She has this laugh." Ellis shook his head. "It's loud and . . . I don't know . . . full of life or vigor or whatever. I miss it. I miss *her*."

Everly tugged at the elasticized waist of her white suit. She'd had no idea her brother felt this way. He'd never said anything.

He missed her. The real her.

And, really, so did she.

She just wasn't sure how to find her way back to that version of herself. Or if there'd be anything left of her once she did.

The sledgehammer weighed more than expected but, god, swinging it at the old CRT TV was satisfying. As the gray screen crunched inward, the whole thing toppled to the floor with a bang.

"Yeehaw!" Everly yelled.

Stanton stopped mid-swing to arch a brow at her. "Excuse me, cowgirl?"

She grinned. "Breaking stuff should always be accompanied by yelling." To prove it, she let out a guttural scream like the final girl from a horror film as she turned and brought her hammer down on a half-broken wooden chair.

"She's not wrong," Becca piped in. She followed up her golf swing at a set of green wineglasses with a Tarzan call.

"Sexy, baby." Ellis winked at his wife.

Everly gagged. "That's my best friend you're making suggestive faces at."

"You know I do more than that with her, right?"

"Oh my god." Everly hauled her hammer over her shoulder and brought it down repeatedly on a cracked concrete block, doing her best to drown out her brother's voice. The rest of them were laughing, but Everly would *not* be joining in. Thinking about your sibling having sex was no better than being forced to recognize that your parents knew each other carnally.

Stanton finally took his first swing at an object, slamming an aluminum bat into a stack of plates in spectacular fashion. Shards of porcelain rained down like confetti as he threw back his head and hollered.

He blew out a breath when he was done and wiped at his brow. "You're naming everything, right?" he asked Everly.

She narrowed her eyes. "What do you mean?"

"Label everything you break. It's part of the process." He spun his grip on the bat and pointed the end at his next target, a large, flat serving platter. "For example, we'll call that one the comics industry. Every imprint that denied my pitches because heroes needed to have 'a certain look.'" He threw air quotes around the last few words before choking up his hands on the bat's neck and landing a stunning strike at the plate's center. Half of it launched in the air, smashing into the closest wall.

Lowering his arms, he scanned the floor. Then he retrieved a computer monitor and placed it on the barrel in front of Everly. "What's this?"

Everly didn't need to think twice about it.

She pictured Grandma Helen as she brought the hammer back over her shoulder. First, how she'd looked for most of Everly's life—tall and round, strong, confident. The way her eyes disappeared into her plump cheeks when she grinned. The way she loved to swear, and to yell, and to laugh, and only grew louder the more Everly's mom tried to shush her. Everly used to look forward to holiday gatherings, not for the gifts or the food, but for the chance to watch her mom squirm beneath the shadow of her own mother's unbridled energy.

Then Everly recalled how all that had been sucked away by chemo. At the end, her grandmother had been so small and frail. Her laughs had turned into coughs, her bright smiles into closed-mouth grimaces. Cancer stole her grandmother's joy, her laughter, her magnetism. Then it took her life.

She slammed the sledgehammer down on the monitor as if it could erase those final images of Grandma Helen from her mind. There was a loud crack, and the plastic stand snapped, but the casing remained intact. She frowned. She'd wanted it to crumble under the force of her blow.

She wanted to have the power to change things. If she didn't, what was the point of being on this show?

Logan had been circling the room, grabbing footage, helping Sady direct everyone into the best spots for filming, all while managing to avoid getting hit by swinging blunt objects and flying debris. His agility was pretty impressive. Everly was sure she would have been bleeding from multiple wounds by now if she'd been in his position.

He paused across from her and, for a second, lowered the camera from his face. "Place it flat," he said.

"What?"

"The monitor."

She stared at it. He was right. There'd definitely be more surface area that way. More room for maximum damage. Flipping it on its side, she glanced up to thank him, but he'd already moved on.

She wound up her swing like a postapocalyptic baseball player in her hazmat suit and, using all her strength, slammed the weapon down on the monitor's back. Tension fled her body, and she couldn't help but grin at the bits of plastic that cut through the air when the hammer's head burrowed into the casing.

"Nice." Stanton patted Everly on the back. "Who was that for?"

"The cancer that took my grandmother."

Stanton gave the pieces a few whacks of his own. "Fuck cancer," he said.

"Fuck cancer," Everly repeated.

After a moment of silence, Stanton summoned Ellis and Becca over and asked each of them to pick an item and place it in front of Everly. "It should represent something you know she struggles with," he explained. "And you need to tell her what it is."

Becca stepped up first with a vase. "Self-doubt," she said.

Stanton touched Everly's shoulder lightly. "Smash it, then say an affirmation."

The crystal exploded into chunks that shimmered in the light like diamonds. "My art is good."

Becca jammed her hands on her hips. "You can do better than that."

"Isn't it against the rules to criticize affirmations?" Everly turned to Stanton for backup.

"Not when she's right."

Everly sighed. "Fine." She said the words in her head a few times before she spoke them aloud. "I'm . . . talented, I guess?" At Becca's glare, she cleared her throat. "I *am* talented."

"What else?" Becca demanded.

"My art is worth showing to the world."

"Better." Her best friend blew Everly a kiss, and Stanton followed up with a high five.

Ellis took his time selecting an object, finally settling on a wine bottle. "Mom."

Everly made a face. "I can't hit my mother with a sledgehammer."

"But you can smash the way she makes you feel," Stanton pointed out.

Everly blew out a breath. This one was harder than her own self-doubt. Her palms grew sweaty against the hammer's handle, making her adjust her grip. She knew her mother loved her, knew that she wanted what she thought was best for Everly. But the years she'd spent buying her daughter baggy, dark clothes, placing her in the back of photos where no one could see her size, encouraging her to be quieter, smaller, had cut Everly down, blunted her edges, whether her mother had intended it to or not.

How did you tell someone that? How were you supposed to make it clear that they were harming you when they thought they were helping?

"Love shouldn't hurt," she said as she took a swing.

Everly was the last to choose an item. She found a tall stack of plates in the corner and cradled them among the shards of glass and plastic. "I don't want to be afraid anymore."

For too long now, she'd let fear determine every path she took. Quitting the Collective, living at her brother's, staying in Monmouth Cove, working as a receptionist, never posting on the *OTPS* forums, never doing anything at all.

Her eyes skipped to Logan, and her heart danced in her chest when she found him staring back at her.

"It's time to do things that scare me," she said, and smashed the stack of plates to smithereens.

CHAPTER 8

Jazzy disappeared into the depths of the closet again. After some fumbling and muttering, she reemerged with a dozen shirts on hangers.

Everly sat perched on the corner of her bed. Over the last hour, her apartment's beautiful honey-wood floors had disappeared under a thick layer of black and navy blue as Jazzy unearthed all of Everly's clothes.

The host brandished the first shirt—a black, long-sleeved lace number—and waited for Everly to comment, one hand propped on her hip.

"My mother bought me that. You couldn't pay me to wear it," Everly said. She still couldn't believe she was *in* one of Jazzy's wardrobe critiques.

Jazzy pulled it off the hanger and angled it against her own body, inspecting the top in the mirror. "I have nothing against a handkerchief hem or a lace shirt, but together—"

"It looks like the devil's doily." If they burned it, accompanied by the right spell, they'd probably actually summon him. It was that sinfully ugly.

"Accurate." With a laugh, Jazzy tossed the top into the growing do- nation pile at her feet.

Somehow, the next two shirts were even worse. One was a loose navy camisole covered in enormous sky-blue polka dots. The other was a green-and-blue-camo-patterned hoodie with rhinestones encrusting the shoulders like epaulets.

Everly grimaced. "I had one of those days last year where after watch- ing a bunch of old *OTPS* episodes, I decided I wanted to diversify my closet. But there's slim pickings for plus-size clothing around here, so those were the best I could do."

Jazzy waved the sales tags on the polka-dotted shirt. "You didn't even wear it."

"Do you blame me?" Everly muttered.

"It's actually not horrible." Jazzy laid the camisole across the bed and grabbed a gray cardigan from their tiny "keep" stack beside Everly. "If you pair it with a solid color like this, it will tone down the pattern." She shook her head. "But I'll never understand the obsession with polka dots in plus-size fashion. And the bigger the better, too. Just because I'm fat doesn't mean I want to look like a walking case of the chicken pox."

"Or a kindergarten art project." Everly inspected the camouflage hoodie briefly before removing it from the hanger. "Embroidery and ran- dom bedazzling can't save a shapeless button-up. It just makes it look like it's been eaten and regurgitated by sentient art supplies." The last time she'd stopped into Monmouth Cove's thrift store, she'd seen a plus-size peasant top decked out in rhinestones, embroidery, *and* gigantic ruffles. She'd wanted to stand there and scream *why* at the top of her lungs.

She shook the shirt in her hand like it might offer her an answer. The second time, she put a little too much power in it, and the sleeve snapped against the lens of Logan's camera. He grunted as it knocked into his face.

Gasping, Everly froze, her gaze cutting to Jazzy, who was stifling a grin. The moment their eyes met, they both burst into laughter.

Logan blew out a long-suffering sigh. Then he lowered his camera to inspect the equipment for damage. His free hand rubbed at his cheek.

Drama queen, Jazzy mouthed.

Everly sniggered. The sound invited a glare for Logan.

She shrugged at him helplessly. She hadn't *meant* to hit him with the shirt, but it was amusing. At least to normal people who weren't vying for the title of the world's top curmudgeon.

"I think we've got plenty of closet shots," he grumbled.

"Just one more thing." Everly balled up the hoodie and heaved it out the open window behind her bed. She didn't want that thing's presence in her house. Too many bad fashion vibes. Its sleeves spread like wings against the wind, catching air for a second before it landed in a nearby tree. The brittle autumn leaves burst around it in a plume of dust. Maybe the neighborhood squirrels would make a nest out of it.

Sharing a satisfied smile with Jazzy, Everly returned to her place on the bed. Part of her wanted to do that with her entire wardrobe. Sacrifice it to the wildlife and start over, even if it left her with nothing but a bath towel to wear to work for the next three weeks.

"Maybe designers think that these weird patterns and shapes will hide the size of our bodies?" Everly shrugged.

"I guess ugly will do that. But I hate that way of thinking. Nothing we put on ourselves is going to change the body we have. A structured jacket or multiple layers is not going to turn this"—Jazzy gestured at her soft midsection and thick thighs—"into an hourglass shape. I'm only going to be miserable because jackets are basically prison cells for your arms."

"Oh my god, *right*?" Coats were the worst. "It's like, do you want a potato sack that fits your arms, or a properly fitted jacket that you can't move in? There's no compromise." Everly was considering buying a poncho this winter, so she could wear a layer over her sweaters without feeling like she couldn't raise her arms past her waist.

"You know our motto. Fashion is supposed to be fun and make us feel good." Jazzy swept another item off a hanger and shook it out in front of Everly. This one was a spandex tunic tank top with a satin sheen. "Okay, please tell me this thing fits neither of those criteria for you."

Everly barked out a laugh. "Why do I have that? It looks like it belongs on a figure skater."

Jazzy glanced down at it. "You're right." Draping it over her body, she danced around the room, moving her arms like she was gliding over ice. "How do I look?"

"Team USA better make room for you in the next Olympics."

Everly's cheeks hurt from smiling. It was so much easier to think about clothes with someone who understood. If she'd tried to make fun of these outfits with Becca, her best friend would have insisted Everly looked good in all of it. Because that was the only way she knew how to deal with their size difference. Instead of acknowledging that Everly was fat, Becca tried to deny it out of existence.

But Everly didn't have that luxury. And with Jazzy she didn't have to try. The same way it had been with Grandma Helen. The weight it lifted off her chest left her almost light-headed.

As Jazzy wandered off to gather the mess of dresses from the top of the bureau, Everly tried to tidy up the bed. Her underwear—mostly cotton hipster briefs in neutral shades—was strewn across the comforter and buried beneath her well-worn beige bras. Just out there in the open. She glanced up, horror tightening her chest when she saw Logan's camera pan over the room.

If there was ever any question of whether she possessed an iota of sexiness, tonight had cleared that right up.

As soon as she thought no one was looking, she stole a handful of panties and scooted them under the sheets.

Jazzy laughed. "I think we're long past bashful, hon." She pointed to the chaos. It would take Everly hours to put the room back together. Her drawers and closet had been organized by style, season, and frequency of use, a system she'd honed through meticulous trial and error over the past few years.

Everly groaned. "I don't understand what my underwear has to do with making me over."

Jazzy sat down beside her. Her signature "wardrobe day" red hand-kerchief was tying back her tight black curls, and she wore black yoga pants and a high-necked trapeze tank in a muted tangerine that looked gorgeous against her deep brown skin. Even this casual, she was more put together than Everly would be in a ball gown.

"What we wear for only a few people to see says more about us than the costumes we put on for the rest of the world." Jazzy swept a hand toward the prints framed above Everly's dresser. They were reimagined covers she'd made of her favorite books: *Alice in Wonderland*, with a shattered tea set before a mirror that reflected back the same tea set, whole. A top hat hanging from the mirror's edge. *A Tale of Two Cities*, with an illustrated guillotine, empty except for a scarf fluttering in the wind. A cup of hot cocoa set before a snowcapped mountain for her favorite cozy queer romance. And for *Wuthering Heights*, Catherine Earnshaw with a round body like Everly's, staring longingly at Heathcliff as rain battered them atop a grassy cliff.

"You're an artist," Jazzy said. "It's clear from your décor that you love color and print. But all I see here," she nodded to the detritus of undergarments behind them, "is someone who wants to blend in. Disappear."

Everly couldn't meet Jazzy's stare. She glanced toward the doorway, like she could somehow disappear through it without having to move.

"And then these . . ." Jazzy grabbed one of her cotton swing dresses. "How many do you have? Seven?"

"They're comfortable." Plus, they always seemed to be on sale.

Jazzy eyed her warily. "And having one or two as staples is fine. But this is like a uniform." She let the dress fall to the floor, where it blended into the mountain of dark fabrics. "It's like you didn't want to think about getting dressed."

Everly had to grip her comforter in her fists to keep from folding her arms over her chest. It was as if Jazzy had stripped her naked, leaving her torn open and exposed. "I don't."

Jazzy cocked her head. "Why not?"

Everly cleared her throat. She spent a good three minutes picking at some invisible lint on her leggings. "Putting thought into what I wear feels like inviting attention. I don't really want that." Not anymore. She already struggled with so many ways that she felt like too much. She didn't need her clothing to add to it.

Jazzy stood and ducked into the living room. When she returned, she was holding the multi-photo frame that hung in the entryway. It was full of pictures of Everly from the end of high school and early college. Setting it in her lap, Jazzy said, "You weren't always that way." She tapped her nail at the center picture.

Staring up at them was a younger version of Everly, decked out in Claymore University's maroon-and-gray colors, squished on a small couch with her arms around her grandmother. She remembered taking this picture after the homecoming game sophomore year. Everly wore a football jersey knotted at her waist and those loose boyfriend jeans that had been all the rage. Under the right pocket and on both knees were big rips that exposed her pale white skin, and the pants were cuffed over heeled Mary Janes with three skinny ankle straps. Her hair had caramel highlights and hung loose around her shoulders in beachy waves, and her minimal makeup brought out her eyes and lips beneath the maroon numbers scrawled across both her cheeks.

Beside her, Grandma Helen beamed, her short blond hair threaded with gray and mussed from a long day outside, her high cheekbones and sharp nose ruddy from the sun. Their features could not be more different, but their smiles, their confidence were the same.

Seeing that tugged at Everly's insides, and tears burned her eyelids. Back then, she'd known exactly how good she looked. She'd known exactly who she was. And she'd been proud to be that person. Loud voice, no filter, and all.

Just like her grandmother.

"What happened to this girl?" Jazzy asked quietly.

Everly turned her head away as a few tears slipped down her cheeks. The loss of her grandmother clung to her like a shadow, always looming. But staring at this former version of herself, remembering for a moment what it was like to have Grandma Helen at her side, gave that grief claws. They dug deep, tore at pieces of herself she'd thought had healed.

Brushing her knuckles under her eyes, she met Jazzy's gaze. Logan moved a few steps closer, presumably to zoom in for the reveal. This was the good stuff, wasn't it? The moments that kept people riveted to their screens.

It took her a second to realize that he wasn't holding the camera. Instead, he offered her a box of tissues. Everly couldn't make out the exact meaning of his tense expression, but his eyes were like ice, freezing her in place.

She took one, then let her gaze drop to her lap. For a second, she sat in silence, folding the tissue over and over on her knee. "My grandmother died. She was my person. And it was like she took a piece of me with her."

Jazzy's face fell. "Oh, honey."

"My mom was always working, so Grandma Helen basically raised Ellis and me until junior high." Her grandmother had been the one that explained periods to Everly. She'd given Everly her first sex talk. When Everly came sobbing to her that Becca had to move to New Hampshire, Grandma Helen had reminded her that there was more to being best friends than living across the street from each other. And the first time someone called Everly fat at school, it was her grandmother who'd taught her that this was their problem, not Everly's.

Her throat tightened with emotion, and her next few words came out hoarse. "She was an amazing person. So generous and honest and so sure of herself. She didn't care that you could hear her laughing from the neighbor's house, or that people thought she was too blunt, or that only I found her jokes funny. That was who she was. Take it or leave it."

Everly had known wardrobe day would be emotional, but she hadn't been prepared for how much it would remind her of her grandmother. Her thoughts kept sliding back to the many times that she and Grandma Helen had hit online sales and thrift stores to help Everly keep up with the latest trends. They'd do fashion shows in her grandmother's giant kitchen, pulling together outfits and commiserating about how hard it was to find good clothes at their size, the same as she and Jazzy were doing now. Grandma Helen always sent Everly home on those nights with arms full of new clothes and a heart full of pride. "We were a lot alike. She used to call us 'two peas in a pod.' It made it so easy for me to feel good about myself around her, because, even though our faces weren't the same, she was my mirror."

Jazzy nodded.

"It was her idea for me to do the Collective. I used to sketch reimaginings of book covers with plus-size characters. Like that." Everly pointed at the reproduction of *Wuthering Heights* over her bureau. "In typical grandmother fashion, she loved them and thought they were brilliant.

She pushed me to consider applying for a booth. She was so sure that my art could change how people saw the world. How they saw themselves." Everly smiled sadly. "She made me believe it, too. We spent the whole summer before my junior year in college preparing the application, gathering the pieces I would show, and brainstorming ideas for new ones. I was even planning to enter one of the art contests. I'd never done something like that before."

"She sounds like she was an incredible lady," Jazzy said.

Everly closed her eyes, swallowing hard against another wave of tears. She hated thinking about those last few months of her grandmother's life. How quickly everything had changed. How fast and unexpectedly cancer had stolen Grandma Helen from her. "She got diagnosed with stomach cancer in September. By November, she was gone."

The idea of doing the Collective without her had seemed unfathomable, but Everly knew how excited her grandmother had been, so she'd tried to push through the fog of grief and pain. She'd added a new sketch of her grandmother to her portfolio, flying in a cape, surrounded by goats and dogs and cats, like the true superhero she was. That was the best way Everly knew to communicate her love. To make visual representations of the people who filled her heart.

But as the art festival crept closer, Everly's nerves had kicked in. It was hard to see her drawings in the same light without Grandma Helen there to remind her of their value. Suddenly, there were flaws everywhere: the designs looked too amateur, the shading was all wrong, the bodies lacked natural form. Who would care about these things anyway?

About two weeks before the Collective opened, Everly had come home to practice her presentation for the art contest. She'd thought she was alone, but her mother must have gotten out of work early. Everly had no idea how long she'd stood there listening, judging. She was just getting to her favorite part, where she explained why it was important to reframe Juliet from Shakespeare's play in a fat body, when her mother had broken in. "You're talking too loud."

Everly had jumped, her surprise becoming discomfort as she registered her mother's presence. "The audience will need to hear me," she insisted.

"Your voice carries *plenty* without you raising it." The words landed in Everly's gut like an arrow finding its target. She pressed a hand to her middle.

Her mother clutched her neck as she studied the *Romeo and Juliet* cover Everly had propped up on the couch. "That's really the one you're going to enter?"

Everly's heart pounded. "It's my favorite."

"But what about the Little Mermaid one? With the shell at the center? It's beautiful."

"There aren't any people in that one."

Her mother nodded. "Exactly. I think it might be better received."

Everly had glanced at her drawing. All the flaws drifted to the surface. She could barely see the image through them. "You don't think people will like it?"

"I just think they might not get it, sweetie."

What her mother actually meant, of course, was that they were too much like Everly herself. Too out there. Too bold. Too loud.

Grief had been hanging too heavy on Everly to fight back. She'd let her mother, let the doubt her mother had sown, win. That night, she tore her *Romeo and Juliet* cover in two and pulled out of the Collective.

Everly shifted toward Jazzy. "I was too exhausted and scared to do the Collective without my grandmother. If she had been my mirror, now I was staring at an empty wall. I didn't know where I fit anymore. The art that had made me so proud looked silly. Weird. I was too afraid people wouldn't understand what I was doing. I knew it would break my grandmother's heart to see me quit, to see me give in to my fears, but it felt safer. Disappearing is safer." She gestured to her quiet clothes, her quiet space above her brother's garage, her quiet life. "Then there's never the chance that I might be all the things I'm afraid I am: too weird, too loud, too awkward." Everly had to take a breath before she spoke the last one. "Too much."

For a moment, no one spoke.

Then, out of nowhere, Logan growled, "Fuck that." His voice was so distinct, so clear, that Everly suddenly understood the phrase "shattering the silence." It was like something palpable broke against the roughness of his voice. Her eyes cut to his face.

"Hey." Jazzy waved at him. "Language and the fourth wall and all that."

"Fuck it. Greg can edit me out. You are *not* too much."

Everly stared at him. Her heart felt like it was doing push-ups against her chest. She hadn't realized he'd thought about her enough to have an opinion, never mind be this put out. His cheeks were ruddy beneath his beard, and his brow had this furrow she wanted desperately to smooth with her fingers.

"What?" he said. Still growling. Still gruff.

"I didn't know you could string so many words together in one sentence." Tears still stained her face but Everly couldn't help grinning. "Are you tired? Do you need water?"

Jazzy laughed, loud and raucous, the sound filling the room. Then she placed her hand gently over Everly's to stop her still-fidgeting fingers. "You may be the first guest he's ever spoken to in multiple syllables. And he's right. You're not too much. You're exactly enough."

Her words summoned a fresh wave of tears to Everly's eyes.

Jazzy pointed to the picture of her younger self, still in her lap. "Did you like this girl?"

Nodding, Everly dragged her palms up her cheeks to dry her face.

"Do you miss her?"

Everly nodded again.

"Do you want to find her?"

One more nod.

Jazzy shook her head. She stood up, then grabbed Everly's hands to pull her to her feet. "I need you to say it. Out loud."

"I want to be that girl again," Everly whispered.

"Louder."

This time, no one yelled at her when she made eye contact with the camera. And Logan on the other side. In a voice she thought she'd silenced long ago, she said, loud enough for Ellis and Becca to hear her in the main house, "I want to be that girl again."

READ-IT FORUM: ON THE PLUS SIDE

Annette98 *4 months ago*

I just read that article about eight secrets from behind the scenes of *OTPS* on Whisper Network and I'm convinced its horse shit.

NO WAY was Stanton policing the guests' food choices or referring them to trainers. That goes against everything the show stands for!!!!!!

987 ♥ 456 👍 811 ✦ 321 👎

CourtK *4 months ago*

Right?! Or the one about how Jazzy doesn't actually do any shopping trips. That its all personal shoppers or whatever

409 ♥ 633 👍 217 ✦ 200 👎

SarahEditsThings *4 months ago*
SAME @Annette98.

I refuse to believe the producers had Alicia play up the drama
with her straight-sized twin sister.

There's already so much actual fatphobia in the world. The
show would not fabricate more.

1030 ♥ 533 👍 899 ✨ 344 👎

FarmGyrlME *4 months ago*
damn straight

they should do an episode on this forum if they need some
fatphobia fodder

2345 ♥ 1200 👍 873 ✨ 666 👎

CHAPTER 9

"Should I even be watching this?"

On the Plus Side's season-three premiere special was set to drop at 8:00 P.M., which, according to Becca's chicken-shaped clock, was mere minutes away.

Everly wedged herself between Bagel and Cream Cheese on the enormous ivory-colored sectional in the living room. The blank screen of the TV gaped at her, like the Grim Reaper waiting for his moment.

"This is like being a musician who listens to their own albums or something." Narcissistic at best. Masochistic at worst. Painful either way.

Becca huffed next to her as she attempted to tame her chin-length blond bob into something akin to a bun at the top of her head. "It's your premiere. Of course you have to watch."

"It's the premiere *special*," Everly clarified. "Logan said it would basically be Jazzy and Stanton talking with some celebrity about the third season. They're going to introduce the new guests with some clips, but otherwise it's more about them hyping up the show and getting fans excited."

Everly did her best to sound nonchalant, but the flush in her cheeks was probably giving her away. It was impossible to say Logan's name without remembering how he'd reacted when she'd told Jazzy about pulling out of the Collective. Protective, almost. Like he wanted to get into a fistfight with her feelings.

"Ah, yes. Logan. The hot cameraman." Becca grinned. She hadn't stopped teasing Everly about her "smoking hot paparazzo" since she'd laid eyes on him at the Wreck-It Room. Her hands fussed with the cuffs of her hoodie, dragging them past her fingers. She'd spent most of high school and half of college doing everything she could to hide her psoriasis. In the last few years, she'd finally realized the skin condition was not something to be embarrassed about, but whenever Becca was excited, she always covered her hands out of habit, even when she wasn't having a breakout.

"I didn't say that."

Becca's smile turned wicked. "You didn't have to."

"He's my permanent shadow. That's it." Maybe if Everly said it out loud enough, it would become true. Because every time she closed her eyes, she saw the heat in Logan's gaze, the sincerity creasing his face when he'd said she wasn't too much.

And each time the memory invaded her head, her heart picked up a little more speed. At this rate, it wouldn't be long before it burst right out of her chest.

She adjusted on the couch, causing Bagel to burrow into her lap. The beast had great aspirations to be a lapdog, and Everly could never deny him, even if it meant her thighs would go numb in a few minutes. Sinking deeper into the cushions, she dropped her head back and played with his ears. "I was not prepared for how weird it would be to have a camera following me around everywhere."

"Especially when the guy carrying it is easy on the eyes."

"Oh my god, stop."

Becca put on her Oliver Twist act, her light brown eyes becoming giant orbs of innocence. "I'm a married lady. I need to live vicariously through someone."

"Oh yes, because eight months of marriage makes you a rusty old ball and chain."

Now Becca was pouting.

"You know I only like James." Despite their disastrous first moment on camera, he'd been stopping by Everly's desk even more than usual. And when they ran into each other in the skincare aisle of the pharmacy after work on Monday, she'd managed not to knock everything off the shelves. She would have sworn Logan looked disappointed.

Though she wouldn't admit it to Becca, Everly had bought the face mask James recommended. It was sitting on the vanity in her bathroom.

She didn't even use face masks. *God,* she was a mess. The last thing she needed to do was add a crush on a second guy to this mayhem.

"Then maybe it's time to do something about that," Becca said.

Everly's palms snapped up as if to ward off a punch. "I can embarrass myself fine on my own. I don't need to go chasing rejection on television."

Becca grabbed the remote from the coffee table and aimed it at the TV. Everly's last minutes of peace were dwindling. "I don't mean during the show. But think about it. All that confidence you'll have afterward. Use it. Take the bull by the balls."

Everly choked on a laugh. "That's definitely not how that saying goes."

Becca waved the remote at her. "You get the point."

Swallowing hard, Everly buried her face in Bagel's neck. "Even if I was to buy into your very flawed theory that James likes me—"

"How is it flawed?" Becca squawked.

"You have never seen us interact."

"And you've always been completely clueless about guys. Remember Adam in high school? He basically had to give you a notarized testimony of his feelings before you believed that he was into you."

Everly grumbled, chastised. Flirting was confusing. The line between being nice and "it'd be nice to kiss you" could get very blurry, and the repercussions of crossing it were often mortifying. Best to stay on the safe side. Color within the lines.

Besides, even on the off chance that Becca was right about James, dating a coworker was complicated and uncomfortable. Either you had to hide it, or everyone knew and was watching you and speculating, and there was paperwork to file with HR, and then if you broke up, you had to file *more* paperwork. It was like work divorce.

It was easier to be work single. To leave James safely in her daydreams. She got everything she needed from him there.

Everly breathed a sigh of relief when the theme song for *On the Plus Side* sang out from the TV's speaker bar.

Suddenly, watching herself on camera seemed far less torturous than this line of conversation.

Twenty minutes later, Becca was holding a pillow over her face to smother her laughter.

A clear shot of Everly and James slamming their heads together had just flashed across the screen.

Damn Logan and his excellent zoom lens straight to hell.

Her friend's laugh was contagious enough that Everly had to fight one off herself, even as her cheeks flushed with embarrassment. "I was nervous! Being recorded talking to someone you like is not fun by *any* stretch of the imagination."

Becca's eyes scrunched up in sympathy, though she couldn't stop laughing. Not that Everly blamed her. She was basically a walking fail video.

It didn't help that this moment between James and Everly was the climactic ending to a series of clips focused entirely on him. There'd been shots from the hosts' ambush where he'd aimed a set of finger guns at her from across the room, causing her face to go red as a tomato. A few of her bumbling her way through a conversation during one of his trips to the break room. And the time he tried to lob a jelly bean in her mouth only for it to bounce off her forehead instead.

The worst, though, were the seemingly endless clips of her following James with her gaze like a lovesick puppy. She hadn't realized she watched him that much, and it was not pleasant to learn this via a TV show.

Logan hadn't missed a thing.

And Sady had stacked it all together in a way that made Everly's crush so obvious it hurt. It had to be some kind of trick of reality TV storytelling.

Right?

Everly had to have at least a modicum of self-preservation in real life.

Thankfully, the show transitioned back to Jazzy and Stanton, and the premiere special's host—Stella Gabriel, fashion designer extraordinaire—asking them to sum up their season-three guests for the viewers.

Stanton clapped his hands in front of him like he was praying. "Holly," he beamed, "who will close out the season, is such a firecracker. The way that girl handles the trolls that invade her online gaming community," he shivered, "burns like ice. We can't wait to show her ways to bring that fire into her everyday life."

Jazzy cleared her throat. "Robbie is our show's first transgender man and we're so thrilled to be a part of his journey. He's the most incredible poet and teacher and we're determined to help him see himself the way his family and friends and students already do."

"Then we have Mya." Jazzy tapped her boots against the stage in excitement, gripping the arms of her chair like they were the only thing keeping her in her seat. "She's out there trying to change the way that people understand food, fatness, and health. Her goal is to open a community center in her neighborhood that teaches people about nutrition through cooking and baking demonstrations. It's something Stanton and I both believe strongly in, and we hope we can encourage Mya to see that she has the knowledge and resources to make it happen."

Everly tried to use the feel of Bagel's soft fur beneath her palms to soothe her beating heart. The dog tipped his head back to look at her, ears flopping everywhere, and licked her fingers. He must have felt her panic rising. She was the only guest left, and her story didn't seem nearly as compelling as the rest of them.

As if to prove her right, Stanton took over. "Finally, there's Everly, who will kick off our season. She's a talented artist and one of the sweetest, funniest humans we've met. Like most of us, she's trying to learn to love herself enough to let someone else love her. We really hope we can help her find the strength to tell her coworker how she feels."

His words were as jarring as someone blasting a horn next to Everly's ear. "What?" she yelped, shooting up straighter on the couch. Did Stanton seriously announce her feelings for James on television? Her boss had sent out multiple emails encouraging everyone to watch the premiere and support her. The entire office probably saw that.

James probably saw that.

Becca paused the show, her head turning toward Everly in slow motion. "What about your art? Your job? The Collective? Why are they so focused on him?"

"I don't know."

Everly wanted to slither to the floor. Through the floor, and the basement, and the foundation, through the topsoil and layers of dirt and whatever else rested between her and the Earth's hot core. Something told her it did not generate nearly as much heat as her face right now.

At Sady's office they'd talked about how important participating in the Cape Cod Collective would be to Everly, about her dream to design a tattoo. Why wasn't any of that included? Had they seen the footage with her goofy heart-eyes at James and decided that was a better storyline? Or . . .

Her gaze shot toward Becca. "Did you tell them about James when you nominated me?"

"I told you it wasn't me," Becca insisted.

Clearly, she was going to keep up this charade until she was free of her NDA.

Before Everly was able to push at the issue any more, the front door swung open, and her brother swept into the room, still shedding his coat. Bagel bolted off the couch and trotted toward him.

Everly's face must have still been red, because the moment he saw her, he stopped mid-step. "What's going on?"

"They're making me look like a fool on *On the Plus Side*."

Ellis glanced at the TV. "Shit, that was tonight? I wanted to watch it with you."

"Too late." Everly sank back into the couch. If she was lucky, it would swallow her whole, the way that bed did to Johnny Depp in that old Freddy Krueger movie.

Ellis folded his arms. "No way. We're watching it again. How am I supposed to properly mock you if I don't see every second?"

Everly did her best impression of Logan as she glared at her brother. "You missed nothing."

"That's not true!" Becca shook her head. "Ev's footage was great."

"It was a disaster."

"Well, that settles it." Ellis spun on his heel. "I'm making cookies and we're watching again."

Becca jumped up. "I'll help." Everly didn't miss the way she grabbed her brother's ass (gross) as they rushed for the kitchen.

With a sigh, she pressed Play. There were only five minutes left, but she needed to remember every little detail. She needed to talk to Sady. *This* could not be her story arc.

There had to be more to her than that.

CHAPTER 10

At seven in the morning on a Monday, Monmouth Cove could have served as the set for a postapocalyptic film.

The empty sidewalks were wet with morning dew, grates drawn tight across the storefronts. A sleepy mist hung over everything like a witch's curse, so that the only noise was the muffled breeze and the rumble of tires from the handful of cars passing through on their way to the highway.

Everly, Jazzy, and Stanton headed down Central Avenue toward Sunny's Side Up, the town's best breakfast place. It was the first time she'd been with both of them at once since they'd ambushed her a month and a half ago, and while she was thankful for the extra reprieve from dealing with the fallout from the premiere special at work, she was not ready to handle their chaotic enthusiasm this early in the morning. Stanton had been quizzing her about the diner's menu for the last three blocks, while Jazzy listed the various alternatives to yoga pants that she planned to dress Everly in for future outings. They were both talking at the same time, and Everly had no idea who to answer. Her poor brain was spinning like a pottery wheel.

Ahead of them, Logan set the pace, walking backward to record their interactions. The stare of his camera pressed against Everly's skin. That premiere special had made it clear how closely he watched her with that lens, and it was hard not to analyze every single thing she did. What did she look like walking? Did she swing her arms weirdly? Were her steps too big? Too small? Did her feet make weird noises? What was her resting face? How did her voice sound outside her own head? Everly didn't know how anyone on a reality TV show ever managed to be themselves.

She hadn't even been able to get comfortable enough alone in her car earlier to do a confessional. She'd been dying to talk about her frustrations with how Sady had framed her in the special. But every time she tried, she ended up muttering "um" and "like" and never forming an actual sentence, then laughing uncomfortably. She was barely out of the driveway by the time she'd given up.

If only she could draw what she was thinking instead of having to talk to a camera. The images would be saturated with angry flashes of color and sharp, steep points, and broken circles.

Stanton linked arms with her and gave her a shake. "How much farther is this place? Rhode Island? I need a waffle before I murder someone."

"Another five or six blocks. You'll know it when you see it."

The entire establishment was egg-themed. Tables in the shape of eggs, seat covers that looked like sunny-side up eggs, curtains decorated with eggs in every possible form, salt and pepper shakers that looked like they'd been birthed by chickens. The sign balanced on the roof boasted a pair of fried eggs big enough to be flying saucers. Basically, if it could be an egg, wear an egg, or look like an egg, Sunny incorporated it into her décor. If the food wasn't so damn good, Everly would have driven to Bourne (or anywhere else) to avoid the eye-searing tackiness.

Stanton groaned like Everly had said they wouldn't be eating for a week, sagging dramatically against her. Shaking her head, Jazzy took up his other arm with a smile. "Distract poor Stanton here by telling us a little more about what you do at the office."

"Uhhh." Everly talked about herself these days about as often as she wore a color scheme lighter than navy blue. "I answer phones and organize travel and prep meetings." She was doing a great job making her life sound like a yawn fest. Viewers were sure to be swarming to change careers after this aired.

Of course, instead of looking over at Jazzy, Everly had spoken directly at the camera.

Logan arched an eyebrow. "Really?"

"Shit." Fighting the urge to slap her hands over her face, she turned to Jazzy and repeated herself.

Unfortunately, because Logan always seemed to be at least slightly within her peripheral vision, Everly cringed when she saw him get too close to the curb, ruining that shot as well.

He paused, and lowering his camera, gave her a long look, one that implied her very existence complicated his universe tenfold.

It was probably not the intent, but those frowns were becoming catnip for her. Everly wanted to see every one. Categorize them on a spreadsheet. Determine which ones were for her alone. Invent new ones along the way.

"What? I didn't want you to fall," she said. "I was concerned."

"He's got it under control, hon." Stanton patted her hand. "Logan has superhuman spatial awareness. Do you know how many times I've tried to trick him into stepping in a puddle? Never once have I succeeded."

"Well, now I have a new goal," Everly deadpanned.

Logan rolled his eyes in that bemused way that she associated with

TV sitcom dads, then, lifting the camera back to his face, twirled a finger in the air as if to say "take three."

Everly was about to list her job skills résumé-style again when an older woman turned the corner with her dog. It was a black Lab, in that floppy, all-legs phase, where he wasn't quite full grown but no longer a puppy. He paused to say hi to Jazzy and Stanton, licking their hands and pressing his head to their thighs.

He was just approaching Everly when he sniffed the air, turned with a jerk, and abruptly dove at Logan, tugging the leash right out of his owner's hands.

With his camera on his shoulder, Logan didn't have time to throw out an arm to protect himself before the dog head-butted him in the crotch at full speed. He grunted loudly, surprise and pain animating his usually stoic features.

Through it all, though, he managed to keep the camera balanced on his shoulder, even as the dog continued to snuffle at him like he'd found buried treasure.

"Odin!" his owner called out, mortified.

Everly beat the woman to Logan's side. Crouching, she puckered her lips in some kissy noises, cooing the dog's name until he pulled away from Logan. His tongue lolled loosely out of his mouth, his tail flapping happily.

"Why don't we leave the poor man's family jewels alone," she suggested, giving the dog some good scratches behind his ears.

Logan smirked. "Thanks."

"Did you wash your jeans in bacon or something?" Even as he basked in Everly's attention, Odin's face kept drifting back toward Logan.

He patted at each of his pockets, one of those deep furrows creasing his brow. When he reached the left one, he swore under his breath and dug his hand in.

It reappeared full of bone-shaped treats.

Everly snorted. "That's a weird thing to keep in your pockets."

He shot her a disgruntled stare, but she would have sworn he was fighting off a laugh. "I have two dogs, remember?"

"I guess that makes it a *little* less weird." She gave him a wide smile.

Odin's owner finally retrieved his leash and began apologizing profusely. The poor woman's face was about four different shades of red, but Logan kept assuring her it was fine. In the fewest syllables possible, of course.

Everly took the time to stoop and give the dog one more round of pats. "You're a good boy," she mumbled. "It's not your fault he's wandering around with delicious things in his pants."

The second she heard herself, she wanted to keel over. *Why* was she talking about Logan's pants and what was in them? And calling them delicious? She was talking about the dog treats, obviously, but god, if someone had heard her, or the camera had picked up her voice . . .

What if they aired *that* on the next episode? Everly would have to change her name and leave the country.

Her cheeks were on fire as she stood and brushed her palms on her leggings.

Logan's gaze tracked her movements. "You must have one, too? A dog? You're good with them."

"Becca and Ellis do. But I want at least three of my own someday."

"Yeah?"

"Animals really help keep me centered. I feel like they're . . . I don't know . . . good at reminding us what matters." She shrugged, and her gaze dipped to her feet. She hadn't said anything that earth-shattering, yet it still felt like she'd given him a glimpse of a secret part of her. She didn't really share her attachment to animals. It reminded her too much of her grandmother. Grandma Helen had owned an animal sanctuary a few towns over, where Everly and her brother had spent most afternoons as kids. Whenever Everly had a bad day, or was feeling a little adrift, she'd head for the goat pen, or sit on the porch with the dogs and cats, and pass hours petting their coats or grooming them.

"Prepare for chaos."

"That's my favorite thing."

Everly took a few steps back toward Stanton and Jazzy, but then Logan shot back, "You'll need to keep lots of delicious stuff in your pants."

She spun around in shock to find him battling a smile. The tiny pull of his lips changed his entire demeanor. He looked younger, softer, more open. And a little too devious to be holding a camera.

Everly's pulse was pounding everywhere in her body. She hardly noticed when Stanton and Jazzy hooked arms with her once again.

"Where were we?" Jazzy's eyes narrowed in concentration. "Oh, right. Work." She looked to Logan for the cue to start.

He nodded, camera and frown back in place.

"We can forget the job for now," Stanton said. He tugged Everly closer to his side. "We know what she *really* wants to do is plan how to bag this guy at work. James?" Stanton's eyebrows danced at her.

"What? No." Everly shook her head so hard it was in danger of rattling off her neck. "That's not what I want at all." She took a deep breath and attempted to reignite the anger that had started to bubble in her chest last night while humiliation kept her tossing and turning. "I actually wanted to talk about the whole James thing."

Everly had already pulled down so many walls for this show. She'd resurrected dreams she'd given up on years ago, faced painful feelings about herself, admitted how much she'd let Grandma Helen down by quitting the Collective. Now Sady was going to scrap it all? What did it say about Everly that the showrunner didn't find her actual story worth telling? That she thought it was better to focus on this fabricated romance instead?

By this time, they'd reached Sunny's, and Sady, who'd been idling beside her shiny Mercedes SUV in the parking lot, hurried toward them on impossibly high canvas wedge sandals. She must have caught the last few words Everly said because she clapped her hands together. "Wasn't it great?" She wore an olive-green sleeveless shirt dress with a woven brown belt cinching her waist. Sunglasses that likely cost more than Everly's car were propped on her head, and gold earrings shaped like leaves dangled from her ears. "The fans loved the premiere so much."

Everly had purposely been avoiding the internet since the special. Which, honestly, had been like trying to pass the day without breathing, given how much time she used to spend on the forums.

She swallowed hard. She wasn't afraid of confrontation, but she didn't exactly enjoy it. Especially when the person she had to confront controlled the editing software. "I'm glad it was so well received," she said as diplomatically as she could. "But I wasn't . . . expecting my segment."

"What do you mean?" Sady ushered them forward into the restaurant.

The entire wall of booths at the back had been reserved for filming. Stanton was immediately fascinated by the egg-shaped knickknacks as he slid into the middle one, Jazzy beside him. Sady directed Everly to the bench across from them.

Everly began to explain but Sady shook her head, a finger pressed to her lips as she pulled over a chair for herself next to the booth. For the next few minutes, they sat in silence while Logan tested angles for the best shot. It felt like an eternity before he was finally in position, and Sady gestured for Everly to speak again.

Not so much reality for something called "reality TV."

Everly had thought she'd at least get to choose when she talked and where she sat.

"There was just so much . . . *James* in it. I thought there would be more focus on our plans for the Collective. Maybe my tattoo. Or at least the fact that I'm an artist. Like with all the other guests?" Everly grabbed a Splenda packet and dumped the contents in her empty coffee cup, then started to shred the yellow paper.

Sady pulled her sunglasses from her head and chewed on one end, studying Everly. "Your art will be a large part of your episodes, of course."

"That wasn't really clear from the premiere special. It looked more like the whole purpose of me being on the show would be to land a boyfriend." She wasn't even sure if she was ready for that right now. She'd spent so much time since Grandma Helen died hiding the parts of herself she feared were embarrassing. It felt like she needed to put herself back together first, before letting someone else in.

But if she was ready, if she did want someone . . . was it James?

Everly had to strain her gaze on the table to keep from glancing at Logan.

At this point, the Splenda packet was a pile of confetti, and she reached for a Sweet'N Low to add a new color.

"But you like him?"

Everly shrugged. "There's more to me than that." Out of the corner of her eye, she noticed Logan lean in a little closer. She cleared her throat. "And next to the other guests, I look . . . I don't know . . . vapid."

"There was definitely an imbalance in the footage. I got other shots besides Everly at work," Logan piped in. "The ones with her family. Or her sketching at lunch. It wasn't all about that guy when she was shooting." His voice got extra rough around the words "that guy." It did something weird to Everly's knees.

"I know, but the James angle is a sharper narrative, don't you think?" Sady glanced over her shoulder at him.

"Not if the guest—if Everly—is unhappy with it."

Her name sounded so lyrical on his lips. Every one of her muscles melted in response.

Sady flicked her gaze to Everly. "I promise, you'll see, as the season gets going, we're going to cast you and your art and your entire arc in the best light. It's the magic I work. Logan knows that."

Sady and Everly both looked at him. His brow wrinkled for a moment, then smoothed over. "She's not wrong. She does good work."

"I know it's hard to let go of control, but audiences are going to love you, I know it, and they're going to connect with your story. Totally eat it up." Sady's eyes were bright, her voice sincere, and Everly wanted desperately to believe her, if only so she had one less thing to worry about.

"Could we please downplay the James stuff a little more?" she asked.

Sady's phone rang, cutting off her words. "We've got it taken care of, don't worry." She offered Everly one more smile before pointing down at her screen. "I've got to answer this." With a few last directions to Logan, she flitted out toward the parking lot.

Everly followed her with her gaze until Sady's SUV backed onto Central Avenue. Her stomach was in knots. When she settled back against the booth, she realized everyone was watching her. "What?"

"I thought you liked James?" Stanton asked.

"I guess. But I don't want to date him."

"Your nominator seemed to think otherwise. The whole application was about helping you build your confidence." Stanton stretched his long arms to emphasize "whole."

Of course Becca would do that. She was convinced that the only thing standing in the way of a potential relationship between Everly and James was Everly's lack of self-esteem.

She sighed and turned her eyes to the table, sweeping the torn sugar packets into a neat little pile. "It's—" Pausing, she looked straight at Logan. "I don't want any of this on camera." She dug her phone out of her pocket and cued up a playlist, angling the screen at him. "I'm prepared to start blaring copyrighted music to mess up these shots if needed."

She expected a fight, but Logan only lowered the camera silently.

"I'm not insecure about dating." She didn't hate herself or the way she looked. She just wanted to stay off people's radar. No one could think she was too much if she was not on their mind. It was a rejection-free approach to life. "You can like someone but not want to be with them."

"Of course." Jazzy tucked some of her black curls back into her hat. "We just want to understand why, so we can make sure we're helping you the way you want to be helped."

"I want to focus on myself," Everly said. "On making things right by my grandmother and doing the Collective, on designing my tattoo. Maybe figuring out what I want to do for a career. I want to learn what makes *me* happy." Adding another person to that equation would complicate things. It introduced the possibility of being rejected. Of not being enough, or maybe too much, or somehow both at once, for someone else. Everly wasn't sure she was ready for that.

James was a great guy. He was hot. And she really enjoyed that, in her own daydreams, she could be herself around him. If she tried to date him and discovered that wasn't true, it was liable to devastate her. That's not what her *On the Plus Side* experience was supposed to be about.

None of that would help her to embrace who she was.

The two hosts nodded. Their affirmation was a shot of helium to

Everly's chest, and she was ready to float away. It had been too long since she last felt heard. Since she'd tried to be.

"You're the important part of this," Jazzy said. "We want you to be happy."

"But," Stanton cocked an eyebrow, "if people happen to fall in love with you in the process, we can't help that."

CHAPTER 11

"What is this place?"

Everly wished she'd known that *On the Plus Side* would repeatedly require her to rise before dawn. That might have impacted her decision to participate. As far as she was concerned, time was nothing but a construct until eight thirty in the morning. And yet here she was, the sun barely cresting the treetops hemming in the village façade in front of her.

"This is King Henry's Feast, New England's most celebrated Renaissance faire." Stanton's grin brimmed with excitement. Clearly, he was unperturbed by the indecent hour. Or, judging by the way he bounced on the balls of his feet like a toddler who didn't know how to contain his energy, his veins were laced with caffeine.

What Everly wouldn't give for the same. Her brain had been too muddled with exhaustion this morning to remember coffee, and at this point, she was fairly confident she could defeat Logan in a grump-off.

At the thought of him, she glanced around, suddenly hyperaware of his absence. "Where are Sady and Logan?"

Stanton waved her off. "They'll be here when the feast opens."

"But they're missing all of this." Everly fanned her hands in front of her face, which was most certainly as droopy and pallid as she felt. The last time this eight-hours-or-more gal had tried to function on less than five hours of sleep, she'd had circles under her eyes as big as tote bags.

Stanton chuckled. "I think they'll survive."

"I don't know. Logan seems to get a lot of joy out of catching me in my worst moments," Everly quipped. She'd been a complete disaster on camera so many times already, she couldn't bring herself to be truly upset about it anymore. She would accept her fate as the Mia Thermopolis of *On the Plus Side*.

"Not worst. Just . . . authentic."

"You should go into PR with that kind of spin."

Stanton laughed again. It was a great sound, robust and low like a tuba, but genuine. You could feel his happiness in it.

He led her past shop windows and doors that had been transformed into ticket booths, toward a hidden entrance at the end of the row. Everly got the sense this place had been here awhile; up close, the white and brown paint had begun to peel, exposing gray, aged wood underneath. Above them, the roof's latticework was crisscrossed with intricate spider-webs.

"Stanton, why are we at a Ren faire?" While Everly loved seeing the incredible work people put into their costumes at places like this, it wasn't really her thing. Neither was historical reenactment.

"Ren faires are full of artists!" He threw his arms out like he was in the middle of the opening number of a musical and he was establishing the setting for the audience. "Metal workers, jewelry makers, costumers, body artists. You're going to meet so many people who share your inter-ests. You never know where that might lead."

Holding up a finger, he checked the time and made a quick call on his phone. A moment later, a man dressed as a court jester opened the door for the two of them, bowing as he waved them through.

Stanton answered the bow with his own. "Good, sir," he said, then turned back to Everly. "These events are also so wonderfully inclusive. It's a perfect place for you to let loose and be yourself."

Picking up their pace, they crossed through the main thorough-fare, a four-sided booth at the center hawking mead, wine, turkey legs, and funnel cakes. The paths branching from it were packed with vendor booths.

One stand displayed beautifully crafted swords and axes; another had bracelets and necklaces dripping in crystals draped from every sur-face. With each turn, the growing sunlight winked in the gems' many faces. Across the way were tables boasting handmade dishware beside racks of intricately sewn corsets and shifts. There was even a cobbler and a haberdasher.

Vendors were getting set up for the day, but Stanton stopped at each booth to inspect the wares like a proper market shopper.

"When I was a kid," he said, "I spent all my time at places like this."

"Really?" Everly didn't remember reading about that in any inter-views or hearing him talk about it on the show.

Nodding, he rubbed at the beads of sweat beginning to stipple over his brow. Even with only a week until Halloween, it was still a bit muggy out. New England weather was so weird.

"Once I got my license," he went on, "I would drive hours to a faire or a con if I had to. There weren't a lot of kids at my tiny high school with any interest in art, so I'd come here to feel less alone. Plus, these kinds of events draw in people of all shapes and sizes. I never stood out the way I did in the real world, even though I was a hundred feet tall and fat. Here, I could dress like a knight or an executioner or a pirate, and no one mocked me or called me a mountain or whatever."

"It's so hard to find those places, when you look like us." Everly paused to admire a pocket watch pendant at one of the jewelry booths. "Especially when you're younger."

"Where were yours?" Stanton asked.

Frowning, Everly fell back into step with him as they made their way deeper into the grounds. "Online spaces, mostly. People who followed my YouTube account or liked my art on social media. My friends in high school were all thin. In college, I found some who looked more like me, but after my grandmother died, those relationships fell away, too." She sighed.

"Why?"

"It was too hard. I lost my drive to do fat activism, and they didn't understand why. So I let those friendships disappear with that part of me." Everly slid her hands nervously down the sides of her leggings. It was so hard to be honest about this stuff, to face the ways in which she let her life get smaller. The ways she'd actively shrunk it with her choices. "Now I only find that kind of connection on the forums for this show."

"But you don't really participate?"

"Just a lurker."

Stanton's expression was sad enough to summon an ache at Everly's center. He knew as acutely as she did what she'd lost.

They wandered down a path to their right. It was narrower and not nearly as crowded with booths, ending a few yards away at a large wooden building. The sign hanging from heavy chains off the overhang read EDMUND'S WARDROBE in sweeping calligraphy, and the shop's barn doors were already thrown open, the light from LED lanterns making the inside glow a soft white.

Stanton stopped before they approached the building, and turned to face her. "I got my first idea for a fat superhero at a faire. Most people come in period costumes, but you get your sprinkling of superheroes and steampunk, sci-fi, or fantasy outfits. I'd driven hours to reach this faire in Maryland and I was sitting on a bench, crowd watching, taking it all in, and this guy walked by me in a vintage Cyclops costume from *X-Men*. The blue spandex with the yellow belts and whatnot." Everly's expression must have betrayed her lack of classic superhero knowledge because he made a *tut* sound with his tongue before moving on. "Anyway . . . he was on the shorter side and had a round belly, but he owned that costume like he *was* the character. It made me think, why *couldn't* Cyclops look like that? How was shooting lasers out of his eyes in any way affected by what his body looked like?" Stanton huffed a breath. Behind his glasses, his dark brown eyes were far away, as if he were somehow back at that particular faire. "It changed the whole trajectory of my life. I hope this place might do that for you, too."

There was a tug at Everly's chest, a wistfulness that felt heavier than a boulder. Until Jazzy and Stanton had burst into her life, she hadn't realized how badly she wanted to change. How much she needed something to nudge her off course. To point her in a direction she hadn't thought possible.

"Me too," she whispered.

Stanton's eyes were glassy, and Everly could feel tears gathering in her lashes. They both laughed as they wiped at their faces, and a companionable quiet settled between them. Eventually, Everly broke it by muttering, "Logan's going to be pissed he missed this moment."

With a chuckle, Stanton waved her toward the building. "We'll give him an appropriately themed heart-to-heart once we're dressed."

She glanced down at her leggings and loose tank. The pants were, of course, black, but the shirt had some white stripes. "I . . . am dressed."

"Oh, not for King Henry's, you're not." Flourishing a hand, Stanton herded her into the building.

Racks of garments filled the floor, and others hung from the walls and the low beams on the ceiling. Most were corsets, shifts, and floor-length dresses, along with belts and coats. A few racks had shirts and pants for more masculine styles.

On a stack of barrels at the back sat an old ornate brass register, and beside it idled a tall, wide-hipped brunette in a cream-colored corseted overdress covered with brocade roses. Underneath the dress was a velvet shift the color of mulberry wine. As Everly and Stanton approached, she paused her conversation with a thin blond man in a pirate's costume that was clearly inspired by Captain Stede from *Our Flag Means Death* to glance their way.

Stanton rushed over and hooked an arm around each one's shoulder. "Everly, this is Meryl and Broden. They'll be our historical style consultants today."

Oh. God. Everly's heart nosedived into her stomach. They were going to put her in a costume.

She'd never been a huge fan of Halloween or other costume-oriented events. Partially because it wasn't quite as fun to play dress-up when nothing was available in your size, but she also wasn't interested in giving the world what it wanted and pretending to be someone else. *Something* else—skinnier, prettier, quieter, invisible. She wanted to be able to exist exactly as she was and how she looked in the moment. That's why she was on this show.

Choosing a dress at random, Everly spread out the skirt and inspected its intricate detail. "I'm going to look ridiculous in one of these."

The woman named Meryl shook her head adamantly. "Renaissance fashion flatters every body type, but especially curves. You're going to look gorgeous."

"I'm going to be a puddle of sweat under all these layers."

"Join the club," Broden said with a smile. "It's part of the whole Ren faire experience."

"Plus, it adds authenticity since people back then didn't bathe nearly as often as we do." Stanton had come to admire the gown with her, and he nudged her arm playfully with his elbow. "But seriously, this is part of the process. Embrace it. We need to shake you out of your comfort zone."

"There's nothing like a corset and eighteen layers to loosen you up."

"Exactly! By the time Jazzy dresses you, you'll be up for anything."

Everly eyed him warily. "That's some twisty logic."

Throwing his arm around her neck, he gave her a squeeze. "Just trust me."

"And me!" a voice yelled from the rear of the building.

With typical *On the Plus Side* flair, Jazzy burst from the dressing room, the curtain flapping wildly in her wake. Logan and Sady ducked out from behind the next one. His camera was already braced on his shoulder. He'd probably been filming since the second they'd walked in.

Maybe earlier if he was sneaky—though something told Everly that wasn't his style. Plaid did not make for good camouflage.

Jazzy rushed forward to hug Stanton and Everly before falling into a deep discussion about the day's logistics with Sady. Everly used the moment of quiet to slip away and browse the racks. She needed a second to wrap her head around the fact that she'd be squeezed into one of these things any second now.

The garments were organized by color, so she beelined for the darkest hues. There was no way Jazzy was going to let her wear something black, but starting with a color she could stomach seemed like the best way to ease into this.

The first corset Everly picked up felt like butter in her hands. The material was soft and pliable, and the detail was subtle: velvet florals in a deep midnight shade overlaying the charcoal fabric. She held it up to her body, expecting it to be far too small, but it looked like the perfect size.

Her hands trembled a little as she returned it to the hanger. She

couldn't remember the last time she went shopping in an actual store and
the item on top was her size. Usually, she had to dig all the way to the
bottom of the pile or the end of the rack. Sometimes, she'd have to ask
a salesperson to get her size from the stock they kept in the back. More
often than not, the stores didn't carry her size at all.

She'd lost count of how many times she'd tagged along with her
friends to the mall with dread clawing at her chest as they meandered
through store after store without plus sizes. Every time an employee
looked her way, Everly would cringe, certain they were laughing at her.
A few would offer to show her the jewelry and shoes, as if accessories
weren't their own minefield to navigate. They're no more one-size-fits-all
than anything else. Shoes were often too narrow for her feet, necklaces
too short, bracelets too tight. Rings were only for tiny fingers. Nothing
in the fashion world was created with larger bodies in mind.

But as Everly continued to find wearable pieces on each new display at Edmund's, as she watched Sady, Meryl, Jazzy, and Stanton, every
one of them plus-size, talk animatedly a few feet away, something warm
spread through her limbs. This was what it was like for your body to be
perceived as normal. To be able to turn any which way, go anywhere,
and know you'll fit.

This was what she'd stolen from herself when she let her fear, her
sadness, her mother, get in her head.

As she moved deeper into the shop, a mannequin on a center display caught her eye. It showcased a long-sleeved gown in dark gray with
a black brocade and silver stitching. Everly reached for it, running her
fingers over the fabric.

Behind her, someone clucked their tongue. Jazzy. That sound was as
unique to her as her various pearls of wisdom. "You want to spend the
day as a widow in mourning?"

Everly let the fabric fall with a satisfying swish. "It's pretty."

"So is color," Jazzy said. "So are *you*."

Tension crept into Everly's shoulders. Her first instinct these days was always to contradict a compliment. But this time, she didn't let herself. She only smiled. If she wanted the show to change her, she had to be willing to change herself, too.

Jazzy folded her arms over her chest. "You believe that, right?"

"I don't think I'm ugly. I just hate the word 'pretty.'" Everly shrugged. "Why?"

"I don't know if I can explain it in a way that makes sense." She forced her feet toward one of the brighter-colored sections, using the extra time to gather her thoughts. "Pretty . . . I don't know . . . feels like one of those things I'm supposed to strive for, something straight-sized people are. Dainty, small, petite. It's a beauty standard I don't want to have to subscribe to." Even when she was at her most confident, "pretty" and "fat" felt like polar opposites. She could look killer, fierce, hot, cute, whatever. Anything but pretty.

Jazzy followed, idly flipping through garments, her dark eyes bright and attentive. Beyond her, Logan's camera captured the two of them like Big Brother.

His expression was impossible to decipher. Everly hated how much she wanted to know what he was thinking as he observed their conversations, recorded them to be shared with the world. It shouldn't matter to her, the same way she shouldn't be thinking about him as much as she was, but it did matter, and she was thinking about him. A lot.

Much more than James, lately.

Fuck.

There had better be a witch at this Ren faire that had a counterspell for catching feelings. She didn't want to fall for someone else. Not now, when she was supposed to be working on herself. Not when he would be gone in a few weeks anyway. He wasn't worth crushing on any more than James.

Turning away from Jazzy, she pulled out a silk corset dress covered in stitched flowers in hues of rose and blush. It was elegant and soft and absolutely beautiful, something she could never imagine on herself. So of course, the minute Everly released it, Jazzy snatched it off the rack.

She was still quiet. Waiting for Everly to go on.

Clearing her throat, Everly fussed with a pile of folded cloaks. "I'm tired of all the words for femininity emphasizing being small and frail. I want to be attractive and strong. Powerful. Like the way you co-opted 'fabulous' and transformed it into something that spoke to bodies like ours."

Jazzy chewed on her lip for a second. She now had three dresses in her hands. Each one a brighter color than the next.

"You're so right," she said. "What is it we always hear? 'You'd be so beautiful if you just lost a little weight.' It's bullshit." She added a pirate-esque striped shift to her pile. "So what do you want your word to be? What's *your* 'fabulous'?"

It was a question Everly had never thought to ask herself.

She mulled it over as she made her first dress selection. Apple red with gold stitching. The farthest thing from black. Jazzy beamed, a proud mother hen, as she watched Everly drape it over her arm.

Everly hadn't realized how much she wanted to see that expression on the host's face. Usually, it wasn't something that happened for guests until the end of their arc.

But she'd already made Jazzy proud.

Everly felt like pumping her fist or doing a touchdown dance.

She chose two more dresses before she finally decided on her word. It was not a synonym for pretty. But there was a power to it. Like people would stop and pay attention. To Everly, that was what lay at the heart of being attractive. Not being invisible.

When she told Jazzy, it was with as much certainty as Everly had heard in her own voice in a long time. "Striking. My word is 'striking.'"

Forty-five minutes later, Meryl was making the final tugs on the ribbons of Everly's first costume and urging her out of the dressing room.

She'd barely reached the wall of mirrors before she started shaking her head. "No. Absolutely *not*."

Jazzy had started Everly off in a tiny embroidered skirt that barely hit mid-thigh, with white lace peeking out of the hem. The shirt beneath had a similar gauzy lace trim that accentuated Everly's ample cleavage, especially with the black-and-gray-striped corset tied up to her bust. "I look like I'm trying to be a sexy milkmaid or something."

"More pirate, I think." Stanton stopped beside her to admire his own Robin Hood outfit in the mirror. "And I don't see the problem."

The point of today was to shake Everly out of her comfort zone, but this was a different kind of discomfort. She'd spend the whole day distracted by trying to make the skirt cover her whole ass. "It's begging for a wardrobe malfunction." She tugged up the shirt before her nipple became a star on national television. "This is . . . it's not what feels sexy to me."

Logan moved in the periphery of her vision, circling the platform to catch them from another angle. Her cheeks flushed red, and, grabbing the end of Stanton's cloak, she draped it over herself like a bath towel. Practically every inch of her skin was on display, and she couldn't stand the thought of what Logan's camera—what he—might see.

"Another great shot, thanks." He spoke the words with a grumble, but his blue eyes sparked, like a gem caught in sunlight. He was teasing her.

And she loved it.

"I have the right to deny the viewing audience an eyeful of my ass cheeks."

Jazzy flanked Everly's other side in a matching outfit. They were similar in size and stature and yet the costume couldn't look more different on them. It was the way they held themselves. Everly curled in, trying to make herself smaller—trying to disappear—while Jazzy took up as much space as she could, legs spread wide in a power stance, her shoulders back and proud. She believed she looked hot. Meanwhile, Everly could hardly look at herself.

Jazzy seemed to recognize it, too. "This isn't it." She unraveled Everly from Stanton and his cloak and urged her back toward the dressing room. "Maybe the red one next?"

The red dress was floor length, with no corset. Instead, the clingy fabric draped out from an empire waist. On Everly's arms, belled sleeves created a similar silhouette. With no embroidery or brocading, the vibrant red color was jarring and unappealing.

"I'm a stop sign," she declared as she stepped out from behind the curtain.

Jazzy pursed her lips, and Everly's stomach clenched. She was being too negative. "It's a nice shape, though," she added hastily.

"Romantic suits you," Jazzy said.

Everly glanced at her reflection again. "Romantic's a good word for it. But I feel like the color's too much. I like muted pastels and neutrals. Something more boho-y."

"Is boho your thing?"

"Kind of." Everly pulled at the skirt of the dress, admiring how the fabric moved. "I never really had a style back before—"

"Swing-dress-aggedon?"

Everly let out a loud laugh. It was a sadly accurate description of her current wardrobe. "Yes. Before that. I used to wear whatever I wanted, any style that looked fun. But I always felt most . . . striking," the word rolled easily off her tongue, "in those loose, flowery tunics and skinny jeans and boots, with lots of draping necklaces or statement earrings."

Jazzy pointed a finger at the mirror. "Look at your face right now."

Everly's gaze shifted to her reflection. She looked so happy. The light from her smile went right up to her eyes.

"That's what I want you to feel all the time." Jazzy held her gaze in the mirror. "Before she passed, my mom always used to say that our faces can't lie, no matter what our mouths are doing. And your face is telling me everything I need to know right now."

She shooed Everly away with instructions to put on the pink dress.

Ten minutes later, Everly was back at the mirrors, the hosts flanking her. Stanton had to keep pulling down her hands whenever she pressed them to her cheeks to hide her blushing.

She couldn't stop staring at herself. This dress was the very definition of romantic. The shift was cream colored and soft, the puffy sleeves falling off her shoulders and gathering in a ruffle at her elbow. Cinched over it was a silk corset in a soft shade of light mauve with petals and flower buds stitched in rose and blush pinks. Cream ribbons served as straps, and another ribbon laced up her midsection. Cascading from the corset was an ankle-length skirt in a shade of blush that matched some of the flowers. The train was gathered in a bustle on one of her hips.

Jazzy had paired the dress with black booties, and she'd gathered half of Everly's hair in a braided crown on the top of her head, a handful of daisies woven in. The rest showered her shoulders in auburn-brown curls. Simple pearl droplet earrings peeked out from under the loose strands.

"Can I wear this every day?" Everly whispered. She felt more like herself in this costume than she did in anything that currently hung in her closet. The old Everly would have rocked this look. Everly could have sworn she could glimpse that girl behind the surprise in her expression, a shadow of the version of herself she thought she'd lost.

"I support this," Stanton said. "We should make costumes a part of everyday dress. I feel like people would be a helluva lot happier."

Everly loved that the hosts had dressed up, too. It made her feel a part of things. Like they'd pulled her inside.

She blinked away a wave of tears. She didn't want to blur this image of herself or chase it away. She wanted it seared into her mind, so that every time she envisioned herself, this was what she saw.

Soft. Romantic . . .

For the first time since she'd hid behind Stanton's cloak, Everly's gaze searched for Logan.

The camera was on her, as always, but it felt like his eyes were as well. They swept over her, something weighty behind that deep blue hue.

Then the corner of his mouth tipped into the smallest of smiles.

Her stomach spun, and heat washed over her like a tidal wave as he mouthed, *Striking*.

CHAPTER 12

Laughing in a corset was a particular kind of torture. It was like Everly's rib cage had a rib cage, and they were vying for dominance.

"You don't even match," she said before erupting into another fit of cackles. Then she groaned.

"Maybe people who need makeover shows shouldn't have opinions about others' style choices." Logan's eyes narrowed at her, but that tiny teasing smile peeked out from his beard.

He walked backward, picking up the pace as if he hoped the heat or the rocky terrain they were navigating in heeled boots might take Everly, Stanton, and Jazzy out one by one, like in a horror movie.

Before they'd left the costume booth, Stanton had presented Logan with a kilt. The cameraman refused to put it on until it became clear that no one would move forward with the production schedule unless he complied.

"You need to blend in," Stanton had insisted, brandishing the garment.

"Because that ship hasn't already sailed with this thing." Logan waved the camera.

Everly then (unhelpfully) pointed out that Logan would look like a time traveler, which Stanton had *loved,* ensuring there was no way Logan was exiting Edmund's Wardrobe without that kilt on.

In the end, he'd done it, but he wouldn't budge on losing his shirt, so he now shuffled ahead of them in a yellow, red, and white plaid shirt tucked into a kilt of gray, tan, and blue tartan. He even had a sporran secured around his waist. And he'd capped it all off with his black Vans.

"This is some of my best work," Stanton declared.

Jazzy hooked her arm with Everly's. "Stanton dresses Logan up for every themed event."

Another little secret about the show Everly needed to share with Becca. She'd *die.* "So when you went to Disneyland?"

"Mickey ears."

"And the beach?"

"Full surf gear. Wet suit and all."

"And the Marvel movie?"

"He was the Hulk."

Everly wondered if he'd worn his plaid shirt under the wetsuit, too. She arched an eyebrow at him. "Why do you give in?"

"It's easier than fighting with them," he mumbled. "They're impossible."

Stanton shook his head. "I think he secretly loves it."

Logan's grunt in response sent them into a new wave of laughter.

One of the best things about being on *On the Plus Side* was seeing proof of the camaraderie among the hosts. So many of the gossip sites claimed there was infighting and backstabbing, but Jazzy and Stanton had been everything Everly had hoped they'd be from the second they'd met.

The faire opened as they approached the jousting arena. Signs had been posted everywhere announcing that the show was filming at today's festivities, and Everly's stomach flip-flopped when she saw the size of the crowd streaming toward their end of the fairground.

There were *so* many people. She was still wrapping her head around the idea of an audience behind the camera. Now she had to deal with a live one.

Sady waved to them from a raised pavilion at the front of the arena, where a bearded man in a crown, who Everly could only assume was King Henry, sat on a throne flanked by women dressed in expensive-looking gowns and dripping with jewels. People in yellow volunteer T-shirts ran around them, adjusting costumes and seating.

Breaking away from the group, Sady strode their way. She wasn't decked out in costume, instead wearing a wide-leg linen jumpsuit in a shade of forest green. Everly was beginning to believe the woman wore business attire to bed.

She smiled as she took in Everly and the hosts. "You all look fantastic." Waving Everly over, Sady took her hand and spun her in a circle so she could admire her dress. "This is perfect. Do you feel like a princess?"

"Actually, I feel like a badass."

Sady's grin widened. "Even better."

She led Everly up the stairs to the pavilion, Jazzy and Stanton right behind them. Everly almost tripped twice on her dress, and every time she glanced back, Logan's lens was right on her. Of course. That man had awkward-Everly radar.

"The faire organizers are so thrilled to have you here today that they want you to participate in the joust. It's their most popular event."

Everly eyed her warily. She loved being with animals, but with her feet firmly on the ground. "Like, on a horse?"

"Not you, no." Sady laughed. "You'll be bestowing gifts upon the winners."

Everly wasn't sure that was much better. She'd had to take a medieval history and culture course in college. The winners of these kinds of tournaments usually received a kiss or the woman's hand in marriage or something else that reminded everyone that women were no different from gold coins back then. Objects to barter or make deals with.

Sady winked at her before stepping out of the frame. "It will be fun, trust me."

As much as Everly wanted to believe her, there was a very good chance that the two of them had diametrically opposed definitions of that word.

The opening ceremony began a few minutes later. King Henry greeted the crowd and introduced the *OTPS* hosts. Stanton began by thanking the organizers for allowing them to crash their event, then spoke briefly about his personal attachment to Ren faires, and Jazzy followed up by introducing Everly and giving a shout-out to Edmund's Wardrobe.

Thankfully, no one asked Everly to say anything. She couldn't do public speaking without note cards (and backup note cards for the original set).

After making a few jokes about their strange speaking habits and poking the lens of Logan's camera like he'd never seen one before, King Henry explained Everly's role for the morning.

"Each of our jousters will compete in a series of increasingly difficult feats. At the end of each round, I will determine the winner, and you, Lady Everly of Winters," he pointed a finger at her, "will bestow upon them a gift of your choice."

A volunteer carried over a small table with three items on it: a rose, a ring, and a handkerchief embroidered with daisies.

Everly nodded in understanding. Stanton echoed the gesture by yelling, "As you wish, good king."

Everly's mouth went dry. Was she supposed to be role-playing? Her eyes scanned the sea of people. She'd been in exactly one play, in junior high, and that had been enough for her to know she was no actress. Someone should have given her a heads-up that there was going to be a performance element today so she could have practiced.

Practice probably didn't make for good TV, though.

The first few rounds of the tournament challenged the knights with various obstacles. They soared their horses over hurdles, captured rings hanging at various heights with their lances, and charged at targets with their weapons.

As they cheered for another knight who had caught all five rings on his jousting pole, Stanton leaned into Everly and whispered, "I have a theory that knights were every bit as gay as pirates. There's no way they spent all this time playing with proverbial phalluses without enjoying the real thing."

Everly couldn't fault his logic.

The winner of the round was a weathered knight in green regalia who was the only one able to hit the last set of three small targets. It was impressive, actually, given that they were barely the size of a fist.

King Henry invited him to the pavilion to receive his reward.

Jazzy and Stanton had to shove Everly to her feet.

Her heart drilled against her chest as she grabbed the rose and crossed to the lower platform, where the knight waited.

"Um . . . hey," she muttered.

His name was Sir Horace, and he had kind, grayish-brown eyes, the color of old driftwood. They squinted in amusement at her stilted greeting, accentuating some of the lines in his brow.

"Great job . . ." Her hands flapped against the folds of her dress. Twice she almost crushed the delicate petals of the rose she held. "You know, with that stuff you did."

Everly's voice was so weak it barely reached her own ears. The crowd hummed impatiently as it waited for fanfare she didn't know how to deliver. Why hadn't anyone given her notes? She was on this show because she was terrified of being seen—how was thrusting her into this unprepared supposed to help her?

She bit her lip. Panic shot through her veins, leaving her jittery.

Logan was a few steps to her right, close enough for her to hear him whisper, "You need to play this up."

"Great. Thanks for the advice," she hissed. Her fingers tightened around the stem of the rose, which thankfully had no thorns, until it snapped in her grip.

Where was that cartoon coyote to saw a hole around her and let her fall through the stage?

Sir Horace cleared his throat. "My lady," he called out, clearly trying to help, "I am humbled by the honor of your gift." He bowed his head and raised his hands, palms flat, ready to receive his winnings.

Everly's arm locked at her side. The rose felt like the only thing tethering her to reality. If she let it go, she'd float away, or worse, burst into tears.

Logan started up again. "You've got those romance novels in your apartment with the knights on the cover."

She shot him a glare, with no care for the fourth wall and how much she'd demolished it. "Now is not really the time for you to judge my choice of books."

"What would one of the ladies from those things say in this moment?" There was no derision in his voice or on his face. His eyebrows were doing that thing with the center crease that made him look worried.

Everly thought of *The Wayward Queen,* sitting half-read on her nightstand. There was in fact a moment like this, where Queen Eleanor was forced to honor a knight from a nearby kingdom, even though he wasn't the man she loved.

She did her best to remember the queen's speech as she faced Sir Horace.

"Your prowess is without rival, good knight. The truest champion has won the day." Everly spoke as loudly as she could, then placed the broken rose in the knight's hands. Its practically decapitated top hung off his palm, raining red petals onto the dirt. Though she wanted to grimace and apologize, then fold in on herself until she vanished, Everly said nothing, only tipped her chin up the way Eleanor would in times of strife.

A storm of applause followed, and with a deep bow, Horace tucked the pathetic flower into his tabard and rode off.

On her way back up the stairs, Everly snuck a glance at Logan. Their eyes locked. There was a glimmer of something bright in his irises.

By the time they left the tournament two hours later, the faire was bustling with activity.

All the shows were in full swing. They passed fire-breathers, laundry wenches, fortune-tellers, animal acts. Patrons gathered everywhere there was space, and the air brimmed with music and laughter and voices hawking wares. More than one person yelled "huzzah" as they wandered by.

Though she'd been in the shade for most of the day, Everly was covered in sweat and exhausted from carrying around the extra weight of her costume's many fabrics and layers. She would have loved nothing more than to find some air-conditioning, but Stanton had something planned at the body art tent and was herding them along at a rapid pace.

In such a big crowd, Logan couldn't really film, so he'd fallen into step next to Everly. Thanks to his quick thinking, the rest of the jousting tournament had gone more smoothly than she could have hoped. She'd borrowed as much dialogue as she could remember from *The Wayward*

Queen, and everyone had seemed impressed by her role-playing. The last knight—Sir Christian—really got into character, and instead of taking the ring she offered, begged her to run away with him, pressing a slow, warm kiss to her palm. As his mouth had met her skin, a rock had tumbled by and tapped his horse's leg, startling it and almost throwing Christian to the ground. When she'd looked behind her to see where it had come from, she would have sworn a satisfied smirk lurked under Logan's beard.

Now she turned to him, not sure what to say. Part of her wanted to show gratitude for his help, but she was also really curious about that rock.

He nodded to a turkey vendor ahead of them. "Look at these two."

There was a couple standing at the booth. She was plus-size and petite, wearing a long floral maxi dress and a flower crown atop a sea of long brown waves. Her arms were crossed over her chest as she argued with the vendor, something about turkeys not being eaten in Europe until the sixteenth century. The guy beside her burst into a laugh that sounded more like geese screaming. He was wearing legitimate plate armor, but it was clearly too small for his tall, super-thin frame, and he had the whole thing duct-taped to his jeans and cardigan. His maroon glasses held up the visor of his helmet so he could see.

"That's a look," Logan said.

"A choice, indeed," she echoed. "I'm surprised you're not filming them for the B-roll."

"They'd have to sign waivers. Too much work."

Everly watched them wistfully until they were out of sight. Neither one seemed embarrassed about his unusual ensemble. That was what she wanted. To be completely and authentically herself again, no matter who was watching.

By the time they reached the body art tent, dust painted the hems of Everly's skirts—and probably the inside of her lungs—but that discomfort quickly dissipated when she saw the room Stanton had brought them to. The walls were lined with pictures of various kinds of art, from face painting to henna to temporary tattoos.

Hefting his camera back to his shoulder, Logan resumed filming.

"Some of these people must do tattoos, don't you think?" she asked as he trailed her around the space. After all the times he'd spoken on camera today, Everly no longer worried about breaking the fourth wall. That thing had been obliterated at this point.

"Probably."

She ran her fingers over a small bird sketch, its wings wide in flight. "It's got to be so . . . I don't know . . . fulfilling, to know that you get to help people turn fleeting memories into something permanent."

"Have you given any thought to yours?"

Everly skimmed the bird with her finger again, then peered at him over her shoulder. "I haven't gotten the drawing right yet, but I'm thinking an open birdcage with a flock bursting out of it."

His expression softened a little. "For freedom?"

Her heart stuttered. "Exactly." He'd been listening while he recorded her.

"One bird for every piece of me I've kept locked up." Her eyes pored over the other pictures, black-lined reimaginings of various mythology monsters, woodland creatures, and flower garlands. "You have one, right?" She'd seen the edge of a tattoo peeking out from under his rolled-up cuffs, but never enough to figure out what it was.

"Yeah. On my forearm."

Everly turned to face him. "What is it?"

His gaze, usually so steady and intense, skipped to her feet. "Paw prints. For each of the dogs I've lost."

Surprise cut through her knees, almost knocking Everly over. When she'd imagined what his tattoo looked like (she might have, once or twice—or more—daydreamed about removing his shirt to see those arms sans all the plaid), she'd always assumed it would be something wilderness related, like an ax or a tree or a mountain, some symbol that aligned with his lumbersexual aura. Not something so vulnerable and soft.

"I'm so sorry. It sucks losing a pet." Her fingers braided through the fabric of her overskirt. "We never had one growing up, but my grandmother had an animal sanctuary, and Ellis and I were there all the time. Whenever she lost one, it was like someone chipped a little piece out of me. The worst was Sheldon, one of the pygmy goats. He'd been my buddy at the sanctuary for years—he'd follow me around and sit beside me while I did my homework every night. When old age finally got him, I sobbed for weeks." The farm had never felt quite the same after Sheldon was gone. He'd left a goat-shaped hole behind no one could fill.

Logan nodded again, but his eyes had finally stopped avoiding hers.

"Can I see it?" she asked softly.

"Sure."

He secured his camera on a shelf behind them, then shoved up his sleeve. It was tight, the fabric not fully giving around his muscles, but he managed to expose most of the tattoo.

He held out his inner forearm. Just below his elbow were four black paw prints about the size of golf balls arranged in a vertical line.

Everly's heart hurt. "You've lost four dogs?"

His eyes narrowed into a squint, and he paused to rub a hand across the back of his neck. "I like to adopt the older ones, which means I don't always get as much time with them." He glanced down at his arm. "I like having a visible representation of the mark they left on me."

"They take a little piece of us with them," she said quietly. That's what her grandmother used to say.

He nodded.

"You have some dogs now, right?" Everly asked. He'd mentioned them a few times. "Alan and . . . Linguine?"

"Ravioli," he corrected her, his head down as he dug his phone out of the pouch on his kilt.

"I knew it was something Italian." Everly watched him poke at the screen. "If you don't name the next one Gnocchi, I will never forgive you."

His lips twitched against a laugh. "Ravioli is the name he came with."

He moved to Everly's side so they could both see his phone and began to flip through pictures of the dogs. She wanted to concentrate on them, but her brain was too focused on the pressure of his arm against hers. The solidness of his biceps. And the effect that both of these things were having on her insides.

Her head jerked up when she heard Stanton suddenly call her name. He was standing in the tent opening, Sady by his side, her phone out as usual.

At the sight of them, Logan's energy fizzled. His face settled into a frown and he turned to grab his camera.

The air around them seemed to deflate right along with his smile.

READ-IT FORUM: ON THE PLUS SIDE

Subject: Season 3, Episode 1

CourtK *20 minutes ago*

OMG THAT FIRST EPISODE!!!!!!!!!!!!!

234 ♥ 168 👍 50 ✨ 4 👎

FarmGyrlME *10 minutes ago*

that last fifteen minutes CHANGED EVERYTHING

100 ♥ 76 👍 98 ✨ 1 👎

Annette98 *3 minutes ago*

WHO WAS THAT GUY????!!!! HE BETTER BE BACK ON
THURSDAY. AND EVERY EPISODE AFTERWARDS. IM AL-
READY IN LOVE!!!!!!

swoons

187 ♥ 103 👍 86 ✨ 11 👎

RosyTea *now*

otps has an otp for sure

131 ♥ 201 👍 83 ✨ 1 👎

CHAPTER 13

Hell was a family gathering without your phone to distract you. Especially when you were the center of attention.

Though it had felt like the right decision at the time, Everly was currently regretting leaving hers in her apartment. With her first full episode of *On the Plus Side* dropping on VuNu in less than half an hour, she'd been desperate to avoid the itch to slide into the *OTPS* Read-It forums and see who was doing a live reaction thread. She didn't need to see how fans were responding to her.

But since her brother apparently felt extra guilty about forgetting the premiere special, he had organized a family viewing party for tonight. So now, instead of facing the opinions of the online masses, Everly was at the mercy of her mother.

Becca had decorated the living room with festive streamers in gold and silver, and the sofa table was packed with a charcuterie spread, platters of tiny meatball subs and pigs in a blanket, a jug of watermelon sangria (Everly's favorite drink), and bottles of champagne and sparkling cider. Everly's mom sat in the middle of the sectional, having tossed aside the streamers and crown that marked it as the seat of honor. She was holding court, waving a flute of champagne like a slightly inebriated symphony conductor.

Everly planted herself on the couch next to her mother and futilely attempted not to roll her eyes at her comments.

"What do they do with you besides follow you around? You'll go shopping, right?" Mom pointed her champagne at Everly. "Hopefully for something other than black or gray."

Good lord. She and Jazzy should conspire.

"And they're going to help me work toward some of my art goals," Everly added.

"Oh?" Her mom sat up straighter. "Are you going to try to get a promotion at Matten-Waverly?"

"I don't know yet. But I can freelance on my own to help build a portfolio and get more experience. I've always loved doing those book covers, and there's definitely a market out there for indie books."

Her mother nodded. "The ones in your apartment are so beautiful."

Her words fizzed through Everly's veins. Her mom hounded her so much about her laugh and her voice and her style—pretty much everything—that it was nice to be reminded she could be proud of her daughter, too.

"And there might be other opportunities. The show has a lot of surprises that they don't share with me ahead of time."

Part of Everly itched to talk about her tattoo, but she already felt so raw and open sitting here, moments from seeing herself on TV, that she couldn't get the words out. Who knew how her mother was going to feel about *that*?

Becca squished herself between Everly and her mom and turned on the TV. A hush fell over the room as she cued up the episode. Even Everly's mother had set down her glass of champagne and settled in.

Grabbing a nearby throw pillow, Everly hugged it to her chest. Her stomach was a rope of intricately tied knots, and nerves slipped under her skin until it prickled. She had no idea what to expect. What if it was more of the same lovesick Everly from the premiere special? This was exactly why she didn't want a party, why she hadn't let Ellis invite anyone but close family. There was no telling what they were about to see.

She needed a distraction, and Bagel and his perfectly fidget-approved ears were in the dining room with a bone, so Everly took her life in her own hands and dared to pet Cream Cheese, perched possessively in Becca's lap.

The cat's fur was soft and smooth, and Everly's muscles relaxed a little with each brush her fingers made across the white Angora's coat. Clearly Cream Cheese sensed Everly's stress, because she only swiped at her hand a few times, and always with her claws retracted. That was as close as this cat got to showing mercy.

After the opening credits, the episode began like the first one did every season—with Jazzy and Stanton introducing themselves and explaining the show's documentary format (minimal edits, a small crew, each of the four guests getting eight episodes—all meant to infuse as much reality as possible into the show). Then it cut to a shot of Everly at the office, answering the phones. Though it had been filmed days after they'd ambushed her, Sady was using it as an establishing shot.

Becca grabbed her arm and gave it a big shake. "Look at you. On *our* show! Oh my god." Her eyes were glassy with excitement.

Everly's vision also blurred. "It's wild."

"It's *amazing*."

Even her mom offered her a smile. "You look nice," she said. Rarer words had never been spoken by Penny Winters.

Maybe this would go okay.

The first half hour or so focused on the hosts surprising Everly at

Matten-Waverly. She remembered their arrival vividly, but watching it unfold from an objective point of view was eye-opening. She'd thought she held it together really well in the moment, but on-screen, she was practically bouncing out of her own skin when Jazzy greeted her. Her face had this manic expression, eyes wide, her smile stretched to its limits, like those fun house entrances with the giant clown face. It was a wonder everyone hadn't run screaming.

Sady was clearly constructing a different timeline, because directly after the ambush, the show cut to Everly sitting down with her for their first interview, as if she'd strode straight from the hallway of the office building to the park across the street. In reality, that had happened hours later. It was a good reminder that even when something was trying to be "real" or authentic, it was still a story being told.

Like one of her English professors used to say, everything was a narrative.

Everly's nerves while talking to Sady were crystal clear in the footage. Though Sady had prompted her with questions, Everly had struggled to say much more than a few words.

After that, things shifted back to the office. It was incredible how well Logan captured the chaos: the loud clatter of pens as Stanton shook them out everywhere, Jazzy treating Everly's poor sweater as a beach blanket and then later, a bath towel. There were multiple close-ups of the horror on Everly's face at the mess.

Most of the day unfolded on the television screen exactly the way she remembered it, except for the last few minutes of the segment. There was this moment as the rest of the crew left where the camera swung back toward James and Everly. James caught her arm gently and gave her a wide smile. Her body visibly loosened in response. The shot remained on them, capturing their eye contact that lingered long after James had released her.

Long enough that everyone in her brother's living room began to murmur.

Her mother leaned over Becca to tap Everly on the knee. "Who's that?"

Everly shushed her, gesturing toward the television, pretending she didn't want to miss a second. Her cheeks were so hot they burned, but she did her best to feign nonchalance (as well as anyone could while desperately clutching a pillow to their chest).

She felt strangely disconnected from the girl swooning over James in that clip. Her heart wasn't dancing at their shared eye contact, and no goose bumps blanketed her arms. Mostly she was embarrassed. She might as well have inscribed her feelings across her forehead in calligraphy.

Ever since the premiere special, Everly had been actively avoiding James (the last thing Sady needed was more ammo for her love story arc), but now she wondered if the distance hadn't had the added bonus of dampening her crush. Especially given how much more real estate Logan was inhabiting in her head these days.

She almost sighed with relief. Filming *OTPS* would go so much more smoothly if she could do it sans James. Then she could worry a little less, and Sady would be forced to focus the show on Everly's art and goals. It would be a win, win, win, all around.

The next segment introduced the town of Monmouth Cove and Everly's day-to-day life. They used a lot of the same clips from the premiere special, only in more extended detail, so, of course, there was plenty of James. Too much, in Everly's opinion. The scene of her knocking everything off her desk and then slamming heads with him went on for decades.

"Not your finest moment," her mother pointed out with a cluck of her tongue. She chased her words with a swig of champagne.

Everly barely heard her. She was too mesmerized by the tiny details in every scene she never would have imagined Logan would catch: a zoomed-in shot of a dog doodle she'd sketched while on the phone; a panning shot over her shoulder while she worked on a logo for Becca's freelance website after closing; a moment of Bagel nuzzling her under her chin; Everly and Becca giggling with their heads bent low; Everly laughing exuberantly after she'd made Logan blush, the fluorescent lights of the office catching in her hair and skin like a halo. In each moment, Everly and her art looked so good.

Striking, even.

Her heart pounded in her chest, and her stomach was full of fluttering wings. He was doing what she'd asked for at Sunny's. He was showing the audience who Everly was. She wasn't prepared for how much she liked seeing herself through his camera lens. Or for how it would make her feel so weightless, as if she were bobbing in a pool of water.

Her family's running commentary was nothing but a low, senseless buzz in Everly's ears. Their words faded against the thrum of her pulse, her mind too full of those perfect pictures of her for anything else.

Maybe this whole experience on TV would be okay. There were only fifteen minutes left in the episode, and the scene had shifted to wardrobe day. Which meant that what she'd shared at Sunny's about not wanting to date James didn't make the cut.

Logan had kept his promise.

The realization left her light-headed. It had been hard to ignore her growing attraction to him when she thought she was just someone he had to point a camera at. But this whole episode had proven to her that she was more than that. She was *real* to him. Someone worth listening to. Worth seeing. How was she supposed to fight her feelings in the face of that?

Everly shook her shoulders to loosen them and smiled at Becca, who had grabbed her hand as Jazzy started rummaging through on-screen Everly's closet and drawers.

"B, I'm having a wardrobe day," she squealed softly. She needed to aim her brain at something else to stop thinking about Logan.

Becca squeezed her hand. "And Jazzy's clearly loving your style choices." She raised an eyebrow at the screen. The camera was scanning across the giant pile of discarded clothes at the host's feet.

"Oh yeah, she let me keep everything." Everly snorted.

At the sound, her mother's eyes jumped to Everly, her face scrunched in distaste. But for once, Everly didn't choke her laugh back or try to hide. She was watching herself on her favorite show, surrounded by her family. If there was anywhere that she should be able to show joy, to be her full self, it should be here.

Their gazes met, and her mother's lips pursed. But instead of making one of her usual comments about Everly's laugh, she tipped her head at the screen. "This is exactly what I've been telling you for ages. The clothes you wear don't do you any service. I can't wait to see what this woman finds for you. I hope she shows you how to layer to camouflage your problem areas."

"No way." Everly had never heard Becca speak so firmly. "That's not what Jazzy does."

"But it's a makeover show."

"One that cares about the guest's happiness, not their size," Everly pointed out.

It was true that most makeover shows dressed their fat guests to mimic the standard hourglass shape. The advice was always about accentuating your waist and hiding your belly and redirecting the eye. But Jazzy and Stanton didn't abide by any of that.

Everly's mom frowned. "But don't you feel more confident when you look slimmer?"

"No. I feel like a fraud. I want to be comfortable as I am." Everly reached for Cream Cheese's soft coat again. Equating feeling good with being thin was her mom's thing.

With a sigh, her mother sat back against her chair.

As Everly returned her attention to the TV, she realized the three of them had talked right over her explanation of Grandma Helen's death.

It was a relief, honestly. She wasn't ready to relive that grief again. Or to deal with how much more judgmental her mother became at any mention of Everly's grandmother. Sometimes, she wondered if her mom was jealous of the relationship Everly and Grandma Helen had shared. Penny Winters seemed incapable of forging that kind of bond with her own daughter or mother. Maybe she begrudged them for forming their own connection in her place.

Suddenly, Logan's voice cut into the frame, and the room snapped into silence.

"Fuck it. Greg can edit me out. You are not *too much."*

Each word, each syllable, spoken in that graveled tone of his, danced shivers down Everly's spine. She'd been there when he'd said it, but hearing him now, when she wasn't distracted by her own emotions, drew her attention to the intensity in his voice.

"Who is *that*?" Her mother's fingers wrapped Everly's arm in a tight grip.

"That's Logan," Becca said. "Ev. Oh my god."

They heard it, too. Everly didn't know why that knowledge set her whole body aflame, but she was burning hot. It was a wonder the couch wasn't smoking. "Oh my god, nothing." She shook her head at Becca. "He was being nice."

"Bullshit." Becca aimed the remote at the TV and jumped back a few seconds to replay the scene. She did it once. Then twice. Then a third time. And again.

Everly kept insisting it was nothing.

But even as she said it, she knew the words were lies. There was something in that moment, in Logan's voice, that made her center go warm. Made her press her knees a bit more tightly together.

He sounded practically feral. On her behalf.

And she liked it.

She liked *him*.

And after hearing him growl those words over and over as Becca replayed the scene, Everly couldn't deny that he just might like her, too.

That was the scariest part of all.

CHAPTER 14

"Oh my god, look at your little pigtails!"

Jazzy pointed at Everly's kindergarten school photo and squealed.

Since *On the Plus Side* needed interviews and footage with her family for future episodes, Everly's mother had agreed to host a barbeque at her house. They'd both figured that would be easier than trying to fit everyone into one of Monmouth Cove's tiny restaurants, and, Everly had now discovered, it offered the added bonus (horror?) of viewing plenty of pictures from her childhood, which the hosts had been meticulously inspecting for the last twenty minutes.

In the photo Jazzy was fawning over, five-year-old Everly wore pink corduroy overalls and a flowered shirt, her reddish-brown hair half-tamed by two braids. She was also missing her front teeth, because the universe was rarely merciful on school picture days.

Logan eased behind Everly to zoom in. Because of course.

She whacked him on the arm in a pathetic attempt to stop him, only to swiftly turn away from the stairs, cradling her hand to her stomach.

Good. God. His bicep was a solid wall.

She tried (and failed) not to think about what those arms could do under the right circumstances. Those were thoughts for later, when he wasn't standing right beside her while her cheeks cycled through multiple shades of red.

"No one needs to see that," she told the floor.

"Everyone needs to see this." He twisted the lens, and something whirred in his camera. Probably to pan in closer, the bastard. "You're adorable."

"I was five. Everyone's adorable at five."

He swept the camera up and down the wall, pausing now and then to focus in on a particular photo. "My school pictures for most of elementary school beg to differ."

Jazzy paused her conversation with Stanton. "Oh. You *need* to see his grandmother's Facebook page. It's like a shrine to awkward Logan."

Everly yanked her phone out of her pocket and cued up Facebook, which she only had because her mother insisted on sending invites for family functions through it. "What's her name?"

"What? No." Logan's rough voice caught on a higher pitch. He swung the camera in Everly's direction.

"I need to see this."

"Everly." Her name on his lips sent a jolt of electricity through her body.

He straightened his shoulders and aimed the lens at her. "How does it feel to have survived three full weeks of filming?" His tone perfectly parroted Sady's during interviews, reminding Everly how many he must have sat through. How all these firsts for her were routine workdays for him.

She took a few steps back only to have him press forward to match her pace. As if the camera were chasing her.

"Fine." With an exaggerated frown, she mumbled, "You win, no

Facebook," and returned her phone to her pocket. His victorious smirk sent her fleeing from the room.

She sought sanctuary outside with her brother, who was tending to the burgers, chicken, and vegetables on the grill. Bagel, who never missed a chance to hang out in her mom's large backyard, wove his way between Ellis's legs, hoping to luck into an errant piece of food.

Everly perched on the end of a lounger. "This is a whole thing, huh?"

"My little sister on TV was definitely not on my bingo card." Ellis flipped one last burger before shutting the grill top. He stared at her over his beer bottle, taking a long slug. "How are you holding up?"

The two of them were close in that way that having only one reliable parent bonded siblings. They'd spent most of their childhood picking up the slack for their father, whether that meant coming up with money to help their mom with the bills or working out their differences without getting into fights that would upset her. Ellis had taught Everly how to drive and was home to meet the first guy she'd dated. He gave her her first beer the summer before she went to college. She'd helped him find a tux for prom. She was his sports buddy. And his supportive shoulder when his heart got broken.

Everly glanced up at the sky. It was overcast, and the stars looked like twinkle lights submerged underwater. "About as well as Gonzo the Great being shot out of a cannon."

Ellis cackled. They'd watched *The Muppet Show* together on repeat during their formative years. When Everly was in fourth grade, their mom had brought home the DVD sets of seasons one and two from a yard sale, insisting she and Ellis would love them. At ten and twelve, the siblings had been horrified that their mother wouldn't pay for a streaming service. Back then, they would have very dramatically sworn they were the only kids in their school who knew what a DVD player was, never mind how to use one. But a few months later, when their father hadn't shown up for his weekend (again), and Grandma Helen had pneumonia, their mom was forced to leave them home alone for the first time overnight. Everly and Ellis had been so afraid to go to sleep that they'd hunkered down together on the couch and, without many other choices, decided to pop those DVDs in. They'd laughed so much that night that they forgot to be scared.

After that, they'd sought out every flea market, yard sale, consignment shop, and Goodwill, looking for the rest of the seasons and anything else by Jim Henson. Whenever they were left alone or feeling down, they'd watched them. Over and over until they knew them all by heart.

Sometimes, when one of them needed a laugh, they still did.

Ellis uncapped another beer, then grabbed his spatula. "It's got to be weird having these people around all the time, just like . . . watching you."

"It is. There are cameras in my car, too, and some in my living room. I swear, the bathroom's the only place I can be alone."

"As far as you know."

"Oh my god." Everly picked up one of the tennis balls their mother kept everywhere for Bagel and tossed it at Ellis. "Don't do that. I have to feel alone *somewhere*."

"Do they watch you in your sleep, *Twilight* vampire style?"

"Ellis."

He laughed.

"I have to talk, too. I'm supposed to be voicing all my thoughts out loud. Which is weird in a whole different way, because who cares what I have to say? And even if I did say something important, I have to run every thought through my mind nine hundred times first. Otherwise, I might blurt out something I can't take back. I don't need to end up an internet meme."

"Imagine." Ellis shook his head, bringing his beer to his lips. "I'd have to disown you." Everly's glare made him snort. "I'm kidding. Honestly, I thought you did great on that first episode."

"I was an awkward chaos magnet."

"You were real and believable. I bet people loved you."

"I hope so." She hadn't bothered to check. Her family's reaction to Logan had been enough to convince her to maintain her internet sabbatical. She didn't need to see a bazillion people shipping them. She was still processing how those last few minutes of the episode felt for *her*. There'd been a protectiveness to how he'd sounded that could only be born of affection. It had turned Everly's body to molten lava. It still did every time she thought about it. (Which was *a lot*.) But her whole purpose for being on *OTPS* was to learn to love herself again. Could she do that if she let herself fall for him? What if a new relationship made her too anxious about the parts of herself that were louder, weirder, too much? She couldn't risk what *On the Plus Side* was offering her. The show couldn't be something else she squandered out of fear like she had the Collective.

Her fingers itched for her charcoal pencils. She could already envision how Logan's face would look on the page, that beard squaring off his strong jaw, the intensity in his eyes, the deep crease between his brows. Seeing him so clearly, even in her head, set her pulse racing. She had to shake herself to make the image disappear.

Balancing her elbows on her knees, Everly sank her chin into her hands. "And now there's already going to be another episode airing tomorrow. And, oh god, Mom's going to be on camera tonight." She exhaled loudly. "How many times will she call me fat without using those exact words?"

Her brother sniffed and adjusted the brim of his Red Sox hat. "She means well." He could never criticize their mother, not even when he knew she was wrong.

"It doesn't come across that way."

"I know. But you saw how Grandma was with her. It's how they communicated. By picking at each other. It's how they showed concern."

"No one picks at you."

He tipped her a grin. "That's because I'm perfect."

This time, she aimed the tennis ball at his head.

By some miracle, dinner passed uneventfully.

With a fire going, it was comfortable on the back deck, and thanks to her mother's endless collection of citronella candles, the bugs kept their distance, so they spread the food out buffet style and gathered among the crowd of patio furniture.

From looking at their house, no one would ever guess that Everly and Ellis grew up eating off-brand cereal, wearing thrifted clothes, and learning that every penny could make a difference. The house had belonged to their great-aunt Rose, who opened her home to them when Everly's father left. Rose didn't have any more money than they did, but her house was paid off, and when she passed away, she bequeathed it to Everly's mother.

Jazzy and Stanton entertained everyone with stories of their celebrity encounters while they ate. As a former makeup and hair stylist on sets, Jazzy had all the gossip on which stars were impossible to work with, who had the strangest demands in their contracts, and who was, in her words, "a complete darling."

Becca screeched when Jazzy mentioned her high school crush, who had gone on to play for the Celtics.

Jazzy wagged a finger at her. "Oh no, honey, that one's a jerk. He was obsessed with me being fat, asking these horrible questions like if it jiggled when I walked and if I was constantly tired and how much I ate daily. His nickname for me was Juicy."

Everly rose from her seat to toss out her paper plate. "Ew."

"Yup. It's hard to feel human when everyone's fixated on your size." Jazzy shook her head, sending her curls dancing around her shoulders.

Logan had positioned himself by the trash can at the edge of the deck, trying to work everyone into a few frames. Everly wasn't sure if he'd eaten anything, so she loaded a burger, some chips, and salad on a plate and stopped beside him.

"Do cameramen eat?"

In the dim evening light, the blue in his eyes was bright and saturated, like shards of stained sea glass on a sandy beach. They hung on her face for a moment before dropping to the plate in her hands. "It's not your job to feed me."

"And yet, here I am doing it anyway." He had to burn a lot of energy lugging that camera around, and Everly had never seen him take a break.

Everyone deserved a break. That was all she was doing. She wasn't over here feeding him because she was so attuned to him at this point that she always knew exactly where he was and what he was doing, his presence heavy enough to take root in her bones.

Nope. It wasn't that at all.

After staring at her for another second, Logan accepted the plate with a grunt that might have been a thank-you. "Now get back in the shot."

"Aren't I in enough of them?" It felt like she was on camera perpetually, even when it wasn't a filming day.

"That's kind of the point." As if to prove it, he slid back enough to get her in view of the lens.

She gave him her best scowl on the way back to the table.

By the time her mom coaxed the group inside for dessert, the sun had dipped below the horizon and the night air had cooled. A reminder that no matter how warm the days might get, they were well into autumn.

Everyone was gathered in the living room for interviews, so Everly hid in the kitchen under the guise of doing the dishes. Really, though, she was eavesdropping. She needed to be ready to pounce the second her mother said something inappropriate or fatphobic.

So far, all she'd heard was cooing, which meant that her mom and Stanton had broken out the baby photos.

Wiping her hands on a towel, Everly peeked around the doorway. The two of them were squished close together on the love seat, a red book splayed open on their laps. Her mother's eyes were misty as she swept a finger back and forth over a page.

"It was after her father left that she started to get rounder," her mother said softly.

Everly's stomach clenched. She didn't want her mother talking about her this way. Like she was a victim of something. Like her fat needed to be explained away, blamed on something, excused. Her body did not need an apology tour.

Stanton nodded. "That makes sense. There's a lot of research out there about the connection between weight gain and stress. I'm sure it was hard for her to figure out what to do with big feelings like abandonment as a kid, so that emotional stress came out physically in her body."

Everly's mother studied the photo album. Her brow furrowed, emphasizing the crow's-feet along her eyes and the line at the center of her forehead. It was only on these rare occasions when she looked vulnerable that Everly was reminded how much her mother had aged over the years.

"I tried to help her." Her mom looked to Stanton almost pleadingly. "I truly did. We went to counseling. The two of us and Everly's brother, too. I made sure they understood this wasn't their fault. That their father left because *he* wasn't enough, not because we weren't. But . . ." She shrugged dejectedly. The movement was bereft of her mother's usual poise and control. It jabbed at Everly's center, jagged as it twisted deeper.

Her mom picked at the edge of the clear plastic that adhered the photos in place. "It does something to kids, when they're missing a parent. Especially when that parent chose to leave. I'm not sure there's any way to fix that."

A thick ball of emotion pushed itself up toward Everly's throat, and she pressed her hands to her chest as if that might hold it in place. Her mother's words rang too true. It always felt a little like her grip on the people around her was fragile. Like if she blinked, they'd disappear. Maybe that was what happened when your father left you behind. You feared you were expendable to everyone else for the rest of your life. Because if one of the two people programmed by biology itself to love you chose not to, it must mean that there was something fundamentally wrong with you to begin with.

Grandma Helen's death only proved to her that you couldn't hold on to anyone forever. So Everly let her world get a little smaller. She stopped trying to fill it back up with new people to replace the ones who were gone. Who'd left her.

If there was no one around you, you couldn't be left behind.

"When Everly started to gain weight, I tried to help with that, too." Her mother pulled a new album into her lap. This one was blue, their photos from high school. There were less of Everly in that one than the other albums. The more weight she'd gained, the more her mother had tried to hide her. The fewer memories she wanted to preserve.

"How?" Stanton asked quietly.

"Showing what clothes would slim her down, counting calories together, going for walks in the morning, not keeping problem food in the house."

Stanton was careful to maintain a neutral expression. "Did that help?"

Everly's mother shook her head, the layers of her blond hair feathering her chin. "She pulled away from me. She thought I was being mean, but I was trying to protect her."

"From what?" Stanton flipped to the next page in the album, then the next one, and the next one. As if he were trying to find Everly.

"The world." Her mom's hands snapped into fists. "The world is cruel. People are crueler." Her mouth tightened. "I know my daughter thinks the sun rose and set around her grandmother, but my mother didn't live in reality. She ignored the way people looked at her, responded to her. Once at a restaurant, she complained to the server about the booths being too narrow, and when I went to the bathroom, I heard him talking to his coworkers about how my mother shouldn't be eating a burger if she cared about fitting in a booth." The expression on Penny Winters's face clearly conveyed how horrifying she found this.

Stanton regarded her, his head tilted thoughtfully to the left, spilling his thick curls across the top of his ear. "What did you do?"

Everly leaned forward a little more, curious to hear the answer. Grandma Helen would have torn them a new one. Everly's mom had probably agreed with the waiter.

"I didn't tip him." Her mother's lips pursed. "You shouldn't talk about people that way."

"What they were saying, though . . ." Stanton seemed to be deliberately choosing his words, as if he were picking his way through a minefield. "That was wrong, too, right? Food doesn't have moral value. We shouldn't be judging what others eat."

Everly's mother tensed. "I know that. But that's not how people act. And not everyone has a thick skin like my mother did. Not everyone wants to be a spectacle. It doesn't feel good. And she encouraged Everly to be the same way." Her fingers smoothed down one of the pictures. "I was trying to save my daughter from being hurt."

Everly backed away from the doorway. She didn't want to hear any more.

When she glanced up, her eyes caught Logan's. She hadn't realized she was in his line of sight. He waved her over, but she turned and ducked outside.

She dropped onto one of the loungers and angled her face toward the sky. There were so many stars visible tonight; they flickered like fireflies against the darkness. She counted them, one by one, anything to chase her mother's words from her head.

Hearing her worry, learning that every time she shamed Everly for her size, for the fat on her body, for who she was, for how she looked, she was doing it out of love, to—in her mind—*protect* her, filled Everly with anger. And the way she talked about Grandma Helen? Her grandmother had never forced her point of view on Everly. All she did was make Everly feel normal. Like she fit exactly as she was. Just because her mother was always fixated on how everyone else saw her didn't mean there was anything wrong with ignoring that.

It was healthier not to care.

Part of Everly wanted to burst into the house, to yell, to force her mother to understand that love should never make anyone feel wrong, feel smaller. Sady would have loved that. Talk about an excellent TV moment. But Sady had left hours ago for a meeting. And some conversations weren't meant for cameras. Some words should not be recorded. They should exist in one moment and then *poof,* disappear. They should be captured only in memories that would never quite get at the truth of them.

Everly refused to bare her soul for her mother, to speak words to her she couldn't take back, for the benefit of an audience.

She'd reached one hundred stars when Logan wandered onto the deck. Everly held up her hand. She wasn't in the mood to be filmed.

He flashed his palms to prove they were empty.

"I didn't know you could exist without your camera."

He shrugged. "Everyone's taking a break."

"Thanks for not pushing me to talk to my mother after what she said to Stanton." Everly's shoulders were bunched at her ears and wouldn't quite drop. "It almost makes how she acts worse, to think she's doing it out of love or something."

"What do you mean?" His voice was so soft Everly had to lean forward to hear him.

She didn't have the energy to detail the endless passive-aggressive comments, the new clothes she'd find on her bed every week that became more and more shapeless, more dated, the frustrated looks she shot Everly whenever her volume rose above a whisper.

"Let's just say it has been my mother's mission in life to find a Mute button for my grandmother and me." She'd never managed it with Grandma Helen, but until *OTPS* wandered into Everly's life, she'd succeeded on her daughter.

Shaking his head, Logan lowered himself into the chair next to her so they were eye level. She could feel every inch of the space between them.

"It's hard when the people who should know you best can't see you clearly." He rubbed his hands together, his eyes skirting her face. "My last girlfriend thought because I was good with a camera and followed her to LA that I wanted to be in the film industry. When I took every PA or photography gig I could get on her sets, and worked overnights, and got shit on by celebrities, that it was all for experience. But it was for her. I wanted to make us work. When she broke things off and I moved back east, she was shocked. It was like she had no idea who I was. What I cared about."

Everly scowled. "Well, she sucks." Without meaning to, she scooted a little closer to him on the lounger. She had no choice about opening up to *On the Plus Side*'s entire viewing audience—which, by proxy, meant opening up to Logan—but this was the most he'd ever shared with her about himself. It made her feel connected to him, as if every word were a thread, a new stitch, knotting them more tightly together.

"It worked out in the end. I met Sady on one of those crappy jobs, and that changed my life." His gaze settled back on Everly's face. "But that didn't make it any less painful."

"How are you so sure it's not true?" The wind practically swallowed her voice. "All the things my mother says about me?" This wasn't the first time he'd suggested Penny Winters was wrong.

"I've been watching people through a camera lens basically since I could carry one. It teaches you to see things differently. See *people* differently. I think it's harder to perform for a camera than an audience. It filters out the false stuff." He cast his eyes over the yard. His hands hung clasped between his knees. "Some people have a light. No matter what shitty stuff they're dealing with, it can't be snuffed out. You have one of those." Everly had never noticed how long his eyelashes were. They brushed against his scruffy cheeks with each blink. "It's kind of . . . I don't know . . . hypnotic."

No one had ever described her that way.

Everly's chest felt cinched, like she was back in that Ren faire corset and someone had tied it to breaking. She couldn't breathe. Her skin blazed.

The urge to wrap her arms around his waist and press her face to his chest overwhelmed her. She'd never so desperately craved the feel of someone else's body. His skin must be warm under that plaid shirt. She wanted to see if it was as hot as hers. If his heart was also drumming so hard it might burst.

She scooted back farther into the seat of the lounger before her instincts took over and pressed her shoulders tight to its cushion.

"You sure that's not my excellent personality?"

He grunted out a laugh.

Hopefully, her voice sounded as breezy as she'd meant it to.

Because inside, she was a tornado. Her pulse and stomach raged with want, with the desire to hear him repeat those words, to make her new to herself, to whisper her name in that voice that was like sand and stone.

But another part of her screamed with panic. She was just starting to stand upright, and falling for Logan would set everything off-balance.

As if she'd opened Schrödinger's box. Torn the top right off.

She needed to figure out how to close it again before it was too late.

Everly Winters: Day 0 Interviews
Sady Sanders
1:02 P.M.

This interview is filmed outside, on a bench in a small park. Everly sits facing the camera, Sady beside it so she is out of the frame.

SADY: I get the sense you're a big fan of the show.

EVERLY: The biggest. There's nothing else out there that really focuses on people who look like me. Maybe there's a handful of TV shows and movies with fat characters. That's about it. And definitely no shows about fashion. What you're doing is amazing.

SADY: Thank you. We wouldn't be filming season three right now without the support of fans like you.

There's a pause, and Everly shifts in her seat. Her eyes dart from the camera to Sady, as if she has no idea where to look. More than once, she starts to straighten her skirt and top but then stops herself.

SADY: We really want to help people celebrate and embrace who they are in the moment, rather than who they were or who they hope to be. I feel like that's the healthiest thing we can do.

Everly's expression loses some of its brightness.

EVERLY: That can be really hard.

SADY: Without a doubt. But that's why we're here. To give you the support you need to make that journey.

Everly nods, her eyes on her hands clasped in her lap.

SADY: Tell us what you want from the show.

Everly's gaze rises, and she looks directly at the camera.

EVERLY: I just . . . I just want to be happy. No caveats. No buts. No regrets.

CHAPTER 15

"Welcome to Graphic Design 101."

Stanton was waiting for Everly at the entrance to Matten-Waverly's conference room when she returned from lunch. Behind him, the portable monitor was centered at the front of the room, the display bright and ready for use. James and the firm's senior designer, Alex, sat across from it.

Everly narrowed her eyes. "I took that freshman year."

Stanton puffed out a frustrated breath through his nose. "Okay, how about Graphic Design in the Real World," he said. Stepping forward, he took her arm and ushered her inside. It was only then that she spotted Sady and Logan standing in the opposite corner.

Everly's breath seized in her lungs. This was the first time she'd seen Logan since the barbeque at her mom's house on Saturday, unless she counted the second episode of the show, which had aired last night.

This one had been entirely focused on the Ren faire, with plenty of footage of Everly trying on costumes and a good five minutes dedicated to her performance awarding the knights during the joust. But the episode's whole narrative was anchored around her conversation with Jazzy about choosing a word of her own. It changed the cadence of everything. Made it about her and her personal growth rather than chasing some crush.

Everly had felt vindicated. Like her plan to keep James off Sady's radar by avoiding him had worked.

Then, in the last fifteen minutes, the showrunner had gone and complicated things.

The segment had started with Stanton introducing Everly to the vendors in the body art tent, where she'd gotten into an extended conversation with a face painter who also did tattoos. She'd given Everly a ton of excellent resources for finding apprenticeships and getting practice equipment. After only a few minutes, though, the scene segued into footage of Everly and Logan. Someone had captured their entire interaction in the tent, both while he was filming and once he'd stopped. Given that the angle was from the doorway, Everly assumed it was Sady. She must have recorded them on her phone.

The idea of being filmed without her knowledge was unsettling, but those thoughts had been quickly shoved aside by Everly's swirling stomach and her brother and Becca yelling, "Oh my god, look how he's staring at you."

There wasn't a second that Logan's eyes strayed from her, as if they were tethered to her face. She'd had her back to him that day, so she hadn't seen his expression. How carefully he was listening. How soft his eyes were. That hint of a smile tugging at his lips.

She wanted him to look at her that way all the time.

But that couldn't happen. It didn't matter if he said all the right things or that he listened attentively when she spoke. It didn't matter that he had eyes with a touch as intense as any hand. Or arms that made her want to order him to pick things up to watch them flex. Or a smile as warm as sunlight. Or a voice that sent shivers down her spine every time it scratched out her name.

Falling for him had the potential to ruin everything Everly was doing on *On the Plus Side.*

She needed a system reset. A return to default settings. A canvas
erased to white. Logan was just the cameraman. She was just the person
he had to point the lens at. If they could remain in those roles, keep those
boundaries clear, no one had to get hurt.

She refocused her attention on Stanton. "What are we doing here?"

"Helping you see what it would look like to go from the reception
desk to the art department." He guided Everly toward the seat Sady had
designated for her beside James.

Because of course.

"Alex also knows some people at a few publishers if that's where you
end up wanting to go." Stanton smiled at the senior designer as he added,
"You should see the cool cover designs in her apartment."

Alex cocked their head at Everly. They had blond hair striped with
pink and a fresh side shave on the left. Like Everly, Alex had their own
uniform, but it was one Jazzy would actually approve of: skinny jeans
and a short-sleeved button-down in zany prints. Today's was olive green
with red and white mushrooms dotted across it. "I didn't know you did
cover designs."

Everly rarely mentioned her art at work. The space under the table
became suddenly appealing. A perfect place to lie down and never get up.

"Not for real or anything." She scrubbed at the heat invading her
cheeks. Alex was destined to be the next head of the department. Next
to them, Everly wasn't sure her own projects could be called actual
designs. "It's just a hobby. It's fun to play around with how I'd represent
the story."

James cast his high-beam smile at her. "She's soooo good, Alex. I
follow her on social media. You should see her stuff."

"Could I?" Alex asked.

Her stomach fluttering against her ribs, Everly pulled up the photos on her phone. Once she found the best ones, she set the device between James and Alex and attempted to back away.

She didn't get far. James looped one of his muscular arms around her shoulders and eased her body against him. Her *entire* right side—ribs, hips, waist, thigh—was pressed to his left, and her heart threatened to explode straight out of her chest.

He'd been taking up less and less space in Everly's head lately, but that didn't change the fact that he was hot as hell, and that she'd spent over a year infatuated with him. The moment he rested himself against her, her body forgot every one of her mature, levelheaded breakthroughs. There was only his warmth, and how solid he was, and how easy it was to lean into him without worrying about falling over.

Her blood burned hot in her veins, her pulse rushing to all the wrong places.

This is not going to happen, Everly yelled silently to herself. *Do not give Sady more fodder for her imaginary romance plot. You don't want this. You don't need it.*

She straightened as much as she could with the anchor of his arm on her. If nothing else, the full-body contact was a nice, momentary distraction from her Logan problem. At this rate, Schrödinger was going to need a bigger box for all these guys she refused to deal with.

"Damn, Everly. These are fantastic." Alex held the phone close to their face, swiping the pictures back and forth and pinching their fingers to the screen to zoom in. "The *Alice in Wonderland* one is spot-on." They cast their brown eyes at her. "People would pay for this."

"It's just a doodle."

"No way, V. No self-deprecating. You're a fantastic artist." James faced her, and because of their height difference, his nose and mouth skimmed her hair. "Whoa, your hair smells good."

Well, she was dead now. He was going to have to *Weekend at Bernie*'s her for the rest of the day.

Everly died again when he didn't immediately move away. "It's like strawberries in a garden or something—"

"Dude, you're in her shot." Logan's voice exploded from the corner, low and deep like a growl. It took physical effort for Everly not to glance his way.

Sady waved her hands at him, her brow furrowed, but he didn't seem to notice.

When James didn't react, Logan inched a step closer. "Hey." The word was a low rumble, thunder about to crash overhead. Everly felt it in her knees, in the sudden goose bumps that speckled her skin. "Let go of her and move out of frame."

James glanced around like he still wasn't sure who Logan was talking to. Before he could say anything, Sady insisted he stay put.

She cleared her throat and turned to Logan. "What are you doing? Why don't you come around this way, so we don't lose this great moment?"

Their eyes locked, something passing between them, though neither said a word. It reminded Everly of the way that Ellis and Becca could have whole conversations with just a stare.

When he finally glanced away, Logan looked humbled and dutifully changed positions. "There's some great footage around Everly's art here, and we shouldn't mess with it. That's all I'm saying."

"We're not." Sady's voice was strained.

Everly took the opportunity to duck out from under James's arm. Turning, she addressed Alex. "Do you really think there's something there?" Logan wasn't wrong that this meeting was supposed to be about her future career, not James cozying up to her.

"Oh, absolutely." They flicked through the images of her book covers one more time. "Are you freelancing?"

"No. I don't even know where to start." In reality, she was too afraid to try to find out.

"I'll put you in touch with one of my friends." Alex handed Everly back her phone. "You have an eye for this, for sure. James has shown me your tweaks to his stuff, too. Honestly, it's only a matter of you deciding what you want to do at this point. The doors are open."

Their words filled Everly's chest with something light, something that pushed at the deadened weight of fear that usually clung there.

Something like hope. Excitement.

For the next half hour, Alex walked Everly through the responsibilities of their job. The whole time, James kept bumping shoulders with her and interjecting with examples of ways she'd already done this or that while helping him with his designs.

The final part of the meeting involved the three of them collaborating on a logo for *On the Plus Side*. At Stanton's urging, Everly took the lead. She assigned Alex to mock up the design, and had James focus on color, while she made sure everything harmonized visually. Once they were finished, she used her smart pen to make final tweaks, highlighting the font and adjusting the shadowing so the show's title was the focal point. As she stepped back to get a better perspective, James gently took her hand in his and guided the pen. "A little bit more, I think, no?"

A grunt issued from the direction of the camera. In her peripheral vision, Everly saw Logan's face was bright red, his mouth a tense line.

Sady nudged his arm, and Everly heard him whisper, "This is supposed to be her design."

Embarrassment tugged at her stomach. Logan was right. How many times had James come to her for help? Now suddenly, they were on TV, and he was acting like her mentor?

And she was letting him.

She reclaimed the pen and erased his work. Even if he was simply trying to help, she was supposed to be the lead designer. "Any more shadowing makes it too dark."

"Everly's right. The words stand out better this way." Alex rubbed their chin as they inspected the final design. "I think it's perfect."

Stanton joined them, mimicking their stance. "Me too." He winked at Everly.

Once they were done, Alex collected their phone and water bottle to head back to their office. "Does Bob know?" they asked, already halfway out the door.

Everly glanced up. "Know about what?"

"That you want to do design."

"No." Another thing tucked snugly in Schrödinger's box.

"Show him your portfolio. He should know we have an up-and-coming talent right in the office."

Except for saying hi when they passed her desk, or the occasional handoff of messages or phone calls, Alex and Everly had never really interacted, and now she regretted it. They were four or five years older than her, and she'd always been intimidated by their talent. It had never occurred to her that she could consult them, get their opinion on things, the same way James had always done with her.

"Thanks, Alex."

Their smile was wide and genuine. "You should stop by my desk sometime so we can chat. And I want to see more of those book covers." With a supportive squeeze of her shoulder, they disappeared toward the design department.

When Everly turned back to the conference room, she heard Stanton exclaim, "I didn't even know this tiny town *had* a bar."

"Oh yeah. Harry's is a good time. Especially when there's a band," James said.

"I assumed this was a whole *Footloose* sitch and you couldn't dance after midnight or whatever."

Everly joined them at the table. "I'm pretty sure that's not the plot of *Footloose*."

"Semantics." Stanton gave her another wink behind his round glasses. "In my version they're vampires."

"I'm here for that." Everly raised her hand to erase the design on the monitor, but Stanton squawked loudly.

"What are you doing?"

"We're done, no?"

His expression was just shy of flabbergasted. "I need a copy of that for marketing. Who says they aren't going to want to hire you?"

Those words sent her body into free fall. Was he serious? She would have spent more time on the logo if she'd known he meant to use it. It was not in any shape to be reviewed by an actual potential client.

"I got you, boss." James nodded at Stanton. Then Everly heard that telltale zip as he sent off an email. Her chance to make tweaks was gone.

Panic tightened her limbs like a vise. In an attempt to stave it off, she asked, "Why are you talking about bars, anyway?"

James smiled at her. "You and your new friends are coming to Harry's with us tomorrow."

CHAPTER 16

From the piles of clothes on the bed, you'd think Jazzy and Everly were having another wardrobe day.

Only this time, Jazzy had brought the clothes, and Everly was rejecting them.

She stood in front of her full-length mirror, staring at the black, sleeveless body-con dress hugging her curves. She looked hot. So hot. Plus, the dress was black. Her favorite color. Who knew Jazzy would ever let her wear it again?

The problem was, it was the absolute wrong vibe for where they were going.

"Have you *seen* Harry's Good Times Pub?" Everly asked.

"Not yet." Jazzy's voice was muffled by the fabric of the dress she was tugging over her head.

Everly gestured at her reflection. "This is an outfit for drinks in Boston or hitting a club in Vegas. This is not for Harry's."

"What does one wear to Harry's then?"

"Jeans. T-shirt. Sneakers."

Jazzy wrinkled her nose. "Can we at least put you in a cute shirt and something dressier than tennis shoes?"

"Just no sequins?" Everly bargained.

Jazzy laughed. "Why don't you look through what I brought and tell me what's Harry's appropriate."

Everly rifled through the tops Jazzy had stacked on the bed until she spotted a promising cranberry-colored one with short flowing sleeves hemmed with ruffles and a faux-wrap waist. Cute, but not too dressy, with just enough cleavage to make it not-safe-for-work without flashing every resident in town.

Jazzy nodded in approval. "Wear the dark skinnies," she pointed to a pair of jeans folded on Everly's nightstand, "and put that dress in your closet. Maybe you can use it for the Collective's gala next month." Her gaze cut back to her own image in the mirror. "I should probably change too, huh?" Jazzy was wearing a skintight halter dress in a ruby red.

"I mean, you're Jazzy Germaine. You can do whatever you want and everyone will be in awe."

"I want you to be the only one standing out tonight." Jazzy guided Everly in front of the glass and stood behind her. After fluffing her hair (which Jazzy had styled in beachy waves), she placed her hands on Everly's shoulders to straighten her posture. "Everyone can be in awe of you, too." She gave Everly an encouraging squeeze. "You just have to believe it."

These first few weeks of *On the Plus Side* had already made that a little easier to do. Sometimes, when she looked in the mirror now, Everly saw herself the way Grandma Helen always had.

Jazzy stepped away to sort through the discarded top options.

Everly watched her through the mirror's reflection. Trading outfits, taking something off and saying, "Oh, this would look better on you," was something she'd never gotten to experience before. She hadn't realized how *normal* it would make her feel. And how much she'd craved that.

Not surprisingly, Jazzy ended up in something only Jazzy Germaine could pull off: a pair of light-wash boyfriend jeans rolled up to her ankles to reveal silver sandals with spiked heels, and a black AC/DC T-shirt cut up and corseted on the sides.

By the time they headed out, the two of them still looked far too good for a night at Harry's, but Everly didn't care. For the first time in a long time, she felt genuinely awesome.

Striking.

No caveats.

Jazzy aimed her phone at Everly as they walked, the same way she'd been doing all night.

"No Logan?" His name was a reflex, tumbling from her mouth before Everly could stop it. She wasn't supposed to be thinking about him. It shouldn't matter where he was.

"He'll catch up with us at the bar. He had some things to take care of."

So much for a night safe from the camera. And the distraction that was Logan. The slap of her black sandals against the sidewalk drowned out Everly's sigh.

"Tell me what you're feeling," Jazzy said.

"I look amazing." Everly did a little pose like she was modeling, causing Jazzy to erupt into a series of catcalls. "And I'm excited to hang out with you tonight." Everly chewed on her bottom lip.

"But?"

"I'm nervous, too."

"Why?"

"I don't know why James invited us. It's not like he and I hang out outside of work." If Stanton hadn't immediately accepted and turned this into a whole *On the Plus Side* moment, Everly would have declined. She didn't want to give the show any more footage for the #Jeverly plotline, and, after working with Alex today, she was ready to focus her energy on her art career and see where the show could help her go.

Jazzy cocked her head. "Well, the whole internet seems to think he's into you."

"The whole internet is wrong." Everly thrust her hand forward like a stopping guard. "Hear me out. We could dodge him and the three of us could get sloshed."

"Or. Hear *me* out. You could stop avoiding things." Jazzy flashed a smile that was too knowing. Too right.

Everly feigned shock. "I don't avoid things." She couldn't even keep a straight face as she said it. Who was she kidding? She was practically a professional avoider. It was the very essence of being comfortable, of staying off people's radars. But, Everly was learning, it was also a surefire way to ensure you never got anything you wanted. And even if she was pretty positive James was no longer on that list, she needed to start chasing the things that were rather than running away.

Rock music bombarded them as they pushed through the doors of Harry's. There was a band playing, so the place was more packed than usual. The square bar that filled the middle of the room and the booths around the dance floor were jammed with bodies. More people leaned against the windows and walls and crowded around pub tables at the back. Twinkle lights framed the ceiling and snaked around the counter, giving everything a soft, fuzzy glow.

Everly had been to Harry's so many times, and it always looked the same. In high school, one of the bartenders had been her friend's brother, and he used to slip Everly and Becca one drink apiece as long as they were walking home. The two of them whiled away most of their summer weekends at Harry's during college, too, dreaming of being back in Providence with its bigger, more modern bars and sophisticated drinks. Now it was the perfect place to drown a stressful workday. Sometimes, a person needed to knock back enough glasses of frosé to make their head spin.

When Everly and Jazzy spotted Stanton waving from the bar, they locked arms and maneuvered through the crowd. Both the same size, they slipped smoothly between people, taking up the same amount of space. Everly couldn't help but think back to all the times she'd been to places like this with Becca and her other straight-sized friends, bumping into everyone as she moved, sucking in her stomach as she'd slid into a booth, praying she'd fit, standing instead of using the barstools because she worried they wouldn't have enough room for her ass.

Everything was an endless obstacle course, and normally she was forced to navigate it alone, but as she and Jazzy reached him, Stanton was shoving aside a barstool, scowling at it like it had insulted his mother.

It was proof the problem wasn't Everly. It was the world.

She needed that reminder sometimes.

"Finally," he said. "I was about to order without you two. What are we getting?"

"A Sour Candy. They're a Harry's staple. It's like drinking a Jolly Rancher." It was also extremely easy to lose count of how many you'd had. Which was exactly what Everly needed tonight. No time for the slow burn of sipping a frosé.

Stanton's mouth made an O of intrigue. "Can they make them virgin? Because I can't deal with a hangover."

"Ugh, same," Jazzy added. "I have to drive to New Hampshire in the morning and I'm not doing that rocking a headache."

"I don't see why not," Everly said. "But make sure mine is plenty boozed up." She was not surviving this night without at least a buzz.

They laughed. Jazzy leaned her ample breasts on the bar to get the bartender's attention, and in less than five seconds she was ordering.

"Only Jazzy Germaine can order two virgins and no one blinks an eye," Stanton joked.

Jazzy tossed her hair over her shoulder. "What can I say, I'm a goddess, baby."

Stanton snapped his fingers in support.

Before their drinks had fully hit the bar, Everly seized hers and sucked it down in three big sips. Her lips puckered for a second, then the sweet lemon-lime taste took over.

Jazzy cocked an eyebrow.

"Liquid courage." Everly was going to need it, too, because as she looked up, she spied James's tall frame bobbing through the crowd in their direction. Panic swelled in her chest.

"Jazzy, use your boobs again." Everly tapped her arm. "I need a shot of something strong, please."

Two seconds later, she had one in hand.

Everly didn't see the label on the bottle so she wasn't sure what the bartender had poured, but its scent burned the inside of her nose as soon as she lifted it to her mouth.

"Wait, let's get this on camera." Jazzy angled her phone above them and squeezed beside Everly. "Our girl, Everly, has survived almost four weeks of filming, so we're blowing off some steam. Here goes nothing!"

Jazzy grabbed her second virgin Sour Candy and the two of them tapped their glasses lightly on the bar as they counted off: four, three, two, one. When Everly knocked her shot back, Jazzy and Stanton cheered.

Except Everly missed her mouth by a good five inches.

As she'd raised her drink to her lips, Logan appeared, the light on his camera already aglow. At the same time, James sidled up to Jazzy's right. In her surprise, Everly tipped the glass too early, splashing her chin and chest with amber liquid.

"Fuck." Now she was going to smell like a gas station all night.

"Everly."

"I know. Another one to bleep out. I'm sorry." She paused in fussing with the wet spot on her shirt long enough to peer up at Logan. She expected to see that expression he wore whenever she messed up a take, a potent mix of frustration and exhaustion. Instead, there was a small smile on his face and a pile of napkins in his hand.

He wasn't teasing her or filming her or giving her a lecture. He was just being nice.

For whatever reason, in that moment, drowning as she was in the caustic smell of grain alcohol, his kindness pushed her over the edge. With her heart in her throat and her brain screaming to find a suitable hiding spot, Everly fled for the bathroom. The one place at Harry's Logan couldn't follow.

She scrubbed her face, neck, and chest raw with paper towels that pilled against her shirt, leaving a dusting of white specks across the already damp fabric.

Shaking her head, Everly sighed at her reflection. She was a mess. She still smelled like booze, she'd washed half her foundation and bronzer off, and thanks to the wet stains on her cranberry blouse she appeared to be lactating. There was nothing to do now but fluff her hair in the mirror, reapply the lip gloss Jazzy had given her, and commit to drinking so much she didn't remember any of this tomorrow.

As if he could read Everly's mind, Stanton had two shots waiting for her when she got back. One was red like a strawberry, the other seemed to be whiskey. He flourished a hand at the tiny glasses. "The boys bought you a few drinks to make up for your . . . accident." He placed the amber one in front of her. "James got you some Southern Comfort."

Everly tossed it down her throat with one flick of her wrist, inviting a celebratory yell from James. The alcohol set her esophagus on fire—she imagined it burning away her humiliation on the way down.

"And Logan got you a Strawberry Bomb."

She flicked her gaze to him—or, more aptly, to the camera—and knocked the shot back. It tasted like someone had melted those strawberry candies Grandma Helen always used to carry.

"You chose this one because I'm so sweet, right?" She did her best to sound sarcastic. Edgy. Hard. But with the amount of liquor already in her system, she could tell it came across more flirty than anything else.

His expression didn't change, but the bar's twinkle lights winked off the amused glint in his eyes. "Oh. Absolutely. Sweet as a lemon."

Turns out, three drinks was all it took before the world got soft at the corners.

Everly had expected James to go back to his friends after saying hello, but he'd stuck around, joking with Jazzy and Stanton and trying to whisper in Everly's ear something that she could never hear because the music was too loud or Stanton kept interrupting or Logan rearranged everyone for a better shot.

The band was taking the stage for their second set when Everly and James first found themselves alone. The hosts were greeting some fans, and Logan had wandered off to get some establishing shots, leaving the two of them awkwardly idling together. Nerves began to itch beneath Everly's skin, but her buzz dulled them enough that she was able to offer him a smile. Without a work project to guide their conversation, she had no idea what to say.

He leaned down, his mouth so close that the heat of his breath warmed the shell of her ear. Chills jumped down her back, and she had to fight off a shiver. Her mind might have decided it was time to call it quits on this whole James thing, but clearly no one had informed her body.

"Are you having fun?" he asked.

She nodded. "Are you?" Someone bumped into her, and she stumbled against James's chest. He hooked an arm around her waist to keep her steady.

Her blood screamed in her veins at his proximity, even as her mind demanded that she back up.

"I'd be having more fun if we were dancing."

Everly used to love to dance. At a party, a bar, in her room, in the car, anytime a good song came on, she had to shimmy it out. It was something else she'd let her fear take from her. Now moving her body that way felt too open, too visible. It begged for attention.

But after so much time on *On the Plus Side,* and with enough booze in her system to obliterate her inhibitions, Everly was ready to let that go. She could dance with James. There was no harm in it. Friends danced together all the time.

Nodding, she let him take her hand, their fingers slotting together. He lifted their arms in the air and picked his way across the bar. Like a knife through butter, they sliced through the crowd, moving in tandem, each of their steps in sync.

The band was playing "Sweet Home Alabama," and the dance floor was packed with people, forcing the two of them close.

Everly didn't know the rules for platonic dancing. How should they touch? Was it okay that their stomachs were pressed together? That their hips swayed in unison? That his hand trailed up and down the small of her back?

She finally forced her eyes to his face, and James smiled, friendly and open as always. It helped to ease her nerves.

This is fine, she told herself. They were two people hanging out. Dancing to a decent band at a dive bar in a tiny Cape Cod town. With the three shots sloshing through her veins and the crowd thickening around them, it was easy to feel a hundred miles away from Logan, his camera, and *On the Plus Side*. Here, in this bubble, for this one moment, there was no pressure for them to be anything more than they were. No pressure for Everly to have anything figured out.

Despite the lack of space, James twirled her like they were doing a two-step, both of them laughing. The song swept into the chorus, and they rocked side to side, singing loudly. At some point, part of his hand had slipped under the loose fabric of her shirt, the pads of his fingers grazing the skin above her belt. Their legs were tangled together, and they hugged each other close. The heat of his body invaded hers, leaving Everly feverish and a little dizzy. The moment felt charged. Heady. Like whatever happened next would change everything.

She lifted her head to look into James's face, and their eyes locked. Neither of them looked away. Or blinked.

His stare was soft and welcoming, and so was the smile on his face.

The way he held her, how he looked at her, summoned something bold in her. She felt loose. Certain. Ready.

For the first time in almost four years, she did something the old Everly would have done.

She eased up on her toes and lifted her face to James's.

HOLLYWOOD SCOOPS, OCTOBER EDITION

"*ON THE PLUS SIDE* BREAKS THE FOURTH WALL, BUT CAPTURES OUR HEARTS"

Sonia Schwartz, Weekend Editor

New Mood Media's reality makeover show, *On the Plus Side*, has always been one for challenging the status quo, not just with its refreshing approach to fat representation, but also with its format. VuNu's most popular original series broke onto the reality TV scene two years ago with a documentary-style format that gave viewers extended screen time with each of the show's four guests. Allowing its audience so much time to get attached to the guests and the show's delightful hosts created a rabidly dedicated fan base.

Now, with its third season just underway, *On the Plus Side* is at it again, this time creating engaging narratives by breaking the fourth wall. In the show's premiere episode, viewers heard the voice of Logan Samuel, the show's cameraman and assistant producer, as he reacted to Everly Winters's heartbreaking story about her grandmother. Fans went wild for the episode, speculating all over the internet about who Logan is and why they left his words in the final edit. Was it an error caused by the exhaustive schedule, which requires episodes to be edited on the fly for almost-real-time consumption? Was it simply a good moment of TV that savvy showrunner Sady Sanders didn't want to squander? Or, perhaps, is the show teasing us of something more to come?

That certainly seems to be the case after watching episode two, where Everly and the gang spend the day at King Henry's Feast. The entire last segment of the episode included not just Logan's voice, but the broody, bearded cameraman (dressed on theme in a kilt!) himself on-screen, having a sweet heart-to-heart with Everly. By now, fans are setting their ships a-sail, and we can only assume that's New Mood's whole plan . . .

CHAPTER 17

Everly had imagined kissing James more times than she could count.

In those daydreams, his arms were strong but gentle as they pressed her to his chest.

His broad frame would stoop to reach her face, so she didn't have to strain.

She would mold herself against his firm body, every part of him built to cradle her. To fit her.

His large hands would drag up and down her back, strong fingers knotting in her waves, tugging at them tenderly.

He'd smell like smoke and fire and something clean, leaving her senses drowning in him.

And his mouth. His mouth would be heaven.

But dreams and reality were rarely the same.

Kissing James in reality was clumsier.

Messier.

More awkward.

He stood stone-still, and his arms were too tight, and it felt like

Everly's organs were going to pop against her ribs as she shoved up on her toes to reach his mouth.

One of them stank like sweat, and some moist pieces of hair had fallen out of his bun and stuck to her cheeks.

His lips were scratchy but wet, and his tongue was too big for her mouth. Though she thought he was kissing her back, they were completely out of sync: her too forceful, him too soft.

A second later, they pulled apart, and Everly stumbled back, knocking into whoever was dancing behind her. The music crashed through her senses like cymbals slamming against her head, and whatever mellow high she'd been riding from the alcohol evened out, leaving the world too crisp and clear.

The surprise in James's eyes was far too vivid.

He kept opening and shutting his mouth, like he wanted to say something but he wasn't sure what.

She stared back at him, her head filled with screeching. Everything about that kiss was so, so wrong. Her skin itched with the discomfort of it. She'd never regretted something so deeply before.

She wanted to bolt from the dance floor, the bar, the whole town, except her feet wouldn't budge. Her muscles had stiffened, as if they'd been dipped in bronze.

She was a statue, frozen forever in this horrible moment.

After another minute of stunned silence, James took her hand. They retraced their earlier path to the dance floor, only this time, their fingers were too stiff to slot together. They didn't move in rhythm, parting the crowd. They were two entirely separate entities shoving their way through people who didn't care they were in a hurry.

He pulled her to the other side of the bar, where two armchairs sat near the front window, miraculously empty. As if they knew James and Everly needed them.

Releasing her hand like it was a hot pan, James dropped into one chair and nodded for Everly to take the other. She wanted to stand, but she sank into the gray cushion anyway.

"V," James said softly.

Thanks to the streetlight outside, she could see his expression. How his golden brows were pinned tautly together, the lines around his mouth. He was worried.

Everly felt sick to her stomach. Every one of those shots had been a worse idea than the one before.

"V," he repeated.

His tone was gentle but tentative.

Everly slid her sweaty palms down the thighs of her jeans and attempted to look him in the face. She'd been bold enough to kiss him. She had to be bold enough to listen.

His hands drummed nervously against his knees, and then fell over Everly's, only to immediately pull back. He dragged them through his hair, clawing most of it out of his bun.

"I've wanted to tell you this for weeks." He shook his head. "It was just . . . the time never seemed to be right."

"Now seems good." Though a month ago, the thought of opening this box would have cracked her in two, Everly was ready for whatever he had to say. She wanted an answer. Something solid to stand on so she could move forward.

His fingers traced another pathway across his scalp.

"V." He took a deep breath. "I nominated you for the show."

Her head jerked. "You what?" Who knew words could give you whiplash?

"I nominated you for *On the Plus Side*."

Everly gawked at him. This made no sense. Becca had nominated her. She was sure of it. James would have had no idea she was a fan of the show.

His palms rubbed together.

Behind her eyes, she was sketching abstract images, reds and blacks tearing across a white page like blood.

"I knew . . . you know . . ." The chafing of his palms quickened. Flint to tinder. So did his words. As if he needed to get them out before they caught fire. ". . . that you had feelings for me. And you're such a great girl. I saw an episode of the show one day at the gym and I thought maybe they could give you the confidence you needed to move on to someone else. Someone who—" His eyes dropped to the floor. "—who feels the same."

Every part of Everly was shaking. She couldn't organize her thoughts in her head. How could he do this to her? She'd thought they were friends. Yet he'd recruited a TV show to help him reject her.

A whole-ass TV show.

It was so humiliating.

So public.

James nudged her hand with a knuckle. "Say something."

"What do you want me to say?"

"What you're feeling."

Everly stared at him. She was too exhausted, and there was too much alcohol in her system to explain herself. He knew how she'd felt about him and he'd kissed her back tonight. He'd flirted with her at work so many times. Then he'd brought a TV show in to shame her for those feelings. He didn't get to hear her thoughts. She wouldn't placate him for whatever guilt was motivating the concern on his face.

Thank god for Jazzy and Stanton. Everly hadn't realized how much they'd already affected her confidence until this moment. If James had said this to her a month ago, she would have fallen apart. She might have been grateful that he'd gone out of his way to help her. She might have thanked him.

But he didn't deserve that. He didn't deserve anything at all.

So Everly walked away.

Harry's was suddenly too full. Too small. Too hot. It felt like she was being pressed in from all sides. Before she could cry or vomit or something worse, she rushed outside.

She wasn't ready to go home, so she sat on the low wall of the small garden that framed Harry's large front windows.

With her palms, she rubbed at her stinging eyes, forcing back the tears still blurring her vision.

When had she become someone everyone else was determined to fix? Her mother and her weight stuff? James's assumptions about her self-confidence? When did she start needing a TV show and two experts to remind her who she was?

She felt like a boat going in circles with only one oar. Or a muddled painting with no focal point.

She heard footsteps behind her. Dragging a knuckle beneath her eyes to catch the last of her tears, she glanced up to find Logan standing there.

Neither of them was tall—in fact they were practically the same height—but the way the light from the streetlamp fell on him cast a giant shadow over her and the white-and-yellow daisies spotting the garden.

Beneath his beard, his cheeks were bright red, and he was breathing hard, like he'd run half a mile (not ten feet) to reach her. Those blue eyes of his flashed.

"Are you okay?" His voice was somehow rough and soft at the same time.

"Just needed some air." Everly's eyes drifted to the pharmacy across the street. Mrs. Hartl stayed open late on the weekends in case anyone had too much to drink at Harry's and needed first aid or aspirin at the end of the night. She could see the older woman's shadow moving around as she restocked shelves. Everly wondered if she had anything for lost souls in there. "I assume you saw what happened." He missed nothing, after all.

Logan was kind enough to only nod as he sat down beside her. There was a whole length of brick between them, and Everly hated how aware of the distance she was.

She raked her hands through the waves Jazzy had spent twenty minutes styling.

"You know you did nothing wrong by kissing him, right?"

Everly could only imagine how pathetic the whole scene was going to look on camera. She'd probably had some goofy, lovelorn expression on her face as she'd leaned toward James. He must have looked horrified. Sady was going to eat it up.

"I'm a fool," Everly mumbled.

She was staring ahead, but she could feel Logan's gaze. Heat sparked in the path his eyes trailed across her cheeks. "Why?" he asked.

She shifted to face him. The moment their eyes connected, the truth Everly had been fighting off hit her with the force of a train at full speed.

James had always been a fantasy. She kept him safely tucked away in a box she'd never planned to open. He was no different from any book boyfriend or hero in the romances she liked to read. He was safe. Never a threat. Because he'd never happen.

But from the second he had grumbled his way into her life, Logan had become something else entirely. He refused to stay in the box she put him in. Or out of her head.

He saw her. More than anyone had in a long, long time. Even with a camera between them.

And though she'd tried like hell to deny it, Everly saw him, too. Right through that gruff exterior to the softness at his center.

"You acted on your feelings. Not everyone is brave enough to do that."

She watched him, not blinking until he stopped talking. His lips pressed together in a straight line. It was still unnerving to look at him without a camera between them. That lens often made her feel naked, but now she felt even more so.

Especially as the words left her lips.

"Did I, though? Because I'm pretty sure I kissed the wrong person."

CHAPTER 18

Logan stared quietly at her.

Everly was afraid he was going to make her repeat herself, or worse, force her to explain what she meant.

But then his tongue slipped out to wet his lips, and his gaze deepened. "We should fix that," he said softly. The gravel in his voice would have buckled Everly's knees if she weren't already sitting.

One of his large hands rose from his lap. Her breath hitched as he reached for her, gently sliding his palm across her cheek before circling the back of her neck and drawing her face to his.

Even after being inside a crowded bar for hours, he smelled like winter, and his lips were soft and supple, minty like a cold breeze.

One of his hands cupped her face while the other continued to cradle her head, keeping her close in a way that felt fragile, ephemeral, like the hold would break the moment she needed it to.

Each push and pull of her lips he answered with equal pressure. Matching her.

Her hands grasped his biceps to steady herself, and holy god they were every bit as solid as they looked. She relished the sensation as her fingers sank into them.

The thump of her heart was so hard against her chest, she was sure Logan could feel it across the space between them. Yet her mind was oddly calm. Serene. Like she was exactly where she needed to be. Doing exactly what she should be doing. She wasn't worried about her body or how it felt to him. She wasn't worried about what he was thinking. There was only the perfect taste of his mouth and the race of her heart and how she wanted more and more of this.

That certainty vanished, though, the moment they pulled apart.

Doubt slammed into her like a tidal wave. What was she doing? Kissing Logan wasn't going to help her fix herself. It was only going to confuse everything further.

"Everly." He took her wrists gently in his hands. Her name was as gentle on his lips. Yet she was shaking enough to rattle her bones.

She didn't remember standing, but suddenly she was on her feet, and he released her from his grasp. "I—I have to go."

Already, she was walking away. It was a fight not to run.

She wasn't ready for this, but she was. She wanted it, but she didn't. Her emotions were being tugged every which way, every part of her yanked to its limits.

This was the second guy she'd kissed tonight. And the second time she'd bolted. Doubt, fear, desire, surprise all swirled inside her like multiple colors on a palette, turning into something murky and gray that urged her to flee.

She snuck one glance at him as she rushed for the street corner, where she could mercifully put this whole night behind her. Logan was on his feet, too, his blue eyes clinging to her, those hands that had, moments ago, cradled her face, hanging uselessly at his sides.

Then she was around the bend and he was gone, and though part of her yearned to go back, she was too tired. She'd been through an emotional triathlon tonight, and despite how fast she was running, she was coming in last.

The light was on in Becca's office when Everly reached the house. She turned from the garage and rushed inside. She had to get her frantic thoughts out of her head so she could sort through them.

She spotted Becca through the open office doorway, sitting at her easel desk. She was coloring in a blue monster, the watercolor pencil in her hand sweeping back and forth to create spikes of cornflower blue fur.

Everly leaned her head against the door and watched for a few minutes. There was something mesmerizing about the way Becca drew. The images poured out of her like magic, spilling across the page as if they'd always been there and she was simply revealing them to the world.

She waited until Becca's hand stopped to whisper, "Hey."

Her friend startled, then spun in her seat. Everly must have looked as rough as she felt because Becca's face creased in concern. "How late is it?"

"A little after midnight."

Yawning, she stretched her arms over her head and cracked her neck. "God, I've been at this for hours." A sleepy smile settled into her features. "How was Harry's? Did you have a drink for me?" Everly had invited her along, but Becca was in the middle of an intense deadline.

"Too many." Everly sagged against the doorframe. Fading adrenaline and too much alcohol hung heavy in her veins, making her sluggish.

"Did you have fun, though? I can't imagine what Jazzy and Stanton are like when they let loose."

"I kissed James." Everly couldn't hold it back any longer.

Becca coughed in surprise. "What?"

"Then I kissed Logan."

"Ev, oh my god."

"I know you're busy. I just had to tell someone." Everly pressed her hands to her temples. "This is all turning my poor brain to soup."

Becca's pencil snapped against the table as she released it. "I'm never too busy for this. Or for you."

Everly slid her back down the molding until she was sitting on the floor. Resting her head against the wood, she gazed up at the office's ceiling fan. "What am I doing?"

"What do you mean?"

"I shouldn't have kissed either of them."

"Hey." An eraser bounced off Everly's shoulder. "Look at me." Another one hit her knee. Everly faced her friend before the next one clocked her in the head. "You should be fucking kissing everyone."

Everly snorted.

"No. I mean it. I hate how, the last few years, you seem to listen to these voices that never would have gotten in your head before. Somewhere you stopped believing in yourself. And I know you're still convinced I nominated you, even though I didn't, but I'm glad as hell you are on that show."

Everly placed the three erasers on her open palm and shuffled them around. "I know you didn't do it. James admitted tonight that it was him."

"What?" A fourth eraser whizzed by her. This one seemed more out of shock than to get Everly's attention.

"He was hoping they'd help me with my confidence so I could find someone who feels the same." Everly ground her teeth. With every echo of his words in her head, her anger swelled. He should have talked to her. They were supposed to be friends. Friends were honest with each other, even when it was tough.

What a coward. And a real asshole, if he thought it was okay to reject someone on TV because he was too afraid to say something himself.

"Wow." Becca came to sit by Everly on the floor. She stretched out her legs, lightly nudging Everly's knee with her foot.

"A real Prince Charming, huh?"

"I hope he kissed like a toad."

Everly cracked a smile. "It wasn't great."

Becca leaned back on her arms. "Do you know why I fell for Ellis?"

"If you're about to start talking about his man bits, I'm leaving." It was probably good Becca wasn't holding any more erasers or Everly would have certainly taken one to the head this time.

"He was the first guy I dated who ever truly made me feel like he understood me." A soft smile spread over Becca's face. "And it wasn't the big things, like when he proposed to me using that graphic novel, or when he brought Cream Cheese home despite how much that cat hates him. It was the tiniest moments. Like how he makes sure to find out if an animal dies before we watch any movie, because he knows I will completely fall apart. Or how he does meal prep the week of my period because he knows my anxiety spikes and I can't make decisions. None of my quirks, the things that feel messy to me, were ever flaws to him. They were just part of who I was. And he's always loved all of me."

Everly grimaced. "He's all right, I guess." She joked around with Becca about it, but she could listen to her best friend talk about her brother forever. They worked in a way that Everly had never seen in another couple.

Becca rolled her eyes. "I feel like you tend to pick guys who don't see you. I was really hoping maybe James was different since he was all about your art, but if he thinks you need a whole TV show to survive his rejection, he doesn't know how strong you are."

Everly hadn't felt strong in a long time. Not since Grandma Helen died. But the way she'd handled James tonight made her wonder if maybe that was changing.

If *she* finally was.

"You deserve an Ellis." Becca threw up a hand before Everly could react. "Not literally. But someone that sees all of you, Ev. And loves you for it."

Everly's thoughts drifted back to that conversation with Logan at her mom's house. The light he'd said she had. And then to the way he'd kissed her tonight, matching her energy, her need, with his own.

If anyone saw her, it was him. His footage from the show kept proving that again and again.

As if reading her mind, Becca wagged an eyebrow. She had such a youthful face that she looked like a ten-year-old trying to tell a dirty joke. "So . . . what about that other kiss?"

Everly's face was instantly on fire. "A very different story."

"Yes." Becca actually pumped a fist in the air, like Everly's love life was a sports game and her team was winning. "Tell me everything. What happened after you kissed?"

Everly averted her eyes. "I ran away."

Becca groaned.

"I know." Everly buried her face in her hands. "I panicked. I had just dealt with all that stuff with James, and I was a mess."

Becca tapped Everly's leg with her foot. "Tell him that. This is salvageable."

"It doesn't matter anyway. I can't be with him."

"Why not?"

"I'm supposed to be focusing on myself. How can I do that if I'm endlessly worried about scaring him away?"

"*Or.*" Becca gave Everly a slightly less gentle kick this time. "Being around him will help you grow even more. That's what happened with me and Ellis."

Everly couldn't fight with that. She'd seen the many ways her brother and best friend made each other better. And though it scared Everly to admit it, she knew, deep down, that Logan had already been good for her.

With no more excuses to hide behind, her fear was her only roadblock. And she'd promised herself, when she decided to do *OTPS,* that she would stop being so afraid to take a risk.

The moment her lips had met Logan's, she'd set the runaway roller coaster down the track. The risk had already been taken. Now she'd have to ride it out.

Starting with facing him next week at filming.

ENTERTAINMENT NOW, BREAKING NEWS

"DID *ON THE PLUS SIDE* CROSS A LINE? SEASON TWO'S SHOCK-ING REVEAL."

Samantha Quain, Media Desk

The lifestyle and makeover show *On the Plus Side* has always had a knack for pushing boundaries, but on last night's episode, they may have taken things a step too far.

Sunday's show marked the midway point in the eight-episode arc for guest Carrie DeLuca, a fan favorite whose experiences as a plus-size child adopted by thin parents have resonated with many. After years of searching, the twenty-eight-year-old had finally found her birth mother, and the show helped her set up a meeting.

Cameras followed Carrie on her trip from Boston to Milwaukee to meet her birth mother. Their encounter was heartwarming, but interspersed between clips of their emotional reunion were pieces of an interview the show conducted with Carrie's adoptive mom, who broke down sobbing when she learned where her daughter was.

As it turned out, Carrie hadn't shared the news about her birth mother yet. The show had revealed it instead.

New Mood Media has already released a statement insisting that this was all an unfortunate accident, but a lot of journalists—and fans—don't buy it . . .

CHAPTER 19

Who knew spreadsheets could be so damn sexy?

After the disaster that was Saturday night, there was nothing more appealing to Everly than sitting at the reception desk, lost in the company's travel details. She had a large coffee, a bagel sandwich, and some aspirin to nurse the effects of her still-lingering hangover, and all she wanted to do on this Monday morning was find the perfect color coding system for these columns and rows.

Overflow text never judged her for her decisions. Pivot tables didn't see her as too much. It was like a portal to a new world: one of numbers and formulas and linear boxes, where everything made sense, and James and Logan and what had happened at Harry's didn't exist.

Tabbing back to her email, she pulled up the itineraries for her boss's next trip. As she transferred over confirmation numbers and other details, her brain sank into a blissful emptiness for the first time since she'd climbed into bed Saturday night.

James's expression when he'd admitted to nominating her, Logan leaning in to kiss her, Logan's hands as he held her, Logan's lips on hers,

Logan's face as she'd run away: the memories had cycled over and over in her mind while she tossed and turned. Then, for a change of pace, she'd begun to panic about what might end up on the show. How would Sady spin it?

It was a miracle she'd gotten any rest this weekend.

After about two hours of focused clicking on the December spreadsheet, she managed to achieve a pink ombré pattern that she was absolutely certain her boss would make her remove as soon as he saw it. But for now, she leaned back in her chair to admire her work. Maybe it could be a nice overture to a conversation about moving her to Design. A first step toward more than she'd let herself have in a long time.

Across from Everly, the front entrance to the office opened. Her welcoming smile froze on her face as she glanced up.

Framed in the doorway was Logan, his camera hanging at his side.

In an act of self-preservation, the first thing Everly had done when she'd dragged herself out of bed this morning was check the production call sheets. According to them, she wasn't due back on camera until the show shipped her off to Boston. She was supposed to have another two days to prepare herself to face him—and the fact that she'd initiated that kiss (at least verbally) and then ran away. "What are you doing here?"

The weight of his gaze turned her muscles to rubber. "Sady told me to come in and get some extra footage."

"Do you do everything she says?" Everly's voice was harsh. Her head teemed with so many worries about that night at Harry's and what might have ended up on camera that the mere mention of Sady's name was enough to turn her into a series of sharp points and edges.

"She's my boss, so yes."

Everything about him was so even, so monotone (except for his loud orange-and-green plaid shirt) that it was impossible to discern his thoughts. Was he upset at Everly for running? Did he feel as awkward as she did? Did he want to turn back time and erase their kiss?

"Okay," she mumbled.

"Do you have a problem with Sady?"

Everly sighed at her monitor. "Maybe? I don't know." She shrugged. "You were there this weekend filming and who knows what you caught on camera. But whatever footage you got from Harry's is going to feed this love story she wants to turn my episodes into. And I have a problem with *that*."

His brow furrowed. "I stopped filming the dance floor the minute you kissed him. And there's only shots of about half your conversation. You looked so upset when he admitted to nominating you that I cut it off there."

Everly's cheeks warmed. That was still more than she would have liked to be on film, but it could have been so much worse. Logan had protected her. She wanted to ask him why, but the sound of heavy footfalls from down the hall trapped the words in her mouth.

A second later, James appeared.

James, who Everly hadn't seen yet this morning, who she'd hoped she might be spared from interacting with if she only focused hard enough on her computer. Clearly, the universe was intent upon punishing her today.

Logan's mouth snapped shut, and his attention dropped to his camera.

Everly's stomach clenched. James was a talker. He'd want to hash this out. But Everly didn't want to remember their kiss, much less talk about it. She didn't want to explain that his nomination had been selfish, and that he'd embarrassed her. She wanted to return to the days of pointless chatter, to meaningless finger guns and silly nicknames, only this time without the pressure of her feelings for him.

She wanted to undo their kiss without messing with Logan's.

But they were so fully intertwined that breaking one would destroy the other. If she hadn't kissed James, she wouldn't have had to recognize that what she felt for him wasn't real. And without that, she would have never considered kissing Logan.

Everly ran her shoe along the carpet below her, secretly wishing to find the ruts of a trapdoor to climb through.

As James drew closer, she pinned her eyes to her screen and concentrated on the last few details she needed to input into the spreadsheet.

"V."

Her shoulders bunched to her ears at the sound of his voice. She felt like a grenade with a pulled pin, ready to go off at any second. "Hi."

"Uh, hey." He sounded sheepish, and when she finally looked over at him, he was scrubbing nervously at the back of his neck.

She sighed. She was a fool for kissing him. No matter how many drinks she'd had or how confident she'd felt, she should never have opened that box.

But part of her, one that had grown increasingly louder over these past few weeks, reminded her that it wasn't all her fault. James knew how she'd felt about him. He'd thought those feelings were so strong she needed a TV show and an entire life makeover to move on from him. So where did he get off dancing so close? Flirting with her? Shouldn't he have to take some responsibility for that? Being nice and leading someone on were not the same thing.

The office was not the place to hash that out, though. Not if she wanted a future here. And especially not with Logan and his camera watching. The best thing James and Everly could do right now was put the other night behind them.

She forced herself to meet his gaze. "Could we not dwell on what happened at Harry's? It's over. It was a mistake, and I want to forget it."

His face lit up. "Yeah?"

She shrugged. She couldn't bring herself to say it again when she knew she was letting him off so easily.

"Thank god." He slapped on one of those charismatic grins. "Because I seriously need your help." He draped himself across the reception counter, like he was so put out he could barely keep upright.

Already, he was invading her personal space again. Everly crossed her arms and leaned back, reclaiming some distance. "On what?"

"That cookies account. They want the print ad to suggest healthy and delicious at the same time, and nothing I've put together is working."

She frowned. Usually she liked helping him, but was that why he'd come over here? Not to make sure everything was okay?

That *she* was okay?

"Dude, are you serious?" Logan's voice held an angry edge. He strode forward so he was almost between them. His knuckles had gone white from his grasp on the camera's strap.

"Oh, hey, man. I didn't see you over there." James retreated two steps from the desk.

"Yeah, you were too busy making Everly do your work."

"Nah, she's just a great brainstorming partner." James's eyes flicked to her. They were wide, expectant, as if he was waiting for her to agree.

Everly gazed back in silence. She'd always thought of their collaborations as practice for her, but Logan wasn't wrong that James seemed to take advantage of that.

And that she let him.

The old Everly *never* would have put up with that.

She shouldn't be putting up with it now.

Logan's frown tugged at the ends of his beard. "Funny, 'cause I haven't seen you offer any ideas. Just take hers." He was standing at the reception counter now, his camera resting on top.

"She's really good."

"Maybe she should have your job then."

The tips of James's ears glowed a bright red to match the flush in his cheeks. "I'm gonna—" He scratched at his head for a moment. "I'm gonna go."

He retreated toward the break room before Everly had a chance to respond. Which was fine, because she had no idea what to say.

Her insides swam, making her a little queasy. How had she never noticed that he was more interested in her help than anything else? How had she thought they were friends? Even with *On the Plus Side,* he didn't nominate her because he knew she loved the show. He did it to squash her feelings for him.

Everly was beginning to think that maybe she shouldn't regret that kiss with James. Maybe it had needed to happen so she could see him more clearly.

She faced Logan. "You're grumpier than usual. And that's saying something, since you're usually a ten on the grump-o-meter."

"How do you expect me to act when you kiss me like that, then run away?" His gaze drilled into her. Apparently, it was time to get to the point.

Everly's heart jammed into her throat. Kissing someone when you weren't 100 percent certain they felt the same was a lot like showing a first draft of a drawing to someone. Raw and scary and way too revealing. She braced her hands on the desk as if they were the only thing keeping her from plummeting.

"Like what?"

"Spectacularly."

Her surprised laugh filled the room. Her mother would have been mortified by her reaction, would have thought it was too much, too loud. But Logan only watched Everly quietly. The same way he always did.

She brushed her fingers over her keyboard, the soft clicks soothing. "I'm sorry I ran."

"I thought you regretted it."

Her head snapped toward him. "No way. It was how much I *didn't* regret it, actually. It scared me." Their eyes met, and she tried to mirror the steadiness of his stare. "*You* scare me."

He frowned, a wrinkle appearing in his forehead. Her fingers itched to smooth it away. "Why?"

"You've been here this whole time. You've heard my mom talk about me, heard about what happened after my grandmother died, seen what a complete mess I can be. I can't really hide from you."

"You're funny. You're quick. You're beau—" He stopped himself. "Striking. There's absolutely nothing you need to hide."

Goose bumps trailed up and down Everly's arms. Everywhere his eyes touched her, shivers danced across her skin.

She didn't know how to explain what it meant to her that he saw her so clearly. Not with words, at least.

He seemed to share the sentiment. Giving the empty room a furtive glance, he nodded to her desk. "Can I come back there?"

"Please." Another shiver chased through her.

She didn't have time to get up from her chair before his palms had cupped her face. They were warm and soft and smelled like evergreen.

His thumbs slipped under her chin to tilt her head up, so he could fit his mouth over hers.

Everly's fingers dragged through the bristles of his beard. A groan shuddered at the back of his throat when she gave his facial hair a soft pull.

Their kiss deepened, and his whole body leaned into her, as if she were a magnet and every part of him were made of metal.

And this time, no one ran away.

CHAPTER 20

The storefront of Kisses and Hugs looked like the entrance to every boutique Everly had been afraid to step into her entire life.

Sleek, modern signage affixed to a pristine white building on Newbury Street. High, plate-glass windows that caught the sun's rays. In each one, mannequins were displayed in loose, floral midi dresses; high-waisted, straight-legged jeans with strategically placed tears; cropped T-shirts; strands of beaded necklaces and bracelets; body-con dresses; wide-legged linen trousers over tightly fitted bodysuits. Around them, antique furniture functioned as stands for hats, pendant necklaces, scarves, and other accessories.

But unlike in those other shops, these mannequins were Everly's size, and some of them were her shape. Everything in this store would fit her.

Her hands trembled hard enough to hurt as she stared at the entrance. Shaking them out, she fisted her fingers and pressed them to her thighs.

This was it. The true beginning of her transformation.

Over the next few days, Jazzy would help her choose her wardrobe, they'd experiment with hair and makeup, she'd meet with Goro to design her tattoo. Then she would work with Stanton to prepare her booth for the Cape Cod Collective. She'd have to decide what pieces to show, how she wanted to market herself, what path she wanted to follow for her career. And it all started here. Stepping through those doors would be like passing through a portal to somewhere new.

A few weeks ago, that idea would have been terrifying. Everly was too attached to being fine. To feeling safe. She was no less terrified now—but she was ready to shed this version of herself. To become someone unafraid to embrace the messy, the uncertain, the possibly amazing.

"After you," Logan said softly.

Though she nodded, her feet didn't move, and he didn't push her.

If she'd needed to wait ten more years, right in this spot, he'd let her, without pressure or impatience. It was like the way he kissed—following her lead, never taking more than she gave.

She hadn't been able to stop thinking about their kiss in the Matten-Waverly office since it happened two days ago. Almost immediately after they'd pulled away, his phone had rung, Sady requesting that he return to Boston, where he'd been ever since. They'd texted a little, but Logan was, no surprise, the king of one-word responses.

Everly glanced back at him. Her whole body tingled with the urge to rush forward. To wrap her limbs around his. Kiss him until their lips went numb from the pressure.

Taking one more breath, she smiled and reached for the door.

If she was going on this journey to a new Everly, at least she got to take Logan with her.

Inside, she spotted Sady and Jazzy speaking to a short, curvy woman around Everly's age with shoulder-length brown curls. She was wearing an incredible romper in a light seafoam green with a pattern of maroon and mauve flowers. Everly made a mental note to ask if it was from their collection.

Jazzy called her name and hurried down the center aisle to greet her. Another cameraman followed. He was older, taller, smiling, and clean-shaven. Basically the anti-Logan.

Her gaze jumped between them. "What's going on? You're not replacing Logan?" Everly would riot. Loudly. She'd show them what too much actually looked like.

"Of course not. Fans are going wild for him." Sady clasped her hands in front of her. She must love the color olive, because today she was wearing a body-hugging sheath dress in that shade of green. A black woven belt cinched her waist, and her giant black sunglasses were shoved into her loose blond hair. "We brought on a second camera so we can grab more footage."

Everly's shoulders tensed. *More footage of what?* she wondered. *Logan?* He'd already featured heavily in the second and third episodes, at the Ren faire and during Everly's graphic design tutorial with Alex and James. Was Sady going to try to construct a love triangle now? From what Becca said, that's what the internet was clamoring for. There were apparently whole forums on Read-It dedicated to #TeamLoverly and #TeamJeverly.

God help her.

Everly watched the showrunner gesture energetically to the two cameramen. Sady and Logan were close. Had he told her about their kiss? Was that the driving force behind this need for "more footage"? Everly refused to have whatever this was between them unfold on camera. It was too much pressure on something that had barely started.

Sady clapped her hands to get everyone's attention. "We only have the store to ourselves for a few hours, so let's meet Sophie and get shopping."

Sophie, it turned out, was the woman in the killer romper. She had friendly coffee-colored eyes and tan skin, and she waved Everly toward the back of the store with a big smile. A sketch pad was tucked under her arm.

Everly nodded to it. "Are you an artist?"

"A designer," Jazzy said.

"Not quite yet," Sophie clarified. "Just an assistant right now, but someday." She said it with such confidence. Like she knew it would happen. Everly wanted that for herself and her art.

"You know this brand, right?" Jazzy flourished an arm to indicate the store.

Everly nodded. Kisses and Hugs was sustainable, high-end fashion and far (far) outside her budget. She used to own one or two pieces she and Grandma Helen had found thrifting, but she'd donated them along with the rest of her flashier wardrobe years ago.

"Then you know they do custom work as well." Jazzy grinned. "We're going to collaborate with Sophie to build you the perfect, just-for-Everly wardrobe with a mix of off-the-rack and custom pieces."

Everly grew warm with excitement. She was going to have a signature style. The thought of that had her eyes already stinging with tears. She was going to be a puddle by the time she started trying items on.

"You've seen the show a million times, so you know the drill," Jazzy said. "We're going to split up for now. You grab everything and anything you like. Don't second-guess yourself. Then we'll work through our piles together, trying everything on, building outfits, figuring out what makes you happy. What defines *you*." Jazzy beamed at her. "Where do you want to start?"

Everly glanced around, searching for the corner of the store with the most floral prints and flowing fabrics. Boho vibes, her favorite. "Over there."

Jazzy and Sophie headed in the opposite direction, the new cameraman trailing in their wake.

Resuming his usual role as her shadow, Logan followed Everly's chaotic zigzags through the aisles to a rack of loose peasant tops.

It had been so long since she'd last put on anything that didn't have the sole purpose of making her blend in like a neutral wall color. What did she want to look like? What was her interpretation of boho? Long, loose dresses? Gauzy layers? Big hats and lots of accessories? Tassels and florals?

Selecting a baby-blue cold-shoulder top with ruffle details, she lined it up against her body. Could she see herself in this? "I never understood this trend. Are shoulders sexy?"

One of those bemused expressions crossed Logan's face. He stepped back a little to make sure both Everly and the shirt were in the frame. His camera was smaller today, something he held in front of him to view the screen. It must have been easier to use in a cramped location like a clothing store.

"Right up there with elbows and pinkie fingers."

Everly laughed. "Good to know." She hooked the shirt back on the rack, then flicked through a few others.

A silk jacket in mauve florals on another display caught her attention. Immediately, Everly could picture it with some dark skinny jeans and booties. Maybe a fitted bodysuit underneath. The joy that always accompanied a good graphic layout or font choice fizzed through her veins. She was on to something.

The fabric felt like cool running water against her skin. She was so lost in the sensation as she ran it through her fingers that she didn't hear Sady approach until the showrunner said, "That's gorgeous."

Everly jumped, then coughed, trying to clear her throat. No one as tall as Sady should be able to move through shadows, assassin-style, especially in heels.

"Right?" Everly laid the garment over her arm. Beneath her ribs, her heart skipped a few beats. Her first selection. Her first step toward the new her.

This was happening.

Sady glanced between Everly and Logan. "You two are talking, right?"

"What do you mean?" Everly's heart hiccupped. How much did Sady already know about them?

"Make sure you narrate to him what you like and don't like. And banter. Both of you. Don't be afraid to break the fourth wall. Viewers are eating it up. They love your energy."

Everly eyed the showrunner warily. "Right. Our energy."

"We're on our way to our highest streaming numbers yet." Sady was practically bouncing on her heels. "I *knew* you were going to be one of our stars this season. It's incredible."

Everly shrugged, then spun around to focus on a set of dresses behind her. She didn't care about ratings or anything like that. She just wanted to be portrayed honestly. As someone with bigger goals than dating.

Sady wandered off with her phone a few minutes later. Once she'd disappeared, Everly motioned for Logan to lower his camera. She stepped close enough that the cotton of his shirt brushed her bare arm, and even though there was no skin-on-skin contact, a little shiver wended its way up her spine.

"How do you feel about this?" Everly glanced toward Jazzy and Sophie on the opposite side of the room.

Logan followed her gaze. "What, Joe? He's fine."

"No. You being incorporated into the show. Sady is clearly concocting another romance plot."

He smirked. "You make it sound like one of those historical shows where the women are all scheming to bed the duke."

"A Regency romance?"

He shrugged. "Sure."

"It sounds like you're a fan, Logan."

Another shrug. The physical equivalent of a grunt if there ever was one. "They're fun."

Suddenly, nothing sounded more appealing than snuggling up with him on the couch under a warm blanket to binge some Regencies.

And then maybe reenact some of the steamier scenes.

There was that one on a staircase . . .

Everly honed her attention on a stack of jeans before her face ignited from the scandalous thoughts in her head. "I just want to know . . . are you comfortable with this . . . thing . . ." She had no idea what to label them, and Mr. Monosyllable did not seem interested in helping her out. ". . . with us being on the show?"

That solemn wrinkle returned to his brow. "What *you* think is more important."

Everly blew out a breath. "I hate it, honestly." She wanted to let what was happening between them unfold naturally. It needed space to breathe. Not the weight of the world's expectations.

Logan sighed. "I don't love it either." He frowned, obviously pained to admit this. As if he didn't want to go against Sady's wishes.

"Yeah?"

"Yeah." His blue eyes flicked to her. A tiny bit of mischief glinted at their center. "I kind of want you all to myself." His voice rumbled, low and husky.

Everly's knees literally gave out. No one had ever talked to her like that.

She stumbled trying to catch her balance and bumped hard into the table. The legs scraped against the wood floor with an earsplitting screech and four stacks of jeans toppled to the ground.

She was a walking hurricane around this man. "Oh, for fuck's sake," she groaned as she kneeled to clean her mess.

Logan erupted into laughter. It was so loud and joyous, something in her core loosened in response. Everly would have given both her kidneys to hear that laugh again. To have it recorded so she could play it on a loop. Make it her ringtone. Drift off to sleep to its (not-so) dulcet tones.

He stooped to help her. Their hands collided as they reached for the same pair of jeans, and a blush spread across Everly's skin.

He studied her for a long moment, his lips pressed together. "What if we give Sady just a little? Some flirting, that banter she wants. Nothing major."

Everly frowned. "What about everybody watching, commenting, thinking they have a right to weigh in on us? You really want to put up with that?"

"I think we can give Sady what she wants and still protect us. Not that she'd do anything to put the show—or its guests—at risk." He gathered the newly folded pants from her hands and stacked them neatly on the table. Then he rose to his feet and reached down to help her do the same. His fingers were warm as they closed around hers.

"She wants this show to succeed. So do I." He put so much feeling behind those last few words it set Everly's heart galloping. "And there's a lot riding on this season. If it performs well, we're looking at a big bump in our per-episode salary. The extra money would help me a lot."

Everly rubbed at her forehead. "This love stuff really makes for good TV, huh?"

"People get invested."

He must have seen the doubt in her eyes because he stepped a little closer. The toe of his shoe tapped hers and stayed there. The most contact they could have at the moment without risking it getting captured on film.

"We can make this work for everyone." His eyes were almost pleading. "We'll be careful," he promised. "Only show them what we're willing to let them see."

"All right."

Everly was willing to compromise with the camera if it meant giving her and Logan a real chance.

"Shouldn't the pattern be on top?"

Kisses and Hugs had a 180-degree mirror in their dressing room, and Sophie and Everly were standing in it. Sophie had her sketch pad open and Everly was staring at herself in a pair of loose-fitting, wide-leg pants in a vibrant (or, if she was being truly honest, *garish*) pink-and-cream floral. Because she was barely average height, the bottoms pooled around her wedge sandals. But she was more concerned about the cream-colored crop top they'd paired with it.

She narrowed her eyes at her reflection. She couldn't decide if she didn't like the outfit or if she simply wasn't used to it. Which was how she'd felt about almost everything she'd tried on so far.

Turns out, obliterating your comfort zone was not such an easy task.

"You are not a fan," Jazzy observed from behind them.

Everly glanced over her shoulder. "What? No. I'm adjusting to it."

Logan threaded through the room, stopping beside Jazzy. "Oh, she hates it." He lifted the camera, zooming in to get a close-up of Everly in the mirror. "Look at your face. It's the same expression you made last week when Stanton brought in sushi, because you'd never tried it, and you could hardly choke it down."

Everly's heart jumped. She couldn't get over how carefully he paid attention to her. How much he *saw*.

"Okay. Fine. I'm not sure it's for me."

Sophie leaned against one of the mirrors and primed her pencil on her sketch pad. "Tell me why."

"The pattern screams the sixties, which might be my least favorite fashion decade. But I also think I'd like some structure somewhere?"

Everly pulled at the pants to show how loose they were, and then did the same with the top. "Even with all those flowy tops I love, I'd pair them with formfitting jeans, or half-tucked in a pencil skirt. Something to control the billowiness."

"Okay. What about this?" Sophie displayed her sketch pad so everyone could see it. "We have a jumpsuit in this shade of cream," she tugged on the sleeve of Everly's shirt, "that I think would be incredible on you. It comes standard at a crop length with short sleeves, but I feel like if we made it wide-legged and sleeveless, it would give that perfect balance of volume and structure."

Everly's eyes roamed the page, already picturing herself in the outfit at work. Except she wouldn't be sitting at the reception desk. She'd be in an art department somewhere. Because the Everly who wore that jumpsuit was not afraid to go after the job she wanted.

"I love it. It looks like something an artist would wear." Everly's voice was whisper soft. Amazed. Somehow, the thought of letting her profession inform her style had never occurred to her. But if she came into a meeting in that outfit, everyone would immediately know she did something creative. It was like another kind of advertising.

"Precisely." Jazzy hooked her arm around Everly's neck and gave her a squeeze. That pride was in her face again, like she could sense Everly surrendering to the process.

After seeing a few more of Sophie's custom designs, Everly shook her head. "Where have you been every time I've gone shopping?"

Sophie laughed. "I'm down any time you want to go."

"Wait. Seriously?" Heat attacked Everly's cheeks. She hated how trying to make friends as an adult conjured the same terror as inviting everyone to your birthday party in first grade and being convinced no one would come. She should know how to do this by now; she'd had decades of practice.

"Absolutely. I need more artists in my life." Sophie entered Everly's number into her phone, then bent to retrieve one of the rejected garments that had fallen off the hanger. "Plus, anything we find that doesn't fit, I can alter." With a playful wink, she disappeared back into the showroom.

It was another hour before they finished going through Everly's selections and moved on to Jazzy's.

The first option was a short, bright orange dress, hitting Everly mid-thigh, with three voluminous layers of skirt, a banded chest, and puffy sleeves.

She couldn't keep the horror off her face as she stared into the mirror. Thank god Jazzy had hung back to organize some outfits in the fitting room.

"I look like Grimace." Everly fluffed the skirt out to really emphasize its layers.

Logan's mouth twitched, like he was trying hard not to react to this monstrosity on her body. "Who?"

"That Philadelphia hockey mascot."

His boisterous laugh echoed off the walls. These rare moments of levity were catnip for her. Everly's body went soft and loose. She wanted to roll around in his joy. In him.

"You mean Gritty."

"Right, that guy." She blew out an exaggerated breath. "I look like Gritty on prom night."

His second laugh was even louder.

They were alone. Everly crept to the edge of the raised platform so she was standing above him, about a head taller. She felt like King Midas. Or one of the twenty billionaires trying to shoot themselves into space. His smiles, his laughs, they were richer than any gold.

She settled her palms lightly on his cheeks and let her fingers explore his beard. She loved how it was rough and soft at the same time, how the bristles tickled her cheeks when they kissed. His hands wandered over the dress's many layers, finally catching them in a gentle fist and urging her toward him.

Their kiss was soft and sweet, mouths closed, only a second long, but it sent a jolt of heat through her limbs.

She wanted to kiss him a hundred more times, but there were too many prying eyes, too many cameras. These soft moments weren't for any audience. And they weren't for Sady.

They were theirs alone.

He cupped her face, keeping her close as their lips parted. "What are you doing later?" he asked.

She shrugged. "Pizza and a book?"

"What about better pizza and hanging out with some dogs?"

She narrowed her eyes. "What makes you assume your pizza will be better?"

"Is that a yes?"

Nodding, she kissed him again, no more than a brush of their mouths, before stepping down from the mirrors.

As she turned away, he said, "Please don't wear Gritty."

Everly erupted into laughter. She waited until she'd opened the door to her dressing room and stepped inside to reply.

"Now I'm wearing Gritty everywhere."

CHAPTER 21

"How do you live here?"

Everly watched Logan balance a giant pizza box on one arm as he dug into his camera bag for his keys. They were on the verge of having cheese-side-down slices for dinner, but she was too in awe of his apartment building to do much more than stare. It was a beautiful brick walk-up with only one unit per floor, and his was on the top. Everything was so clean and well-polished and orderly. She had no idea cameramen earned this much money.

Her mouth fell open. "Oh my god, do you still live with your parents?"

He cocked his head. "What if I do? You basically live with your brother."

"Touché." Everly took the pizza from his overburdened hands. "But seriously, I'm not prepared for parents."

"Good lord, I don't live with my parents. This was my grandfather's place. I'm the only grandkid, so he left it to me in his will." He cringed as the barking inside the apartment reached a crescendo with the slide of his key in the doorknob. "That's one of the reasons I moved back here. No rent."

He popped open the door, then took the pizza from her so they could maneuver their way inside. "No matter how cute they look or how much they bark and whine, you cannot give them attention until they sit down," he instructed.

The front door led into a narrow hallway that was basically an acoustic blast zone for his two dogs. One was tiny, no more than eight pounds, with a white, wiry body, black fur around his ears and eyes that was trimmed in brown, and the curliest tail Everly had ever seen. She recognized him as Alan from the pictures Logan had shown her at the Ren faire. The other, Ravioli, was an English bulldog, old enough that he'd gone gray around the muzzle and head. He was a thick boy covered in wrinkly skin, his folded ears flopping with every waddle at Logan's heels.

Though she wanted desperately to drop to the floor and snuggle them, Everly respected the rules and paid them no mind while they hopped in circles. Alan had escalated from barking to yowling, as if they were murdering him simply by denying him pats.

The first to plop his butt down was Ravioli, who gazed up at Logan with liquid brown eyes and a big, drooling smile.

Logan set aside the food to shower the bulldog with praise. The way he cooed was so diametrically opposed to his typical gruff nature that Everly choked on a laugh.

Alan finally stopped his baying and also sat, earning him a good scratch from Logan under his chin.

Everly eased to the floor so she could pet him, too. "Do you sing to them?" She'd assumed it was something every animal enthusiast did until Logan frowned.

Panic ignited in her chest. Was this his threshold for "too much"? Singing to dogs?

His jaw tightened as he watched Alan, who'd rolled over onto his back, his paws kicking every time Logan found that perfect spot. "Only at dinnertime." He spoke the words so quietly they were almost inaudible.

Everly cracked a grin. Either she wasn't a weirdo or they both were, and she was fine with that. "At my grandmother's farm all the dogs had their own songs for everything. Meals, walks, bath time." She *might* have made most of them up herself.

Logan's expression softened. "Oh man. A farm. That's the dream."

Her heart picked up speed. She kept discovering that they loved the same things: dogs, tattoos, a good Regency romance, visual arts, farms. Each one became a little knot stringing them invisibly together.

She'd never had anything more than Matten-Waverly in common with James.

"Not a surprise, given your aesthetic." She gestured to his shirt.

His eyebrows dipped low. "Plaid is classic."

"On flannel, it reads more like lumbersexual."

"That's not a real word."

"Look it up."

He actually pulled out his phone, but Alan started gnawing on the corner of it, and he gave up. These dogs had him wrapped around their paws. "Tell me about this farm," he urged.

Everly wasn't sure where to begin. With the expanse of bright green fields that stretched out from every side of Grandma Helen's two-story white farmhouse like oceans of grass? With the wraparound porch where the barn cats had their meals, then poured themselves bonelessly into the wooden rocking chairs to nap? With the tractor her grandmother let her drive way too early? With the way that, back then, she'd never felt more herself than when she was running across the fields, covered in mud, followed by herds of goats and packs of dogs, singing at the top of her lungs?

She could only imagine how Grandma Helen would have reacted

to Everly being on *On the Plus Side*. The whole town would have been over to her house twice a week for rowdy watch parties. She would have made her granddaughter feel like a rock star, a celebrity, someone to be proud of, instead of a walking potential embarrassment like her mother.

"It was the best." Everly rested on her palms, her gaze drifting to the ceiling as if she might find sketches of her memories in the white paint. "She had all this land. You couldn't even see any of her neighbors' houses. It was like being on our own little island. Only the sea was maple and fir trees."

"Freedom." Logan said the word softly. Carefully. Like it was breakable.

Everly nodded. "Grandma Helen turned it into an animal sanctuary after my grandfather died. I didn't find out until she passed that her friend June, who worked there with her, was actually her girlfriend." It was this whole other side to Grandma Helen that Everly wished she'd gotten the chance to know. But her grandmother had always been so private. She kept the things that mattered most to her locked tightly inside. "She and my mom never got along, but that woman was my favorite person in the world." Logan had been there when she'd opened up to Jazzy on wardrobe day. He already knew this. But Everly wanted to say it again, to him, as if that might tether them closer together. "I hope *OTPS* helps me be more like her. I want to care so little about what others think that I can't even hear them."

"She sounds great."

Everly blew out a long breath. Grandma Helen had died almost four years ago, yet the loss was as fresh as an open wound. Some grief clung to you like a ghost, never quite disappearing.

Tears bit at the corners of her eyes. She blinked them back and concentrated on scratching Alan, who had squirmed into her lap and lay belly-up, flapping his tail.

"You two would have gotten along well. She loved plaid, too." And monosyllables.

Logan snorted. "I'm going to tell Jazzy to build your entire new wardrobe out of plaid now."

Everly straightened her shoulders and shot him a flirty smirk. "And I'd look incredible in all of it." The words felt like another kind of freedom on her tongue. Because she meant them. She'd never looked in the mirror and hated what she saw. It was more that she hadn't wanted to see anything at all. And she didn't want anyone else to, either. But these last few weeks on the show had changed that. She was ready to be visible again. To be seen.

And right now, there was no one she wanted to see her more than Logan.

His blue eyes caught hers, and the weight of his stare buckled her knees. This man could dismantle her with a mere glance.

"Yeah, you would." His voice was soft but rough. Feathers and sandpaper. Every rumble reverberated through Everly's core.

Heat rushed to her face, and she almost fell as her arms went slack. They were too close together for him to be talking to her in that tone. Like he wanted to devour every inch of her. She was liable to pounce on him and do unconscionable things to this man she'd only kissed three times.

She stumbled to her feet and cleared her throat. "Does your fancy apartment come equipped with water?" Her whole mouth was dry as sand.

"We should probably eat, too, before the pizza gets cold." His face had regained that stoic expression, except for this tiny tip to the right corner of his lips that told her he knew *exactly* what effect he'd had on her, and he was enjoying it.

As he unearthed some glasses and plates, Everly wandered a little deeper into the apartment. The open floor plan was sparsely filled and decorated in neutral shades of gray and blue with white accents. The few pieces of furniture that filled the space were mostly sleek and modern, everything clean lines and leather and steel. She would have believed she was standing in a store showroom rather than a home, if not for the dog toys and blankets strewn everywhere, which added a lived-in feel. On the walls, New England sports memorabilia and movie posters (mostly older action films like *Die Hard* and *Predator* and *Con Air*) hung in perfectly symmetrical lines and rows.

The sound of shuffling behind her pulled Everly's attention to her feet, where she spotted Alan face-deep in her purse. She tried to shoo him away, but he emerged with a pen and beelined for an open doorway off the living room.

Logan was setting plates on the bar that separated the kitchen from the dining area. "Oh, that's going in the toilet," he said.

His words were followed by the distinct *plop* of plastic meeting water. Everly ducked into the (incredibly clean) bathroom to retrieve her pen, only to have the Chihuahua mix prance back in behind her, this time with her compact in his mouth.

She pried the silver case from between his teeth and returned to the kitchen. "Your dogs are oddballs," she declared as she moved her purse safely to the counter. "I'm surprised you don't come home to find everything you own in the toilet."

"I leave them with a babysitter to avoid that fate."

"What's the worst thing he's thrown in there?"

Logan scratched at his beard. The skritching sound sent a pleasant tremor up Everly's spine. "He likes to 'help' me unpack the groceries," he threw some air quotes, "so probably a loaf of bread."

Everly crouched in front of Alan. "Not the bread. Bread is sacred, buddy."

Alan balanced his front paws on her knees and licked the tip of her nose. A valid response.

Everly felt Logan's gaze settling on her. "He doesn't do that for everyone. Just the really good people."

His tone suggested there was more to what he was saying than the words that came out of his mouth. Her stomach flipped. Not knowing what else to do, she gathered the plates and set them at the four-seat glass table in the dining area.

He followed with the pizza, and for a few minutes, they were quiet as they ate.

"Hey, this is kind of our first date." It was, after all, the first time they'd shared a meal. Everly held out her half-eaten slice for a toast.

Logan frowned. "I'm sorry." He rubbed at the back of his neck. "It's been a long day. I just wanted to come home. I didn't even think—"

"What are you talking about?" Everly loved pizza and dogs and being around Logan. She had everything she needed. Except maybe his face on hers.

But they'd get there.

"You probably wanted to go out somewhere in the city. Put on one of those new dresses and have a nice meal or whatever."

"Good god, no." She reacted without thinking, her voice loud and emphatic. It bounced off the empty walls of the dining room, but she didn't let herself cringe. Everly was so tired of being embarrassed of who she was. And Logan had never made her feel like she needed to be. "I've been peopling all day. All I want to do is take off my bra and flop down in front of the TV."

His left eyebrow arched at the mention of her bra, and Everly wanted to climb under the table. She coughed, then took a big bite of her pizza. The time it took to chew gave her the space to find a suitable non sequitur.

"You said this apartment was only one of the reasons you came back east. What could possibly ever drag you back to the land of winter?"

Cold was fine, but snow and ice were Everly's nemeses. They made driving precarious and walking outside an extreme sport, and what started out as a beautiful blanket of soft white too soon transformed into a desolate gray landscape right out of a dystopian novel. She would not choose to live somewhere that looked like the world of *1984* for half the year if she had options.

He chuckled. "Just wait. I'll teach you to love snow."

Her heart hiccupped. It was only the beginning of November. Her filming would be over long before the snow came. But Logan didn't seem to think they would be.

"Doubtful." Trying to sound indifferent was a task when her body buzzed with his words and what they implied.

"You've yet to experience Ravioli *basking* in a pile of snow. It changes everything."

Everly looked down at the wrinkly monster lounging at their feet. Dammit. That would do it.

Logan folded a circle of pepperoni into his mouth. "Not paying rent was big, but really it was for Sady. When she got this gig, she asked me to come with her, and we'd been working together long enough at that point that it only made sense."

"You two are close, huh?"

His lips pressed flat, and his eyes skipped to the window. "She gave me a purpose."

"What do you mean?"

Logan rose abruptly and dragged his chair halfway around the table so they were sitting as close as possible. His knee pressed gently against hers. "I don't know if we're at the place yet where we're talking about exes . . ."

Everly snorted. "You told me about LA girl like two weeks ago."

That little smile she loved so much teased the corner of his lips. His leg sank a little more solidly into hers, like he wanted to feel her there. "When I moved out west with Annie, I thought we were it. Looking back now, I know how dumb it was, but I was eighteen and thinking with my heart, not my head. I was lost after that. I made a lot of bad choices, threw away a lot of money partying and running with people who didn't care about anything but what I could give them."

For once, Everly didn't fight the urge to smooth the wrinkle between his eyebrows. His head angled forward, drawn to her touch. When she stopped, he took her hand in his and brushed his mouth lightly to her knuckles. He seemed grateful to have her there. To be able to talk. To have someone listen. The tautness in his frame softened with every word, melting into her wherever their bodies met.

"The first time I was a PA on one of Sady's sets, she randomly chose me to help with some filming, and then she kept calling me back for more episodes, more shows. The next thing I knew, she was asking me to be her DP on a new project. It got canceled, but it's where we realized how well we worked together."

He shrugged, and his eyes lifted to Everly's face. "She saw something in me, like your grandmother with you. I owe her everything. And she still gives me room to do what I really want, no matter how crushed our schedule gets."

Everly didn't realize she was leaning toward him until she could feel the warmth of his breath on her nose. "What do you mean, what you really want? This isn't it?" It seemed like such a fun, exciting life. Always going to new places, meeting new people. Not sitting at the same desk day in and out because it was safe.

Logan shook his head. "A buddy of mine and I are starting a facility for dogs."

Everly coughed in surprise. "Wow, you're *truly* a dog person, huh?" She wondered if he had socks and underwear with prints of various breeds. Then, of course, she was picturing him in *just* socks and a pair of boxers, the image painting heat into her cheeks.

"It's like you said. They help us remember what matters." He ran the palms of his hands over his beard. "I had a pretty shit childhood. My parents were strict. There was no pleasing them." His frown turned into something deeper, more like a grimace. The pain in it squeezed Everly's heart. She increased the pressure of her knee on his to remind him she was there. "We had a dog for a long time, and he was the only good thing about that house." His voice hitched, and he cleared his throat loudly. There seemed to be more to this story, but his whole body had stiffened, his expression shuttered, as if he wasn't ready to share the rest.

Everly didn't push him. She just leaned closer. "That's why you need the show to do well. More money for the facility."

He nodded. "Dogs rely on us. Brian and I want to make sure more of them get adopted, and that those who don't, live comfortably. He's a vet, so we're going to make it part clinic, part rescue, part daycare." His eyes dipped to Alan and Ravioli. "That way, as many as possible can get the care they deserve."

Everly pulled back from him enough to dig her phone out of her pocket. "What's it called?"

"It's not open yet, but we'll probably name it something boring like the Wheaton-Samuel Center for Dogs."

That sounded more like a research center. Or a college building. It made Everly's brain yawn. "Logan." She braced her hands on his arm. "We can do better than that. I work for a *marketing* firm."

His cheeks reddened beneath his beard. "I was actually thinking about asking you to help us with branding, but I didn't know . . ."

"Are you kidding?" She couldn't stop herself from literally bouncing in her seat. This felt like the first time since her grandmother that someone was taking her seriously as an artist. And she loved that it was him.

He slid his arm out of her hands so he could lace his fingers in hers. His palm was warm, wide, and smooth, and it felt like their fingers were two ends of a dovetail joint. Carved to fit only each other.

He watched her excitement, his stare unmoving. This man and his eye contact were going to be the death of her. "I've seen your work. I know how good you are."

She didn't have the words to respond, so she kissed him instead.

This time, it wasn't rushed or nervous or uncertain. They were alone. No cameras. No prying eyes. At first, it was a slow brush of their mouths. His lips growing gentle but sure as they kissed again. And again.

Each one was longer and added more pressure. Then he nipped at her bottom lip.

As Everly opened her mouth to him, he rose eagerly from his seat, grasping at her waist and pulling her to her feet. She grabbed for the front of his shirt, balled it in her fists.

His tongue swept softly into her mouth, and little bursts of heat exploded at her center, below her waist. She suddenly couldn't get him close enough, and she tugged on his shirt, pressing her body more tightly against him.

They stumbled back toward the couch, refusing to separate, the sound of kissing turning to occasional moans. The sun had begun to set and the only light left in the apartment was over the dining room table, shrouding them in semidarkness as their legs tangled and they fell together onto the couch.

Everly was wearing a dress, and it was both a blessing and a curse when he settled between her legs. The only thing standing between her and the hardness pressing against the fly of his jeans was her increasingly damp underwear, and it was an effort to keep herself from writhing against him.

It had been too long since she'd been touched by anyone but herself, and her body ached with the want of it.

The want of *him*.

Their kisses grew hungrier, their mouths open, their tongues dancing in a perfect rhythm of pressure and release.

His hands roamed her body, sliding up her sides, curving around her waist to her back, and coasting over her ass. His mouth got the same idea, leaving her lips swollen and her breath gasping as he traced the softest of kisses down to her jawbone and over her neck.

"I want to touch every part of you," he whispered into her collarbone. "Taste every part of you." The low gravel of his voice rumbled over her skin.

Oh god. He was a talker in the bedroom. The irony.

"Do it. *Please.*" There was a shudder in her voice, and she arched herself against him.

His mouth dipped to her breasts, kissing between them, below them, across her nipples, over the fabric of her dress and bra. If Everly had had a match, she would have lit her clothes on fire so those lips, those hands, could be on her skin.

Soon he'd reached her belly button. The peak of her thighs. He was slow. Methodical. Torturous. As he slid the hem of her dress up to her waist, his fingers moved like he was performing delicate surgery.

They teased the elastic of her panties, lifting it lightly off her skin, exposing her most sensitive parts to the cool air, only to let it settle back down a second later.

His mouth found the same spot, and this time Everly couldn't hold back the sound that slipped from her lips. Somewhere between a groan and a sigh. A plea.

"Please," she whispered again.

Her hips bucked, trying to angle his face where she wanted it.

He complied with one of those butterfly kisses, so soft she wasn't sure it was real. He inched her underwear to the side before he applied any pressure, and she was seconds from erupting when his mouth finally rested firmly against her.

She made the loudest moan as his tongue parted her. Her skin grew hot and humid, and it felt like a warm wind was blowing across her face.

At first, she couldn't place the sensation. Maybe she'd never had sex so great before, and this was what it felt like. You hallucinated as all your blood raced to one part of you.

Could that create phantom scents, too? Because something smelled vaguely like meat and pond water.

Logan slowly dragged his tongue up the length of her, and then softly back down, urging another moan from her. Everly's body crept quickly toward an orgasm. Everything hot, tight, throbbing.

Just as he found that perfect spot, she turned her head and opened her eyes.

Only to find herself staring at Ravioli's gaping mouth, his dog breath fanning her face. Before Everly could react, he eased forward and planted a giant, slobbering kiss across her cheeks.

She let out a shriek and accidentally slammed Logan's head between her knees as her legs snapped together. Like someone had tossed a bucket of freezing water on her, all that heady lust and need was zapped away, leaving behind nothing but hot cheeks and a tangled dress and laughing.

So much laughing.

Logan sat back and swiped a hand over his face. He was staring daggers at Ravioli. "My dude," he muttered. "What did I ever do to you?"

"Doggus interruptus," Everly mumbled.

They both fell into another fit of laughter.

CHAPTER 22

After Ravioli had murdered the mood with his unwelcome participation, Logan and Everly had spent the rest of the evening finishing off the pizza and indulging in some Regency romance movies, which, it turned out, he was quite a fan of. He kept track of the characters' names and complicated love triangles far better than Everly did.

When it got late, he'd offered to let her crash on his couch, or as he put it, "wherever she was comfortable," but the show had paid for a rather swanky hotel room, and she'd felt too guilty not using it. Besides, after how quickly things had ignited between them, Everly could use a little alone time to simmer down. Otherwise her hormones would likely get the best of her.

He'd called a ride share, then joined her for the trip across town to make sure she got to the hotel okay. The whole time, he'd held her hand, his thumb painting the crest of her palm with soft strokes, back and forth, back and forth, until Everly's nerves were buzzing like live wires. At her hotel room door, they'd kissed, long and slow and deep, her back flush against the wood, his broad frame curled around her. It had demanded every ounce of Everly's willpower not to pop the door open and tug Logan inside with her.

There's time for all of this, she'd had to remind herself as they shared one last kiss before he disappeared down the hall. The filming might be creeping toward its final three weeks, but Everly and Logan were only at the beginning.

Now she stood bleary-eyed in the entrance to Goro's tattoo studio, repeating those words once again. Though Logan was on the opposite side of the room, deep in discussion with second-cameraman Joe, Everly's mind was preoccupied with the memory of Logan's hands on her skin, his mouth finding all her sensitive spots.

How was she supposed to exist in the same space with him and have anything but impure thoughts after last night? The universe was a cruel mistress.

Turning away, she gave herself a mental realignment. She was here for *her.* Her first tattoo. A potential new career path.

Her lady bits would have to wait.

The walls of the room were lined with Goro's art: oil paintings, water-colors, some pencil sketches and marker drawings, and, of course, photo after photo of his tattoos.

Because of the intricacy of the details, each piece looked different from every angle. What, from far away, might appear to be a flower petal glistening with water, up close had a smiling face embedded in it. A seemingly abstract design revealed words as you approached. Fan art unveiled more and more Easter eggs the longer you studied it.

There was so much precision. So much inventiveness. Tension tugged at Everly's shoulders as she wandered among the framed images. She wanted to be this skilled. But she'd wasted so much time hiding herself and her art that she was worried it was too late. She hadn't been producing anything but doodles. Hadn't been putting herself out there for feedback. Hadn't been trying to grow or *do* anything. She'd been coasting, treading water since college.

She pressed a palm to the wall and leaned closer to inspect a reproduction of Ghostface from the *Scream* movies. The sketches of her tattoo in her purse, the ones she'd lovingly pored over for the past two weeks, suddenly seemed like senseless scribbles. She no longer wanted to show them to Goro.

The thought left her chest tight, and she headed for the set of chairs by the door. As she passed Logan, their index fingers hooked around each other. It was only for a second, barely a whisper of contact, nothing anyone would have seen. Yet it felt like a reflex, some natural response to his presence. They'd been doing their best to keep a professional distance all morning, but every time they got near each other, their arms brushed or their hands caught. As if their bodies couldn't help but keep tangling together.

"What are you feeling right now?" he asked.

"Overwhelmed." Everly dragged a hand through her hair. She needed to say more. That was the only way to make the audience connect with her, to help them feel what she was feeling. If she could get them behind her, Sady wouldn't need to force a love story into her episodes. Then Everly and Logan wouldn't have to worry about hiding. They could just *be.*

She cleared her throat. "His work is so . . . incredible. I know he's been at it longer than I have, and that I have plenty of time to improve, but it feels like some people are born with this spark that you can't practice into being. Some people just have *it*. You know? Goro has it." Her eyes traced over a thigh tattoo of an intricate garden that looked like something out of *Alice in Wonderland*. "Maybe I don't." Those last words hurt leaving her mouth, jagged glass dragging across her tongue. She was too afraid they might be true.

"You *do*." Logan's mouth had pulled tight, but there was a softness in his eyes that now never faded around her. An affection he couldn't grump away.

Everly glanced over her shoulder for Joe, to see if he was filming. This was exactly the kind of moment Sady would want to splash all over her episodes. Like when Logan had called Everly striking at Kisses and Hugs, when he'd helped her perform at the joust tournament: every sweet thing that left his mouth seemed to make it to air. It was harder to feel like those moments were Everly's when they got shared with the whole world. She wanted a few to herself.

Thankfully, Joe was preoccupied with filling his water bottle and didn't have his camera in his hand.

She smiled uncertainly at Logan. "We'll see what the world-renowned artist has to say about that."

Logan repositioned himself, so he wasn't blocking the door to the rest of the studio. "You think he hasn't already seen your work? Do you think I would ask my friend to do this, or that he would agree to help, if you didn't have talent?"

Somehow, Everly hadn't considered that Logan would give Goro a sample of her art. What did he show him? Why didn't he consult her?

Her mind ran back through everything she'd posted on social media over the past few years, and she had to fight off a grimace. A lot of it was from late high school and early college, her many body-inclusive book covers and character designs. She'd drawn princesses with thick waists and thighs in formfitting gowns, women with small breasts in low-cut necklines, short girls in maxi dresses pooling around their feet, curvy figures in crop tops and boxy sheaths without any belts to define their waists or jackets to hide their fat. To Goro, they'd probably looked so amateur. So visionless.

The sudden appearance of Sady and Stanton from the hallway drove the worries out of Everly's head.

A short-statured Japanese man stood between them. He had dark hair, even darker eyes, and a well-trimmed chinstrap beard. Everly recognized him from his social media accounts, which she scrolled through pretty much daily.

Goro Adachi.

Her pulse burst into a gallop, the jump in her veins so frantic it must have been visible beneath her skin. This was happening. It was a huge step. The biggest she'd taken in a long time toward figuring out who she wanted to be.

Stanton beelined for her and spun her in a circle. "Excuse me. *Look at you.*"

There'd been a box of outfits waiting for Everly in her hotel room when Logan had dropped her off. A note resting on top read *Let yourself be seen.* And, in a move that was classic Jazzy Germaine, everything Everly had packed for herself (minus her PJs and underwear) had disappeared. Which meant she'd be wearing what Jazzy picked out, whether she liked it or not.

Not that there was any chance Everly wouldn't like her choices. Jazzy had a magical eye for dressing people.

Everly had whiled away a good hour trying everything on and peacocking in the mirror. Every piece had made her smile a little wider, from the tan hoodie with leopard-print sleeves, to the cerulean-blue cropped T-shirt with a floral print, to the formfitting joggers and perfect boyfriend jeans. Stylish but casual, with a hint of boho. Exactly the vibe Everly had been daydreaming about since she'd agreed to this wild adventure.

She'd chosen the cropped tee and the joggers for her tattoo consultation. Leaving her room that morning had taken a fit of bravery (there might have been a literal, out-loud pep talk, *Friday Night Lights* style), and nerves had spun her stomach like a Ferris wheel, but then she'd caught a glimpse of herself in the reflection of the elevator doors. She'd looked *fierce*. The joggers hugged her hips and ass perfectly. The top was loose, exposing a small sliver of skin above her waistband, the gauzy fabric emphasizing the shape of her ample breasts.

"I might live in this forever," she said to Stanton, smiling. She felt a million miles away from her uniform of blacks and grays and formless swing dresses.

"I support this choice." He gave Everly one final twirl.

By now, Sady and Goro had reached them. The tattoo artist was wearing a plain gray T-shirt, which accentuated his sleeves of tattoos. Instead of a series of distinct pieces, his were seamless, each image blending into the other, all working together to tell a single story.

Goro narrowed his eyes at Stanton. "How do you have this much energy before eight A.M.?" His voice was playful, though as far as Everly was concerned, it was a legitimate question. Stanton's endless stores of energy continued to amaze her.

"I'm pretty sure he's secretly a windup toy," Logan muttered from the corner.

Stanton winked at him. "You wish you could turn my dials."

"That's not how—" Logan paused mid-sentence and waved a hand, cutting himself off. "Forget it."

Goro slapped Stanton congenially on the back. "Have you ever noticed that our friend's sense of humor diminishes by a factor of ten for every hour before noon?"

Everly had a million questions. How did Goro and Logan know each other? What embarrassing stories did Goro have to share? Had he done the paw prints on Logan's arm? But those were things for Logan to tell her, when and if he wanted.

Instead, she asked, "Wait, he has a sense of humor?"

Goro let out a hearty laugh. "Everly." He stuck out his hand, his grip firm but gentle when Everly shook it. "I can already tell you're going to be everything Logan said you were."

Oh god. Her gaze shot toward the cameraman, who only shrugged, that ghost of a smile haunting his mouth. Her mind spun with the possibilities of what he might have said.

Goro waved them toward the hallway. "Let's head to my office. I'm dying to hear about this tattoo of yours."

There were only two rooms behind the waiting area, one with a tattoo chair, the other a small but spacious office. Both had a southern wall of wide windows that bathed the faux wood floors in sunlight.

Everly and Stanton sat opposite Goro at an angled table with a large tablet inlay. Sady and Joe positioned themselves behind Goro, and Logan stood behind Everly, so he could capture whatever happened on the tablet.

A scanner sat on a small table beside the desk. Goro fed Everly's sketch into it, then pulled up the drawing on the tablet's screen.

"I know this is sacrilege to some artists, but I like to start my pieces electronically. It's more forgiving while I'm figuring out the right approach. Especially when collaborating with someone."

Collaborating. Like they were on the same level. The word yanked the breath from Everly's lungs.

"This is cool." With some twists and turns of his hand, he zoomed in to inspect the image from every angle.

Everly held her breath. Silently, she noted every crooked line, the skewed perspective between the tipping cage and the flock of black birds in silhouette erupting from it. She should have used a ruler to get the bars just right, should have scaled down the birds to match the cage.

Goro had to be seeing those same things.

"Everlyyyyyy," Stanton squealed, "yessssss." His long fingers clamped down on her shoulder, and he gave her an excited shake.

"That's killer." Logan's voice was soft as it filled her ears from over her shoulder.

Sady waved her hands. "Wait, wait." She squinted at Logan. "Lean closer to Everly and say that again. Without your camera blocking your face." Then she turned to Joe. "Make sure to zoom in."

Everly's stomach clenched. Was Sady really *staging* a moment between her and Logan? Actually, not even staging, *redoing*. As if the reality hadn't been good enough.

She peeked at Logan, wondering if he felt the same. But he was smiling, pride in his eyes. He leaned down, so close she could feel the soft bristles of his beard sweep her cheek. "That's killer." The roughness in his voice danced down Everly's spine. If he wasn't bothered, then maybe she shouldn't be either.

Besides, in the grand scheme of things, this was better than Sady making stuff up. God, imagine the scenarios she'd concoct. Everly twisted toward Goro again before she let that thought go further.

He picked up a stylus and traced the lines of her drawing. "I hear this is your first tattoo."

"It is."

"Why now?"

Everly fought the urge to shrug. This was another opportunity to show the viewers who she was. "It's something I've wanted to do forever, but I couldn't figure out exactly what to get. Tattoos tell a story, and I feel like I'm just starting to understand what mine is." She watched the screen as Goro's pen flashed across it, faster than should be possible. "Or maybe it's more that I'm only now figuring out what I want it to be, thanks to this show." Out of the corner of her eye, Stanton's smile was brighter than a firework. "It's been . . . I don't know . . . really freeing to think that I can be whoever I want. That all I have to do is make it happen."

Goro sat back and stared at the image "Freedom." He tapped the corner of the screen. "Like this."

She nodded.

He didn't blink for a whole minute as he studied the series of thick black lines. "This is a great start. But I feel like you can tell your story even more clearly with a few more details." Pressing down on his stylus, he erased the open door and drew a new one, closed, at the center of the cage. "What if they're breaking out of the bars, instead of through the door?" In the gap left behind by the original door, he etched a series of bent, broken bars, curling them away from the last bird, still half in the cage, about to make his escape. Another bird carried a piece of metal in its talon.

Everly's heart squeezed. There was something beautiful in the violence of it. A reminder that change never came easy, but that it was worth it in the end.

It was exactly the first story she wanted to tell on her skin.

"You should mention to Goro you want to do tattoos, not just get one."

Logan lowered the laughably large menu in front of him, seeking out Everly's gaze with his intense blue eyes.

She forced herself to meet them, though his stare always felt like being pinned under a spotlight.

Nowhere to hide. Every part of her on display.

Thankfully, the restaurant's sound system was booming out classic rock, making it hard to focus on anything other than some guy screaming about pouring sugar on him. Neon lights danced from gaudy signs on the walls, and TVs flashed music videos from decades ago.

It was all, quite frankly, amazing.

When Logan had asked if she wanted to go for lunch before she headed back to Monmouth Cove, she'd been almost embarrassed to request they go to Sparky's. A chain restaurant where the aesthetic of Planet Hollywood met a menu of Cheesecake Factory proportions, it was not exactly fine dining. But she loved places where, if she wanted, she could order potstickers and lasagna at the same time. There was no pretension.

Still, most people thought Sparky's was tacky. And Logan's gruff demeanor didn't exactly scream "loves restaurants with an overabundance of flair and three pages' worth of appetizers."

Hence her shock when he'd agreed. "God, I love that place," he said. "Where else can you order four different kinds of egg rolls, with fillings from four different cuisines?"

Now they were poring over the menu, trying to determine how many appetizers was too many.

Everly's eyes dropped to her left forearm. Already, she could imagine her tattoo there, that first bird, in full flight, wrapped partially over the front of her arm. "I know. I meant to tell him my plans today, but then I chickened out."

"Why?" Logan's eyes drilled into her. This man should have been a detective or something. He could draw confessions out of people with nothing but a quiet stare.

"Because he's a fucking master and who am I to tell him I want to do what he does?"

"We all have to start somewhere. I didn't burst out of my mother's womb already understanding camera angles and focal lengths."

Everly waved her hand in front of her, batting the words about. "This is more like me waking up one day and deciding I'm going to write horror stories and then driving to Maine to find Stephen King and ask him to mentor me."

That concerned crinkle stitched into Logan's brow. "You said you've wanted this for a long time—"

"I have." Everly dragged her hands through her hair. If she'd learned anything over the past few weeks, it was that a part of her had been hiding long before Grandma Helen passed away. For all the confidence she had in herself and how she looked and who she was, she'd never actually believed in her art. Not enough to commit to anything. To try. To open that box. "But I've never done anything about it."

Setting down his menu, Logan reached across the table and rested his hand over hers. "That's what you're doing now." He waited in silence until she looked up at him. "Brian and I talked about the shelter project for years before we finally got going. We kept waiting for the right time, like we were going to get some sign from above or something. Finally, we just had to do it. There's no right time except the time when you decide to go for it."

His voice was gentle, but there was nothing tentative about it. Why should there be? He was right. It wasn't too late to try.

She twisted her hand so her fingers could fit between Logan's. The warmth of his strong grip seeped into her skin.

"You're right. You're right." She had to stop letting fear steer her life. It had yet to get her anywhere.

It was time to open Schrödinger's box, even if it might be empty.

Not every one would be.

On the Plus Side had shown her that. In just a few weeks, she'd been given so many new opportunities. Met so many new people who understood her.

And then there was Logan.

Everly had not been prepared for Logan. But that was what she loved about him. He'd knocked her totally off-balance. And it was exactly what she'd needed.

"I figure I'll do it while he's tattooing me. It will be a good distraction."

Logan nodded. His expression told her he'd hold her to it.

They returned to their menus, settling on the rangoon platter (of crab, buffalo chicken, and cheesesteak varieties), pulled pork nachos, and some hamburger sliders.

The waiter left the specials and dessert menus behind, and Everly began idly flipping through them.

Across from her, Logan fiddled with a straw wrapper. "Have you ever had their donut dippers?"

Everly shook her head.

She couldn't imagine being hungry for dessert after the smorgasbord they'd ordered, but it felt like a way to keep them here, together, for a little longer. Truth be told, she would have superglued their asses to the seats if given the opportunity. Her head was so quiet when he was around. No matter how loud her voice, her ideas, her presence, it was always okay with him. She didn't have to worry about finding her proverbial volume button and toning it down.

"We're getting them, then." A gentle command. As if his mind were wandering in the same direction as hers.

"Deal." She set the menu aside.

Logan replaced it with a rose he'd fashioned out of paper.

Everly gasped. Taking it carefully in her fingers, she raised it closer to her face. It was one straw wrapper, woven intricately around itself to create the illusion of petals and a stem. "How did you do this?"

He shrugged. "I spent a lot of time with Brian at his parents' Chinese restaurant when we were in middle school. His mom would set us up at the bar with a giant box of straws and a plate of crab rangoon and have us fold paper roses for drinks while we watched reruns of cop shows." He dragged his cup in front of him and took a long pull. "I *loved* his family. Those nights were some of the best of my life. I guess my fingers revert back to that ritual when I'm nervous."

"I make you nervous?"

"Incredibly."

It was the last answer Everly expected. "But I'm like a human Muppet." Sometimes, she seriously wondered if she and Fozzie Bear shared genetic material.

Logan's fingers were already at work on a second rose. "That word you came up with at the Ren faire . . . striking? That's why. It describes you perfectly."

She wanted to reply in some cool, composed way, but all her face seemed capable of was gaping at him.

"I mean, you're fucking hot, but it's not just that. When you forget to hide yourself, like when we showed up at your office . . ." He shook his head. "And then that laugh of yours. Everly, I can't breathe when you laugh. You're . . ." Again, he shook his head, letting the rest of the sentence die on his lips, as if there weren't words to finish it. Not adequate ones, anyway.

"Logan—" Hearing him talk was like watching his camerawork. He kept showing her that he saw her in ways no one else did.

"And you say these things sometimes that are so damn funny. But in a smart way. And you're quick. And my dogs love you. And . . . like this place. You get it. You get—"

"Me," they said in unison.

Everly's heart felt too big for her body. Not knowing what else to say, she grabbed a pen from her purse, then reached for his tattoo-free arm, shoving up the cuff of his sleeve to expose his inner forearm.

With a slightly trembling hand, she sketched a little cartoon cameraman, one with a dark beard and a plaid shirt and a frown on his face. The same one she'd been doodling lately on the corners of her notebooks, on receipts, and in one of her most monstrous moments, on the inside cover of the romance she was reading.

"I think you're pretty great, too," she said softly.

It was the only thing she could think to give him. A piece of art for his rose. A piece of herself for a piece of him.

Everly had anticipated a lot of things about being *On the Plus Side*. As a fan, she knew to expect new clothes, new adventures, a new sense of self. She'd known she'd laugh. That Jazzy and Stanton would make her feel heard.

But she'd never expected to feel so understood. Not by the hosts. And certainly not by this man sitting across from her. Yet every step she took, he was right there beside her. First with his camera.

And now with his heart.

CHAPTER 23

There's nothing quite like an evening in with your best friend and your rabidly judgmental mother to put a girl on edge.

All Everly had wanted to do when she got back from Boston was lounge around her living room daydreaming about the last two days with Logan, but instead she'd spent a good two hours obsessively scrubbing down her apartment in preparation for the imminent arrival of Becca and her mom so they could watch the fourth episode of *On the Plus Side* (damn Ellis and his fantasy football cult for taking over their normal viewing space).

Her mom now stood at the center of the living room, eyeing the pristinely vacuumed floor as if an army of dust bunnies was about to burst from the corner at any moment.

"Make yourself comfortable, Mom." Everly did her best to sound welcoming as she flopped down on the couch.

Her mother pursed her lips. "You're going to ruin the couch sitting that way."

"This thing was Ellis's in college. It was ruined when it got here."

Her mother's ability to disapprove of *everything,* including mundane stuff like how Everly sat, was impressive.

Practically a superpower.

A part of Everly itched to say that. God, what a relief it would be to be honest with her mother about how she made Everly feel. Because even if her actions were some misguided form of love, they hurt just as much.

But Becca arrived with Chinese takeout before Everly could organize her thoughts. Then her mother was on her feet and in the kitchen, and the moment passed.

Everly's stomach sank. She was almost positive tonight's episode would feature the family barbeque, and she wasn't sure she had the energy to sit quietly with a smile on her face while she listened to her mother tell Stanton that every dig, every criticism, every word that had come out of her mouth for the past twenty-four years had been to protect her daughter.

As if that somehow absolved her.

Becca grinned as she handed Everly a plate of fried rice and General Tso's chicken. "Sooooooo. Are we going to see more of Logan tonight?" Her best friend was terrible at winking, but Becca tried anyway, which basically translated to blinking awkwardly while trying to look conspiratorial.

Everly had a *lot* to fill her in on, but not with her mother and her inhumanly keen hearing in the vicinity.

"I suspect so." She tried to play along, being coy, but with a mouth full of fried rice, she sounded like she was trying to talk underwater.

"Any more kissing?" Becca kept her voice low.

Not that it mattered.

"Who are you kissing?" Everly's mother yelled from the kitchen. Every syllable dragged up Everly's spine like a knife.

There was no sense in lying. The episode would probably be full of scenes between them. Who knew what kind of footage Sady had strung together?

"Logan." A smile crept across Everly's face, even as she braced for the fallout. She couldn't *think* about Logan, never mind say his name, without smiling anymore. If she wasn't the one experiencing it, she'd think it was gross.

Her mother rounded the sofa, handing Everly and Becca each a can of sparkling water. Her expression was blank. "Who?"

"The cameraman from the show."

"The one who looks like he belongs on a roll of paper towels?"

Everly and Becca exchanged a look, both of them failing to fight off their laughter. It was such an accurate description. Logan would probably spontaneously combust without plaid somewhere on his body.

"Yes. Him." Honing her attention on her dinner, Everly awaited her mother's inevitable disapproval. Something about his line of work being too menial or how he looked too old for her or wasn't tall enough or any number of other petty criticisms that Penny Winters always had stored in her arsenal.

Lowering herself into the armchair, her mother raised an egg roll to her face and inspected it. "Good for you. He's handsome. And he seems kind."

"What?" Everly choked on a grain of rice.

Her mom glared at her like she was being childish. "He was early to the barbeque, and he helped me set up. He didn't say much, but he was very polite. He wouldn't let me lift anything."

"That sounds like him."

"Wait. Are you two a thing now?" Becca asked.

Everly feigned deep interest in a piece of broccoli on her plate. "We're seeing how it goes."

It had only been a week. Far too early to define anything. Even if

Everly already knew she was all in. James never crossed her mind anymore, and every love interest in the novels she read had Logan's face. Indisputable proof that she was falling hard.

"Oh my god. We should double-date," Becca said.

"First, you have to invite this man over for a proper dinner so I can meet him under the right circumstances," Everly's mother piped in.

Clearly neither of them understood what "seeing how it goes" meant. It was not the time for meeting the family or the best friend. Even if Logan already had, in a different capacity. Sady was putting enough pressure on them by including Logan in the show. Everly didn't want to add to that until she knew they were solid.

Or at least had a clearer sense of where Logan stood.

For all she knew, this was a fling to him. A way to pass some time while he was stuck hanging out in Monmouth Cove.

Thankfully, eight o'clock rolled around, shutting down their questions as Becca pressed Play and the theme music from *On the Plus Side* sang out from the television speakers.

Saved by the internet.

The episode began at her mother's house, and after a second of enthusiasm for seeing herself on TV, her mom launched into a diatribe on the many ways Logan could have better captured the interior of every room.

"Why would he film from that doorway? You can see all the dust balls on the top of the armoire."

"Why wouldn't they get a southern view of the kitchen? My granite island is the best part and you can't even see it."

From the way she was talking, you'd think *OTPS* was a home design show.

"Me and this Logan of yours will need to have a chat about what rooms in the house are best to shoot in— Oh." Her hands flew to her mouth, cutting off her sentence.

The scene had segued into Everly's mom and Stanton poring over the photo albums.

"I didn't think they'd air this," she said quietly.

"Of course they would. It's 'good TV.'" Everly threw in some air quotes, the gesture sharp and swift. Her muscles had already snapped taut, every move she made robotic.

Her mother's face paled. "You heard us?"

"Parts of it."

Snatching up the remote from the couch, Everly's mom paused the show with a shaking hand. "What parts?"

"The ones where you talked about fat-shaming me to protect me."

The words were harsh, but true. And having the truth sitting between them, out in the open rather than coiling around them like a snake strangling their air, already felt like a step toward healing.

"I—" Tears shone in her mother's eyes. When she cut herself off, a few slipped down her cheeks.

Becca rose. "I'm going to go walk Bagel."

Everly placed a hand on her friend's arm, giving it a squeeze as she passed. Though she'd love for Becca to stay, Everly had to open this box on her own. Just her and her mom, without Ellis or Becca or Grandma Helen to intervene.

The *snick* of the door closing echoed in the quiet room. The glow of the TV painted Everly's mother's face a ghoulish shade of white. On the end table beside her, her food sat untouched, the fork and knife abandoned in the middle of her egg roll like an unfinished archaeological dig.

Then, with a small cough, she straightened her shoulders and lifted her chin, finally meeting her daughter's gaze.

"I was chubby as a teenager." She tucked a strand of her blond hair behind her ear. "When I told Stanton people could be cruel, I was speaking from experience." Lifting the paper towel from her lap, she dabbed her face dry. "The fashion back then was short skirts and sheer cropped tops, and like most girls, I wanted to look cool, but when I wore those things, other kids laughed at me. One day in gym, some of the more popular girls stole my clothes from my locker, and I had to walk the halls in spandex shorts and a sweatshirt because they were all that fit me from lost and found. After that, the boys nicknamed me 'dump truck' for the rest of the year because I carried my weight in my back end, and it was on display in those shorts. It was a small school. There was nowhere to hide. I cried every day."

"Did you tell Grandma Helen?" Everly couldn't imagine her grandmother letting her mom hurt that way if she'd known what was going on.

Her mother's posture stiffened. "Your grandmother told me to ignore it. That those awful kids didn't deserve my tears or my energy." She shook her head. "Maybe she was right, but not all of us are built that way. I wanted to have friends. To fit in. To be liked and accepted." She frowned, her knuckles white from how tightly her hands were fisted against her thighs. "There's nothing wrong with that, you know."

"Of course there isn't, Mom." Everly set her plate on the coffee table and shifted to face her mother fully. She rested a hand on her arm. "You never told me any of this."

Her mother fussed again with the ends of her hair. Talking about this seemed to physically pain her. "My senior year I started helping your grandparents out on the farm and dropped a lot of weight. It changed things for me, and I just wanted to put those terrible years behind me."

This explained why there were so few pictures of her mother from before college in their family home. Her mom had always insisted they got lost in one of their moves, but Everly wondered if maybe she'd destroyed them. Or had avoided cameras to begin with.

"I'm so sorry. No one should have to go through that."

"I know you think I don't love you—"

"Mom, that's not—"

"But it's because I love you that I never wanted you to suffer like I did." She patted the top of Everly's hand, then folded her fingers in her lap. "I still don't."

Everly hated that her mother knew intimately what it was like to be fat-shamed. And she hated even more that those feelings had turned her fear into a wedge between them. Because no matter how much she loved her, Everly's mother had never been able to see past Everly's body. And because of that, she'd never truly known her daughter.

Everly sighed. "I never cared what other people thought of me. I knew the kinds of things they said, but who gives a shit? They were strangers who disappeared from my life the minute I left high school. I loved myself. That was all that mattered."

Everly would never forget what Grandma Helen had said to her in seventh grade, when she'd found an amazing sequined shirt at a thrift store but was worried about wearing it to school. She'd been afraid kids would call her a disco ball, and her grandmother had sized her up and said, "If you love it, that's what matters. You don't need anyone's permission to be yourself." Everly had worn that shirt with pride. Every day afterward, until she got to college, she'd repeated those words in her head when she woke up in the morning: *I don't need anyone's permission to be myself.* If only she'd never stopped.

She and her mother had been taught the same lessons by Grandma Helen, and yet they'd internalized them in opposite ways. Everly had learned to accept herself; her mom had learned that accepting herself might mean others didn't. It had caused them to turn into two entirely different people.

She fought the urge to reach out and hug her mom. She wanted to bury her head in her neck the way she used to when she was small, and whisper everything that scared her into her mother's vanilla-scented skin. But she wasn't that little girl anymore, and her mother wasn't a sanctuary, and if Everly hugged her right now, she'd never get the rest of what she needed to say out of her mouth. "But *your* opinion mattered to me. You're my *mom*. And the way you talked about my body, the way you looked at me, tried to hide me, tried to teach me to hide myself, that hurt. *That* damaged me."

Fresh tears leaked down her mom's face. Everly could feel some of her own sketching warm paths down her cheeks. But she felt lighter now. As if she'd set every word she'd spoken free from her chest like the birds in her tattoo.

"Was that why you stopped . . ." Her mother hesitated, clearing her throat. ". . . being yourself?"

Everly blew out a breath. "It was part of it. And losing Grandma was part of it. And I was, too." She had to take some responsibility for letting her mother's voice drown out her own.

Her mom pressed her fingers to her temples. She was fully crying now, her chest heaving with emotion. "I thought I was doing the right thing. I thought I was protecting you. I wanted your life to be easy. Everything with your father leaving was hard enough. I didn't want you to have to deal with this, too."

"I know." Everly wanted to say she forgave her; she wanted to be able to move on. But loving someone who didn't show you love the way you needed was complicated and messy, and their issues weren't going to magically vanish because of one open conversation. Not after twenty-four years of ignoring what hurt.

Her mother reached out and squeezed her elbow. "I'll try to do better."

It wasn't an apology. But it felt like a start. People couldn't change overnight. That didn't mean her mother wasn't willing to try.

Everly pulled her into a hug. They still had a lot of work to do, but tonight felt like progress.

A beginning.

A seed.

A promise.

Another way Everly's life was changing.

Subject: Season Three, Episode Four

Annette98 *2 hours ago*
OKAY FRIENDS

Where do we stand? TeamJeverly? Or TeamLoverly?

231 ♥ 453 👍 98 ✨ 10 👎

FarmGyrlME *1 hour ago*
james is the worst get him off my screen

LOVERLY 4EVA

210 ♥ 46 👍 345 ✨ 3 👎

Nan312 *35 minutes ago*

I am relatively new here, but I guess I just don't feel like Everly and Logan go together? He's so built. I feel like he belongs with someone who has a similar life style.

45 ♥ 21 👍 15 ✨ 500 👎

RosyTea *now*

my dude do you even watch this show? that is the exact attitude the hosts are trying to erase

589 ♥ 691 👍 180 ✨ 40 👎

Schuylersisters *now*

I'm with Nan. Everly needs to get to a gym if she wants to hook a Logan. Or a James. Neither of them belong with her.

4 ♥ 10 👍 18 ✨ 213 👎

CHAPTER 24

Nothing about the Seahorse Inn had changed in Everly's lifetime.

It still had the same starfish-shaped sign at the parking lot entrance, the announcement board underneath declaring FREE CABLE TV COMING SOON. The knockers on the exterior room doors remained giant clamshells, the curtains decorated with seascapes, the carpet's itchy blue piling faded to gray.

Every prom party Everly had attended had taken place in one of these rooms. Half her high school friends had lost their virginity on the creaky queen-sized beds. And for the first month after their father had moved out, Everly and Ellis used to spend Saturday nights sitting at one of these chipped Formica tables, eating vending machine snacks while their father sat on the bed silently watching TV.

Now Everly stood in the doorway of Logan's hotel room, admiring the movement of his muscles as he cleaned his equipment off the beds. The steam from the bag of fried shrimp and French fries clutched in her hand coaxed perspiration to her palm.

"Wow. The studio got you a hotel right next to Monmouth Cove royalty," she said as she set the bag on the bureau beside the TV. "No one fries sea creatures like Ollie's."

Logan was head-deep in the closet arranging his bags and boxes and his voice wafted, muffled, from the floor. "I'm honored to partake in his wares."

Okay. Seriously. The man consumed too many period pieces.

"As you should be." Everly spread out the to-go containers and organized the piles of ketchup packets and cups of tartar and cocktail sauce. Then she pulled the bottle of malt vinegar from her purse and set it next to the other condiments.

Logan snorted. "Do you have a whole grocery store in there?"

"Just a live lobster and a family-size lasagna."

That earned her another snort.

"Fries and malt vinegar are OTP," she told him.

Logan folded his arms, his head shaking slowly. "Does Jazzy know she needs to get you purses big enough for a complete mis en place?"

"Shut up. I grabbed it on the way out because I knew we were getting Ollie's." The moment he tasted one of those salty, starchy fries drizzled with a bit of tangy vinegar, he'd be eating his words. To prove it, Everly shoveled a few on a plate and topped them with a small shake of vinegar. "Try it."

He gingerly picked one up. "What's wrong with ketchup?"

"This is better." Everly hoped he wasn't a finicky eater. She already had more than enough of that with Becca.

Eyeing her like she was Snow White's evil queen offering him a poisoned apple, he nibbled the smallest bite off the end of a fry. "Shit." A second later, he was scooping them all in his mouth. "That's so good."

Everly pumped her hand in the air before dousing the rest of their fries and bringing them over to the bed. "Tell me one of your food things."

"I don't have any. I eat whatever."

"Then give me a food opinion. I *know* you have those." She grinned.

His brow furrowed, his lips dipping in a thoughtful frown. She loved how he took every question she asked him seriously, regardless of how silly it was. It made their conversations feel precious. Like something he didn't want to squander.

"Ice cream shouldn't have stuff in it," he declared.

"Stuff?"

"Cookies, candy, dough, all those lumps. It should be smooth. Creamy. You shouldn't have to chew it."

She gaped at him for a moment, then stood up. What was this nonsense coming out of his mouth? "I don't think I can see you anymore." Her hand reached down to grab her tote bag from the floor.

"Wait. Are you serious?" Logan jumped to his feet.

Everly laughed loudly. The worry on his face was adorable.

Excavating a folder overflowing with sketches and printouts from her bag, she dropped it back beside the bed. "I mean, I'm pretty horrified by that ice-cream hot take, but no. I wanted to show you these."

She gently eased open the folder. Technically, she was here to watch the fifth episode of *On the Plus Side,* but with the Cape Cod Collective just over two weeks away, she wanted Logan's thoughts on the pieces she and Stanton had selected.

"What's this?" He moved behind her and wrapped an arm around her waist, resting his chin on her shoulder so he could see the contents.

The press of his body against hers was so relaxed, so natural that a shot of adrenaline bulleted through her veins. She hoped his touch never stopped feeling like electricity.

Pausing on each one so he could see them, she flipped through the prints. "Stanton and I were thinking I should focus my booth at the Col-

lective on book covers and marketing mock-ups, since I don't have a tattoo portfolio yet." After working on the *OTPS* logo with Alex and James,
and mulling over branding for Logan's dog shelter in her free time, Everly
was ready to say she wanted to give a job in marketing a try. But she'd
still do book covers, and hopefully someday tattoos, on the side.

She'd gone so long without any dreams; she was ready to have too
many for a while.

Logan's beard tickled her neck as he angled his head forward.
Against the small of her waist, his fingers ran in circles, tracing patterns
with a feather-light touch that was causing all sorts of chaos to her insides.

His free hand reached over to page back through the images again.
"Where's the book cover with the hot chocolate?"

"Stanton thought it would be best to keep with a theme, since that
one is a contemporary romance and the rest are classic literature."

Logan made a surprised noise in the back of his throat.

"What?" Everly stepped out of his arms so she could see his expression.

"Stanton knows this stuff better than me. I just really loved that
one. There's so much atmosphere. I actually went out and bought it after
seeing the cover in your apartment."

Everly's knees threatened to dump her on the floor. She dropped
back onto the bed. "Are you serious?" She'd never thought her little pet
projects could have that kind of impact.

Logan crossed to the closet and dug in one of the bags. When he
faced her again, he was holding a copy of the sapphic holiday romance
in his hand.

Everly swallowed. "I might need to add it back in the mix then."

"Only if it makes sense."

He followed the words with a dismissive shrug, but Everly caught the flash of softness in his expression.

As if he cared about her opinion every bit as much as she did his.

"What. The. Hell."

Everly jabbed at the Pause button on the remote so hard she cracked a thumbnail.

"I didn't say any of that." On the screen, she was standing next to James, the two of them frozen in a laugh. "At least not in that context."

In the episode, she'd just lamented how the show had made a big deal about her crush. It was something she'd ranted about in one of her car confessionals, not to James's face. Yet here it was, spliced over a random shot of her and James in the conference room at Matten-Waverly. Then Sady had taken audio of James saying that they'd have to see where this goes and placed it in the clip as he turned his back to the camera, so no one could see his mouth wasn't moving.

Not one element of that scene was real.

Logan's warm hand settled against Everly's knee. "Calm down. This isn't—"

"Calm *down*?" One of Everly's least favorite phrases. It always had the exact opposite effect. Rather than taking a deep breath and relaxing, she itched to find another wreck-it room and smash something. "She's making things up now. Forget misrepresenting me. This is fiction."

She jumped to her feet and began pacing the tiny space between the beds. "Can she do that?"

Logan's mouth was a tense line. "If she's got the footage and audio, she can do whatever she wants with it."

Everly raked her fingers through her hair. She'd been trying so hard to give Sady compelling footage, to steer her away from the need for a James plot. And yet here the showrunner was, concocting her own nonsense instead. At this rate, how long before she began using body doubles to stage Everly in illicit moments? Sex sells, right?

Her steps quickened. Logan caught her hand, trying to still her. "I know it's not exactly how things happened, but Sady's just establishing some narrative. It's nothing to worry about."

Everly growled. It was the only accurate summary of her current state of mind. "Except it's a narrative I told her I didn't want."

There'd been so much more focus on Logan in episodes three and four that she'd thought—she'd hoped—that if Sady was going to push a romance story on Everly's part of the season, it would be with Logan. At least there'd be some truth to that.

But the arc was back to James. Back to everything Everly wanted to put behind her.

"What about that other thing I'd said?" *You can like someone but not want to be with them.* Sady had snuck that line in before James responded. It almost sounded like an apology, an attempt by Everly to explain away her feelings. "I never said that to James either. That was from Sunny's. You said you stopped recording that day." She yanked her hand out of Logan's and backed away until her ass was pressed to the bureau. She needed some distance so she could think.

Logan was so loyal to Sady. They had so much history. And a month ago, there'd been nothing between him and Everly. It would have made total sense for him to pretend to turn off the camera to earn her trust. To get the good TV. That was his job, right?

"Whoa. Hey." He held up his palms in surrender. "Of course I turned it off." Everly wanted to believe him. He looked as confused as she was. Then his expression crumbled. "Shit."

Everly braced herself. "What?"

"Your mic. I didn't even think. We've never turned off your mic."

Her shoulders slumped. He was right. She'd become so used to the damn thing that it felt like a vital organ. More than once, she'd strapped it on out of habit, only to get to work and realize it wasn't a filming day.

He slid around the bed so they were facing each other. "I'm sorry," he said, reaching for her hands.

Everly's heart was still slamming against her chest, but she let him take them. She let her fingers slip between his.

"I'll be more careful."

"We both will," she echoed firmly.

Logan guided her forward, then down onto the bed beside him, so they were sitting hip to hip. His thumbs drew lines up and down her knuckles. "I know this looks bad, but Sady's not trying to misrepresent you. She just wants to make sure people pay attention. That's her whole 'good TV' schtick. She'd never do anything to hurt you or the show. Not on purpose."

"But she did." Everly nodded at the TV. "I wanted my episodes to be about me growing as a person, as an artist. Obviously, that wasn't enough for her. Or I'm not enough for her." Everly tugged her hands back and pressed them to her knees. "I know this thing with us is really new, but I hate that you're taking her side."

The furrow in Logan's brow was deeper than Everly had ever seen it. Even though they disagreed, even as mad as she was at Sady, at all of this, her fingers ached to trace the paths between them. To smooth them against his forehead. "I'm not." He gently took her chin in his hand and turned her face until their eyes met. So close, she could see shards of silver among the blue in his irises. "I know her better than you do. That's all. But I'll talk to her. I'll make sure this doesn't happen again."

Everly's muscles eased a little. Logan had never lied to her before. He'd always been honest and straightforward. There was no reason to think any of that had changed, no matter how much she didn't trust Sady.

"Yeah?"

"Yeah."

He leaned in closer, as if to seal the deal with a kiss.

Everly pressed a finger to his lips.

"One more thing."

His frown dipped lower.

"Could you accidentally back your truck over that expensive purse of hers?"

Everly Winters: Dash Cam
Week 5, Day 2
7:51 A.M.

Footage opens with Everly in her car, staring at the camera.

EVERLY: I've been sitting here so long trying to figure out what to say that now I'm going to be late for work.

Sighing, she shoves her sunglasses up on her head.

EVERLY: There's two weeks left of filming, and for a long time, I thought I'd be relieved to get here. To have some privacy back, to have a say again in how I publicly present myself, what I let people see of my life. But now that we're almost done, I'm not relieved at all.

Her voice hitches, and she stops to wipe at her face with the side of her hand. She's chewing on her bottom lip.

EVERLY: I'm not good with change. I like things to feel stable and secure. I like what's familiar. There's a reason I went to college barely an hour from home, why I moved back to this town after graduation, why I live above my brother's garage. Doing this show was so scary because I knew it would introduce all these new things to my life.

She blows out a breath.

EVERLY: I've finally learned to embrace that newness. I'm so excited to try this whole tattoo thing. I think I want to go for it the next time a designer position opens up at work. I'm letting new people in. Having new experiences.

Pink tinges her cheeks.

EVERLY: In two weeks, everything is going to change again. Jazzy and Stanton will be gone. Any changes I make after that, I'll have to do myself. And I keep thinking . . . what if I'm not strong enough? What if this growth I've experienced is only because they were here to catch me if I fell?

She shakes her head.

EVERLY: What if I'm not ready to fall on my own?

CHAPTER 25

It was nine in the morning on Saturday, and Logan was idling in a black pickup truck in Everly's driveway.

"What's on the agenda?" she asked, popping open the passenger door.

There was nothing specific on the call sheet for today. Sady and the hosts were currently on their way back from a convention in Chicago, and Everly had no idea what they could film without them.

Though she'd seen him multiple times this week, settling into the cab next to Logan still caused her heart to flutter. She would have sworn his eyes were bluer than she remembered, his beard more perfectly groomed, his face more handsome.

She leaned across the console to kiss him, and Logan met her halfway, his hand doing that thing where it cradled her cheek, his palm against her jaw as his fingers cupped her ear and threaded into her hair. He smelled like winter and coffee, and the wisps of his beard tickled her skin. His mouth was warm and welcoming on hers.

It would be so easy to disappear into this man's kisses forever.

She practically groaned in disappointment when they finally pulled apart.

"Interviews around town," he said. "Sady wants me to take you to some of your favorite places and have you reflect on the journey so far. Filler stuff, basically."

Everly nodded, but internally she was scowling. Ever since Thursday's episode, the thought of Sady left a bad taste in her mouth.

She fought to keep those thoughts off her face as she smiled at him. "We could go to the beach. There's a spot not far from here that's only for residents, so it doesn't get too crowded on weekends, especially this close to winter."

He reached out his hand for hers. "To the beach, then."

The trip was only a few miles, and they crossed town in a comfortable silence interrupted only occasionally by Everly pointing out the best ice-cream shop (The Banana Splits), the best market (AJ's always had her favorite pens and the best variety of laundry detergents), and the only thrift shop in town (which rarely had her size but got excellent selections of cute jewelry).

Once he'd turned off the main drag, she pulled their clasped hands into her lap.

"How was your trip to New Hampshire?" Sady had sent him to scout locations for their next guest the day before.

He shrugged. "Fine."

He'd been so open lately that Everly's hackles immediately sprang up at his one-word answer. "What's wrong?"

His grip tightened on the steering wheel, and on her fingers. "I . . . don't want to think about a next guest. Because that means I won't get to spend my work days doing this." He waved their hands between them.

Everly watched them move. "Yeah, maybe don't hold *all* the guests' hands. I prefer to be hand monogamous, unless it's, like, a family member, or Ravioli. You can always hold Ravioli's hand."

"Ravioli has paws."

Everly never tired of the way she could derail him simply by babbling long enough. It had become one of her new favorite games. "Even better. Then they're not subject to the agreement at all."

He shook his head. "That's not what I meant. I'm not going to get to see you every day at work soon."

She knew what he'd been implying, but her heart jumped at his honesty all the same. Then it plummeted to her stomach. He was right. Soon Logan wouldn't be here every day. Neither would the hosts. Over the last few weeks, she'd grown accustomed to being surrounded by people who looked like her, who made her feel like her best self. It had started to feel . . . real. *Normal.*

She wasn't ready to give that up.

To give anything up that this show had given her.

She squeezed his hand back and tucked it to her chest. "We'll figure it out. I can come to Boston, or even New Hampshire. And one of the other guests is in Rhode Island, right? That's not too far."

"I know we'll figure it out, but that doesn't mean I have to like it." There was a red light ahead, and he eased the truck to a stop. Then he glanced over at her. The look in those blue, blue eyes was solid, sure.

"But let's get one thing straight. Nowhere is too far to be with you."

They'd been ambling across the beach for about fifteen minutes when a patch of gray clouds rolled in overhead.

Everly shook off a thick pile of wet sand slurping at her sneaker. "So maybe the beach wasn't the best idea."

Logan was keeping closer than usual while filming on account of the wind, which shoved at their limbs and slapped the water against the shore.

"But it's all so tropical. The dark gray sky, the quicksand beneath our feet, the freezing wind." He grinned at her.

"I figured this *was* tropical for you lumbersexual types. Do they even make flannel in short sleeves?"

Logan huffed out a low laugh. "I do wear other fabrics."

"Lies." Everly paid *very* (very, very) close attention to him and had seen nothing but plaid shirts for a month.

He shook his head, a smile twitching at his lips. "Assuming the sun actually shows itself here, why do you love this beach so much?"

Casting her gaze out across the water, Everly fought back the loose strands of hair whipping around her face. "It's a lot of things. The artist in me likes the different textures. The sand and the water and the rocks. And sea glass. I keep mason jars of sea glass all over my apartment. One day I want to do some kind of collage or mural with it."

"On the shelves above your TV?"

She nodded. He never missed a detail.

"But more than that, there's something comforting about all this space." She stretched her arms out to indicate the length of the beach. "When I was younger and had a really shitty— er . . . crappy day—"

He snorted. "Nice save."

She gave a little curtsy, then blushed when it summoned a full smile from him. One where his eyes crinkled and that furrow in his brow smoothed out and he looked five years younger.

"Anyway, when I had a crap day I'd come here and look out at the water, the way it expands out to the horizon with no end in sight, and I'd realize that the world is bigger than whether I'm wearing the right brand of shoes, or have to get the free lunch, or the C on my math test, or whatever was upsetting me. There's all this out there," she gestured again with her arms, "and that moment of being upset is just that: a moment."

They were moving away from the houses that lined the shore to the craggy rocks at the border. Everly got as close to the water as she dared, scanning the ground for sea glass.

A crescent-curl of lilac caught her eye against the grayish-brown sand, and she bent to pick it up.

A few steps away she spotted a small sea-green piece, and farther still, a flat sphere almost the same color as Logan's eyes. She placed them on her palm to show him.

"Why sea glass?"

She shrugged. "It's pretty. Whenever I see it, my mind instantly wants to make something. Or draw something. And I love that they have a story, you know?"

"What do you mean?"

She picked up the blue circle. "At some point, this was the bottom of a bottle. Now look at it. It's something else entirely." He offered his hand, and she pressed it to his palm. Her fingers lingered for a second against his skin. "Transformation. It's like what this show does." Her hand fell back to her side. "What I hope it's doing for me."

He opened his mouth to say something, then closed it again. "How have you felt about being on the show so far?" he asked instead.

She exhaled, long and slow. That question felt like another reminder that everything was coming to an end. "There's things I've loved as much as I knew I would. Like meeting the hosts, shopping with Jazzy, Stanton making me get myself together at work. Even him talking with my mom that day at her house, it opened up a space for us to be more honest with each other." She scuffed her shoe against a mound of sand. "I don't think we'll ever have a perfect relationship but I think we understand each other a little better now. And I think, over time, that will help. And the tattoo stuff. That tattoo is my dream . . ." Everly let her voice fade into a strong gust of wind that buffeted against them. Logan had been a huge part of her transformation as well, but with the camera on, she couldn't get the words out. It was too intimate. Too much of an acknowledgment of what was growing between them to give to an audience.

To give to Sady.

She looked away from him, toward the sky, which was much darker. The smattering of clouds had thickened to a charcoal canvas, and the threat of a thunderstorm pressed against her skin.

"We should probably—"

The words hadn't fully left her mouth when the first raindrop splashed against her shoulder.

CHAPTER 26

Water dripped from Logan's long eyelashes onto his cheeks, slipping off the smooth skin under his eyes and catching in his beard.

Everly watched the tracks it drew over his face as the two of them sought shelter in his truck. It had been at least ten minutes, and the drum of the sudden storm against the windshield and roof had not let up.

The rain had started too quickly, catching them in the downpour. Logan had been forced to tear off his plaid shirt to protect the camera, leaving him in nothing but a thin black T-shirt as they ran for the truck.

By the time they reached it, they'd been soaked to the bone. And soaked they remained, even with the heat blasting from the vents. The fabric of Everly's dress clung to her skin, and her hair was plastered to her scalp. Logan was not faring much better: his T-shirt shed water over the seats, and dripped more moisture onto his already soaked jeans. Everly cringed. There were few things worse than wet jeans.

She held her hands in front of the heat. "This isn't stopping any time soon."

"Agreed."

"There's a dryer in the garage at my place. We could warm up and get those—" She motioned vaguely toward his lap, then immediately flushed in embarrassment. Were they at the point where she was allowed to acknowledge his lap and what it contained? "—dry."

He scratched the back of his neck, a sheepish smile dawning on his face. As if he was wondering if they were in lap territory, too. Or what activities they might participate in that involved his lap.

Her blush deepened tenfold.

As he navigated back to her house, Everly fiddled with her phone. She couldn't remember how long it had been since she'd opened the Read-It app, and yet that itch remained. Part of her was dying to see what her favorite contributors thought of her episodes.

Resisting the urge, she dropped the phone in the cupholder. She needed to stop letting other people decide how she felt about herself. She'd become so worried about everyone else's opinion of her that she'd lost sight of her own. Reading what they had to say, good or bad, was going to mess with her head. If they liked her, she'd panic about how to keep that going. And if they didn't, she'd believe them. Neither was useful to the new Everly she was trying to become.

Logan's eyes strayed briefly from the windshield, finding her phone and then her face. He didn't say anything, but she saw the furrow in his brow that she now knew preceded a question.

"Have you read any of the things people are saying about me?" Everly smoothed her hands over her wet skirt. Droplets of cold water raced over her knee and down her leg. "About us?"

"I refuse to feed the trolls."

"I've been trying to do the same, but Becca told me about some stuff she's come across, and it's . . ." Everly's shoulders stuck at her ears in a half shrug. ". . . brutal." Last night, the two of them had been sitting at the kitchen table, waiting for their chocolate-chip cookies to bake, and Becca had pulled up the forums. "I don't want you to stumble upon these by surprise," she'd said. She'd also offered a few creative (and probably physically impossible) things that these trolls could do with themselves.

Everly cleared her throat. "There's the usual comments about my weight—which, no surprise, people online aren't exactly known for their originality—but then there's stuff about how you and me make no sense."

"We make perfect sense." His tone was so serious, so *sure,* that her bones liquefied.

"They don't think so. Because I look like . . . well . . . me . . . and you look like you." Everly didn't buy into that bullshit that people's appearances had to match. Tens with tens, and all that. Nor did she think fat people couldn't be hot or have hot partners. But she'd be lying if she denied that it stung to have outside observers doubt what felt so right to her.

"We look pretty excellent together." They were stopped at a red light, so Logan grabbed her phone from the cupholder and leaned in, his cheek cradled against Everly's soggy scalp, and snapped a selfie.

He handed the phone back to her.

They were a mess: hair matted, clothes soaked, cheeks red from the truck's heat. And yet they were beaming.

He was right. They looked perfect.

"Anyone who doesn't think this works is an idiot," he said.

She angled over the center console to kiss his cheek.

The downpour was still in full swing when they reached her house. The two of them dashed from the cab of the truck to the side door, which, bless her brother, had an awning, since it took Everly more than one try with her slippery fingers to get the key in the lock.

Goose bumps popped up along her skin at the chilled air in the garage.

No one actually parked in there, and for a hot minute before he married Becca, Ellis had tried to make it his man cave, but now it was where things went when no one knew what else to do with them.

They'd cleaned out enough of the clutter to create a little laundry area for Everly so she didn't have to go into the main house if she didn't want to. There was a counter to fold clothes on and a drying rack for delicates and an old couch so she could read while she waited.

Logan idled in the middle of the space, hugging his arms to himself to keep warm.

"I'll go find us some blankets or something," Everly said, heading upstairs. "And then we'll get our clothes dry."

Of course, this was her weekend for laundry, and the few extra blankets she had were stuffed in her hamper from the last time Becca had crashed up there.

Everly rushed to her room, her body buzzing, cognizant of every second she left Logan alone downstairs, as if he might disappear if she took too long. Digging through the carcass of a wardrobe Jazzy had left behind, she found a cozy oversized tunic and a pair of leggings for herself. But for Logan? She was stumped. He was too stocky to fit into anything of hers, and the idea of borrowing something from her brother felt way too weird.

Thankfully, in the bottom drawer of her dresser, she came across a maroon Claymore hoodie Jazzy had dug out of the back of Everly's closet. It was oversized and cozy, and she'd passed many long nights of studying at the library buried in it. It would have to do.

Logan hadn't moved from where she'd left him, except to empty his phone, wallet, and keys from his pocket onto the couch.

She offered him a towel and the hoodie. "This was all I could find."

"I'd take a dry napkin at this point," he quipped.

As she tossed him the clothes, thunder rumbled over their heads, and a shiver raked through Everly's body.

"Okay, I need out of this wet dress." She'd been spread out on his couch half-naked a week ago, so she thought nothing of grabbing the bottom of her sweater dress and pulling it up.

Logan, however, choked on his surprise.

And because she was the least smooth person in existence, the wet fabric of her dress got tangled in her arms, knotting around her shoulders and trapping her. She couldn't even blame the camera for this disaster.

"You okay over there?" His voice was playful.

"I'm grand. This is my favorite way to wear this dress." She struck a pose, bending a knee and popping one hip like they always did on *Top Model*.

She could hear him laugh softly.

But his gaze was serious when he pulled the dress down past her face and their eyes locked. He didn't so much as blink as he brushed his palms up her arms to reach the tangled fabric. With each bit he unknotted, he eased a little closer, until they were hip to hip, chest to chest, his breath spreading hot across Everly's face and neck.

Her body melted at his touch, and she couldn't help but back up until her spine hit the washing machine. Something to keep her upright.

Her heart was hammering against her ribs, and her head had emptied in that perfect way, where there was nothing but him and her. Nothing but this one moment. The thunder outside went silent. The proximity of her brother's house disappeared. The thrum of the rain became a whisper that was barely a breath beneath the scream of her blood. The pulsing need at her center.

"There," he breathed, and her dress went slack against her shoulders. Everly raised her arms so he could guide it over her head.

She didn't hear the fabric hit the floor because his hands were cupping her face and guiding her lips to his, and all she could think was how much she wanted to kiss him.

And as much as she wanted to be patient, to wait until his lips found hers, the hunger won.

She leaned forward until their mouths slotted together, and her hands burrowed into the hem of his wet T-shirt, yanking it taut against his chest. Everly's skin burst to life at his touch, at the gentle scratch of his beard against her cheeks.

His tongue teased the seam of her lips, and she parted them slowly, enjoying the way she ached for him. To touch him. To have him touch her. For their bodies to come together wherever they could.

She lifted herself onto the washer and let her legs slide apart. Logan moved between them, and the bulge in his jeans pressed against her exactly where she needed him. A moan stole its way out of her mouth, which only encouraged him to grip her waist and arch her closer.

She wore nothing but her bra and underwear, and he was fully clothed—and still damp. They needed to change that. She wanted the feel of his warm skin against her everywhere.

Deepening their kiss, she ran her hands along his shoulders and down his back. Taking a handful of the cotton in her fists, she dragged his shirt toward his shoulders.

With a start, he jumped away, yanking the hem back into place.

Embarrassment barreled through her. Had she completely misunderstood what was happening? Everly snapped her knees together and crossed her arms over her chest, hiding herself as much as she could.

"Shit. I'm sorry," he said.

She struggled to hold his gaze. "What did I do? I thought—"

"You didn't—"

"—you wanted this."

"I *do*." He moved back toward her, anchoring his hands on either side of her against the washer, palms down, so she had to look him in the face. "I *really* do."

"Then what . . . ?" The rest of the question died between them.

Sighing, he tipped his head back toward the ceiling. It was a minute before his gaze returned to her, but when it did, it had regained that solidity. That sureness. "I have my own . . . stuff, with my body."

She laid her hand tentatively on one of his perfect biceps. "What do you mean?"

Another sigh. "The last girl I dated, a year or two ago, when we hooked up the first time, I took my shirt off, and she stopped, in the middle of things, and just said . . . 'Oh.'"

"*Oh?*" Everly's eyes narrowed.

"Yup." He paced away from her. "I asked what was wrong and she told me, 'With your arms, I thought you'd be more . . . fit.'"

Anger ricocheted through Everly. What the hell. Who would *say* that to someone? And not just anyone. This man? Who was kind and honest and funny. Who gave weird dogs a good home. Who saw to the truth of you when you couldn't see yourself.

She dropped from the washer to her feet. "What's her name? I just want to talk." What Everly really wanted to do was kick her. In both shins.

That yanked a laugh out of Logan. "Everly." He really hit all the syllables this time, like he knew exactly what it did to her. "It's fine."

"It's *not* fine. You're perfect. She's a fool. And an asshat."

He laughed again. "You haven't even seen me."

Everly was the one with the steady gaze this time. "Then show me."

His brow furrowed so deeply that for a moment she thought he'd refuse. But then he gripped the bottom of his T-shirt and pulled it over his head. From the tension in his arms, it seemed like he was fighting the urge to cross them over his chest.

Her eyes traced over him.

Those beautiful biceps. A light layer of dark hair across his chest, a little roundness in his belly. She was right. He was perfect.

She approached him, and this time she explored him with her hands, her mouth. The ridges of his arms, the expanse of his broad chest and shoulders, the softness of his stomach. With each kiss, she whispered the word "perfect" into his skin.

It seemed to ignite something in him, because when she looked up, his blue eyes were ablaze.

Their mouths collided, and as they kissed, he pushed Everly back toward the machines again. Her eyes were closed and her mind was occupied by all the ways they were touching each other, but she could tell he'd slid her up onto the dryer.

His hands unhooked her bra, and as soon as her breasts were free, he buried his face in them. One of his arms locked around her waist to keep her close, while the other fought with his belt and zipper.

The sound of it lowering was a shot of lust to her system, and her hands fumbled to help him drag the damp denim down his legs. Now there were just his boxers and her underwear between them as they rocked together.

His hands and mouth teased her nipples, and her own fingers traveled beneath the elastic waistband of his shorts to grip him in her palm. The feel of him was enough to summon another groan from her lips.

Everly couldn't remember the last time she'd wanted someone inside her so badly. "Do you have a condom?" she whispered into his neck. She wasn't sure she had it in her to go all the way upstairs for one.

"Mmmmm."

"Is that sex for yes?"

His laugh was heady and low, almost a growl, and somehow the fire inside her rose to a new level of heat.

"I'm taking my time." His hand maneuvered between them, and she could feel his finger exploring the edges of her panties. He kept teasing her with light pressure and then taking it away, the trace of a finger over her, the heel of his hand pumping against her in exactly the right spot, and then nothing. Just her writhing, aching.

He must have seen how close she was getting just from want, and he stepped back to gather her dress and his clothes from the floor.

"Is this really a time for chores?" she muttered. She could barely hold still in his absence, and she was about ten seconds from taking care of things herself.

His eyes locked on her and stayed there as he crouched to open the dryer door and toss the garments in. As he stood, his mouth traced a hot path up her leg. When he reached her center, he pressed his lips to it once, then his tongue, before rising to his full height.

He pulled her against him, one arm anchoring her waist, the other fooling with the dials of the dryer.

She didn't realize what he was up to until the dryer started, and where she was sitting began to buzz, warmth spreading across it.

It was like sitting on a fucking vibrator.

She was going to die of pleasure. This man was going to kill her.

He slipped her underwear off in that same slow, methodical way he did everything else. By the time he'd shed his own boxers and put on the condom, Everly couldn't imagine how ready her body was for him.

The moan she released when he entered her was so loud she didn't recognize her own voice.

She'd had sex with a few other men: two high school boyfriends, one in college, and a regrettable one-night stand a few weeks after graduation. But sex had never felt like this. Her entire body thrummed with need. She was like a live wire. A fuse that had been lit. She was aware of every piece of herself and where it met him, and how it felt.

Her hands memorized his angles and edges like she would an object for sketching. Light etches at first to feel out his shoulders, his back, the impeccable curve of his ass, the fine-hewn cliffs of his biceps. The length and width of him.

Each touch grew deeper, more certain, until she could feel his shape. Understand it.

His hands couldn't seem to let go of her. If she was sketching, he was molding. Cupping her breasts, cradling her ass, palming her thighs.

They were moving faster now, and like everything else with them, they matched each other. Moving in rhythm, even breathing in time together. Keeping pace. Giving the other what they needed.

Right before she went over the edge, his mouth rested at the shell of her ear. In a deep, graveled voice, he whispered, "I hope you know you're perfect, too."

CHAPTER 27

"Sady will probably be pissed you didn't get this on camera," Everly quipped.

She and Logan were lying together on the old couch in the laundry nook, her Claymore sweatshirt draped over them like a makeshift blanket. The rain's patter filled the silence, blending with the rumble of the dryer as their clothes tumbled inside it.

Everly's face flushed. She'd never be able to think about doing laundry the same way again.

Logan let out a gruff laugh. "She's not looking to direct porn."

"But sex is 'good TV.'" Everly raised her arms enough to throw air quotes before nestling them back under her head, which was pillowed by his chest. "She must have tried to get you on camera endlessly when you two dated." She'd always wondered if there were feelings fueling his intense loyalty for his boss, but joking around about it was the only way Everly felt comfortable fishing for that particular truth.

Logan let out a noise somewhere between a snort and a grunt. "We never dated. Sady has a type, and I am not it." He spoke it matter-of-

factly, no different than if he were describing the weather or a particularly unexciting wall color.

Everly angled her face so she could see him. "So what you're saying
is she has no taste."

The warm breath of his laugh brushed through her hair. "I'm not tall
enough, or jacked enough, or rich enough."

None of that said he wasn't interested—or had never been interested—
in Sady. Just that she would never date him. Everly's stomach twinged at
the thought, but she tried to chase it away. He was here with her. And he'd
never made her feel like that was a concession.

She pressed a light kiss to his collarbone, savoring the way he grasped
her hip in response, his fingers digging gently, but firmly, into her skin.
"Again, no taste."

"Says the woman who used to be infatuated with a clone of Thor."

Everly pursed her lips. She didn't want to think about James. They'd
barely acknowledged each other since the day after Harry's, and the more
distance she got, the more she realized her feelings had been nothing
more than a defense mechanism. Another way to stay safe.

Fine.

Hidden.

"First of all, Thor, like Ryan Reynolds, transcends sexuality. They're
hot to everyone, regardless of preferences."

Logan merely shook his head, but the little smile on his face told her
he didn't disagree.

"Secondly. I've come to my senses. My type is clearly mountain man/
lumbersexual."

His expression softened further, and he leaned forward to kiss the
top of her head. Everly guessed it was as close as someone that grumpy
would get to melting.

Her cheeks flushed. She didn't want to keep harping on this, but now that they'd proverbially invited Sady and James into the room, Everly needed to know where Logan stood on what was happening on the show. "Does . . . does Sady know we're doing this?" She gestured between them. And squawked when she realized what her question sounded like. "Not the sex, obviously, but us dating?"

He chuckled, and his eyes pored over her, slowly, like she was a book lying open for him to read. "I haven't told her, but I think she might have her suspicions. Why?"

Everly sat up to face him. Outside of their little bubble, the air was still cold, and it dragged chilly fingers up her skin. Snatching the shirt she'd brought down for herself, she shrugged it on. "It feels . . . I don't know . . . shady for her to bring James back into the show when what you and I have going on is . . . real." In five episodes, Everly's arc had gone from unrequited love, to a growing connection between her and Logan, to a love triangle which, judging by Thursday's episode, Sady was literally writing herself. Everly didn't want any of the fiction to impact what was actually happening between her and Logan.

"She's not—" He stopped, his eyes narrowing as he heard himself. "What I mean is, I know she can come across a bit overbearing, and her methods may seem a little unorthodox." Everly cocked her head, her retort already poised on her tongue, but he rested a hand lightly on her thigh to quiet her. "Especially when you're the one she's editing. But she knows how to make waves. How to get people to notice what she's doing. I trust her process because I've seen it work. And I believe in what she's doing with this show."

Everly crossed her arms. "I do, too, obviously. You don't have to tell me how revolutionary this show is—I've been waiting for something like it my whole life. After I watched the very first episode, I wore leggings outside the house for the first time in a year. Jazzy's rant about how clothes should be for everyone hit me exactly where I needed it." She sighed. "I know the show needs new viewers and high ratings. But it feels like Sady's desire to grow her audience is more important than representing me or my life authentically." She swallowed against the lump in her throat. "I spend a lot of time wondering why she picked me if she doesn't think people will care about my story without all these embellishments."

Everly was proud of her diplomacy, because she had some less-than-kind words for what she thought of Sady's edits. Her fingers tugged at the waist of her shirt.

Logan laid a hand over hers to still them. "She picked you because your story is real, and raw, and relatable." His fingers slipped between hers, and he gave them a squeeze. "Everyone has felt the way you do."

He slid closer and set his legs on either side of her, then wrapped his arms around her waist. Leaning down, he snuck his face beneath the collar of her half-buttoned tunic, brushing the ghost of a kiss to her clavicle. "So I lied earlier. I have looked at the comments."

Everly jerked back. "What? Why?"

He shrugged. "I'm on the show, too, now. I was curious what people were saying."

She rolled her eyes playfully. "The allure of fame comes for all of us. Even the lumberjacks."

With a shake of his head, he kissed her neck again, this time adding a tease of teeth. A love bite for her oh-so-biting sarcasm, obviously.

"And under the romance stuff, there are a lot of people who really connect with you. Who have felt like they were too much or chose to hide to feel safe or who didn't know how to follow their dreams." With one last kiss, he eased back so he could gaze into her face. "Some of them talked about doing things they were scared to do after watching you do the same. The story you're telling matters, and it's making a difference, even through all the . . . noise . . . of Sady's approach."

His words gave Everly that naked, torn-open feeling, even as they buoyed her. The idea that people were seeing the truth of her in the episodes—and that it *helped* them—filled her heart to bursting, but it also felt like a lot of responsibility. What if she failed? What if she couldn't handle a tattoo artist apprenticeship and get a design job? What if no one liked her book covers? What if she did all those things, but she was bad at them? What kind of impact would that have on the viewers who supported her, and on the show and what it stood for?

She leaned her forehead on Logan's shoulder and settled her body against his. The arm with his tattoos was draped across her lap, and she traced a finger over each of the paw prints. "What were their names?"

"Cashew, Jewels, Toby, and Sundae."

"Sundae? Like the dessert?"

He nodded.

"Oh my god." Another incredible dog name. Someone needed to give this man a trophy. "Please tell me about this dog."

He rested his chin on her head. "He was the best dog who ever lived."

"Ravioli and Alan will be pretty put out when they hear that."

He laughed. "You love every dog a little bit differently. Your heart grows to make room for them, because they each take up their own spot." He ran a finger over the shell of her ear. "Sundae was my dog when I was a kid. I told you I had a pretty shitty childhood."

Everly gave his arm a gentle squeeze to signal she remembered.

His Adam's apple bobbed against a hard swallow. "My parents . . ." Logan scratched his beard, his eyes shifting to the floor. "They fought a *lot*. And they took their anger out on me. It sucked. That dog was the only one who made me feel loved." He blew out a breath, and his jaw flexed, like the words were hard to get out of his mouth. "Sundae and I would sneak out for a walk when they started yelling. When one of them called me lazy or useless for leaving a shoe in the wrong spot or a dish on the counter, he'd let me cry into his neck until I felt better." Logan's eyes sank shut, and he paused for a long time, gathering himself.

"They didn't want the hassle of an aging dog, so they surrendered him when he got old. I visited the shelter every day. It was the only thing I could do." His body stiffened, and he cleared his throat. Everly's stomach twisted. A part of her knew what was coming, and she wished she could press her temple to his, absorb the next details so he didn't have to share them out loud. "No one ever adopted him. He died in that cage. And even though I was, like, thirteen at the time, I swore I'd do better by others someday. To make it up to him."

"That's why you adopt the older ones." Everly pressed a hand to his heart. The pain in his voice was palpable, and a sadness sat heavy on her bones. She knew firsthand how much animals could comfort kids. She couldn't imagine what it must have been like for him to have to say goodbye to his dog in such an awful way when his life was already so tumultuous. She deepened her touch. It was the only way she could think to make sure he knew she was there. That she was hearing him.

That she was listening with her whole self.

"Exactly," he said softly.

"My grandmother started the sanctuary for similar reasons. She wanted animals to have a place to live out whatever was left of their lives, comfortable and in peace."

"That's why this thing Brian and I are doing means so much to me. If we can get it off the ground, it could give so many dogs a chance. Make sure they're healthy. Socialize them. We'll hire trainers to work on behavioral issues caused by abandonment or bad owners. We'll give them that love until they find a new home."

An idea popped into Everly's head. She rose up onto her knees in excitement. "Sundae's Sanctuary."

His brow wrinkled. "What?"

"The name for your program. Sundae's Sanctuary."

Logan's eyes grew glassy, but a smile pulled at his lips. "It's great."

Everly sat back on her heels, her head racing as quickly as her heart. The joy on his face was a shot of helium into her system. She wanted to make him look like that all the time. Every second of every day. "Send me pictures of Sundae, or at least some reference photos of what he looked like, and I'll work him into the logo." The graphic was already forming in her head: a dog curled up in a ball, sleeping peacefully, his expression soft and relaxed, with the name above him in a dreamy cloud.

Grabbing a pen and a novel she'd left next to the couch, she flipped to one of the blank back pages and sketched it out. The happiness in Logan's face shone a little brighter with each line she scratched across the paper.

"We could make Sundae a kind of mascot. Cartoony but with the essence of your dog. He could show up on different pages of the website, on your cards and materials. Maybe you could have some stuffed animals made for brand awareness."

Logan pulled her in for a kiss. She sank into the sensation of his mouth on hers, letting herself get lost in it. In him.

When they pulled away, he shook his head, almost dumbfounded. "You're brilliant."

"I'm all right."

But in her head, she was already creating a style sheet for the company, a presentation for her boss.

Because for once, she didn't want to wave Logan's compliment away. She didn't want to deny it.

Because she believed it.

CourtK *3 days ago*

Ex

cuse

me

Did Everly just kiss JAMES???? What about Logan??? This is bullshit.

430 ♥ 237 👍 112 ✦ 219 👎

Annette98 *3 days ago*
Listen, I am TeamLoverly as much as the next person, but I say,
take it where you can get it, girl. People hardly believe someone who is fat can get one person, so if E wants to pull two, I
say more power to her.

409 ♥ 98 👍 75 ✨ 55 👎

KelseyisHere *3 days ago*
I get what youre saying @Annette98

but Logan is so clearly all in

he deserves better than this

211 ♥ 287 👍 168 ✨ 15 👎

FarmGyrlME *3 days ago*
I may have broken my tv from throwing the remote at it

if it is broken, everlys getting the bill

no one treats our plaid cinnabun this way

341 ♥ 766 👍 112 ✨ 67 👎

CHAPTER 28

Everly Winters: I'm not saying a word until you switch my mic off.

Logan was standing two feet in front of her, but Everly sent the text anyway.

They'd ducked into an alleyway around the corner from the restaurant Stanton had chosen for Everly and her mom to have a bonding moment. But her mom was stuck in a meeting, Stanton was running late, and Sady was on the phone putting out a production-related fire (metaphorically—Everly hoped).

When Everly and Logan realized they were on the sidewalk alone, Logan had powered down his camera and waved her toward the relative privacy of the alley. But now that she knew Sady's secret to catching stolen moments, Everly didn't plan to give her any more.

Her phone pinged.

Logan Samuel: Turn around.

She obeyed, angling her back toward him, and lifted the hem of her white sweater so he could access the battery pack hooked to the waistband of the maroon corduroy skirt Jazzy had picked for this outing.

It was quiet enough between the restaurant and the small boutique furniture store next door that she could hear the telltale *click* when he found the Power button.

Before she could face him again, he slid his palms along her bare stomach. His skin was hot against hers, and that familiar shiver of want danced through her.

Everly twisted in his arms until they were face-to-face, and his roaming hands trekked across her back. Their mouths collided in a kiss, hard and deep and hungry, full of all the things they wanted to do right now but knew they shouldn't.

The threat of getting caught by a passerby or someone from the show only increased the thrill. Everly's blood raced, lava hot, and the ache at her center swelled when Logan's hands tightened on her ass, pressing her more firmly to him and the hardness below his belt.

For a moment, she gave in. Everly let herself forget that they were in public, that Sady could catch them, could film this, could *air* it. She let go of her anger with Sady for the last episode of the show, where they'd spliced together clips of James and Everly at the bar, the two of them dancing, their kiss, smiling as they'd taken shots. To anyone who didn't know the truth, it looked as if they'd gotten together, and from what Becca had told her, everyone online saw it that way. And tons of them were mad at her for betraying Logan.

At least she didn't have to deal with the fallout from James, since they were still barely speaking. Who knew if he was watching anymore? And quite frankly, who cared? Everly was more concerned about why Sady continued to feel that downplaying her actual story was the only way to keep ratings high.

But as Logan staggered back against the stairs of a fire escape and pulled one of Everly's legs around his hips, as his hands navigated the fabric of her skirt to get underneath, her mind emptied of everything but him and how much she wanted him to touch her in all the right places. How much she wanted him in every single way.

His fingers snuck between her legs for one perfect second before the moment was shattered by the sound of a familiar voice far, far too close by.

Sady called Logan's name, and a second later, his cell phone rang. She strode to the mouth of the alley and hollered, "What the hell are you doing down here?"

Logan and Everly sprang apart, and she aimed her back at Sady as she tugged wildly at her skirt. Logan was scrambling for his camera.

Sady's phone was in her hand, but who knew if she'd actually recorded anything, since that thing seemed to be one of her vital organs.

A smirk crossed her face. "Dammit. Save that stuff for the camera, you two. That would have been such a juicy shot."

"Funny," Logan muttered.

But Everly wasn't ready to dismiss the comment. "I thought you were back on the whole James thing after last episode."

"The more footage we have, the more we can play up the love triangle, which viewers are living for."

Everly's muscles clenched. How could Logan not see that this woman's motive was ratings or bust? "I think you're doing plenty with the footage you've got."

Cocking her head, Sady folded her arms over her chest. "What do you mean?" Even with sunglasses on, her expression was innocent, like she truly had no idea what Everly was getting at.

"Sunday night's episode was more fiction than reality, don't you think?" Everly mirrored Sady's stance. Logan rested a hand on her arm, but she ignored it. She was not about to settle down.

Sady smoothed her hands over the front of her black-and-white-striped sheath dress. "All of that happened."

"But not in that order, or in that context. People think James and I are a thing now—"

Sady's face brightened. "Isn't it amazing? Don't you see what we're doing here? How huge this is?"

"We're lying to people." As if the only way for Everly to be happy and feel good about herself was to have as many guys chasing her as possible.

"We are doing something so much more important." Sady's phone pinged, but she shoved it in her purse. "When have you ever seen a fat person in a love triangle? As the point of that triangle? With two hot guys?"

Unless Logan and James were also hot for each other, it was more of a V than a triangle, but this didn't seem like the time to point that out. Especially since this so-called triangle was actually just a straight line between Logan and Everly.

"I know we're going in a different direction than we'd planned, but think about how revolutionary this is. Fans of all shapes and sizes are invested in this. You're their Lara Jean and Peter and John Ambrose. Their Nick, Kaitlyn, and Shawn. The purpose of *On the Plus Side* has always been to show that fat people have all kinds of stories, and you're having one that the world has always insisted we couldn't."

God, Logan was right. Sady's passion was infectious. Everly could already feel doubts pinching at the back of her mind. Making her wonder if she was overthinking this. If she was missing the point.

Still, she tried to hold her ground. "But what always drew me to this show was how real it is. How much it spoke to me. Your guests' lives are my life. They say the things I'm feeling, have lived through the same shit I have."

Sady's lips flattened into a line. "A lot of those moments were edited, too. But that doesn't make them any less authentic, right? It spoke to audiences regardless. Spoke to *you*."

Everly's defenses faltered a little more. She'd bought into the reality of the last two seasons, but maybe that was naïve on her part. She should have known better than to believe the truth in anything the media produced.

Was she making a bigger deal out of this than she should? Logan seemed to think so. He trusted what Sady was doing. And Everly trusted him. So shouldn't she trust Sady, too, by extension?

"James and I barely speak anymore, after his confession about nominating me." It was the last vestige of an argument Everly had left.

"I promise no one cares about that." Sady rested a hand on Everly's arm. "This will end in a way that looks good for all of us. You'll have an amazing booth at the Cape Cod Collective to show your art, you'll end up with an incredible guy, and we'll have taken the audience on a ride they won't forget. I think you'll be happy with it. And the fans will be, too." Sady gave Everly's forearm a gentle squeeze. "We can all get what we want here."

Everly glanced at Logan, who nodded in encouragement. He was obviously on her side. He wouldn't let her do anything that would reflect poorly on her.

She sighed in resignation. "I'd be more comfortable if you'd at least stop fabricating stuff. What if James sued?"

"The contracts he signed—happily, at that—don't let him." Sady gave her arm one more squeeze before dropping it. "If we wanted to, we could make him look like a serial killer and there's nothing he could do."

The right to defame clause. Sady had taken it out of Everly's contract, but not James's, it seemed. Did that mean she'd had this plan from the start?

"Well, don't do that." Everly tried to make her voice light.

Sady laughed. "I promise, we've got you." With a wave for them to follow, she headed out of the alley. "Now let's go. Your mom and Stanton are finally here, and that fresh gnocchi you're making will wait for no one."

Logan and Everly trailed behind her. His palm slipped into Everly's, and his fingers tightened reassuringly.

Before she disappeared around the corner, Sady glanced back at them. "You know," she said, "we could lighten the James side of the triangle if you two would give me a little more to work with." Her eyes narrowed, dancing with mischief. "No more hidden make-out sessions."

Everly snuck a look at Logan, and they shook their heads in unison.

Never going to happen.

CHAPTER 29

"Young man, put that camera away and sit down."

Everly's mother gestured to Logan and wagged her finger at the empty chair beside Everly.

Everly groaned, dropping her head in her hands.

Tonight was the last time filming with her family. They were supposed to be aiming for something celebratory, highlighting how much she'd accomplished over the past few weeks. All the changes and critique and self-reflection.

Sady had ordered them a fancy meal from a steak house two towns over and instructed Becca and Ellis to plate it family style, as if they'd worked together to make the whole thing from scratch. Which was exactly what Everly thought they'd done in previous seasons during the family dinner scenes, which only reinforced what Sady had said yesterday. So little about reality TV was actually real.

Everly peeked at Logan through the space between her fingers. "Mom, he's working."

"He can take a break and get to know your mother a little." She held out a bowl filled with the gnocchi left over from their cooking lesson. The one thing on the table any of them had cooked.

Everly accepted it and added some to her plate. "I think he's gotten to know you pretty well over the past few weeks, given all the hours he's had to film here."

"Where are your brother and Becca with that wine?" Everly's mother straightened her placemat. Everly had never seen her fidget this much. "Hand me your water. I'm parched."

There was a cup of water, perfectly full, sitting right in front of her mother.

As Everly passed her glass over, her eyes slipped to the camera. Everyone watching would know who was behind it, so she saw no reason why she couldn't give the guy she was dating a meaningful look when her family was being insufferable.

"Logan, why are you still standing there?" Everly's mom watched him steadily over the rim of her glass.

"I'm back," Ellis declared, bustling into the room with two bottles of wine and Becca, her hands full of stemware, in tow.

It was about damn time. If her brother couldn't be a mom buffer, what use did he have?

He pointed at Logan. "Sit, man, and explain to me your intentions for my sister."

Everly held out her hands in surrender. "You're not helping."

"Well, I'm not going to eat all this food in front of Logan while he's starving," Becca piped in.

"Et tu, Brute?"

Becca shrugged, a smirk crinkling her features.

"What if you marry him?" Ellis said. "And we were so rude. He'd never forgive us. Family dinners will be so awkward."

Everly squawked. What the hell was her brother doing bringing up marriage? Good god. She and Logan hadn't even discussed being exclusive yet.

"Why doesn't your boyfriend want to join us?" Everly's mother asked with a frown.

Her family was trying to kill her. Murder by mortification. It better be a felony charge. "Oh. *My.* God. He's not my boyfriend." Her eyes cut to Logan's face. "Right?" Her voice hitched at the end. Having a "define the relationship" talk in front of her whole family was not her most inspired choice, but now that the thought was in Everly's head, she needed an answer. "No pressure," she added with a wince. She didn't want him to think he couldn't be honest. "Wherever you are in this, I'm happy to be there, too."

Logan's gaze was a boulder. A rock. Something unbreakable. The weight of that stare pinned Everly to her seat.

"I'm all in," he said softly.

Everly's heart bashed against her ribs. For a second, she forgot they weren't the only ones in the room as she took in his unmoving expression, the heat in his eyes. "Me too," she whispered.

"Then sit down, for crying out loud." Her mother's shrill tone demolished the moment.

"Mom," Everly groaned.

Logan laughed. "How about if I set the camera up for a few minutes and sit, then get back to work? I can't have an entire segment of stationary shots, but a few are fine."

Digging a tripod out of his equipment bag, he positioned the camera a few feet back from the head of the table and came to sit by Everly.

While her mother pestered Ellis about his wine selection, Everly scooched closer to Logan and whispered, "Are you sure you're okay with this? This will all be fair game for the show. Plus, the stuff with my brother talking about marriage. Which, I am *so* sorry. I have plans to smother him with his cat tonight while he sleeps." As if she'd heard her, Cream Cheese came sashaying through the room, stopping to *meow* loudly at each of them. Ellis, though, got a hiss. Like the cat was already on board for Everly's plan.

Logan pressed a reassuring hand to her knee. "This is what she's asking for, right? So she'll lay off the James stuff?" Sady *had* said she'd love to see more between Everly and Logan. And this felt like it was on their terms. There was no hidden footage or stolen audio. Just the two of them, deciding how they wanted the world to see them.

A smile that screamed trouble settled on his face. "Besides, better to give her a cute family moment than us humping each other in an alley."

"We were n—" Everly clamped her mouth shut, her skin glowing red. Denying it would be a big, gigantic lie.

"What are you conspiring about over there?" Ellis chimed in.

"Just choosing the wedding date," Logan deadpanned. Despite being an only child, he clearly understood the art of sibling warfare.

On cue, Ellis choked on his sip of wine.

Everly swallowed back a triumphant laugh. "I'm getting a tattoo," she declared. Anything to stop further talk of weddings and prevent her mother from—god forbid—starting in on the grandbabies Everly had no plans on giving her. That was a conversation for her thirties. "In two days."

"Wait. No way!" Becca's mouth fell open. "I want one."

Everly looked at Logan.

He shrugged. "If it's small, and not something custom, Goro can probably squeeze her in, too. We have him booked for most of the morning, and small tats don't take that long."

"We're leaving at the ass crack of dawn," Everly warned. Becca, like Everly, was not a morning person.

"I don't care. I'll hook up an IV of coffee and sleep in the car." Becca reached across the table (somehow managing to avoid the food spread) and grabbed Everly's arm. "What are you getting and where?"

"On the inside of my left forearm." Everly grabbed her phone to pull up the sketch she and Goro had recently finalized and set it on the table for them to see.

"Oh. My. God." Becca pressed her hands to her face like she was re-creating the *Home Alone* poster.

Ellis let out a long whistle. "This is badass, E."

"It's beautiful." Her mother pointed at the screen. "You drew this?"

"In collaboration with the tattoo artist." Everly ran her finger over the design. "It represents freedom. How I want to be myself and stop hiding. Get out of my cage, so to speak."

Her eyes drifted toward Logan. He was one of the first people to encourage her to give in to this process.

To open Schrödinger's box.

She'd had no idea she'd find him inside.

Logan's hand was flat against the placemat, mere inches away from hers.

Everly thought about what he'd said. How they could choose what to show Sady. Control the narrative. She might not be ready to have her whole love life on film, but she could do something small. She could share something real with the viewers.

With the camera pointed right at them, and her whole family watching around the table, Everly pressed her palm over Logan's knuckles and wove their fingers together.

Everly was working on some designs for Sundae's Sanctuary on her lunch break when she heard a throat clear behind her.

She spun around in her chair. James stood there, looking uncomfortable, a hand extended to offer her a cup containing something frozen and pink. "It's your favorite smoothie from the place across the street."

"Uh. Thanks."

She accepted it hesitantly. What was this going to cost her? The two of them hadn't exchanged more than an awkward hello in days. He must be desperate for help on a project if he was not only talking to her, but had come bearing cold drinks.

"No camera today?" His gaze skittered around Reception.

"They do postproduction on Tuesdays."

"Cool."

Silence settled between them. When James didn't say anything else, Everly set the cup on the desk and turned back toward her computer.

"V." James rounded the reception counter. He waited until she looked up to speak. "I miss us."

Once upon a time, Everly would have believed they were some kind of "us," but now she wasn't so sure. More likely, there had been a her, and a him, and the things she could do for him.

"Then maybe you shouldn't have used a whole-ass TV show to tell me to stop crushing on you."

He jolted at her words as if she'd physically smacked him. "That's not what happened."

"Isn't it?"

She'd learned that James was one of those people whose niceness was dangerous. They didn't understand boundaries and it could make the signals they sent wildly unclear. Flirty and nice weren't the same. And when you were someone who looked like him, who the whole world wanted to flirt with, you could forget that.

His golden eyebrows pulled together, and he frowned deeply.

Guilt soured her stomach, but Everly tried to swallow it down. Why should she feel bad? He was the one who'd wrecked them. If there ever was a them.

"I appreciate you nominating me for the show. It's been a really great experience in so many ways." She took a deep breath. "*But*"—his frown cut further into his face—"it wasn't okay for you to decide you knew what was best for me. You should have talked to me, not submitted me to be on TV."

He scrubbed at his face, then opened his mouth. She kept talking, though. It had been so long since she'd spoken her mind so openly, and now that the words were out of her, she didn't want them back in. It was like someone had finally carved away the mountain that had been sitting on her shoulders all this time.

"Do you know how embarrassing it was to have you say that stuff to me on camera? I know I had no business kissing you, and for that I'm sorry, but you had no business touching and complimenting me when you didn't mean it, never mind grinding up on me at the bar."

His chin fell to his chest, and he scratched at the back of his neck. "I know it's no excuse, but I got caught up in the moment, I guess. You're fun to hang out with. We were having a good time. The music was great. You're a good dancer. But your guy over there," he gestured to the empty section of wall where Logan usually stood, "let me know how shitty I was being."

"What?" This was news to her. Everly jerked back against her seat in surprise.

"Yeah. He let me have it. Totally ripped into me about leading you on and being a coward."

Everly bounced a knee nervously beneath her desk. The same part of her that adored a good romance novel loved that Logan was trying to defend her, but she wanted to fight her own battles. She should have been the one telling that to James.

James cleared his throat. "I didn't mean to lead you on or embarrass you. But I can see why you felt this way."

She appreciated that he recognized it now, but in some twisted way, Everly was glad this had happened. She'd needed the distance from James this whole debacle had given her to see that he was never the one for her. That made it easier for her to get the next words out. "Why do you always ask me to help you with projects? Is it because you know I'll do it?"

"What? No. You're just better than me. And we're friends. Friends help each other out. I'm sorry if it felt like something else." The expression in his eyes was genuine.

Everly nodded. "I want credit from now on, since I'm hoping to be back there in Design with you all soon."

For the first time since they'd started talking, James smiled.

She couldn't bring herself to return it. She was glad he'd apologized, but it didn't fix anything. He'd still nominated her for *On the Plus Side* for all the wrong reasons. He'd still led her on because he didn't want to think harder about the implications of his actions. She knew now that James was someone she needed to be careful around, someone who needed a proverbial fence. Clear boundaries.

Once he'd walked away, she stood and gathered the materials sitting under her purse. Speaking so plainly to James had motivated her to do the other thing that she'd been putting off.

She left the smoothie on her desk, the contents untouched.

Bob Matten was in his office, forking pasta salad into his mouth as he watched recaps from a Red Sox game on his computer. When Everly knocked, he waved her in, a smile appearing under his salt-and-pepper beard.

Though he was probably only a few years older than her parents, there was something grandfatherly about Bob. It might have been the round bifocals, or how he wore golf shirts and khakis instead of suits, or the way he just always seemed happy to see her.

Everly perched on the edge of the chair across from his thick mahogany desk. "Do you have a second to talk?"

He smiled again. "I have many seconds for you."

She blew out a breath. "I know that in the past the company has done pro bono work for fledgling charities and organizations, and I was wondering if you'd consider taking on another one."

He encouraged her to go on with a wave.

She wrung her hands together in her lap. "I have this friend—well, no, boyfriend actually—" It had been a few days since the family dinner, but Everly could still hear Logan's words in her head. *I'm all in.* She could still feel the delicious pressure of his mouth on hers when they'd snuck from the dining room to make out on the back porch. It had felt new somehow, sharing kisses as a full-fledged couple. "Logan, the cameraman? I think you've met him."

Bob nodded. His patience bordered on superhuman.

"Well, he has this dog sanctuary that he and a veterinarian friend of his are trying to get off the ground. It would be a place for dogs without homes to be taken care of, and trained, and hopefully adopted out to families. But if not, then they'd have a safe, comfortable place to live out the rest of their years. They also want it to be a daycare and training facility and even some kind of doggie café, where the animals could be supervised while being exposed to people regularly."

"It sounds like a really great project," Bob said.

"It is. And they've got some funding in place, but their branding is very . . . homespun?"

"Ah."

Everly set her stack of papers on his desk so he could see what she'd been working on. Dummy website pages, sample logos, merchandise, social media graphics.

"If we could take them on," she said, "I'd like to do the branding work." She swallowed hard. This last part was so scary to say out loud. It was her making a decision. Finally taking a real step toward a career path, not a job. "And I hope it could be used toward possibly being considered for the next designer position that opens up."

Bob shuffled through her work, giving each page a thorough inspection. A moment later, he handed them back, and his warm brown eyes met Everly's. "Tell your Logan we're happy to take on Sundae's Sanctuary. Then finalize these and we'll have you present them to the rest of the team."

"Wait. Really?" Everly's enthusiasm raised her voice four octaves.

"Absolutely."

She jumped to her feet, clutching the papers to her chest. "Bob, thank you so much."

She was halfway out the door when he said her name.

"I've seen the work you do in your free time at your desk. And how you guide James. It's about time you asked to be promoted to designer." He gave her one more smile. "You're ready."

She was practically floating as she made her way back to her desk.

Everly had taken a lot of chances over the past few weeks, but this felt like the biggest one.

Everly Winters: Outtake
Week 6, Day 6
3:45 P.M.

The camera zooms in on Everly's arm, slowly panning over her new tattoo. Her skin is irritated from the needles, giving a red shadow to the black and gray lines. The ornate birdcage takes up about half her forearm, starting from the elbow. The top and bottom of the cage have intricate floral designs woven into the metalwork, and scrolling stretches between the bars. One side has burst open, bent bars hanging out of the cage or folded inward. A flock of blackbirds erupts from the opening. The ones closest to the cage have the most detail: outlines of feathers, wild-eyed stares, beaks thrown wide in song. The farther the birds get from the cage, the more they become shadow as they loop toward the front of Everly's arm.

She inspects Goro's work, and a large smile breaks across her face. Her eyes shine, glassy with tears.

Becca crams into the shot to show off her own tattoo: a small etching of a bagel smothered in cream cheese on the top of her foot.

Everly wrestles Logan's camera from him so she can take some footage of the new logo she designed for Sundae's Sanctuary, which he's had inked on the back of his left shoulder.

As they leave the tattoo studio, Goro is heard off camera telling Everly that he'll see her in January for the start of her apprenticeship.

She calls back, her face bright, "And maybe my second tattoo."

CHAPTER 30

Everly stared at her reflection in the dressing room mirror.

All around her hung colorful, stylish clothing that would soon follow her home to her own closet. Shiny, luxurious silks. Soft jerseys and cottons. Bright patterns. Fun silhouettes. Even without trying any of it on yet, she could already see how different she would feel.

No. "Different" was the wrong word. *More* was how she felt; more like herself. Her outside reflecting how she'd begun to feel on the inside.

She fluffed the ends of her new hairstyle.

They'd spent the morning at a nearby salon, where Jazzy and the color artist had added copper highlights to Everly's auburn-brown hair. Jazzy had cut off a few inches and added long sideswept bangs and some face-framing layers. Her loose waves now barely brushed her shoulders. Everly had cried when Jazzy turned her to the mirror. Both because she hadn't had hair this short since she was a toddler, and because she loved it.

She looked sophisticated and polished.

She looked like the person she wanted to see every time she caught her reflection.

After a quick makeup tutorial, Everly had been rushed over to Kisses and Hugs so she could try on an outfit with her new hair and makeup before lunch.

While Jazzy, Stanton, and the crew waited outside the dressing rooms, Everly studied the racks of clothes. Jazzy had said to pick whichever one she wanted, but there were too many choices. Everly wanted to see herself in all of them.

Not knowing how else to decide, she chose the nearest option: a linen maxi dress with a goddess neckline in vertical stripes of gray, pink, and cream. Jazzy had paired it with stacks of bangles, black gladiator sandals, and cream-colored clay statement earrings.

After getting dressed, Everly gathered the leggings and T-shirt she'd arrived in and plopped them in a different changing room so they wouldn't get lost among the other garments.

The fitting rooms at Kisses and Hugs were set apart from the showroom and organized in two rows of curtained stalls that ended in a raised platform with a 180-degree mirror. Everly couldn't help but walk to the mirror like she was striding down a runway. Hips swishing, shoulders back, chin tilted up.

When she climbed the two steps up to the platform and saw her reflection fully for the first time, she burst out laughing.

It was loud. Joyous.

Just enough.

Jazzy's eyebrows flew up her head. Joe was filming from the floor, out of the way of the mirror, and he swung his camera toward the host to catch her reaction. Logan lowered his own camera, peering at Everly from his spot beside her, where he'd been filming close-ups.

Sady and Stanton gasped from the doorway to the dressing area.

"Do you hate it?" Jazzy asked.

Everly shook her head. Her hair brushed soft against her bare shoulders with the movement. "I can't believe how fucking good I look." She cringed. "Language, sorry," she said to Logan.

He shrugged, that little affectionate smile on his face. "That ship sailed day one." His smile grew. "Plus, you do look fucking fantastic."

"Fuck yeah," Stanton yelled.

Everly waved her hand in front of her face to keep her tears at bay. It was wild seeing herself the way others saw her. The surge of confidence and happiness threatened to overwhelm her. She would have paid a million bucks to be able to lie down on the floor, but Jazzy would murder her if she wrinkled this dress. Linen was such a bitch to iron.

Jazz snapped her fingers in agreement. "Amen, girl." Joining Everly at the mirror, she pulled her into a tight hug as they stood together to assess Everly's reflection. "You're totally striking." Both of them were battling tears.

Sophie appeared, squeezing herself between Stanton and Sady. "Car's here for lunch," she announced. Then she pointed at Everly. "Oh shit. You look *incredible*."

In a move Grandma Helen would have been proud of, Everly grinned and said, "I know."

Stepping down from the mirrors, she headed for the changing room. "Let me get out of this and we can go."

"Nope." Jazzy blocked her path. "Lunch is for the rest of us. A certain cameraman has something planned for you here."

Everly glanced to her right. "Joe, you shouldn't have."

Logan snorted.

"That's all ready for you by the register," Sophie told Logan before disappearing back into the store.

Everly had no idea how much the show had to pay Kisses and Hugs to close for so much of the day, but soon the hosts and crew (and Sophie) had left, and Logan and Everly were alone in the boutique. Their footsteps echoed off the walls as they wandered the store.

At the back, beside the register, was a stack of three pizza boxes.

Everly pointed to them. "What's this?"

"Better pizza than our first date."

It was like someone had set off a series of firecrackers in her stomach. She couldn't believe he remembered her little comment at his apartment. That was weeks ago. So much had happened since then. She tried to sound cool and nonchalant as her heart battered her chest. "You were that desperate for pizza, huh? The rest of them are probably going out for some kind of fancy meal."

"This *is* fancy. It's from the North End. There's no better pizza." He flipped open the first box. "Plus, I wanted to spend some time with just you. We've barely seen each other since your family dinner."

And the sleepover they'd had at her apartment afterward. Her mic was still on, so Everly kept that detail to herself.

"Well, now pizza's my favorite meal," she said.

With a bright smile, he removed a slice and offered it to her.

Everly looked down at her dress. Pizza sauce and light colors were never great friends. "I should change first. I don't think I even technically own this yet."

Logan set the pizza back down and wiped his hands on a napkin. "Need any help?" His blue eyes flashed with mischief.

Already, Everly could feel a familiar loosening at her center. "I think I do. This tie was really hard to reach." She gestured to the lace that secured the neckline, sitting on her shoulder. She could easily grab the end and pull, but instead she strode toward the dressing rooms.

She ducked into the stall where she'd stashed her clothes and, seconds later, Logan's arms were around her. His hand coiled her mic out from under her dress, and he flicked off the Power switch and set it aside.

Pulling her close, he kissed her like it had been months, not days, since the last time they'd touched each other.

His mouth opened hungrily to hers, and his hands roamed her ass, her back, her arms. Everly tugged at his belt because she didn't know how long they had, and she wanted him as close to her as possible, touching her skin everywhere.

Now.

It wasn't until that moment, as her hands fought with the buckle, and her leg hooked around his hip, as her pulse throbbed in every one of her veins, that she truly understood the meaning of the word "need." It was something deeper than want, than desire. Something primal. Something heady that thrummed from deep inside her.

He released the bow at her neck with deft fingers, and Everly gasped as the fabric fell forward, exposing her breasts to the air for barely a second before they were in his mouth.

His belt buckle was loose a beat later, then his zipper dropped, and his pants were at his ankles as she guided Logan back onto the dressing room bench.

Her mind had found that place again, the quiet, perfect bliss that always came with his presence, his touch, and as she gathered her skirt around her waist and pushed her panties to the floor, the only thing she was thinking about was how good it felt to be with him.

Not a blink later, the condom was on and she was sinking onto his waist. They rocked together, his arms anchoring her to him, their eyes locked on each other.

He rested his forehead against Everly's as their speed increased, and before she knew it, they were going over the edge together.

CHAPTER 31

"Where are they opening this place? Can I send Bagel there?" Becca asked as she flipped through Everly's final designs for Sundae's Sanctuary.

On Wednesday, Everly would be presenting them to Bob Matten and the design team, and then, that weekend, incorporating them into her display for the Cape Cod Collective. After that, filming would be done. Her time with *On the Plus Side* would be over.

She felt ready. For this new opportunity. For this new version of herself. And for whatever else the universe had in store. For the first time in a long time, not knowing what was next didn't scare her.

If anything, it was exciting.

The exact opposite of safe or fine.

"I don't think they've found a location yet, but you can ask him when he gets here."

She hated that, after next week, Logan wouldn't regularly be driving down to Monmouth Cove from Boston for days at a time. But she reminded herself that this also meant that their lives would be theirs again. No more worries about cameras and Sady and her machinations.

Everly's mother accepted each page from Becca as she finished inspecting it. "These are beautiful." She pointed to the dummies from the website. "I love how you use the same dog on every page, doing different activities. It's so smart."

Everly's heart knocked against her ribs. "Thanks, Mom." There were few better feelings than having someone look at one of her designs and see exactly what she was trying to accomplish. It meant she'd nailed it.

She could do this. Be a graphic designer. Be an artist. Be whatever she wanted.

"Can you really do this *and* tattoos? Aren't they two separate careers? And Stanton said you might start designing book covers, too?" Her mother's eyes narrowed skeptically.

"The tattoos and covers would be for nights and weekends. The stuff I do for fun."

"When would you have time for yourself?"

"Doing what I love is for myself." Everly had wasted too long being afraid to explore professional avenues for her art. She wasn't ready to choose only one. Not until she had the chance to experience them all. Maybe not even then.

There was so much pressure as a kid to know what you wanted to be when you grew up. To choose one path, and follow it, full steam ahead. But that path didn't have to be one-way. You could turn back. You could try a new one. Or retrace your steps later on.

Everly didn't have to deny herself anything unless she wanted to. And she was done with that.

Becca popped up from her seat. "We've got five minutes. Popcorn time."

Everly dropped her eyes to her phone. There were no messages from Logan, even though he should have been there by now.

She shot him a text.

Everly Winters: Everything okay?

By the time the show started, he still hadn't answered.

"Where's Logan?" her mom asked.

"Stuck in traffic," Everly lied. Given the chance, her mother would concoct at least five explanations for his absence that would send Everly into a panic spiral. No one needed that.

Besides, there was a good chance Logan *was* stuck in traffic and had simply silenced his phone for safety.

"I hate how Sunday Cape traffic bleeds into the fall now," Becca said. "You can't get anywhere anymore unless you leave egregiously early or egregiously late."

"It's absurd. I had to go to the big grocery story in Falmouth and it took me two hours because of everyone on the road." With that, her mother launched into a dramatic tale of no one properly using their blinkers or understanding the purpose of a yield sign. "It doesn't say stop, for god's sake," she moaned.

Everly could have kissed Becca. Years of being her best friend and Ellis's partner had given Becca impeccable "redirect Penny Winters" skills. Everly nudged her elbow lovingly as she grabbed the remote and flipped on the television.

The arc of this episode seemed focused on resolving the "Jeverly" plotline and shifting to the budding connection between Everly and Logan. Between footage of Everly shopping at Kisses and Hugs (including, of course, her demolition of the jeans display, as well as the Gritty dress, which looked even worse on camera) was a clip of James and Everly after they'd kissed at Harry's, James angled toward her and Everly sitting pin-straight as he told her that he wanted her to find someone who felt the same. From there, the episode cut to them at work the next morning with Everly insisting that she and James forget what happened at the bar, capped by Logan's angry challenge when James immediately asked for Everly's help on a design.

Though it pained her to admit, Sady had done a good job. She'd wrapped up the James story in a way that didn't vilify either of them but made clear that it was over. Relief eased Everly's pulse. Hopefully, this meant that the faux love triangle was truly and fully behind her.

The last few minutes of the show homed in on Everly and Logan. It was mostly comprised of small moments between them: Logan and Everly laughing together between takes, locking eyes across the room, a few times where he put the camera down to kiss her on the temple, or let her rest her head on his shoulder when she got tired.

They were all the things they'd tried to hide from the camera, and yet there they were on-screen. But unlike with James, what she saw between Logan and herself was exactly what she felt when they were together. There was nothing fabricated or performative. It was all real. And that shone through.

Becca and Everly's mother kept cooing whenever she and Logan were on the screen.

"He really is a nice guy, isn't he?" her mom observed.

Everly nodded, her eyes stinging. Not just because it was true, but because her mother had noticed. She didn't always notice the good things. "There's no one like him." And no one that made Everly feel the way he did. Not the boyfriends she'd had in high school and college. Not James.

"What are you going to do when filming is over? He lives far away, doesn't he? And he'll be traveling to work on episodes for the other guests." There was concern, rather than criticism, in her mother's voice, which Everly appreciated.

"Boston is only an hour away," she pointed out. "And all of their guests this season are in the New England area."

Becca leaned into her. "You'll figure it out. Plus, there are plenty of marketing firms in Boston." She raised an eyebrow.

The thought had, of course, crossed Everly's mind. She enjoyed working at Matten-Waverly and living so close to Becca and Ellis, but those choices had been made out of convenience. They were safe. If she was leaving safe behind, she could leave Monmouth Cove, too.

Her mother's lips pursed, considering her next words. As someone who tended to wildly blurt out her thoughts, consequences be damned, this was a new development. "Have you two talked about that?"

"Not yet. Things between us are still pretty new." Everly picked up her phone to discover the screen still empty, and her stomach dropped. The episode was practically over, and Logan was now officially two and a half hours late. "We've got time to figure it out." She had to clear her throat against the hitch of worry in her voice.

Thankfully, her mom was distracted enough by the show to let this line of questioning go. "You took him to Bleaker's Bend," she noted, pointing at the screen.

"Just before it poured." That was absolutely all the information her mother needed to hear about that particular day. "He helped me find sea glass."

As if on cue, the camera lowered toward the sand, following Logan's hand as he reached for a speck of green. At the same time, the tide washed in and soaked his Vans. Like some sort of found footage movie, you could hear the unfiltered rush of the sea and see splatters of ocean water on the lens, and, in the background, Logan half mumbling curses as he tried to shake the wetness off. A second later, Everly's laughter came through clear as a bell. The scene cut out right after he retaliated with a gigantic splash of water that darkened the hem of her dress.

"You two are really cute together." Becca squeezed Everly's arm. "It comes across so different on camera than the stuff they added with James."

Everly smiled. She couldn't remember the last time she'd felt this calm, this relaxed, this ready for whatever came next.

She was days from showing her boss that she could be a designer. With her tattoo, Everly had fulfilled one of her biggest dreams. And next year she would get to pursue another one when she started working with Goro. It was slow going, and painful at times, but she and her mother were working on things. She had a hot, sweet lumberjack of a boyfriend. And for the first time in years, she was comfortable in herself, inside and out.

Maybe Everly was too much. But for her, and the people who loved her, she was *just* enough.

Typically, she and Becca avoided promos for future *OTPS* episodes, as they were both very anti-spoiler, but no one had turned the TV off, and after the credits rolled, the familiar dressing room of Kisses and Hugs caught Everly's eye.

The grin faded from her face.

Her back was to the camera. It captured her and Logan from a high angle as he kissed her, his hands visibly roaming her body both in the shot and the reflection from the room's mirror.

There was no sound, but Everly knew exactly what was coming.

Though she dove for the remote, she wasn't fast enough. Before she could hit the Power button, she was on the screen, pointing to the lace at her neck.

A second later, the fabric fell from her skin, revealing her bare back to the world.

CHAPTER 32

Voicemail.

Voicemail.

Voicemail.

Every time Everly dialed Logan's number, the call went straight to voicemail. She didn't leave a message. She couldn't. Her thoughts were too wild to articulate.

Sady had filmed them. Everly didn't know how. But it was the only explanation that made sense. Joe had gone to lunch with everyone. Logan had left his camera in the showroom.

He'd *sworn* they could trust *On the Plus Side*'s showrunner, and look what she'd done. She was trying to turn them into porn stars. She'd betrayed them both.

And for what? Her precious ratings? A bigger paycheck?

When Everly dialed Logan's number again, only to hear his voicemail message immediately kick in, the tears that had been clinging to her lashes finally broke free.

She barely felt comfortable kissing on camera. How could Sady ever think *this* was okay?

"You can sue for this, right?" Becca waved a hand at the TV even though it was off. "This has to break some kind of indecency laws." She knelt on the couch, watching Everly pace behind it.

Everly's mother shook her head. "They've humiliated you." Her eyes were wet when she looked at her daughter. "I was afraid something like this would happen."

Everly raked her hands through her hair. "I could lose my job. At the very least, they'll never consider promoting me now. I can only imagine how this will look to them."

How was it that a one-minute video clip was about to topple her whole world? Destroy everything she'd built?

Though she knew it was useless, she dialed Logan's number again. Voicemail.

Everly squeezed her eyes shut and tossed her phone on the couch. Panic pushed in, clouding her mind with doubt. Had Logan seen this promo? Would it be enough to get him to understand why Everly had never trusted Sady? Or what if he wasn't picking up her calls *because* of the promos?

No. Everly refused to follow that line of thought. Logan had never given her a reason to question him before. She wouldn't start now, no matter how freaked out she was. He was in that footage, too. This would be just as bad for him. He'd be on her side. The same way he always was.

There was a knock at the door, and then his rough voice, muffled by the wood, saying her name.

She rushed forward and threw it open.

He was already talking when he stepped inside. "I'm so sorry. The sitter was late and then traffic was a nightmare. My phone died, and

Ravioli had chewed through the cord on our last trip to the vet so I couldn't charge it—" Leaning in for a kiss, he paused, his eyes scanning Everly's face. "What?" Her silence pushed him back a step, and he spotted Becca and Everly's mom standing beside the couch, their expressions stricken. "What's going on?"

Everly's mom pursed her lips. "We were hoping you could tell us."

"Mom. Logan didn't do this." Everly nodded toward the open door. "But he and I need to talk."

Logan's brow dipped deep into a furrow. "Do what?"

"Come on, Penny." Becca hooked arms with her mother-in-law. "We'll give them some privacy. I have those Girl Scout cookies you love at the house."

Everly's mother glared at Logan as they passed.

Becca gave Everly's arm a supportive squeeze on the way out.

Thank you, Everly mouthed. The last thing she needed right now was another audience. Especially one that included her mother.

When they were gone, she rested her back against the closed door. Suddenly, she was bone tired, like she hadn't slept in days.

"Everly, what's happening?" Logan approached her. His arms were open, but they were too far apart to embrace.

"You haven't seen tonight's episode yet, right?"

He shook his head. "We were supposed to watch it together." His hands dropped to his sides. "What did Sady do now?"

"What about the promo for Thursday? Have you seen any of that?"

"No." He moved close enough to gently clasp her wrists. "Why the interrogation?"

She took a deep breath. Just thinking about that footage tightened her muscles as if they might fold in on themselves. She'd never wanted to disappear this badly. Not even when she'd quit the Collective.

"The promo has footage from Friday at Kisses and Hugs."

"You trying stuff on?"

"No. Footage from our lunch." She blinked rapidly against a new wave of tears. "From the dressing room."

"Wait." Realization dawned on his face. "Like you and me?" Wide-eyed, he watched her nod. "Are you fucking serious? She put that on TV?" His jaw flexed. "*All* of it?"

"It was only a quick clip in the promo, but it showed us making out, and then you untying the top of my dress."

"What the *fuck*?"

"Here." Everly grabbed the remote and clicked back to the show. She rewound the last three minutes of the newest episode and hit Play. Then she turned away. She didn't want to re-experience the visceral horror of seeing herself in such a compromising position. Instead, she studied Logan. With each second that passed, his frame grew tauter.

When the promo was over, she hit the TV's Power button, her stomach lurching.

Logan's expression was hard as stone. He stood so rigidly that she was afraid he might crack if she touched him.

"How would she have gotten that?" she asked quietly.

"I have no clue. I didn't give it to her. I would never film us like that. You know that, right?"

"Of course I know that."

"Then why do you seem mad at me?"

"I'm not. I'm just confused."

"About what?"

He moved toward her, and she fought the urge to retreat. She was done running. Done hiding. Done leaving boxes unopened because she was afraid of what she might find inside.

"You and Sady."

He frowned. "Everly—"

"I hate that, for even a second, I wondered if you weren't answering my calls because you knew about the promo. Which is so irrational, because you're in that clip, too. Why would you do that to yourself?" She shook her head. "But you always defend her. No matter what. And I don't understand why. I feel like I can't one hundred percent trust in you—" Her eyes skipped from his face to the floor, and her hands fretted at the stretchy material of her leggings. She would have given anything right now for Bagel or one of Logan's dogs to pet. "—trust in *us*—until I understand what she is to you."

Logan lowered himself to the arm of the sofa. He reached for her, and when she offered her hands, he drew her between his knees, curling their locked fingers to his chest. "Everly. God. Okay. I guess I need to be clearer about some things." He didn't say anything else until she looked at him.

Which was painful, after everything she'd said. She felt a little too raw. More naked than she had been in that video.

"I'm sorry about Sady. And I'm sorry about dismissing your worries." His eyes drifted to the TV as if a ghost of that clip still clung to the screen. His gaze didn't return to her. "I could never make my parents happy. I think a part of me looks for that from Sady. Like her approval cancels out their disapproval or something." His shoulders slumped forward. "That probably sounds ridiculous, but I was pretty young when I met her, and she opened up this whole new path for my life that I never would have thought possible. She's always been like a sister or a mentor or something . . ."

Everly rested a hand on his cheek and guided his face forward. Their eyes locked. "It's not ridiculous," she said softly.

"I'm not okay with what she did. This is fucked up." Anger roughened his voice.

She exhaled sharply. "What are we going to do? I can't be having sex on TV. I'll lose my job. It would follow me everywhere. You, too."

He wrapped his arms around her waist. "We're going to figure this out," he said. "Together."

Everly let herself melt against him. The closer she was to him, the easier it was to believe things would be okay.

"But first . . ." He scooped her phone off the couch. "We're going to call in reinforcements."

"I brought wine," Stanton announced as he pushed past Logan into Everly's apartment. His paisley button-down looked recently pressed.

"And I have coffee," Jazzy chimed in. She trailed behind Stanton, decked out in a faux-fur leopard-print coat over a jogging suit in a subtle shade of pink, a giant tote bag hooked over her shoulder.

Everly arched her eyebrow. Apparently these two never went anywhere unpolished. "I hope you don't expect to drink them together."

Stanton shed his coat onto the back of one of the kitchenette chairs. "That would be horror-movie levels of disgusting."

"We weren't sure if this was a 'get buzzed' kind of emergency or more of a 'pull an all-nighter scheming' situation. Logan was vague on the phone," Jazzy added.

Logan had made one quick call, and Jazzy and Stanton had come running like the cavalry. Everly's heart felt too full. It reminded her that no matter how much Sady staged and edited *On the Plus Side,* its hosts were genuine. They were *real.*

Jazzy dropped her tote on the kitchen counter. "I also brought popcorn and ice cream because they're antidotes for all ills."

She emptied the bag, handing off two pints of ice cream—one cookie dough and one caramel swirl, because Jazzy Germaine had impeccable taste in everything—to Everly.

Everly eyed the two hosts as she unearthed her small supply of stemware for the wine. She didn't know their relationship to Sady, beyond the fact that she ran the show, so Everly had no idea how they'd react to this news. "So, tonight's episode . . ."

Stanton waved her off. "We don't watch those things during filming. We need some kind of work-life balance." He settled himself at the kitchenette and poured a glass of wine.

Jazzy's gaze jumped between Everly and Logan. "Why? Did something happen?"

"Look up the promo for episode seven." Logan nodded tightly at the phone in her hand.

Jazzy typed out a few words on her screen, then scrolled. She set the device between her and Stanton, both of them leaning close. Everly knew they'd reached the clip in question when Stanton muttered, "What the fuck, Sady?"

With an abrupt flick of her finger, Jazzy cleared the screen. "This is not okay," she said simply.

"Has she done anything like this before?" Everly asked. She wasn't sure what she wanted their answer to be. If they said yes, it confirmed her suspicions, proved her intuition right. But it also meant that this show that she loved so much, that had helped her feel seen and normal, was harmful to others.

Jazzy and Stanton exchanged a glance. "Nothing explicit that we've ever seen," Jazzy said.

"But there've been rumors." Stanton set his elbows on the table and balanced his chin in his hands.

"Like with Carrie's adoptive mother." Everly remembered reading so many think pieces on that episode and not wanting to believe that the show would exploit someone's pain that way. "And Veronica's complaints about how she was made a villain?"

Jazzy nodded. "There was also speculation around season one that Sady coerced that sorority to let Nelly pledge."

Everly winced. She'd seen how the forums had celebrated that moment. Nelly had never felt like she belonged anywhere, and then suddenly she had a house full of potential sisters.

And there was a chance none of it was real. What had happened to Nelly once the show ended? Was she okay?

Anger roiled in Everly's insides. Sady couldn't keep messing with people's lives this way. No matter what good she claimed to be striving for. "She can't do this to us. She can't air that episode."

"How do we convince her of that?" Taking a sip of her wine, Jazzy leaned back in her chair. "Logan, you know her best. What's most likely to sway her?"

Logan combed his fingers through his beard, thinking. "Ratings, obviously. Legal stuff. Threats?"

"The triumvirate," Stanton joked darkly.

"I could probably find some legal arguments." Everly stood to retrieve her laptop from the coffee table. "I did a ton of research while I was looking over the contract." And she might, perhaps, have organized it all in a spreadsheet. A beautiful, color-coded one.

"I can see what the fans are saying," Logan offered. "If they're as pissed as we are, it might change Sady's mind."

Jazzy waved a hand between her and Stanton. "We'll check with our agents, see what recourse we might have. I don't want to be associated with a show that exploits its guests and crew like this."

Stanton nodded in agreement. He was quieter and more subdued than Everly had ever seen him. "I'm sorry this happened."

"We'll fix it," Jazzy promised. As if it was their problem. They'd never been anything but kind and generous to Everly. She hated that they'd had to drag the hosts into this.

Still, she couldn't stop herself from asking, "But what if we can't?" She had to be prepared to protect herself from any possible scenario. Sady might be swayed by their arguments. But she also might not care about anything but ratings records.

"Then we go nuclear," Logan said softly.

Everly turned to him with wide eyes. "Quit?" She couldn't do that. She'd signed a contract. They could sue her.

And what about the Collective? She and Stanton had worked so hard on her display pieces and her booth. She was so close to making this happen. To finally doing right by her grandmother and proving that she was the person Grandma Helen had always believed her to be. Her transformation wouldn't be complete without doing the art show. Everly couldn't back out. Not for a second time.

"Could I still do the Collective?" she asked.

Logan took a breath. "I don't know. Sady secured a prime booth based on promises of advertising. Without the show's backing . . ."

"They probably wouldn't want me." Her grandmother's superhero portrait deserved to be hanging on a wall in that convention hall, along with the book covers that she'd loved so much. "I can't give this up." The very thought of it carved a hole in her chest. She pressed a hand there as if that might seal it over.

"We're going to do everything we can to make sure you don't have to." Jazzy squeezed her hand. Her face was hard with determination, but Everly thought she saw doubt clouding her eyes.

When the hosts left an hour later, Everly and Logan moved to the couch. She rested her back against him as she pored over searches on her laptop, while he scanned Read-It on his (finally charged) phone.

He found a ton of online comments that showed plenty of viewers who were invested in "Loverly" without more than a kiss on camera, others who were troubled by the explicit nature of the promo footage, and still more asking about Everly's tattoo.

Each one he showed her gave Everly a little more faith in her beloved Read-It forums. Hopefully, when the show was over, she'd feel ready to pop back in there, and maybe participate for once.

She'd read some news articles about former reality TV participants who'd won civil cases against shows for misrepresenting them, and now she was scanning her contract for evidence that Sady had truly removed the right to defame clause, which seemed like the best chance they had of changing the showrunner's mind. Showing Everly having sex on TV seemed like a prime example of defamation, at least as far as Everly understood the word.

"Wait. Here it is." She angled her computer screen so Logan could see it. The section entitled "Right to Defame" had been struck through, with a comment in parentheses at the end that read "Not a Precedent."

Logan's eyes scrolled over the page. "Perfect. Print it out."

She stared at it for a long moment, then turned to him. "You could lose your job, if this goes sideways. And what about Sundae's Sanctuary? What if you can't find something else that gives you the time and money you need for it?" Everly refused to be the reason he couldn't get this project off the ground.

Logan leaned forward and pressed a kiss to her forehead. "Brian and I will figure it out. I won't stand by while she does this to you."

"To us."

He kissed her lips this time. "To me, you're what matters."

Everly dropped her head against his chest. "I'm so sorry you have to do this. I know she's important to you," she said into his plaid shirt. Gray and black this time. The perfect color scheme for their somber mood.

"My relationship with Sady isn't what I think it is if she'd do this to us." Placing his knuckle beneath Everly's chin, he raised her face to his. "More importantly, I don't know if you know this, but I'm falling in love with you. Hard. So when I say you're what matters, I mean it."

Everly peered at him. Tears blurred her vision. It had been such a long, emotional night. She hadn't been able to predict how it would end, but she'd never expected this. More support than she'd planned for. A profession of love that literally curled her toes.

She imagined drawing him, right in this moment. The way the overhead lights lit fires in his irises, how affection carved lines into the corners of his eyes and mouth. The love on his face was plain. She wished she could capture it. Use that drawing as a confession of her own.

But she didn't have her charcoal pencil or her paper. All she had were words. He deserved to hear them. "I'm falling in love with you, too. I'm pretty sure I have been since the first day you grumped your way into my life."

Logan gave her that same expression he had the day they'd met. The one that, at the time, she'd struggled to read. Now she could parse every inch of it.

Setting her laptop aside, Logan brought his face to hers again. The weight of his body urged her down into the couch, and, as he settled on top of her, he kissed her into oblivion.

CHAPTER 33

Logan gripped his camera in one of his hands.

His other hand held tightly to Everly's.

Together, they strode through the lobby of New Mood Media's Boston offices. Logan's face was full of stony determination, and he navigated the cubicles and hallways with the confidence of someone who'd spent a lot of time there. It reminded Everly how long he'd worked with Sady, and what it meant that he was willing to put that at risk for Everly.

If the showrunner wouldn't listen to reason, Logan had a lot to lose as well. Typically, as a cameraman, he was hidden. Invisible. Untouched by everything that could befall a guest on reality TV. But if Sady aired this footage, it could tarnish his reputation, too. He was trying to get a nonprofit off the ground. What if potential investors didn't want to be associated with someone who'd hooked up on TV? There'd be no way for anyone to know Everly and Logan hadn't consented to it being filmed. Or being aired.

Her fingers pressed deeper into his palm, and their eyes locked. He offered her a small, bracing smile. A promise that, whatever happened, they were doing it together.

They stopped at Sady's office at the back of the suite. A redheaded girl sat at a desk near the door as if she were guarding it.

"Chrissy," Logan said with a nod as they approached. Behind her assistant, through the glass, Sady was visible, her back to them, and her phone pressed to her ear.

Just seeing her caused Everly's heart to roar.

"Hey, Logan." Chrissy glanced at her computer screen. "She's pretty booked today . . ."

"She's going to make time." His voice was matter-of-fact. Commanding. Strengthening his grip on Everly's hand, he strode past the girl's desk and shoved through the door to Sady's office.

"I'm on a call." There was irritation in her voice as she spun to face them. "Oh." Her expression cleared quickly. "I've got to call you back," she mumbled into the phone. Then she hung up and dropped the device on her desk. "Hey, you two, to what do I owe the pleasure?"

Logan released Everly's hand so he could heft the camera on his shoulder and steady it. He pointed the lens at Sady.

The showrunner's eyes narrowed. "What are you doing?"

"Collecting proof."

"Everly, what's wrong?" Sady's tone and expression were all innocence and confusion, but it couldn't possibly be genuine. She couldn't be naïve enough to think that Everly would be on board with having her privacy completely violated.

Everly folded her arms over her chest. "You can't air that footage from Kisses and Hugs."

Sady's lips pressed together. "Take a seat." She flicked her gaze to Logan. "And for Christ's sake, Logan, put that thing down."

"Why?" Everly cocked her head. "Do you not like having things filmed that you'd rather people not see?"

Sady steepled her fingers, observing them quietly for a moment. "This is about the promo."

"Of course it's about that promo," Logan said. "Where did you get that footage?"

"I had Joe install some small cameras in the dressing rooms, in case Jazzy wanted to use them instead of the big one-eighty mirror for try-ons."

"Wait. You've been filming me changing my clothes?" Everly's pulse screamed in her ears loud enough to make her dizzy. Had she been on camera naked all season without knowing it?

Sady gaped at her in disbelief. "Of course not. I was clear that he shouldn't put any in the dressing room with your outfits. Just the empty ones."

One of which Everly had thrown her own clothes into, so she could find them later. The very stall she and Logan had later used to "change." God. Was this her fault?

No. Sady could have chosen not to use the footage, and that placed the blame squarely on her.

Everly stared her down. "I don't want that recording used in my episodes."

Sady frowned. "It's already been in the promo. And have you seen the responses? People are loving it. Our ratings will probably be the highest ever." She said it like this was some kind of victory.

Everly didn't care about ratings. She didn't care what anyone on the internet thought. She didn't even care what happened to her favorite show, at this point. All that mattered was her and Logan, and what this might do to them. She dug her fists into her lap. Otherwise, she was likely to plant one in Sady's face.

"There are plenty of viewers who are *not* on board," Logan said.

Everly pulled the file folder with the online comments out of her bag and dropped it in front of Sady. The showrunner flipped it open and began to thumb through it.

Logan nodded to the stack of papers. "This is a collection of viewer comments, in case you need to see them." He fussed with a button on the camera, and Everly heard it whirl. "But even if no one cared, don't you think what your guest wants should be more important than anything else? Everly's not comfortable with that being released. Neither am I. We did not consent to this." He said the words clearly and firmly to make sure the camera caught the audio.

Everly did the same. "I don't want to be shown hooking up on TV. It could ruin my career. My life."

Sady shook her head. "Obviously, I'm not going to air the *whole* thing. That violates all sorts of content laws. But don't you see what a win this is? It shows how desirable you are. How desirable all fat people are."

"No." Everly straightened her shoulders and tipped up her chin. Stanton had called them power stances when they'd practiced for her presentation at Matten-Waverly. And if she ever needed to feel powerful, it was right now. "I don't want any of that on TV. My bare back. The sides of my breasts. My ass. I did not consent to having my body shown with so little clothing on." She would keep repeating the word "consent" until Sady got it through her head how violated she felt.

"Then don't have sex in public." Sady's words were a slap to the face. Everly jerked back from the shock of them.

"Whoa." Logan stepped closer to Sady's desk. "We didn't. We knew that store was empty. It was locked. Everyone was gone."

Sighing, Sady pushed her black-framed glasses up into her hair and rubbed at her eyes. "I'm sorry you're both so upset about this. That was not my intent. But I can't cut this. It is a perfect end to a groundbreaking series of episodes." Her smile was solemn. "Everly, I wish you could see this the way I do. We are changing minds. Breaking barriers. Your story is forcing everyone to see fat people as heroes in their own stories. Their own romances."

"This is not my story. It's yours. Half of it isn't even real," Everly shot back.

"There are already articles about your arc coming out online. People beyond the fandom are talking about it. This could be the beginning of so much change in the discourse." Her eyes grew bright, and a smile pulled at her lips. "Can't you see it? We are redefining how fat people are represented. Right now. In this moment." She leaned over her desk, eager to hold Everly's stare.

Everly hated that it was working. That she couldn't look away. These were things that she cared about, too. But she didn't want to have to sacrifice her dignity to make it happen.

Sady spread her hands wide. "We could be on our way to romcoms helmed by fat performers, without weight loss plots or endless self-deprecation. We could have fans swooning over love triangles with fat people at the center. All because of you. But not if we don't follow through on the story. Not if we don't prove to the world how desirable you are. This footage with Logan does that."

"Sady." Logan's tone was angry and sad at once.

"Logan, we're on the cusp of doing exactly what we've been striving toward. With the right ratings, we can do whatever we want. Create shows we want. You have to see that."

"No." Everly spit the word out. "*I* am a fan of your show. I'm living proof that you were already changing minds. People flock to *On the Plus Side* because they see themselves. They don't need some sort of forced storyline. They just want to see themselves represented on TV as human beings, not jokes or villains or stereotypes. You're doing that already. Don't cheapen it."

Sady shook her head, disappointed. "This is so much bigger than that. We are reaching beyond the fan base, finally. Nothing will change until we can make an impression *outside* the fat community."

"What about the rest of *this* season?" Everly asked. "Are you going to do the same thing to your other guests? Viewers are going to expect more romance and drama, and it's going to destroy the amazing messages those guests are sending and all the work they're doing."

For a second, Sady seemed chastised. She sat back in her chair quietly, like she was mulling over Everly's logic.

"Sady." Logan's voice was close to losing its edge.

Sady folded her hands over the stack of online comments. "We'll have enough clout from your episodes. We can figure the rest out as we go."

Everly rose to her feet. Her knees were shaking, and her eyes burned as she fought off angry tears. She knew what she needed to do. But it was going to break her to do it.

"I refuse to film the rest of this season."

"That's a breach of contract."

Everly shrugged. "As far as my lawyer and I are concerned, you breached it first." She didn't actually have a lawyer yet, but thanks to her online research, she had a list of them that she could call. A few who'd won similar cases.

Sady blanched. "Wait—"

"I know I don't have the authority to stop you from using that footage, but I don't have to give you anything for the last episodes. I do not consent to how I'm being represented. And I will sue if you put any of it on the air."

Sady's jaw tightened. "What about the Collective? You need the show for that."

Everly hoped that her grandmother could forgive her for quitting again. This time, at least, it was for the right reasons. "I do not consent to being represented this way," she repeated.

She'd have a booth at the Collective someday. On her own terms.

"I guess I'll see you in court." Sady grabbed for her phone.

Logan lowered the camera. "You're going to need a new cameraman, because I quit."

Even though she'd known he was going to say it, Everly's heart jumped at his words. As always, it felt like he was matching her, step for step. Always marching to the same beat.

"Logan." For the first time, Sady looked stricken.

"You used to care about more than ratings." His mouth pressed into a taut line. "You used to care about people."

"You're not this naïve. You've been in this business long enough. Ratings and money make the world go round."

He shook his head. "We did season one on a shoestring budget. Look where it got us."

Sady threw up her hands. "And we can't stay here if we're tiptoeing around everyone's feelings. I'm trying to make a difference."

Logan homed his icy blue eyes on her. Everly could see the emotion pulling at his face, even as he fought it back.

He was sacrificing so much more than a job right now. He was losing a mentor, a friend, someone he'd held up on a pedestal. "Thanks for teaching me everything I know about TV. It's been . . . enlightening."

His voice cracked, forcing him to turn his back on Sady.

"Everly's not the only one in that footage. I'll be seeing you in court, too."

With that, he took Everly's hand firmly in his, and they left Sady and the show behind.

OTPSfan23456 *3 hours ago*
I'm Everly, a longtime lurker and fan.

For years, this forum was the only place I felt like I had any community, and you have no idea how much your company, your honesty, and your stories have helped me to feel seen. To feel normal. Just like OTPS when I started watching it.

Which is why it kills me to write this post, but I can't keep silent. Not after what I've been through while filming my episodes.

By now I'm sure you've seen the promo for Thursday's episode, and specifically, the clip of Logan and me in the dressing room.

Neither of us consented to be filmed in that private moment. We thought we were alone, and were not aware that the show's second cameraman had installed small cameras in most of the dressing rooms at the request of Sady Sanders, the showrunner.

I have never felt so violated. I've had to call out of work the last few days because I can't face my coworkers. I'm getting harassed on social media. I'm struggling to leave my house.

Logan and I made clear to Sady that we wanted the footage removed from the promo, and that we didn't want it included in the final episodes. She refused to comply.

This short clip will follow Logan and me for the rest of our lives. I didn't consent to being intimate on camera or to have that footage shared publicly. My lawyer and I believe that, by airing these clips, Sady Sanders and the New Mood Media production company are defaming me, which is a breach of contract. I will not be continuing with the show or finishing out my series of episodes.

For the record, Sady also wildly misrepresented my relationship with James. We never dated, and he never had any feelings for me. The entire love triangle aspect of my story arc was fabricated.

Logan and me, though, we're the real deal. And that is part of what makes it so hard for me to write this post and share it. My experiences with Sady have been pretty terrible, but I gained a

lot of wonderful things from OTPS—a reminder of my worth, a
new look that makes me feel more confident, a renewed desire
to chase my goals and dreams—and not least of all of these is
my new relationship. I would not have found Logan without this
show. Or rediscovered myself.

But I no longer trust Sady Sanders with OTPS and what it stands
for, nor do I believe she will approach the rest of season three's
guests with the care and sensitivity they deserve, so I had to
speak out. I hope this helps to give some clarity to whatever
happens with the show from here.

Also, what happened to me is not in any way a reflection on
Jazzy and Stanton. They have been as wonderful, as welcoming, and as kind as they seem in every episode. And they have
all fully supported my decision to write this letter and to leave
the show. Please don't take your anger out on them.

Thank you to everyone who has made it to the end of this post.
I don't know what will happen now, but I'm so grateful to have
somewhere to share my story free of any edits or manipulation.
    xoxo,
    Everly

16k ♥ 8k 👍 11k ✨ 3k 🍄

Annette98 *3 hours ago*
EVERLY I WISH I COULD HUG YOU RIGHT NOW. I hate that
they've done this to you. And for what it's worth, I was dis-

gusted by the inclusion of that footage in the promo. That's never been what OTPS was about.

700 ♥ 350 👍 123 ✨ 109 👎

KelseyR0305 *3 hours ago*
Same. It felt totally gross. I'm pissed. I hope they get what they deserve.

655 ♥ 211 👍 78 ✨ 49 👎

RosyTea *3 hours ago*
wat the fuccckkkk

sue their asses for all their worth

896 ♥ 311 👍 671 ✨ 258 👎

FarmGyrlME *3 hours ago*
i never felt like that James stuff was right

the editing was off

and there was no chemistry, not like with you and Logan

it figures u TV show would do this shit for ratings

702 ♥ 568 👍 213 ✨ 108 👎

CourtK *3 hours ago*

My heart is broken for you. I've loved watching you grow in your confidence over these past few weeks, and nothing shows that growth more than you coming on here to share your truth, even though there might be consequences. Thank you for trusting us enough to tell us what happened. We love you and I hope someday you'll stop lurking and say hi. <3

931 ♥ 450 👍 887 ✦ 221 👎

Bridget80 *3 hours ago*

You are wonderful and no one deserves this. I'll be calling New Mood Media as soon as I post this to voice my anger. I hope everyone else does the same.

798 ♥ 257 👍 871 ✦ 390 👎

RachelG *3 hours ago*

I'm right there with you.

329 ♥ 101 👍 153 ✦ 76 👎

. . . 4500 more comments . . .

SophieA *2 hours ago*

Everly. The moment I saw that promo I called my boss. She talked to marketing and they are going to pull support from the show unless they remove that scene. I can't believe they did this to you two.

Text me if you need anything. I'm here for you.

566 ♥ 840 👍 376 ✦ 179 👎

Allison Avery *1 hour ago*

The rage I feel on your behalf is immense. This is such a viola-tion. Plain and simple.

And for all you fools on here saying that she brought this on herself by messing around with Logan, get your heads out of your asses. She could consent to being intimate without con-senting to voyeurism or exploitation. One does not equate to the other.

2k ♥ 922 👍 1456 ✦ 431 👎

SarahEditsThings *1 hour ago*

Everly, you're a warrior. Thank you for sharing your truth with us, and sticking up for all the other people the show could hurt. Please let us know how else we can support you.

994 ♥ 811 👍 769 ✦ 280 👎

CHAPTER 34

The conference room at Matten-Waverly felt significantly smaller when Everly was standing at the head of it.

She straightened her denim pencil skirt and flattened the front of the loose, floral-printed peasant shirt Jazzy had styled her in. "A perfect mixture of professional and creative," Jazzy had insisted. As she'd wrapped Everly in a hug, she'd added, "A perfect representation of you."

Now Jazzy was at the end of the table, with Stanton on one side, and the company's entire design team on the other. Everly's boss sat closest to her, and behind Jazzy, his camera blocking half his face, was Logan.

This device was smaller, with fewer bells and whistles, but he promised the picture and sound would be just as clear. Jazzy planned to post the footage, sans edits, on her website after Everly's presentation. A response to whatever Sady tried to cobble together to finish out Everly's episodes.

Apparently, ratings had plummeted for the last episode of *On the Plus Side*. Everly was staying far (far, far, far) away from anything *OTPS* related these days, but Logan, Becca, and the hosts kept her in the loop.

From what they reported, her post had had the impact she'd hoped. Fans were calling out Sady for her methods and boycotting the rest of Everly's episodes. And not one blip of that footage would be aired. Everly's lawyer and the legal team at Kisses and Hugs had made sure of that. It had taken the fashion company stepping in to make Sady comply.

The last four days had been the longest of Everly's life. She'd been dragged from one end of the internet to the other and gotten such a large outpouring of support that she couldn't fit it all in her heart.

There'd be no Cape Cod Collective. No chance to honor Grandma Helen in the way she'd hoped. No new wardrobe reveal. But in some ways this felt like a truer end to Everly's season. All she wanted now was to finish her presentation and see where it took her.

Tiny baby steps away from safe and fine.

She clicked forward to the next image in her slideshow, which displayed the four website pages she'd created. In one, a cartoon Sundae relaxed in a tub full of bubbles, a rubber ducky perched on his head, framed by a menu of grooming services. The next had Sundae chasing a ball, another dog hot on his heels, above a list of the various programs offered through the facility—daycare, training, rehabilitation, socialization, foster and shelter services. Then there was a page with Sundae being patted by a group of kids, his tail wagging enthusiastically, and another with him sitting and staring up at someone, clearly waiting for a treat.

"I feel like a large part of this organization's success is going to depend on brand awareness and recognition, so I wanted to create branding that would immediately invite a consumer in. You can never go wrong with a cute dog, and incorporating Sundae's image into the various services offered will help remind consumers what Sundae's Sanctuary does. There's even the potential for merchandise to increase recognition: T-shirts, stuffed animals, dog toys, you name it."

Though she'd love nothing more than to cower under the table,

Everly forced her shoulders back (power stance time) and let her eyes pan out over the room. James offered her a small smile and a thumbs-up. There'd been no more finger guns or morning chats, but the two of them were back to at least saying hello, and brainstorming designs now and then (with the proper credit to her). It felt like the right kind of boundaries for a work acquaintance who might soon be her peer.

Beside him, Alex nodded thoughtfully, then turned to Logan. "I know you're only one partner, but how do you feel about Everly's approach?"

"It's exactly what we're looking for. And will definitely help get us attention. Hopefully from donors and potential customers."

Logan wasn't one for empty compliments, so she knew he meant every word.

Their eyes locked, and he smiled, instantly melting her insides. Maybe someday his attention wouldn't liquefy her, but today was not that day.

Logan cleared his throat. "And I know Brian likes them, too."

Alex nodded. "I have a few small suggestions for tweaks, but nothing major. Overall, I think you've got a strong concept here," they said to Everly.

The rest of the designers agreed.

Bob Matten beamed at her from his spot near the head of the table. As far as practice interviews went, this felt like it was going pretty well.

Everly's first design job. Her first client.

Once she'd finished up the presentation, everyone slowly filed out, stopping on their way to offer compliments and thoughts. Alex said to come see them later to get their notes.

Bob was the last person from the office to leave. He shook her hand. "Get your application materials together, because I have it on good authority that there'll be an assistant design position opening up very soon."

"You got it," Everly promised, blinking back tears.

In a reenactment of their first meeting, Jazzy and Stanton surrounded Everly, jumping up and down and cheering as they swallowed her in a huge hug. "We've got a meeting in Boston, so we've got to get going, but, girl, you killed it." Stanton grabbed her arm and yanked it up and down. "I expect a business card when you get that new job, and a redesign of my website."

"It's going to cost you," she said with a laugh.

He hugged her again. "Worth every penny."

Jazzy was already crying as she pulled Everly into a hug. Everly's own tears weren't far behind.

"I'm so proud of you."

"You helped me so much. I couldn't have done it without you."

Jazzy shook her head, her dark curls bouncing around her shoulders. "You did the hard work." Glancing over her shoulder, she called out to Logan, "You'll email me the footage?"

"As soon as it's uploaded."

Jazzy hooked her arm in Everly's and they walked together toward the door. "I had all the clothes delivered to your apartment. And the makeup, too."

Everly's mouth dropped open. She'd assumed that by leaving the show, she'd forfeited her right to the perks. "How? The show pays for that."

Jazzy grinned at her. "Sophie got Kisses and Hugs to donate all their garments, and Fatulous covered the rest." Fatulous was Jazzy's website for style and brand consulting.

Everly's cheeks were soaked. Even after she'd imploded their show, Jazzy and Stanton's generosity knew no bounds.

"Don't you be a stranger," Jazzy said.

"I hope you like texts because I'm going to be sending them." Everly smiled at her idol.

With one more hug, Jazzy disappeared through the door.

Everly watched it swing closed. The last eight weeks had flown by. Standing in the middle of Reception, the summery smell of Jazzy's perfume still hanging in the air, it was almost possible to believe it had all been a dream.

Except nothing about Everly was the same.

Behind her, Logan fussed with his camera on her desk. As she faced him, he looked up and flashed her a bright smile. The furthest cry from the unsmiling grump who had walked in here not two months ago.

It was amazing how fast everything could change. And how quickly they could adjust. How what once seemed impossible was now something Everly couldn't live without.

His blue eyes locked on her. "You ready for lunch?"

"I'm ready for everything," she replied.

He met her by the door, taking her hand in his, and they disappeared into the hallway, leaving his camera behind.

"*ON THE PLUS SIDE* REEMERGES FROM HIATUS WITH A NEW
SHOWRUNNER, NEW FORMAT, AND NEW ENERGY."
Samantha Quain, Media Desk

After the fallout from the show's most recent PR nightmare, viewers thought the groundbreaking makeover show might be gone for good. Scandal hit the show when the first guest of season three, Everly Winters, came to the ON THE PLUS SIDE Read-It forums to share how the show had mistreated her.

In particular, Winters purported that the show had gained access to and aired explicit content without her consent, or the consent of Logan Samuel, a cameraman also in the footage, who she'd formed a relationship with during filming.

After some legal threats, and a lot of bad press and disappointed fans, New Mood Media pulled the footage in question, and soon, the whole season, from its streaming platform, VuNu. According to the production company, they wanted to take a closer look at the show and would return in time to air the rest of season three.

Meanwhile, Jazzy Germaine and Samuel bought the rights to all recordings from Everly's season. The newly edited versions, which are streaming through Germaine's website Fatulous, remove the fabricated love triangle with Everly's coworker James, and refocus the story on Everly's pursuit of her art and desire to find her confidence. Woven in are small smatterings of her developing relationship with Samuel, which this viewer found delightful. Germaine even aired two previously unseen episodes to cap off Everly's season.

Fans speculated that this would be the permanent new home for the show, but New Mood Media has just announced that ON THE PLUS SIDE will return to VuNu in the winter with Germaine and her fellow host, Stanton Bakshi, as showrunners. According to Germaine's statement, the show will be given a new format that will "place more emphasis on community and help to further develop ON THE PLUS SIDE's themes of self-love and body inclusivity . . ."

EPILOGUE

One Year Later

A chorus of barking ricocheted off the cinder-block walls and battered Everly's eardrums as she strode through the large warehouse.

The doggy daycare at Sundae's Sanctuary had been sectioned off into four large pens, separating the dogs by size, energy level, and socialization skills.

She peeked over the wall of the small-dog room and immediately spotted Alan leading a pack through a series of laps. Sometimes, at lunch, the janitorial staff let him drop a few random items into the toilets after they'd cleaned them.

Shaking her head, Everly made her way deeper into the warehouse, smiling and waving at staff as she passed. Every one of them wore a gray T-shirt with the logo she'd designed on the back. It had been almost a month since she'd left Matten-Waverly to work full-time at Sundae's Sanctuary in marketing and publicity, and a giant smile still crossed her face every time she saw someone wearing *her* design.

She did that.

She'd even designed some of the staff's tattoos.

Sometimes it was hard for Everly to remember that, over a year ago, none of this was real. She'd been living above her brother's garage, working at a job that didn't suit her dreams, hiding in clothes that didn't suit her style, all because she was too afraid that she was too much.

Now she probably *was* too much, and that was exactly how she liked it.

Logan was crouched in the solitary pen at the back of the warehouse. He'd texted her earlier to come meet the sanctuary's newest addition.

Pushing through the gate, she stepped into the pen and joined him on the floor. In front of them sat an open crate with a cowering gray-and-brown dachshund inside.

He'd come to them a week ago, too thin and scared to be adopted out any time soon.

Which meant Everly and Logan already loved him.

They'd spent most of last night inhaling pizza (he was right that the North End's was the best) and rearranging their apartment so they could fit another dog crate.

Logan took Everly's hand and set their entwined fingers in his lap. Then he pressed a kiss to her temple.

"So what do you think?" he asked her. "Do we take him home?"

"On one condition."

That worried wrinkle creased his brow. "What's that?"

She raised one finger to smooth it away. "We have to name him Gnocchi."

ACKNOWLEDGMENTS

I am so proud of *On the Plus Side* and its cast of wonderful characters—Everly's journey, in particular, is near and dear to my heart, as someone who, on occasion, still feels that she is too much—but this book took a long and arduous road to get to this final version. *OTPS* definitely did not burst out of my head fully formed (in fact, it came out in a completely different point of view and tense. . . .), and I'm so grateful to everyone who supported and lifted me up during what would prove to be my toughest year of writing yet.

I am eternally grateful to my editor, Sarah Grill, for her sharp insights, invaluable editorial notes, and unwavering patience (and, of course, for her expertise in all things related to reality TV!). I felt lost for a lot of this journey, and (if I may mix a metaphor) Sarah was both my road map and my lighthouse beacon, helping me to find where I was going and get there in one piece. Sarah, you loved the idea of this book from the beginning and you helped me to turn it into something I love just as much. Thank you for believing I could do it. Thank you for *everything*. You make my writing better, my stories better, with each and every draft.

I would not have successfully navigated the stormy waters of debut year and writing book two without my agent, Katelyn Detweiler. Katelyn, you were a dream agent of mine long before we signed together, and your continued belief in me and my stories keeps me going even on the worst days. Thank you for reading this book just days before your maternity leave because you knew I needed it. Thank you for every email, every soothing reassurance, every piece of feedback, every Little Pete factoid (and thank you for 90s Con, which I will cherish forever!). You are a true champion for your writers, and I cannot wait to see where we go next on this wild ride called publishing.

This book would not have its excellent title without Rosiee Thor's unmatched punning skills. I will forever be in awe of your wit, Rosiee.

My earliest readers—Sam Markum, Annette Christie, and Katie DeLuca—helped to push me through the first draft of this book when I was stuck, and I credit them with that draft ever making it to "The End." Thank you, Sam, for reading every messy chapter I tossed at you and finding something to celebrate in it. You kept me going. Annette and Katie, thank you for reminding me that this story was full of gems even when I couldn't see them. It would have been easy to give up without your enthusiasm.

The finished cover of *On the Plus Side* brought me to tears. It so perfectly encapsulates the heart of this story, and Everly looks so beautiful and confident. I cannot thank Vi-An Nguyen and Olga Grlic enough for their incredible design. And thank you to Omar Chapa, for the beautiful interior pages! Holding this book and flipping through it gives me so much joy!

My team at St. Martin's Griffin is the absolute best, and I would be lost without them. Meghan Harrington, Kejana Ayala, Marissa Sangiacomo, Chrisinda Lynch, Lisa Davis, Janna Dokos, and Soleil Paz—thank you for answering all my questions, creating all my beautiful graphics and other promotional materials (and tolerating my ridiculous attempts at graphic design), and for your seemingly endless supply of enthusiasm and support for my books. I am so grateful for all that you do to help get my books out into the world and in front of readers.

On the Plus Side went through a point-of-view change, a tense change, and lost a few major characters, and my copy editor, Christina MacDonald, deserves a special thank-you for helping to make sure none of that slipped through into final production. Thank you for catching everything I managed to miss no matter how many times I read the manuscript. And thank you for fixing all my misuses of *farther* vs. *further* (Someday I swear I will learn this!). Not all superheroes wear capes, but you deserve one.

Gianluca Russo's *The Power of Plus* and Pete Tartaglia's *Creating Reality* helped to acclimate me to the world of plus-size fashion and reality TV, respectively, and informed my conception of the book's eponymous makeover show. I learned so much from both these books, and any inaccuracies or unrealistic depictions are the fault of my imagination alone.

I am so inspired by my colleagues who are doing the hard work to get positive fat rep into the world. To Olivia Dade, Alechia Dow, Sheena Boekweg, Crystal Maldonado, Talia Hibbert, Sarah Hollowell, Lora Beth Johnson, Lisa Fipps, Danielle Jackson, Helena Greer, Jodie Slaughter, Mary Warren, Jenna Miller, Leanne Schwartz, Cassandra Newbould, Kelly deVos, Denise Williams, Tristen Crone, Sarah Kapit, and so many others, I am so honored to see my books beside yours on shelves.

Julie Murphy, thank you for *Dumplin'*. I was in my thirties when it came out, but it still changed everything for me.

So much of *On the Plus Side* is about finding community, and I have been lucky enough over the past year to discover so many new safe spaces and communities for plus-size people. I am so grateful for Mary Warren and her Fat Girls in Fiction community, to everyone who has joined us on the Writing While Fat Discord server, and to the many, many creators on social media who are challenging fatphobia and making the world safer for fat people through their thoughtfulness, vulnerability, and tenacity. Please know your work has value and is helping people. I am one of them.

I decided debut year would be a good time to start therapy, and I had no idea at the time how good a decision that would turn out to be. Rachel, thank you for helping me to learn coping mechanisms, establish boundaries, recognize patterns of destructive perfectionism, and realize that I could, in fact, do all the things, even when it felt nigh impossible.

I am not always my best self when I am in the thick of it with drafting and revising and so, to all my friends and family who lend me an ear when I need to vent, who stick by me when I am not my best, who let me be a hermit and disappear when I need to work, and who have shown up for me and the release of *The Make-Up Test* with more enthusiasm, kindness, and support than I could ever have imagined, you all mean the world to me. Thank you from the bottom of my heart for everything you do, and for believing in me every step of the way.

Look, Mom, I did it again! I hope you know that without you, I would not be here writing another book. And thank you for all those years of hunkering down on the couch with me and watching *What Not to Wear*. That was a huge inspiration for this story.

There is not enough space in this book for me to thank my husband, Kevin, for everything he does, so I am going to keep it simple. Kevin, it is a joy to choose you every day. Thank you for choosing me, too, and for taking this journey with me, by my side, holding my hand.

Finally, to every reader, blogger, reviewer, librarian, and bookseller who picked up *The Make-Up Test,* who messaged me about it, who shared it on their social media accounts, and gave this new author a try, thank you. You keep me going. You make me want to write. And you remind me why I continue telling stories, even on the days when that feels so, so hard. My heart is full, and I appreciate every one of you.

ABOUT THE AUTHOR

Anastasia Aranovich
Photography

JENNY L. HOWE first started scribbling down stories when she was in junior high and never really stopped. In college, she decided to turn her love of books into a career by pursuing a Ph.D. in literature. Now, as a professor, she teaches courses in writing, literature, and children's media. When she's not writing and teaching, Jenny spends her time buried under puzzle pieces, cross-stitching her favorite characters, and taking too many pictures of her rescue dogs, Tucker and Dale. She is the author of *The Make-Up Test* and *On The Plus Side*.